MW01166489

The whole question of *why* men fight wars, of why we choose the hard road of destruction instead of the smoother highway of cooperation, is a challenging one for science fiction, one which has not been adequately explored or exploited.

Considering the geometrically escalating power-curve of modern weapons, is this something the human race can afford? Even if war is part of the normal order of the universe, even if Darth Vaders and Deathworlds do exist, can we—as men—afford to meet them in our present disarray, divided by our own hostilities and weakened by our self-destructive wars, great and small?

It would, at this stage, be futile to call for a Declaration of Interdependence, but sooner or later, if we are indeed to reach the stars and, come what may, survive among them, we will have to proclaim one, and, in one way or another, enforce it.

A great deal of science fiction has shown us the alternatives.

—Reginald Bretnor
From his *Introduction*

THE
FUTURE AT WAR

VOL III
ORION'S SWORD

Edited by
**REGINALD
BRETNOR**

BAEN
BOOKS

THE FUTURE AT WAR, VOL. III: ORION'S SWORD

This is a work of fiction. All the characters and events portrayed in this book are fictional, and any resemblance to real people or incidents is purely coincidental.

Copyright © 1980 by Reginald Bretnor

All rights reserved, including the right to reproduce this book or portions thereof in any form.

A Baen Book

Baen Publishing Enterprises
260 Fifth Avenue
New York, N.Y. 10001

First Baen printing, February 1989

ISBN: 0-671-69807-9

Cover art by Eddie Jones/RPG Agency

Printed in the United States of America

Distributed by
SIMON & SCHUSTER
1230 Avenue of the Americas
New York, N.Y. 10020

ACKNOWLEDGMENTS

In A Good Cause by Isaac Asimov
Copyright © 1951 by Henry Holt and Co., Inc. First published in *New Tales of Space and Time* [edited by Raymond J. Healy.] Reprinted by permission of Isaac Asimov.

Time Piece by Joe Haldeman
Copyright © 1970 by Universal Publishing & Distributing Corp. First published in *Worlds of If*. Reprinted by permission of Joe Haldeman.

Inhuman Error by Fred Saberhagen
Copyright © 1974 by Conde Nast Publications. First published in *Analog Science Fiction/Fact*, October 1974. Reprinted by permission of Fred Saberhagen.

Early Bird by Theodore R. Cogswell and Theodore L. Thomas
Copyright © 1973 by Random House, Inc. First published in *Astounding: John W. Campbell Memorial Anthology [edited by Harry Harrison.] Reprinted by permission of Theodore R. Cogswell.*

Inside Straight by Poul Anderson
Copyright © 1955 by Fantasy House, Inc. First published in *The Magazine of Fantasy and Science Fiction*, August 1955. Reprinted by permission of Poul Anderson.

Superiority by Arthur C. Clarke
Copyright © 1951 by Fantasy House, Inc. First published in *The Magazine of Fantasy and Science Fiction*, August 1951. Reprinted by permission of the author and the author's agent, Scott Meredith Literary Agency, Inc., 845 Third Avenue, New York, N.Y. 10022.

Steel Brother by Gordon R. Dickson
Copyright © 1952 by Street & Smith Publications. First published in *Astounding Science Fiction*, February 1952. Reprinted by permission of Gordon R. Dickson.

City of Yesterday by Terry Carr
Copyright © 1967 by Galaxy Publishing Corp. First published in *Worlds of If*, December 1967. Reprinted by permission of Terry Carr.

When I Was Red Rover by Dean Ing
Copyright © 1957 by Street & Smith Publications. First published in *Astounding Science Fiction*, September 1957. Reprinted by permission of Dean Ing.

Field Test by Keith Laumer
Copyright © 1976 by Conde Nast Publications. First published in *Analog Science Fiction/Fact*, March 1976. Reprinted by permission of Keith Laumer.

Chips On Distant Shoulders by Hal Clement
Copyright © 1980 by Hal Clement. Published by arrangement with the author.

Couldn't We All Just Be Dear, Dear Friends? by Keith Laumer
Copyright © 1980 by Keith Laumer. Published by arrangement with the author.

An Alien Sort of War by Katherine MacLean
Copyright © 1980 by Katherine MacLean. Published by arrangement with the author.

World of the Wars by Jon Freeman
Copyright © 1980 by Jon Freeman. Published by arrangement with the author.

Outguessing the Unknown: Psychological Aspects of Future War by Alan E. Nourse
Coyright © 1980 *by Alan E. Nourse. Published by arrangement with the author.*

The Wizard Warriors: Computers and Robots in Warfare by G. Harry Stine
Copyright © 1980 by G. Harry Stine. Published by arrangement with the author.

Encased in the Amber of Fate by Robert Frazier
Copyright © 1980 by Robert Frazier. Published by arrangement with the author.

CONTENTS

To the memory of my friend, L. Macleod, sometime Captain, Royal Highlanders (the Black Watch).

Brave men will always be needed.

INTRODUCTION

Orion's Sword is the third volume of *The Future at War*. Volume 1, *Thor's Hammer*, dealt primarily with war on Earth and in near space; Volume 2, *The Spear of Mars*, with invasions of Earth, warfare in the Solar System, and finally from there out. *Orion's Sword* takes up where they left off. Its concern is with the infinitely vaster theatre of interstellar and intergalactic space, where so many of science fiction's wars have been, and are being fought.

The question central to the theme of *Orion's Sword* is not whether we will explore stars and their planets, galaxies and the space between them, but whether, if we do so, we will take the wars of Earth with us as an export or, perhaps, find other beings' wars awaiting us. As I said in the introduction to *The Spear of Mars*, the final part of the question is one we cannot answer from the bottom of the gravity well in which we live. However, we can and should examine its first part, and that means examining the nature of war, the nature of mankind, and the relationship between war and man.

Terrible as war can be, perhaps the most terrible thing about it is that almost universally we refuse to recognize its nature and its genesis. It is too easy to exteriorize this purely human and, when it starts, entirely voluntary process. Our ancestors accomplished this by imagining war gods: Thor and Mars, Hachiman and Ku, and how many more? Even the Supreme Being of Christianity, Judaism, and Islam is recognized, among

1

His other attributes, as Lord of Hosts. But even more insidious than this religious and mythological exteriorization has been our tendency, especially since the Eighteenth Century, to consider war as a devastating natural force, somehow as independent of human volition as a lightning strike or a meteor shower. So our historians and sociologists speak of the *causes* of war—of economic causes, for example—as though these were as far removed from our area of decision as, say, the movements of the San Andreas Fault.

There can be only one true *cause* of war between men: an initial act of military agression, which must invariably be voluntary. There are no others. There are *reasons*—sometimes good reasons. And there are *pretexts*.

We, as a race, have been fighting wars on one pretext or another since before the dawn of history—and almost always the pretexts have been made to appear as causes; almost always, the differences have seemed irreconcilable; then, after the appropriate blood-baths—and often even without any clear-cut politico/military decision—those differences have lost their venom, have spent their force, and often have been almost totally forgotten.

Who, during the terrible Thirty Years War, would have ventured to prophesy the ecumenical movement of today?

During the past year, I watched many of the episodes in that superb British documentary, *The World at War*, produced by the BBC in cooperation with the Imperial War Museum, and narrated by Lord Olivier. Strikingly fair in its military judgments, it covered every major theatre of World War II, availing itself of any number of Allied and Axis film clips, and of the testimony of surviving servicemen, high commanders and enlisted men alike, and of civilian personnel and civilian victims on both sides.

Technically, it was of course intensely interesting—I, for example, had had no idea of the scale and intensity of Japan's desperate *kamikaze* attacks during the closing months of the war—but the one factor that, for me, overshadowed everything was the almost incredible volume of *destruction*, not of life alone, but of men's cities, factories, works of art, machines, crops, forests, by air bombardment, by artillery on land, by man's old enemy and ally, fire. Much of this, only too obviously, was without any legitimate military justification—terror raids on non-military targets, for example. A great deal more, though seemingly justified militarily, was essentially duplicative. (As J.F.C. Fuller has pointed out, the levelling of Japanese cities by air bombardment achieved little that the United States Navy had not already accomplished with its submarines and air arm by shattering the merchant fleet upon which Japan and Japanese industry were almost totally dependent.)*

Watching this record of destruction, I was once again reminded of those Pacific Northwest Coast Indians who engage in the ceremonial contest called the *potlach*. Potlaches, in most cases, involve a crazy—to our minds—competition in giving away valuable property, the greatest giver acquiring the most status. However, among certain groups they have taken a more destructive turn: instead of vying to see who can give the most property away, the contestants compete by burning it. Blankets, canoes, paddles and pots and fishing-nets all feed the flames.

The question came to mind: do we really fight our wars for politico/military objectives, or are these simply our rationalizing pretexts for potlaches infinitely more appalling than the Indians' relatively innocuous destruction of their property?

Granted: I am over-simplifying—but if there were no such underlying destructive drive in humankind, why would so few major wars result in what Clausewitz said was their true purpose—a more perfect peace? Why would our politicians and our statesmen continue with their interminable futilities—disarmament agreements,

*Major-General J.F.C. Fuller, *The Conduct of War, 1789-1961, a Study of the Impact of the French, Industrial, and Russian Revolutions on War and Its Conduct*, London 1962.

treaties of alliance and enmity, non-aggression pacts, and such grotesqueries as the mad United Nations/ Third World disco? Why would the Russians, who but for us would have been defeated in the Hitler War and whom even now our grain nourishes and our industrial technology assists—why would they be preparing so cynically and openly for all-out war?

The question should be examined very thoroughly before we venture too far into space. It is conceivable that beings *may* be there who, more civilized than we, would take a dim view of potlach-wars and of those who practice them.

It is also possible that beings may be there who would just love to be invited to one, beings as far ahead of us technologically as we are of the potlach Indians.

The whole question of *why* men fight wars, of why we choose the hard road of destruction instead of the smoother highway of cooperation, is a challenging one for science fiction, one which has not been adequately explored or exploited. Perhaps we might start with one observed fact:

When we think and communicate in symbols that describe the realities of structure and process accurately enough to ensure predictability—when we employ the sane symbolic systems of the exact sciences—then we can indeed reach for the stars.

But if we continue, in everything governing relationships between man and man, nation and nation, to employ the primitive, imprecise, and more often than not false-to-fact symbolic systems inherited in our everyday languages and evolved in the specialized languages of the social pseudosciences and of diplomacy, we are probably doomed to the perpetual recurrence of our potlach-wars.

Considering the geometrically escalating power-curve of modern weapons, is this something the human race can afford? Even if war is part of the normal order of the universe, even if Darth Vaders and Deathworlds do exist, can we—as men—afford to meet them in our present disarray, divided by our own hostilities and weakened by our self-destructive wars, great and small?

It would, at this stage, be futile to call for a Declaration of Interdependence, but sooner or later, if we are indeed to reach the stars and, come what may, survive among them, we will have to proclaim one and, in one way or another, enforce it.

A great deal of science fiction has shown us the alternatives.

Reginald Bretnor
Medford, Oregon
October 26, 1979

Disunity has always been one of the most dangerous enemies of the human race: the refusal of many men and many nations to forget their private quarrels and form a united front against far greater perils. In the 16th century, the Spanish conquest of Mexico was made far easier by alliance with and against the warring natives. In the 13th century, when the Mongols conquered virtually all Asia and swept unimpeded to the very gates of Vienna, the rulers of Europe never did unite against them, and the West was saved only by the death of Ogotai, the son of Genghis, and the Mongol law that princes of the blood and generals such as Subutai return to Mongolia to choose a new Khakhan.

Unless things change, it now seems that we may very well carry this all-too-human trait with us into space. Then, if we encounter beings as quarrelsome and as rapacious as we ourselves—but beings who have never known disunity or internecine warfare—how will we contend with them, and what will the result be?

In this powerful novelette, the author of the famous Foundation *series explores some of the possibilities.*

Isaac Asimov

"IN A GOOD CAUSE—"

In the Great Court, which stands as a patch of untouched peace among the fifty busy square miles devoted to the towering buildings that are the pulse beat of the United Worlds of the Galaxy, stands a statue.

It stands where it can look at the stars at night. There are other statues ringing the court, but this one stands in the center and alone.

It is not a very good statue. The face is too noble and lacks the lines of living. The brow is a shade too high, the nose a shade too symmetrical, the clothing a shade too carefully disposed. The whole bearing is by far too saintly to be true. One can suppose that the man in real life might have frowned at times, or hiccuped, but the statue seemed to insist that such imperfections were impossible.

All this, of course, is understandable overcompensation. The man had no statues raised to him while alive, and succeeding generations, with the advantage of hindsight, felt guilty.

The name on the pedestal reads "Richard Sayama Altmayer." Underneath it is a short phrase and, vertically arranged, three dates. The phrase is: *In a good cause, there are no failures.* The three dates are June 17, 2755; September 5, 2788; December 21, 2800;—the years being counted in the usual manner of the period, that is, from the date of the first atomic explosion in 1945 of the ancient era.

None of those dates represents either his birth or

7

death. They mark neither a date of marriage or of the accomplishment of some great deed or, indeed, of anything that the inhabitants of the United Worlds can remember with pleasure and pride. Rather, they are the final expression of the feeling of guilt.

Quite simply and plainly, they are the three dates upon which Richard Sayama Altmayer was sent to prison for his opinions.

1—June 17, 2755

At the age of twenty-two, certainly, Dick Altmayer was fully capable of feeling fury. His hair was as yet dark brown and he had not grown the mustache which, in later years, would be so characteristic of him. His nose was, of course, thin and high-bridged, but the contours of his face were youthful. It would only be later that the growing gauntness of his cheeks would convert that nose into the prominent landmark that it now is in the minds of trillions of school children.

Geoffrey Stock was standing in the doorway, viewing the results of his friend's fury. His round face and cold, steady eyes were there, but he had yet to put on the first of the military uniforms in which he was to spend the rest of his life.

He said, "Great Galaxy!"

Altmayer looked up. "Hello, Jeff."

"What's been happening, Dick? I thought your principles, pal, forbid destruction of any kind. Here's a bookviewer that looks somewhat destroyed." He picked up the pieces.

Altmayer said, "I was holding the viewer when my wave-receiver came through with an official message. You know which one, too."

"I know. It happened to me, too. Where is it?"

"On the floor. I tore it off the spool as soon as it belched out at me. Wait, let's dump it down the atom chute."

"Hey, hold on. You can't—"

"Why not?"

"Because you won't accomplish anything. You'll have to report."

"And just why?"

"Don't be an ass, Dick"

"This is a matter of principle, by Space."

"Oh, nuts! You can't fight the whole planet."

"I don't intend to fight the whole planet; just the few who get us into wars."

Stock shrugged. "That means the whole planet. That guff of yours of leaders tricking poor innocent people into fighting is just so much space-dust. Do you think that if a vote were taken the people wouldn't be overwhelmingly in favor of fighting this fight?"

"That means nothing. Jeff. The government has control of—"

"The organs of propaganda. Yes, I know. I've listened to you often enough. But why not report, anyway?"

Altmayer turned away.

Stock said, "In the first place, you might not pass the physical examination."

"I'd pass. I've been in Space."

"That doesn't mean anything. If the doctors let you hop a liner, that only means you don't have a heart murmur or an aneurysm. For military duty aboard ship in Space you need more than just that. How do you know you qualify?"

"That's a side issue, Jeff, and an insulting one. It's not that I'm afraid to fight."

"Do you think you can stop the war this way?"

"I wish I could," Altmayer's voice almost shook as he spoke. "It's this idea I have that all mankind should be a single unit. There shouldn't be wars or space-fleets armed only for destruction. The Galaxy stands ready to be opened to the united efforts of the human race. Instead, we have been factioned for nearly two thousand years, and we throw away all the Galaxy."

Stock laughed, "We're doing all right. There are more than eighty independent planetary systems."

"And are we the only intelligences in the Galaxy?"

"Oh, the Diaboli, your particular devils," and Stock

put his fists to his temples and extended the two fore-fingers, waggling them.

"And yours, too, and everybody's. They have a single government extending over more planets than all those occupied by our precious eighty independents."

"Sure, and their nearest planet is only fifteen hundred light years away from Earth and they can't live on oxygen planets anyway."

Stock got out of his friendly mood. He said, curtly, "Look, I dropped by here to say that I was reporting for examination next week. Are you coming with me?"

"No."

"You're really determined."

"I'm really determined."

"You know you'll accomplish nothing. There'll be no great flame ignited on Earth. It will be no case of millions of young men being excited by your example into a no-war strike. You will simply be put in jail."

"Well, then, jail it is."

And jail it was. On June 17, 2755, of the atomic era, after a short trial in which Richard Sayama Altmayer refused to present any defense, he was sentenced to jail for the term of three years or for the duration of the war, whichever should be longer. He served a little over four years and two months, at which time the war ended in a definite though not shattering Santannian defeat. Earth gained complete control of certain disputed asteroids, various commercial advantages, and a limitation of the Santannian navy.

The combined human losses of the war were something over two thousand ships with, of course, most of their crews, and in addition, several millions of lives due to the bombardment of planetary surfaces from space. The fleets of the two contending powers had been sufficiently strong to restrict this bombardment to the outposts of their respective systems, so that the planets of Earth and Santanni, themselves, were little affected.

The war conclusively established Earth as the strongest single human military power.

Geoffrey Stock fought throughout the war; seeing action more than once and remaining whole in life and limb despite that. At the end of the war he had the rank of major. He took part in the first diplomatic mission sent out by Earth to the worlds of the Diaboli, and that was the first step in his expanding role in Earth's military and political life.

2—*September 5, 2788*

They were the first Diaboli ever to have appeared on the surface of Earth itself. The projection posters and the newscasts of the Federalist party made that abundantly clear to any who were unaware of that. Over and over, they repeated the chronology of events.

It was toward the beginning of the century that human explorers first came across the Diaboli. They were intelligent and had discovered interstellar travel independently somewhat earlier than had the humans. Already the galactic volume of their dominions was greater than that which was human-occupied.

Regular diplomatic relationships between the Diaboli and the major human powers had begun twenty years earlier, immediately after the war between Santanni and Earth. At that time, outposts of Diaboli power were already within twenty light years of the outermost human centers. Their missions went everywhere, drawing trade treaties, obtaining concessions on unoccupied asteroids.

And now they were on Earth itself. They were treated as equals and perhaps as more than equals by the rulers of the greatest center of human population in the Galaxy. The most damning statistic of all was the most loudly proclaimed by the Federalists. It was this: Although the number of living Diaboli was somewhat less than the total number of living humans, humanity had opened up not more than five new worlds to colonization in fifty years, while the Diaboli had begun the occupation of nearly five hundred.

"A hundred to one against us," cried the Federalists, "because they are one political organization and we are a hundred." But relatively few on Earth, and fewer in the Galaxy as a whole, paid attention to the Federalists and their demands for Galactic Union.

The crowds that lined the streets along which nearly daily the five Diaboli of the mission traveled from their specially conditioned suite in the best hotel of the city to the Secretariat of Defense were, by and large, not hostile. Most were merely curious, and more than a little revolted.

The Diaboli were not pleasant creatures to look at. They were larger and considerably more massive than Earthmen. They had four stubby legs set close together below and two flexibly-fingered arms above. Their skin was wrinkled and naked and they wore no clothing. Their broad, scaly faces wore no expressions capable of being read by Earthmen, and from flattened regions just above each large-pupilled eye there sprang short horns. It was these last that gave the creatures their names. At first they had been called devils, and later the politer Latin equivalent.

Each wore a pair of cylinders on its back from which flexible tubes extended to the nostrils; there they clamped on tightly. These were packed with soda-lime which absorbed the, to them, poisonous carbon dioxide from the air they breathed. Their own metabolism revolved about the reduction of sulfur and sometimes those foremost among the humans in the crowd caught a foul whiff of the hydrogen sulfide exhaled by the Diaboli.

The leader of the Federalists was in the crowd. He stood far back where he attracted no attention from the police who had roped off the avenues and who now maintained a watchful order on the little hoppers that could be maneuvered quickly through the thickest crowd. The Federalist leader was gaunt-faced, with a thin and prominently bridged nose and straight, graying hair.

He turned away, "I cannot bear to look at them."

His companion was more philosophic. He said, "No uglier in spirit, at least, than some of our handsome officials. These creatures are at least true to their own."

"You are sadly right. Are we entirely ready?"

"Entirely. There won't be one of them alive to return to his world."

"Good! I will remain here to give the signal."

The Diaboli were talking as well. This fact could not be evident to any human, no matter how close. To be sure, they could communicate by making ordinary sounds to one another but that was not their method of choice. The skin between their horns could, by the actions of muscles which differed in their construction from any known to humans, vibrate rapidly. The tiny waves which were transmitted in this manner to the air were too rapid to be heard by the human ear and too delicate to be detected by any but the most sensitive of human instrumentation. At that time, in fact, humans remained unaware of this form of communication.

A vibration said, "Did you know that this is the planet of origin of the Two-legs?"

"No." There was a chorus of such no's, and then one particular vibration said, "Do you get that from the Two-leg communications you have been studying, queer one?"

"Because I study the communications? More of our people should do so instead of insisting so firmly on the complete worthlessness of Two-leg culture. For one thing, we are in a much better position to deal with the Two-legs if we know something about them. Their history is interesting in a horrible way. I am glad I brought myself to view their spools."

"And yet," came another vibration, "from our previous contacts with Two-legs, one would be certain that they did not know their planet of origin. Certainly there is no veneration of this planet, Earth, or any memorial rites connected with it. Are you sure the information is correct?"

"Entirely so. The lack of ritual, and the fact that this planet is by no means a shrine, is perfectly understandable in the light of Two-leg history. The Two-legs on the other worlds would scarcely concede the honor.

It would somehow lower the independent dignity of their own worlds."

"I don't quite understand."

"Neither do I, exactly, but after several days of reading I think I catch a glimmer. It would seem that, originally, when interstellar travel was first discovered by the Two-legs, they lived under a single political unit."

"Naturally."

"Not for these Two-legs. This was an unusual stage in their history and did not last. After the colonies on the various worlds grew and came to reasonable maturity, their first interest was to break away from the mother world. The first in the series of interstellar wars among these Two-legs began then."

"Horrible. Like cannibals."

"Yes, isn't it? My digestion has been upset for days. My cud is sour. In any case, the various colonies gained independence, so that now we have the situation of which we are well aware. All of the Two-leg kingdoms, republics, aristocracies, etc., are simply tiny clots of worlds, each consisting of a dominant world and a few subsidiaries which, in turn, are forever seeking their independence or being shifted from one dominant to another. This Earth is the strongest among them and yet less than a dozen worlds owe it allegiance."

"Incredible that these creatures should be so blind to their own interests. Do they not have a tradition of the single government that existed when they consisted of but one world?"

"As I said that was unusual for them. The single government had existed only a few decades. Prior to that, this very planet itself was split into a number of subplanetary political units."

"Never heard anything like it." For a while, the supersonics of the various creatures interfered with one another.

"It's a fact. It is simply the nature of the beast."

And with that, they were at the Secretariat of Defense. The five Diaboli stood side by side along the table.

They stood because their anatomy did not admit of anything that could correspond to "sitting." On the other side of the table, five Earthmen stood as well. It would have been more convenient for the humans to sit but, understandably, there was no desire to make the handicap of smaller size any more pronounced than it already was. The table was a rather wide one; the widest, in fact, that could be conveniently obtained. This was out of respect for the human nose, for from the Diaboli, slightly so as they breathed, much more so when they spoke, there came the gentle and continuous drift of hydrogen sulfide. This was a difficulty rather unprecedented in diplomatic negotiations.

Ordinarily the meetings did not last for more than half an hour, and at the end of this interval the Diaboli ended their conversations without ceremony and turned to leave. This time, however, the leave-taking was interrupted. A man entered, and the five human negotiators made way for him. He was tall, taller than any of the other Earthmen, and he wore a uniform with the ease of long usage. His face was round and his eyes cold and steady. His black hair was rather thin but as yet untouched by gray. There was an irregular blotch of scar tissue running from the point of his jaw downward past the line of his high, leather-brown collar. It might have been the result of a hand energy-ray, wielded by some forgotten human enemy in one of the five wars in which the man had been an active participant.

"Sirs," said the Earthman who had been chief negotiator hitherto, "may I introduce the Secretary of Defense?"

The Diaboli were somewhat shocked and, although their expressions were in repose and inscrutable, the sound plates on their foreheads vibrated actively. Their strict sense of hierarchy was disturbed. The Secretary was only a Two-leg, but by Two-leg standards he outranked them. They could not properly conduct official business with him.

The Secretary was aware of their feelings but had no choice in the matter. For at least ten minutes, their

leaving must be delayed and no ordinary interruption
could serve to hold back the Diaboli.

"Sirs," he said, "I must ask your indulgence to remain longer this time."

The central Diabolus replied in the nearest approach
to English any Diabolus could manage. Actually, a
Diabolus might be said to have two mouths. One was
hinged at the outermost extremity of the jawbone and
was used in eating. In this capacity, the motion of the
mouth was rarely seen by human beings, since the
Diaboli much preferred to eat in the company of their
own kind, exclusively. A narrower mouth opening, however, perhaps two inches in width, could be used in
speaking. It pursed itself open, revealing the gummy
gap where a Diabolus' missing incisors ought to have
been. It remained open during speech, the necessary
consonantal blockings being performed by the palate
and back of the tongue. The result was hoarse and
fuzzy, but understandable.

The Diabolus said, "You will pardon us, already we
suffer." And by his forehead, he twittered unheard,
"They mean to suffocate us in their vile atmosphere.
We must ask for larger poison-absorbing cylinders."

The Secretary of Defense said, "I am in sympathy
with your feelings, and yet this may be my only opportunity to speak with you. Perhaps you would do us the
honor to eat with us."

The Earthman next to the Secretary could not forbear a
quick and passing frown. He scribbled rapidly on a
piece of paper and passed it to the Secretary, who
glanced momentarily at it.

It read, "No. They eat sulfuretted hay. Stinks un-
bearably." The Secretary crumpled the note and let it
drop.

The Diabolus said, "The honor is ours. Were we
physically able to endure your strange atmosphere for
so long a time, we would accept most gratefully."

And via forehead, he said with agitation, "They cannot expect us to eat with them and watch them con-

sume the corpses of dead animals. My cud would never
be sweet again."

"We respect your reasons," said the Secretary. "Let
us then transact our business now. In the negotiations
that have so far proceeded, we have been unable to
obtain from your government, in the persons of you,
their representatives, any clear indication as to what
the boundaries of your sphere of influence are in your
own minds. We have presented several proposals in
this matter."

"As far as the territories of Earth are concerned, Mr.
Secretary, a definition has been given."

"But surely you must see that this is unsatisfactory.
The boundaries of Earth and your lands are nowhere in
contact. So far, you have done nothing but state this
fact. While true, the mere statement is not satisfying."

"We do not completely understand. Would you have
us discuss the boundaries between ourselves and such
independent human kingdoms as that of Vega?"

"Why, yes."

"That cannot be done, sir. Surely, you realize that
any relations between ourselves and the sovereign realm
of Vega cannot be possibly any concern of Earth. They
can be discussed only with Vega."

"Then you will negotiate a hundred times with the
hundred human world systems?"

"It is necessary. I would point out, however, that the
necessity is imposed not by us but by the nature of your
human organization."

"Then that limits our field of discussion drastically."
The Secretary seemed abstracted. He was listening, not
exactly to the Diaboli opposite, but, rather, it would
seem, to something at a distance.

And now there was a faint commotion, barely heard
from outside the Secretariat. The babble of distant voices,
the brisk crackle of energy-guns muted by distance to
nearly nothingness, and the hurried click-clacking of
police hoppers.

The Diaboli showed no indication of hearing, nor was
this simply another affectation of politeness. If their

... for receiving supersonic sound waves was far
..e delicate and acute than almost anything human
ingenuity had ever invented, their reception for ordinary sound waves was rather dull.

The Diabolus was saying, "We beg leave to state our surprise. We were of the opinion that all this was known to you."

A man in police uniform appeared in the doorway. The Secretary turned to him and, with the briefest of nods, the policeman departed.

The Secretary said suddenly and briskly, "Quite. I merely wished to ascertain once again that this was the case. I trust you will be ready to resume negotiations tomorrow?"

"Certainly, sir."

One by one, slowly, with a dignity befitting the heirs of the universe, the Diaboli left.

An Earthman said, "I'm glad they refused to eat with us."

"I knew they couldn't accept," said the Secretary, thoughtfully. "They're vegetarian. They sicken thoroughly at the very thought of eating meat. I've seen them eat, you know. Not many humans have. They resemble our cattle in the business of eating. They bolt their food and then stand solemnly about in circles, chewing their cuds in a great community of thought. Perhaps they intercommunicate by a method we are unaware of. The huge lower jaw rotates horizontally in a slow, grinding process—"

The policeman had once more appeared in the doorway.

The Secretary broke off, and called, "You have them all?"

"Yes, sir."

"Do you have Altmayer?"

"Yes, sir."

"Good."

The crowd had gathered again when the five Diaboli emerged from the Secretariat. The schedule was strict.

At 3:00 P.M. each day they left their suite and spent five minutes walking to the Secretariat. At 3:35, they emerged therefrom once again and returned to their suite, the way being kept clear by the police. They marched stolidly, almost mechanically, along the broad avenue.

Halfway in their trek there came the sounds of shouting men. To most of the crowd, the words were not clear but there was the crackle of an energy-gun and the pale blue fluorescence split the air overhead. Police wheeled, their own energy-guns drawn, hoppers springing seven feet into the air, landing delicately in the midst of groups of people, touching none of them, jumping again almost instantly. People scattered and their voices were joined to the general uproar.

Through it all, the Diaboli, either through defective hearing or excessive dignity, continued marching as mechanically as ever.

At the other end of the gathering, almost diametrically opposing the region of excitement, Richard Sayama Altmayer stroked his nose in a moment of satisfaction. The strict chronology of the Diaboli had made a split-second plan possible. The first diversionary disturbance was only to attract the attention of the police. It was now—

And he fired a harmless sound pellet into the air.

Instantly, from four directions, concussion pellets split the air. From the roofs of buildings lining the way, snipers fired.

Each of the Diaboli, torn by the shells, shuddered and exploded as the pellets detonated within them. One by one, they toppled.

And from nowhere, the police were at Altmayer's side. He stared at them with some surprise.

Gently, for in twenty years he had lost his fury and learned to be gentle, he said, "You come quickly, but even so you come too late." He gestured in the direction of the shattered Diaboli.

The crowd was in simple panic now. Additional squadrons of police, arriving in record time, could do nothing more than herd them off into harmless directions.

The policeman, who now held Altmayer in a firm grip, taking the sound gun from him and inspecting him quickly for further weapons, was a captain by rank. He said, stiffly, "I think you've made a mistake, Mr. Altmayer. You'll notice you've drawn no blood." And he, too, waved toward where the Diaboli lay motionless.

Altmayer turned, startled. The creatures lay there on their sides, some in pieces, tattered skin shredding away, frames distorted and bent, but the police captain was correct. There was no blood, no flesh. Altmayer's lips, pale and stiff, moved soundlessly.

The police captain interpreted the motion accurately enough. He said, "You are correct, sir, they are robots."

And from the great doors of the Secretariat of Defense, the true Diaboli emerged. Clubbing policemen cleared the way, but another way, so that they need not pass the sprawled travesties of plastic and aluminum which for three minutes had played the role of living creatures.

The police captain said, "I'll ask you to come without trouble, Mr. Altmayer. The Secretary of Defense would like to see you."

"I am coming, sir." A stunned frustration was only now beginning to overwhelm him.

Geoffrey Stock and Richard Altmayer faced one another for the first time in almost a quarter of a century, there in the Defense Secretary's private office. It was a rather strait-laced office: a desk, an armchair, and two additional chairs. All were a dull brown in color, the chairs being topped by brown foamite which yielded to the body enough for comfort, not enough for luxury. There was a micro-viewer on the desk and a little cabinet big enough to hold several dozen opto-spools. On the wall opposite the desk was a trimensional view of the old *Dauntless*, the Secretary's first command.

Stock said, "It is a little ridiculous meeting like this after so many years. I find I am sorry."

"Sorry about what, Jeff?" Altmayer tried to force a

smile, "I am sorry about nothing but that you tricked me with those robots."

"You were not difficult to trick," said Stock, "and it was an excellent opportunity to break your party. I'm sure it will be quite discredited after this. The pacifist tries to force war; the apostle of gentleness tries assassination."

"War against the true enemy," said Altmayer sadly. "But you are right. It is a sign of desperation that this was forced on me."—Then, "How did you know my plans?"

"You still overestimate humanity, Dick. In any conspiracy the weakest points are the people that compose it. You had twenty-five co-conspirators. Didn't it occur to you that at least one of them might be an informer, or even an employee of mine?"

A dull red burned slowly on Altmayer's high cheekbones. "Which one?" he said.

"Sorry. We may have to use him again."

Altmayer sat back in his chair wearily. "What have you gained?"

"What have *you* gained? You are as impractical now as on that last day I saw you; the day you decided to go to jail rather than report for induction. You haven't changed."

Altmayer shook his head, "The truth doesn't change."

Stock said impatiently, "If it is truth, why does it always fail? Your stay in jail accomplished nothing. The war went on. Not one life was saved. Since then, you've started a political party; and every cause it has backed has failed. Your conspiracy has failed. You're nearly fifty, Dick, and what have you accomplished? Nothing."

Altmayer said, "And you went to war, rose to command a ship, then to a place in the Cabinet. They say you will be the next Coordinator. You've accomplished a great deal. Yet success and failure do not exist in themselves. Success in what? Success in working the ruin of humanity. Failure in what? In saving it? I wouldn't change places with you. Jeff, remember this. In a good cause, there are no failures; there are only delayed successes."

"Even if you are executed for this day's work?"

"Even if I am executed. There will be someone else to carry on, and his success will be my success."

"How do you envisage this success? Can you really see a union of worlds, a Galactic Federation? Do you want Santanni running our affairs? Do you want a Vegan telling you what to do? Do you want Earth to decide its own destiny or to be at the mercy of any random combination of powers?"

"We would be at their mercy no more than they would be at ours."

"Except that we are the richest. We would be plundered for the sake of the depressed worlds of the Sirius Sector."

"And pay the plunder out of what we would save in the wars that would no longer occur."

"Do you have answers for all questions, Dick?"

"In twenty years we have been asked all questions, Jeff."

"Then answer this one. How would you force this union of yours on unwilling humanity?"

"That is why I wanted to kill the Diaboli." For the first time, Altmayer showed agitation. "It would mean war with them, but all humanity would unite against the common enemy. Our own political and ideological differences would fade in the face of that."

"You really believe that? Even when the Diaboli have never harmed us? They cannot live on our worlds. They must remain on their own worlds of sulfide atmosphere and oceans which are sodium sulfate solutions."

"Humanity knows better, Jeff. They are spreading from world to world like an atomic explosion. They block space-travel into regions where there are unoccupied oxygen worlds, the kind *we* could use. They are planning for the future: making room for uncounted future generations of Diaboli, while we are being restricted to one corner of the Galaxy, and fighting ourselves to death. In a thousand years we will be their slaves; in ten thousand we will be extinct. Oh, yes, they are the common enemy. Mankind knows that. You will find that out sooner than you think, perhaps."

The Secretary said, "Your party members speak a great deal of ancient Greece of the pre-atomic age. They tell us that the Greeks were a marvelous people, the most culturally advanced of their time, perhaps of all times. They set mankind on the road it has never yet left entirely. They had only one flaw. They could not unite. They were conquered and eventually died out. And we follow in their footsteps now, eh?"

"You have learned your lesson well, Jeff."

"But have you, Dick?"

"What do you mean?"

"Did the Greeks have no common enemy against whom they could unite?"

Altmayer was silent.

Stock said, "The Greeks fought Persia, their great common enemy. Was it not a fact that a good proportion of the Greek states fought on the Persian side?"

Altmayer said finally, "Yes. Because they thought Persian victory was inevitable and they wanted to be on the winning side."

"Human beings haven't changed, Dick. Why do you suppose the Diaboli are here? What is it we are discussing?"

"I am not a member of the government."

"No," said Stock, savagely, "but I am. The Vegan League has allied itself with the Diaboli."

"I don't believe you. It can't be."

"It can be and is. The Diaboli have agreed to supply them with five hundred ships at any time they happen to be at war with Earth. In return, Vega abandons all claims to the Nigellian star cluster. So if you had really assassinated the Diaboli, it would have been war, but with half of humanity probably fighting on the side of your so-called common enemy. We are trying to prevent that."

Altmayer said slowly, "I am ready for trial. Or am I to be executed without one?"

Stock said, "You are still foolish. If we shoot you, Dick, we make a martyr. If we keep you alive and shoot only your subordinates, you will be suspected of having turned state's evidence. As a presumed traitor, you will be quite harmless in the future."

And so, on September 5th, 2788, Richard Sayama Altmayer, after the briefest of secret trials, was sentenced to five years in prison. He served his full term. The year he emerged from prison, Geoffrey Stock was elected Coordinator of Earth.

3—December 21, 2800

Simon Devoire was not at ease. He was a little man, with sandy hair and a freckled, ruddy face. He said, "I'm sorry I agreed to see you, Altmayer. It won't do you any good. It might do me harm."

Altmayer said, "I am an old man. I won't hurt you." And he was indeed a very old man somehow. The turn of the century found his years at two thirds of a century, but he was older than that, older inside and older outside. His clothes were too big for him, as if he were shrinking away inside them. Only his nose had not aged; it was still the thin, aristocratic, high-beaked Altmayer nose.

Devoire said, "It's not you I'm afraid of."

"Why not? Perhaps you think I betrayed the men of '88."

"No, of course not. No man of sense believes that you did. But the days of the Federalists are over, Altmayer."

Altmayer tried to smile. He felt a little hungry; he hadn't eaten that day—no time for food. Was the day of the Federalists over? It might seem so to others. The movement had died on a wave of ridicule. A conspiracy that fails, a "lost cause," is often romantic. It is remembered and draws adherents for generations, *if* the loss is at least a dignified one. But to shoot at living creatures and find the mark to be robots; to be outmaneuvered and outfoxed; to be made ridiculous—that is deadly. It is deadlier than treason, wrong, and sin. Not many had believed Altmayer had bargained for his life by betraying his associates, but the universal laughter killed Federalism as effectively as though they had.

But Altmayer had remained stolidly stubborn under it all. He said, "The day of the Federalists will never be over, while the human race lives."

"Words," said Devoire impatiently. "They meant more to me when I was younger. I am a little tired now."

"Simon, I need access to the subetheric system."

Devoire's face hardened. He said, "And you thought of me. I'm sorry, Altmayer, but I can't let you use my broadcasts for your own purposes."

"You were a Federalist once."

"Don't rely on that," said Devoire. "That's in the past. Now I am—nothing. I am a Devoirist, I suppose. I want to live."

"Even if it is under the feet of the Diaboli? Do you want to live when they are willing; die when they are ready?"

"Words!"

"Do you approve of the all-Galactic conference?"

Devoire reddened past his usual pink level. He gave the sudden impression of a man with too much blood for his body. He said smolderingly, "Well, why not? What does it matter how we go about establishing the Federation of Man? If you're still a Federalist, what have you to object to in a united humanity?"

"United under the Diaboli?"

"What's the difference? Humanity can't unite by itself. Let us be driven to it, as long as the fact is accomplished. I am sick of it all, Altmayer, sick of all our stupid history. I'm tired of trying to be an idealist with nothing to be idealistic over. Human beings are human beings and that's the nasty part of it. Maybe we've *got* to be whipped into line. If so, I'm perfectly willing to let the Diaboli do the whipping."

Altmayer said gently, "You're very foolish, Devoire. It won't be a real union, you know that. The Diaboli called this conference so that they might act as umpires on all current interhuman disputes to their own advantage, and remain the supreme court of judgment over us hereafter. You know they have no intention of establishing a real central human government. It will only be a sort of interlocking directorate; each human government will conduct its own affairs as before and pull in various directions as before. It is simply that we will grow accustomed to running to the Diaboli with our little problems."

"How do you know that will be the result?"

"Do you seriously think any other result is possible?"

Devoire chewed at his lower lip, "Maybe not!"

"Then see through a pane of glass, Simon. Any true independence we now have will be lost."

"A lot of good this independence has ever done us. —Besides, what's the use? We can't stop this thing. Coordinator Stock is probably no keener on the conference than you are, but that doesn't help him. If Earth doesn't attend, the union will be formed without us, and then we will face war with the rest of humanity and the Diaboli. And that goes for any other government that wants to back out."

"What if *all* the governments back out? Wouldn't the conference break up completely?"

"Have you ever known all the human governments to do *anything* together? You never learn, Altmayer."

"There are new facts involved."

"Such as? I know I am foolish for asking, but go ahead."

Altmayer said, "For twenty years most of the Galaxy has been shut to human ships. You know that. None of us has the slightest notion of what goes on within the Diaboli sphere of influence. And yet some human colonies exist within that sphere."

"So?"

"So occasionally, human beings escape into the small portion of the Galaxy that remains human and free. The government of Earth receives reports; reports which they don't dare make public. But not *all* officials of the government can stand the cowardice involved in such actions forever. One of them has been to see me. I can't tell you which one, of course— So I have documents, Devoire; official, reliable, and true."

Devoire shrugged, "About what?" He turned the desk chronometer rather ostentatiously so that Altmayer could see its gleaming metal face on which the red, glowing figures stood out sharply. They read 22:31, and even as it was turned, the 1 faded and the new glow of a 2 appeared.

Altmayer said, "There is a planet called by its colonists Chu Hsi. It did not have a large population; two million, perhaps. Fifteen years ago the Diaboli occupied worlds on various sides of it; and in all those fifteen years, no human ship ever landed on the planet. Last year the Diaboli themselves landed. They brought with them huge freight ships filled with sodium sulfate and bacterial cultures that are native to their own worlds."

"What?—You can't make me believe it."

"Try," said Altmayer, ironically. "It is not difficult. Sodium sulfate will dissolve in the oceans of any world. In a sulfate ocean, their bacteria will grow, multiply, and produce hydrogen sulfide in tremendous quantities which will fill the oceans and the atmosphere. They can then introduce their plants and animals and eventually themselves. Another planet will be suitable for Diaboli life—and unsuitable for any human. It would take time, surely, but the Diaboli have time. They are a united people and . . ."

"Now, look," Devoire waved his hand in disgust, "that just doesn't hold water. The Diaboli have more worlds than they know what to do with."

"For their present purposes, yes, but the Diaboli are creatures that look toward the future. Their birth rate is high and eventually they will fill the Galaxy. And how much better off they would be if they were the only intelligence in the universe."

"But it's impossible on purely physical grounds. Do you know how many millions of tons of sodium sulfate it would take to fill up the oceans to their requirements?"

"Obviously a planetary supply."

"Well, then, do you suppose they would strip one of

their own worlds to create a new one? Where is the gain?"

"Simon, Simon, there are millions of planets in the Galaxy which through atmospheric conditions, temperature, or gravity are forever uninhabitable either to humans or to Diaboli. Many of these are quite adequately rich in sulfur."

Devoire considered, "What about the human beings on the planet?"

"On Chu Hsi? Euthanasia—except for the few who escaped in time. Painless I suppose. The Diaboli are not needlessly cruel, merely efficient."

Altmayer waited. Devoire's fist clenched and unclenched.

Altmayer said, "Publish this news. Spread it out on the interstellar subetheric web. Broadcast the documents to the reception centers on the various worlds. You can do it, and when you do, the all-Galactic conference will fall apart."

Devoire's chair tilted forward. He stood up. "Where's your proof?"

"Will you do it?"

"I want to see your proof."

Altmayer smiled, "Come with me."

They were waiting for him when he came back to the furnished room he was living in. He didn't notice them at first. He was completely unaware of the small vehicle that followed him at a slow pace and a prudent distance. He walked with his head bent, calculating the length of time it would take for Devoire to put the information through the reaches of Space; how long it would take for the receiving stations on Vega and Santanni and Centaurus to blast out the news; how long it would take to spread it over the entire Galaxy. And in this way he passed, unheeding, between the two plainclothes men who flanked the entrance of the rooming house.

It was only when he opened the door to his own room that he stopped and turned to leave but the plain-clothes men were behind him now. He made no attempt at violent escape. He entered the room instead and sat down, feeling so old. He thought feverishly, I need only hold them off an hour and ten minutes.

The man who occupied the darkness reached up and flicked the switch that allowed the wall lights to operate. In the soft wall glow, the man's round face and balding gray-fringed head were startlingly clear.

Altmayer said gently, "I am honored with a visit by the Coordinator himself."

And Stock said, "We are old friends, you and I, Dick. We meet every once in a while."

Altmayer did not answer.

Stock said, "You have certain government papers in your possession, Dick."

Altmayer said, "If you think so, Jeff, you'll have to find them."

Stock rose wearily to his feet. "No heroics, Dick. Let me tell you what those papers contained. They were circumstantial reports of the sulfation of the planet, Chu Hsi. Isn't that true?"

Altmayer looked at the clock.

Stock said, "If you are planning to delay us, to angle us as though we were fish, you will be disappointed. We know where you've been, we know Devoire has the papers, we know exactly what's he planning to do with them."

Altmayer stiffened. The thin parchment of his cheeks trembled. He said, "How long have you known?"

"As long as you have, Dick. You are a very predictable man. It is the very reason we decided to use you. Do you suppose the Recorder would really come to see you as he did, without our knowledge?"

"I don't understand."

Stock said, "The Government of Earth, Dick, is not anxious that the all-Galactic conference be continued. However, we are not Federalists; we know humanity for what it is. What do you suppose would happen if the rest of the Galaxy discovered that the Diaboli were in the process of changing a salt-oxygen world into a sulfate-sulfide one?

"No, don't answer. You are Dick Altmayer and I'm sure you'd tell me that with one fiery burst of indignation, they'd abandon the conference, join together in a loving and brotherly union, throw themselves at the Diaboli, and overwhelm them."

Stock paused such a long time that for a moment it might have seemed he would say no more. Then he continued in a half a whisper, "Nonsense. The other worlds would say that the Government of Earth for purposes of its own had initiated a fraud, had forged documents in a deliberate attempt to disrupt the conference. The Diaboli would deny everything, and most of the human worlds would find it to their interests to believe the denial. They would concentrate on the iniquities of Earth and forget about the iniquities of the Diaboli. So you see, we could sponsor no such exposé."

Altmayer felt drained, futile. "Then you will stop Devoire. It is always that you are so sure of failure beforehand; that you believe the worst of your fellow man—"

"Wait! I said nothing of stopping Devoire. I said only that the government could not sponsor such an exposé and we will not. But the exposé will take place just the same, except that afterward we will arrest Devoire and yourself and denounce the whole thing as vehemently as will the Diaboli. The whole affair would then be changed. The Government of Earth will have dissociated itself from the claims. It will then seem to the rest of the human government that for our own selfish purposes we are trying to hide the actions of the Diaboli, that we have, perhaps, a special understanding with them. They will fear that special understanding and unite against us. But *then* to be against us will mean that they are also against the Diaboli. They will insist on believing the exposé to be the truth, the documents to be real—and the conference will break up."

"It will mean war again," said Altmayer hopelessly, "and not against the real enemy. It will mean fighting among the humans and a victory all the greater for the Diaboli when it is all over."

"No war," said Stock. "No government will attack Earth with the Diaboli on our side. The other governments will merely draw away from us and grind a permanent anti-Diaboli bias into their propaganda. Later, if there should be war between ourselves and the Diaboli, the other governments will at least remain neutral."

He looks very old, thought Altmayer. We are all old, dying men. Aloud, he said, "Why would you expect the Diaboli to back Earth? You may fool the rest of mankind by pretending to attempt suppression of the facts concerning the planet Chu Hsi, but you won't fool the Diaboli. They won't for a moment believe Earth to be sincere in its claim that it believes the documents to be forgeries."

"Ah, but they will." Geoffrey Stock stood up, "You see, the documents *are* forgeries. The Diaboli may be planning sulfation of planets in the future, but to our knowledge, they have not tried it yet."

On December 21, 2800, Richard Sayama Altmayer entered prison for the third and last time. There was no trial, no definite sentence, and scarcely a real imprisonment in the literal sense of the word. His movements were confined and only a few officials were allowed to communicate with him, but otherwise his comforts were looked to assiduously. He had no access to news, of course, so that he was not aware that in the second year of this third imprisonment of his, the war between Earth and the Diaboli opened with the surprise attack near Sirius by an Earth squadron upon certain ships of the Diaboli navy.

In 2802, Geoffrey Stock came to visit Altmayer in his confinement. Altmayer rose in surprise to greet him.

"You're looking well, Dick," Stock said.

He himself was not. His complexion had grayed. He still wore his naval captain's uniform, but his body stooped slightly within it. He was to die within the year, a fact of which he was not completely unaware. It did not bother him much. He thought repeatedly, I have lived the years I've had to live.

Altmayer, who looked the older of the two, had yet more than nine years to live. He said, "An unexpected pleasure, Jeff, but this time you can't have come to imprison me. I'm in prison already."

"I've come to set you free, if you would like."

"For what purpose, Jeff? Surely you have a purpose? A clever way of using me?"

Stock's smile was merely a momentary twitch. He said. "A way of using you, truly, but this time you will approve. . . . We are at war."

"With whom?" Altmayer was startled.

"With the Diaboli. We have been at war for six months."

Altmayer brought his hands together, thin fingers interlacing nervously, "I've heard nothing of this."

"I know." The Coordinator clasped his hands behind his back and was distantly surprised to find that they were trembling. He said, "It's been a long journey for the two of us, Dick. We've had the same goal, you and I— No, let me speak. I've often wanted to explain my point of view to you, but you would never have understood. You weren't the kind of man to understand, until I had the results for you.—I was twenty-five when I first visited a Diaboli world, Dick. I knew then it was either they or we."

"I said so," whispered Altmayer, "from the first."

"Merely saying so was not enough. You wanted to force the human governments to unite against them and that notion was politically unrealistic and completely impossible. It wasn't even desirable. Humans are not Diaboli. Among the Diaboli, individual consciousness is low, almost nonexistent. Ours is almost overpowering. They have no such thing as politics; we have nothing else. They can never disagree, can have nothing but a single government. We can never agree; if we had a single island to live on, we would split it in three.

"But our very disagreements are our strength! Your

Federalist party used to speak of ancient Greece a great deal once. Do you remember? But your people always missed the point. To be sure, Greece could never unite and was therefore ultimately conquered. But even in her state of disunion, she defeated the gigantic Persian Empire. Why?

"I would like to point out that the Greek city-states over centuries had fought with one another. They were forced to specialize in things military to an extent far beyond the Persians. Even the Persians themselves realized that, and in the last century of their imperial existence, Greek mercenaries formed the most valued parts of their armies.

"The same might be said of the small nation-states of pre-atomic Europe, which in centuries of fighting had advanced their military arts to the point where they could overcome and hold for two hundred years the comparatively gigantic empires of Asia.

"So it is with us. The Diaboli, with vast extents of galactic space, have never fought a war. Their military machine is massive, but untried. In fifty years, only such advances have been made by them as they have been able to copy from the various human navies. Humanity, on the other hand, has competed ferociously in warfare. Each government has raced to keep ahead of its neighbors in military science. They've had to! It was our own disunion that made the terrible race for survival necessary, so that in the end almost any one of us was a match for all the Diaboli, provided only that none of us would fight on their side in a general war.

"It was toward the prevention of such a development that all of Earth's diplomacy has been aimed. Until it was certain that in a war between Earth and the Diaboli, the rest of humanity would be at least neutral, there could be no war, and no union of human governments could be allowed, since the race for military perfection must continue. Once we were sure of neutrality, through the hoax that broke up the conference two years ago, we sought the war, and now we have it."

Altmayer, through all this, might have been frozen. It was a long time before he could say anything.

Finally, "What if the Diaboli are victorious after all?"

Stock said, "They aren't. Two weeks ago, the main fleets joined action and theirs was annihilated with practically no loss to ourselves, although we were greatly outnumbered. We might have been fighting unarmed ships. We had stronger weapons of greater range and more accurate sighting. We had three times their effective speed since we had anti-acceleration devices which they lacked. Since the battle a dozen of the other human governments have decided to join the winning side and have declared war on the Diaboli. Yesterday the Diaboli requested that negotiations for an armistice be opened. The war is practically over; and henceforward the Diaboli will be confined to their original planets with only such future expansions as we permit."

Altmayer murmured incoherently.

Stock said, "And now union becomes necessary. After the defeat of Persia by the Greek city-states, they were ruined because of their continued wars among themselves, so that first Macedon and then Rome conquered them. After Europe colonized the Americas, cut up Africa, and conquered Asia, a series of continued European wars led to European ruin.

"Disunion until conquest; union thereafter! But now union is easy. Let one subdivision succeed by itself and the rest will clamor to become part of that success. The ancient writer, Toynbee, first pointed out this difference between what he called a 'dominant minority' and a 'creative minority.'

"We are a creative minority now. In an almost spontaneous gesture, various human governments have suggested the formation of a United Worlds organization. Over seventy governments are willing to attend the first sessions in order to draw up a Charter of Federation. The others will join later, I am sure. We would like you to be one of the delegates from Earth, Dick."

Altmayer found his eyes flooding, "I—I don't understand your purpose. Is this all true?"

"It is all exactly as I say. You were a voice in the wilderness, Dick, crying for union. Your words will carry much weight. What did you once say: 'In a good cause, there are no failures.'"

"No!" said Altmayer, with sudden energy. "It seems your cause was the good one."

Stock's face was hard and devoid of emotion, "You were always a misunderstander of human nature, Dick. When the United Worlds is a reality and when generations of men and women look back to these days of war through their centuries of unbroken peace, they will have forgotten the purpose of my methods. To them, they will represent war and death. *Your* calls for union, *your* idealism, will be remembered forever."

He turned away and Altmayer barely caught his last words: "And when they build their statues, they will build none for me."

In the Great Court, which stands as a patch of untouched peace among the fifty busy square miles devoted to the towering buildings that are the pulse beat of the United Worlds of the Galaxy, stands a statue . . .

I have it on the highest authority—his own—that there's not much to say about Isaac Asimov.

He was born in the USSR in 1920, came to the United States in 1923, has been an American citizen since 1928, went to Columbia University, got three degrees up to a Ph.D. in chemistry in 1948. He is now Professor of Biochemistry at Boston University School of Medicine, but doesn't work at it. He is a full-time writer.

Dr. Asimov published his first science fiction story in the March 1939 issue of *Amazing Stories*, and he has never stopped. His first book was published in 1950, and on the 30th anniversary of that event his 212th appeared. About 150 of these have been non-fiction, on every imaginable subject, including *Asimov's Guide to the Bible* and *Asimov's Guide to Shakespeare*.

Isaac Asimov now lives in New York with his second wife, a psychiatrist. He has two children by his first wife.

Everything else that he has to say about his life and career can be found in the two volumes—totaling 1500 pages—of his autobiography, *In Memory Yet Green* and *In Joy Still Felt*.

There are three main ways of imagining extraterrestrial beings: by deriving them from known life-forms on this planet—exaggerated ants and super-wasps, for instance; by pilfering them from the clutter of our own mythologies and monster-lores and coming up with otherworldly satyrs and Medusas and (almost certainly nonfunctional) centauroid beings; and finally by developing them carefully, according to what we know of evolution and the laws of survival, out of the probable chemistries and ecologies of very different planets circling very different suns.

The last method is the one Hal Clement follows, and his ETs, in such splendid novels as Mission of Gravity and Needle, have therefore been far more plausible than most of those we encounter in sf. Now he takes the method a step further and develops his ideas of what may ensue when we first come into contact—and possibly into conflict—with such strangenesses.

Hal Clement

CHIPS ON DISTANT SHOULDERS

This is not a doctoral thesis. I am trying to stay within the scope of physical laws and military realism. Nothing so brief and so dependent on extrapolation and speculation can, in my opinion, really qualify as a work of scholarship. I do hope that it performs the normal function of the hypothesis: to serve as a basis for experiment and a foundation for deeper thought. If it also manages to provide seed for a few good science fiction stories I will be delighted. Even a playable war game traceable to this source will be gratifying.

The first part of this chapter will be brief. It will deal with reasons why the whole matter is more than academic—why there will probably still be wars long after mankind has mastered interplanetary and even interstellar travel. If you do not need to be convinced on this point, or do not want to be convinced, or feel sure that you can't be convinced, skip to Part II right away.

I

The notion that war is bad is shared both by the utterly selfish and the purely idealistic—though only the latter seem to have the idea that war is invariably the worst possible choice in any situation. Many of both types seem sure that it will be ended once and for all in the fairly near future, usually by universal adoption of some specific religion or social policy.

Presumably it was idealists of this sort who booed and walked out on Robert Heinlein at the 1977 World Science Fiction Convention, when he expressed the opinion that mankind would always have to fight for *freedom*. The reaction was more or less understandable, but was rather silly if "freedom" includes liberty to do what one thinks right. The chance of the entire body of humanity's accepting *any* particular religion or political scheme as undeniably "right" seems infinitesimal—I would be unscientific and call it zero—in spite of the common human tendency to use the word "obviously." As long as the system in power is not universally regarded as right, there will be people who consider it an infringement on their liberties. Some of these, beyond serious doubt, will use violence; so, most probably, will the system.

Of course the words "always" and "never" are pretty sweeping generalizations. While I think Mr. Heinlein was essentially right, I would not have chosen just the words he did. I would simply say that man is pretty certain to reach the stars before he gets rid of war. I can be as idealistic and even as patriotic as anyone; I spent over thirty years in the U.S. Air Force Reserve, and risked my neck in the skies over Europe opposing the late A. Hitler. However, my reasons for the agreement above are on what I consider a realistic and practical level.

I think that interstellar flight, while difficult, may be achieved without an actual breakthrough—that is, a really new discovery of basic physics. One would, I admit, help—it would be nice if the speed-of-light law weren't true after all—but we *could* get there on straight engineering improvements, and our rate of progress along such lines has been very impressive for the last few decades.

Getting rid of war, on the other hand, seems to me far more difficult. It demands at least one, and probably two, psychological developments radical enough to be called breakthroughs, and our progress in developing and utilizing the psychological sciences has so far been disappointing.

The really necessary advance would involve some method of eliminating the almost universal human attitude that one's own rights are as important as anyone else's.

Not *more* important. *As* important.

I am not saying that people shouldn't feel that way, or don't have a right to feel that way, or that it's immoral or even unreasonably selfish. I simply say that unless and until it changes, conflicts of interest will continue to lead to violence in the name of right, freedom, and The People. What specific situation starts things off—the population of a landlocked country believing it has the right to a seaport of its own, women believing they have the same rights as men, or junkies believing they have the right to a fix at public expense—is trivial beside the general principle that my right is as important as yours. If a way were actually discovered to alter this bit of human nature there would be screams against the dangers of psychological research; and if a government or some other group tried to apply the techniques, plenty of people (including me) would fight for their right to their own minds.

Please note that death, destruction, and mayhem are not primary aims of war. They may be secondary ones, as when a cannibal tribe attacks its neighbors for meat, but more usually they are just inconvenient by-products. The aim and end of war is to *impose one's will on an opponent*.

I assume that this is stressed elsewhere in these volumes, but I will come back to the point several times. This is partly because I encouraged people to skip this section, and partly because the fact itself seems curiously unknown to the general populace. Anyone with professional military knowledge is aware of it, of course, and it has never been kept a secret from the masses. However, some writers and speakers have allowed their (understandable) dislike of all things martial to color not only their words but their thinking. Some seem actually to believe that the professional military person typically regards killing as an end in itself. There are, of course, people who can see no other solution to a given problem; but these would not be particularly competent military types, and are in fact found pretty often in other fields.

Unfortunately, imposing one's will on another includes the situation in which *your* will is merely that he not impose *his* on *you*. The human species has an amazing skill at convincing itself that this is the current situation, and that they are merely resisting some form of aggression. Whether nonhuman intelligences turn out to share this variety of self-righteousness remains to be seen. If most, or even many, of them do, the Galactic Patrol is going to be kept very, very busy, whether it's the Edward E. Smith or the Poul Anderson variety of organization.

II

Within the Solar system (also without it, but one thing at a time) the basic sets of possible conflicting species can be arranged in a spectrum. I will use the numbers 0 and 1 to denote the extremes of this range, with intermediates expressed as decimal numbers. With the small number of worlds, and probably still smaller number of intelligent species, available within this system, the spectrum is a discontinuous one. With the galaxy to draw from later, it may look pretty smooth.

I have expressed widely and frequently my opinion that Jupiter is the most likely body, not excepting Earth, to harbor native life. The other gas giants may be like their big brother in this respect, but I regard their chances as poorer.

Since Jupiter pretty certainly lacks a solid surface, its life forms should be of the flying/floating/swimming type (see Arthur C. Clarke's "A Meeting With Medusa"). A conflict between such beings and our own species would represent one of my extremes, which I am arbitrarily calling the 1 or high end of my strangeness spectrum. I am quite aware that this may require revision when we get to the stars. This involves pairs of species which cannot come anywhere near to living under each other's conditions and would presumably have no interest in acquiring either territory or property of the other. In the present example, the Jovians might be unable even to grasp the concept of territory. They might find it easier to communicate with dolphins than with mankind.

An intermediate situation (about 0.3, maybe?) would involve Saturn's big moon Titan and possibly—we don't know much about the place yet—Neptune's satellite Triton. If I had been writing this fifteen years ago I would have included Mars. These are all fairly small bodies, but Titan quite certainly has a fairly dense atmosphere and, a little less certainly, complex local chemistry. I regard it as the third most likely place in the Solar system to have native life.

Titanians could be relatively humanoid to the extent that they would be adapted to existence at a solid/gas interface, possibly with liquid also present. Face-to-face contact and hand-to-hand combat could occur between human and Titanian beings. The fact that one party or both would need space suits is minor compared to the human-Jovian differences; hence the low estimate for the strangeness spectrum number.

Zero strangeness would involve human-against-human or Jovian-against-Jovian conflict. In one way, it is likelier to be more complex than the higher-level situations. I cannot, of course, say that no human beings would sympathize with Jovians or Titanians in a higher-strangeness conflict; the negative chauvinism, or Ugly American complex, or whatever one wants to call it which has been so widespread in this country for the last decade or two could easily expand to cover our whole species. However, the whole who's-for-whom question can get much more mixed up in an all-human or all-Titanian war.

Some examples—by no means an exhaustive list—of various strangeness situations and their implications for strategy, tactics, or both, will form the rest of this section. They will have some relevance to Part III as well, since certain factors are common to any kind of conflict; but interstellar war has one quality which requires us to consider it separately.

Some people might feel that the Category 1 situation would not permit warfare at all because of the mutual exclusiveness of the environments; the parties could never cross each other's paths or have conflicts of interest. Sorry, this is too idealistic even for me.

It is easy to imagine the Ugly Earthman using up his supplies of organic raw materials—petroleum and coal— even if he outgrows the present idiotic practice of burning them. Jupiter is rich in hydrocarbons and, by tonnage if not by percentage, in compounds of nitrogen, sulfur, oxygen, phosphorus, and probably anything else one could want. After we settle our Type Zero wars over local resources, we may very well start sending automatic collectors—ramscoops or something like that—into the Jovian atmosphere to accumulate the local equivalent of plankton for use as organics. The Jovians might reasonably resent such devices plowing through their equivalents of orchards, gardens, and flocks, not to mention their families and themselves. If they have the scientific competence to figure out where the things come from and to do something about it, war would seem a very likely result.

(If one prefers virtuous Earthmen, of course, it would be easy enough to work out a situation in which the Jovians were the heavies. There is no need to pursue both lines, which differ mainly in who does what, and with what, to whom.)

This war, like any space conflict prior to the development of instantaneous unlimited-distance teleportation, is being conducted at very long range. This automatically means very high cost. This last word is to be taken, throughout this article, as a measure of fraction of available effort, not some supposedly absolute unit like the dollar, the ruble, the Scrooge, or anything else which can have its quantitative meaning reduced indefinitely by inflation.

In the present situations the Jovians have a vast cost advantage; their logical strategy would be to make the most of it. After all, they win if humanity merely stops coming.

Tactically, they would reasonably remain in their own atmosphere (leaving it might be prohibitively expensive for *them*) and simply prevent the return of as many ramscoops as possible. The quantitative effect of this would depend on the cost of the scoops. If each one were the equivalent of a missile submarine or even a Boeing 747, even a very low batting average might give a Jovian victory. Of course, if the scoops were more in the family-car class, the process might take longer or might not work at all.

In this connection we must remember that the scoops may well represent a most unusual, and possibly very valuable, *concentration* of elements from the Jovian viewpoint. If they understand clearly enough what is going on at the human end of the line (perhaps too much to expect) the Jovians might deliberately arrange a capture rate low enough to avoid discouraging the suppliers, and accept losses and damage at the Jovian end as a reasonable price for the treasure coming in from space. What would be an acceptable price for either species would of course depend on their psychologies. I don't see how this is to be predicted. I myself belong to a race apparently quite willing to spend several tens of thousands of lives a year for the convenience of privately-owned transportation equipment, but reluctant to pay a fraction of one percent of this price for a continuous and reliable energy supply (yes, I am pro-nuke). In other words, I find human psychology incomprehensible, and suspect that the Jovian variety would be even more so.

The foregoing situation should, ideally, be worked out as trade rather than war, but the parties involved will have to get into intelligible conversation first. This, unfortunately, is not a prerequisite for combat.

The high-strangeness category carries another serious implication. Neither opponent can make direct use of

the other's home world. The destruction of that world,
or at least of its habitability, is therefore a matter
for strategic consideration, assuming its technical feas-
ibility. Either species might have moral objections to
such a course, but unless Jovians are much more moral
than Earthmen this would probably not be a decisive
consideration.

On the practical side, Jupiter would have an enormous advantage; not only does it have over a hundred
times Earth's surface area, but it would be difficult to
confine the effects of any destructive technique to the
Jovian "surface."

Just what the technique might be will depend, of
course, on the scientific and technical capacities of the
warring species. The most predictable from the basis of
our present knowledge would be biological agents, with
radioactive dusting a very poor second from the human
viewpoint. I don't really see how we could hope to
contaminate Jupiter effectively with anything not self-
replicating.

The physical destruction of planets, as practiced in
some of our more advanced space operas, really calls for
a breakthrough of some sort.

With Situation 0.3, more "normal" causes of war can
be envisioned, such as competition for the same real
estate. Titanians and Earthmen might well be interested simultaneously in, say, the larger moons of Jupiter.
Conflict, however illogical, is embarrassingly easy to
foresee in such a case.

Just for variety, we will let the aliens be the villains
this time. The Titanians have decided that thermal
pollution from human settlements or scientific bases is
having (or *may* have, which would be quite enough for
some human beings) an unacceptable effect on the
Callistonian environment. They issue a Monroe Doctrine to the effect that no organism whose body temperature is above the freezing point of water (or perhaps
ammonia) is to land on any celestial body composed
mainly of ice. They blow up the power station at a

human outpost, letting the occupants freeze to death. Earth resents.

This time, both parties are a long way from home, and both are in unnatural environments. From the human viewpoint the Titanians might seem to have some advantage, since Callisto and Titan have about the same size and mass. The chances are, however, that beings from the Saturn system could no more survive unprotected on Callisto than a human being on Luna or Mars. Titan seems to have a fairly dense atmosphere, which would presumably form an essential part of the pressure and chemistry of its native life forms' environment. The temperatures of the two bodies might be comparable, since while Saturn is nearly twice as far from the sun as the Jovian system the Titanian atmosphere could have a substantial greenhouse effect; but even if they didn't need personal refrigerators the Titanians would pretty surely need pressure suits and an air supply.

This is critical to the tactical situation; all infantry operations (including guerilla maneuvers) will have to be carried out in space suits.

This will hamper operations very severely, no matter how sophisticated the suits. This fact has often been overlooked in science fiction stories. Certainly there will be vast improvements over the first PLSS units to walk on Luna, but anyone who had military training between Workd War I and the late 1940s—I can't speak for later years—knows what even a simple gas mask, with no attempt at temperature or pressure control, can do to hamper movement. The much smaller oxygen masks which I knew better in the Air Force were bad enough, even when one wasn't trying to move around in the aircraft. Both sets of troops on Callisto will therefore be operating at *much* less than peak personal efficiency.

If more than walking distances are involved, both armies will need not merely transport but mobile support units to recharge life support equipment—a tanklike equivalent of the torpedo boat's mother ship. What will happen if these units come in contact with each other is one of those essentially statistical problems faced by tactical commanders, science fiction authors, and war game buffs.

All this assumes, of course, that the mother planets can bear the cost of supplying all this equipment—and transporting it.

Just what this cost will be depends, of course, on the general technological background. Also, unless both species have mastered the art of space flight so thoroughly that an Earth-to-Pluto or even an Earth-to-Mercury flight (the latter is much more expensive in energy) is the equivalent of a family car trip to the supermarket, some facts of celestial mechanics are very relevant. (If the above state *has* been reached, all bets are off; see part III.)

For any given type of spacecraft and relative positions of two planets, a specific combination of fuel and payload exists. Periodically there will be orbital arrangements which maximize payload; we call these launch windows in the present state of the art. If two worlds are flying to the same third one, launch windows will differ in frequency and duration for the two planets of origin. In the Earth-Titan case, we have launch windows to Jupiter about every thirteen months; the Titanians have them about every twenty years (chopped into sixteen-day units by Titan's travel around Saturn). The latter windows are, however, much wider—that is, Saturn and Jupiter stay within a stated energy difference of payload maximum for a much longer time than do Earth and Jupiter.

Titan also has another advantage; the difference in both potential and kinetic energies between the Saturn and Jupiter orbits is much smaller than that between Earth and Jupiter even at the best of times. Both, of course, are less than the Earth-to-Saturn difference; but somewhere along the spectrum of technical competence comes the possibility for human and Titanian to attack each other's home worlds directly.

In this case, frequency and duration of one party's

launch windows matches that of the other provided soft landings are intended at each end. The Titanians, falling toward the sun, pick up a velocity which must be gotten rid of at the Earth end; the human beings must build up that same velocity to reach the Saturn system. If the Titanians merely plan to attack *en passant*—scattering radioactives or biologicals and returning immediately to Saturn—they have a huge energy advantage. Even biologicals can be sown at meteor speeds; small enough particles can enter atmosphere at such velocities without being overheated, since they have a very large radiating-area-to-volume ratio.

This brings us fairly smoothly to Situation Zero, that of interworld conflict between essentially identical life forms. Mother Earth has taken umbrage at the Martian colony's Declaration of Independence, or something of that sort. The colony has, of course, become self-sufficient before this could happen, so with sufficient emotional bitterness there *might* be total-destruction attempts on the "home" worlds. Since each one *can* use the other's territory, of course, however, this seems a bit less likely if only for reasons of economy.

However, the situation mentioned earlier obtains here—the division may not simply be between planets. Different nations or subcultures on each of the worlds may support different sides in the war. One can easily imagine a transport rocket's lifting off from Nation X with critical supplies for the Martian Independence Forces, with Nation Y making every possible effort to block the delivery.

A report from the Operations Officer of Y's 3754th Tactical Space Interdiction Group would make interesting reading.

"The six rockets of the 449th Interceptor Squadron lifted successfully and achieved intersection orbits with the target. They were sighted when they started to make velocity corrections for actual rendezvous, and two of our craft were destroyed by rocks. The others evaded the gravel clouds and closed succesfully, but depleted their combat laser batteries without ascertainable effect. Incendiary projectiles were used in attempts to ignite the enemy's fuel, and solid missiles to puncture his tanks. The only measurable result after exhausting the supply of these munitions was seventy-one punctures in the target hull; fuel apparently remained inert and in the tanks. It is believed that the crew are neutralized, as the Squadron Evaluation Officer reports the hull to be at radiation equilibrium temperature. The cargo is of course still en route to Mars, since no significant change in the target's orbital elements was achieved.

"The surviving attack craft depleted their fuel reserves below direct-return point in their successful efforts to avoid the enemy rocks, and are also committed to the Mars orbit. They have sufficient reaction mass to enter closed orbit around that planet. If they can secure enough additional supplies, energy, and reaction mass from our Martian sympathizers, they will be available for another action in approximately thirty-one months."

The numerous cost implications in such a report hardly need stressing, even with rocks being used as missiles. This is not meant to imply that space warfare will return to stone age tactics, however. The late Malcolm Jameson, in an article entitled *Space War Tactics* (*Astounding Stories,* November 1939) described a "mine field" of steel ball-bearings scattered in the path of an oncoming space ship. Contact at several miles per second would be extremely effective. Mr. Jameson used steel so that magnet-equipped "minesweepers" could clear out the menace to navigation later on. My own opinion is that the volume of space involved makes sweeping superfluous and, more important, impossible. My sense of economy therefore substitutes a payload of a couple of metric tons of medium gravel, carried in a low-performance rocket and scattered at the desired time by a small bursting charge. The resulting cloud of small stones could be extended enough to be very hard to dodge (or at least, require inconvenient amounts of fuel for the maneuver, as the report suggested) and still concentrated enough to make dodging a necessity if relative velocities are still high.

Throughout the range of strangeness possibilities, both reasonable strategy and possible tactics obviously depend critically on the level of technology available to the combatants. *Level,* not *levels;* there will not ordinarily be much difference, if the word *war* is really applicable. (Of course, any imaginative author can come up with exceptions to this generality; but it *is* a reasonable generality.) This would seem offhand to imply that the winner of any war could be predicted mathematically from a study of the technology availability to the two sides. The fallacy of this conclusion lies in the impossibility of keeping any significant item of technology a secret by either side for any significant length of time.

A sort of statistical magnifying glass, moreover, is represented by individual encounters between fighters, armed with stone knifes or jet aircraft as the case may be, and between intelligence operatives equipped with keen ears, telescopes, cameras, or spy rays. The result of a single such encounter may have an incredibly large effect on the general outcome. This makes war games fascinating, and may have a good deal to say about why people fight.

A possible relevance of the "strangeness spectrum" outlined here may be that as the strangeness number becomes greater, the likelihood of individual encounters goes down.

III

The discussion so far has been confined to our own planetary system, and many people feel that human activity will always be limited to that volume of space. It is certainly true that interstellar distances are vast. They are far greater than the ordinary mind can visualize in terms of anything familiar. Only our artificial symbol systems permit us to "think" about such quantities at all, and many human beings cannot manipulate or cannot believe such symbols. Many people apparently feel that human beings are for some mystical reason not subject to the laws of arithmetic. I have seen the term "population explosion" decried in print as atheistic propaganda; I have seen the city of Boston plastered with stickers advocating "forty hours pay for thirty hours work;" I live in a nation whose governing individuals seem to believe that it is possible to get more than the maximum amount of available effort by constantly reducing the value of the cost symbols. The failing is not confined to Christianity and Socialism, or even to religion in general; it seems to be an example of the wishful thinking so typical of our species. I suspect, sadly, that the common science-fiction belief in the possibility of faster-than-light travel may be an example of it, too.

But even below light speed, interstellar travel seems technically possible, however expensive. If it is possible, we should and probably will do it, since mankind has a built-in need for basic knowledge. Really this is two needs: there is an emotional (spiritual?) urge to *understand* things, which some can satisfy with the subjective certainty of religious Fundamentalism but for which most of us need some pretense of objectivity; and there is a life-and-death practical need—no rational human being could claim that humanity's present collective knowledge is enough to keep four billion of us alive and fed for more than a few years. For one reason or the other, and probably both, we will head for the stars when we develop the requisite abilities.

And having reached them, we will disagree, probably violently, with the people we send and the people we find.

At such vast and expensive distances, it may be harder than usual for even the confirmed cynic to find a crudely economic basis for interstellar war. Unfortunately, there doesn't have to be such a reason. I have been told, more or less convincingly, that Richard the Lion-Hearted and Peter the Hermit had some drive other than pure religion to send them on the Crusades, but they wouldn't

have had much company if the population of western
Europe had not been intensely religious. Even Hitler,
with Germany's burning urge for more material power
and possessions, had to use the essentially religious
"superman" mythology to override general German recognition of the ethical fact that the rest of the world was
not theirs to take.

With over fifty years of human history in my personal
memory, I find it quite easy to believe that the natives
of Delta Pavonis III might be willing to employ extreme violence to keep themselves from being cor-
rupted by some such immoral human practice as, say,
fiction writing. Beyond much doubt, the strangeness
figure will be well away from zero on the spectrum, and
they won't care personally what happens to Earth as a
planet. Everything said earlier about this situation still
applies, but a major additional factor now complicates
all strategic considerations.

The corruption, or whatever they don't like about
humanity, is going to continue to flow from the Solar
system for at least forty years after the Pavonians decide
to take action, no matter how drastic the action. It will
take a couple of decades for the doom to reach Sol, and
a couple more before ships which started before the
end finally reach Delta Pavonis. This creates a major
planning problem which may reduce the mere question
of obliterating Earth to the attention of a small subcommittee of the Chiefs of Staff. The main body will be
concerned with short-range defense—the *will* is that
the Pavonian population not be defiled; destruction of
the source of evil, while important, is incidental.

The subcommittee has the problem of finding a method
of destruction which will take care of Earth's population
quickly and completely enough to prevent any possible
retaliation. How this is to be done, especially if humanity has colonies scattered on several bodies of the
Solar system, defeats me for the moment. I could, of
course, invent a space-opera technique, but right now
I'm trying to keep within the range of reasonable
extrapolation.

Bacteriological warfare seems most likely to destroy human technological culture, but is very chancy. It has the advantage that any agent developed for the purpose would offer no danger to the makers; the virus or bacterium probably couldn't survive on their planet even if it did get loose from the lab, because it would need, say, six amino acids not present in any of the local life forms. However, it would take a good deal of time to infect all the enemy species no matter how efficient the delivery, and there is a near-certainty that some of the proposed victims would be immune. Even if there were too few survivors to *maintain* Earth's technological culture, enough of it would probably survive for a while to permit the retaliation which *must* be avoided.

I'm dubious about psychological warfare, though it would probably be worth trying. If humanity could be persuaded that it didn't *want* to travel to the stars—

Maybe we're under attack already. I doubt it; we're still talking slower-than-light, remember, and I doubt that beings limited in this way would have had the chance to learn enough about human psychology to use it as an efficient weapon. Obviously an infinity or two of special situations could make me wrong on this point, but again the story-tellers will have to take over.

This may be wishful thinking again, but it seems to me that the most effective strategy for both sides, once interstellar contact has been made and grounds for dislike, distrust, and general suspicion have been found or devised, is for both species to commit all possible resources to the search for a faster-than-light drive. If this is in fact impossible, it will at least keep them from actual combat and will produce lots of useful knowledge as spinoff. If it does turn out to be possible to get around the relativity restrictions, the species mastering the art first will be on the right side of such a huge technological gap that it should feel little need for immediate drastic action against the other (it probably *won't* feel that way, of course; realism would dictate that the other species would be bound to make the same discoveries—probably quite soon, since now they would *know* solutions to the problem were possible—so something drastic should still be done. If so, it will probably *be* done; but the result won't be a war).

If ways are found through or around the speed-of-light limit and the appropriate technology does spread widely in the galaxy, the effect on warfare can only be speculative. Real extrapolation is hardly possible. The different conceivable natures of the solution each have their own possibilities. If ships in transit are practically impossible to detect or, as with interplanetary travel, to intercept except near the start or finish of their flights, then we have the Category Zero situation described in Part II, or something very similar.

If the Galactic Patrol situation of the late E. E. Smith proves a more accurate description, with space craft able to traverse interstellar distances in hours, to detect each other parsecs away, and stop or reverse flight direction with no time lag, then space war will tend to come back to the essentially two-dimensional ground-and-air wars of the mid-twentieth century, as Dr. Smith himself pointed out. Most of the rules for such warfare will apply. One example would be the unwisdom of advancing major forces through basically hostile territory with a large concentration of enemy troops to one's rear. This kept the officers of Charles I from getting their battalions to London in the 1640s; it kept the Galactic Patrol's Grand Fleet out of the Second Galaxy until Boskone's fleet had been annihilated, in Smith's *Gray Lensman* published in 1939; it kept the Hanoi army at An Loc, a hundred kilometers short of its Saigon goal, in the "Easter Invasion" of 1972. This is not, of course, the only rule of tactics; others may combine to offset it, as Bernoulli's effect offsets gravity to make the airplane possible. Edward III of England could ignore it, in his looting journey through France which culminated at Crêcy in 1346, because he had friendly territory (Flanders) *ahead* of him.

Other probabilities—total defense against a determined attacker will probably remain as impossible in interstellar war as it was at Schweinfurt in World War

II and at Hanoi three decades later. Going underground will help.

If, on still another hand, interstellar travel proves to consist of jumping into and out of "hyperspace" defense is even more difficult and a lot of the rules of ground warfare will also have to be revised. Of course, there may be some restrictions on the nature of the "jumps," and these restrictions would have tactical and strategic relevance. Maybe one can't emerge with gravity fields above a certain intensity; maybe the jump can't be made within two kilometers of the fields of a 100 KW transformer operating above 20 Hertz; maybe—we're back with the story-tellers, for now.

IV (Summary)

This has not been a text on space warfare; none can be written yet, in the sharply limited state of the art. I have tried to suggest classification schemes for situations which may arise in interplanetary and interstellar conflict, but can't claim to have done a very complete job. I think the strangeness spectrum and the time-delay factors mentioned will prove useful for giving realism to stories, for designing war games, and as a basis for authors who want to point out how wrong I am. I will be rather unhappy if they end up as the nucleus of a real manual of space war practice; my pessimistic opinion expressed in Part I is not a hope.

For those who want to carry the thinking farther, read up on military history and physics, especially the former, if your hope is to prove me wrong somewhere.

Just remember that history books, unlike directly observed physical facts, have been written and edited by people.

Hal Clement was born in Somerville, Massachusetts, in 1922, attended public schools in Arlington and Cambridge, and received a B.S. in astronomy from Harvard in 1943. He served with the 8th AAF in World War II, flying thirty-five missions over Europe as copilot and pilot in B-24 bombers. After the war, he took his M.Ed. at Boston University, and has been teaching since then, except for two years of active duty in 1951-1953. He has since acquired an M.S. in chemistry, and is still a colonel in the Air Force Reserve.

He sold his first story to *Astounding* while a sophomore at Harvard and has produced a fairly steady flow of sf ever since. He has also published scientific articles in various periodicals, mostly under his real name (Harry C. Stubbs).

He is or has been a member of such scientific organizations as AAAS, New England Association of Chemistry Teachers, Bond Astronomical Society, and the Meteoritical Society. He was a charter member of the New England Science Fiction Association and served for two years on the Nebula Awards Committee of the Science Fiction Writers of America.

Married since 1952 to the former Mary Myers of Atlantic City, N.J., he has two sons and a daughter. His titles include:

Iceworld, 1953 (Gnome)
Needle, 1953 (Doubleday)
Mission of Gravity, 1954 (Doubleday)
Cycle of Fire, 1957 (Ballantine)
Close to Critical, 1959 (Ballantine)
Natives of Space, 1965 (Ballantine)
Small Changes, 1969 (Doubleday)
First Flights to the Moon, 1970 (Doubleday)
Starlight, 1971 (Ballantine)

Joe Haldeman's award-winning The Forever War *considers the effect on soldiers and on society of a war fought against alien enemies by troops transported at velocities so much higher than the speed of light that during a year of campaign and combat more than four normal centuries elapse on Earth.*

In that framework, this story tells of a man fighting against the strange weapons of a stranger foe—and of the fact that the world he fights for, when he returns to it, seems stranger still.

Joe Haldeman

TIME PIECE

They say you've got a fifty-fifty chance very time you go out. That makes it one chance in eight that you'll live to see your third furlough; the one I'm on now.

Somehow the odds don't keep people from trying to join. Even though not one in a thousand gets through the years of training and examination, there's no shortage of cannon fodder. And that's what we are. The most expensive, best trained cannon fodder in the history of warfare. Human history, anyhow; who can speak for the enemy?

I don't even call them snails anymore. And the thought of them doesn't trigger that instant flash of revulsion, hate, kill-fever—the psyconditioning wore off years ago, and they didn't renew it. They've stopped doing it to new recruits; no percentage in berserkers. I was a wild one the first couple of trips, though.

Strange world I've come back to. Gets stranger every time, of course. Even sitting here in a bogus twenty-first-century bar, where everyone speaks Basic and there's real wood on the walls and peaceful holograms instead of plugins, and music made by men. . . .

But it leaks through. I don't pay by card, let alone by coin. The credit register monitors my alpha waves and communicates with the bank every time I order a drink. And, in case I've become addicted to more modern vices, there's a feelie matrix (modified to look like an old-fashioned visiphone booth) where I can have my brain stimulated directly. Thanks, but no thanks—always

58

get this picture of dirty hands inside my skull, kneading, rubbing. Like when you get too close to the enemy and they open a hole in your mind and you go spinning down and down and never reach the bottom till you die. I almost got too close last time.

We were on a three-man reconnaissance patrol, bound for a hellish little planet circling the red giant Antares. Now red giant stars don't form planets in the natural course of things, so we had ignored Antares; we control most of the space around it, so why waste time in idle exploration? But the enemy had detected this little planet—God knows how—and about ten years after they landed there, we monitored their presence (gravity waves from the ships' braking) and my team was assigned the reconnaissance. Three men against many, many of the enemy—but we weren't supposed to fight if we could help it; just take a look around, record what we saw, and leave a message beacon on our way back, about a light-year out from Antares. Theoretically, the troopship following us by a month will pick up the information and use it to put together a battle plan. Actually, three more recon patrols precede the troop ship at one-week intervals; insurance against the high probability that any one patrol will be caught and destroyed. As the first team in, we have a pretty good chance of success, but the ones to follow would be in trouble if we didn't get back out. We'd be past caring, of course: the enemy doesn't take prisoners.

We came out of lightspeed close to Antares, so the bulk of the star would mask our braking disturbance, and inserted the ship in a hyperbolic orbit that would get us to the planet—Anomaly, we were calling it—in about twenty hours.

"Anomaly must be tropical over most of its surface." Fred Sykes, nominally the navigator, was talking to himself and at the two of us while he analyzed the observational data rolling out of the ship's computer. "No axial tilt to speak of. Looks like they've got a big outpost near the equator, lots of electromagnetic noise there. Figures . . . the goddamn snails like it hot. We requisitioned hotweather gear, didn't we, Pancho?"

Pancho, that's me. "No, Fred, all we got's parkas and snowshoes." My full name is Francisco Jesus Mario Juan-José Hugo de Naranja, and I outrank Fred, so he should at least call me Francisco. But I've never pressed the point. Pancho it is. Fred looked up from his figure and the rookie, Paul Spiegel, almost dropped the pistol he was cleaning.

"But why . . ." Paul was staring. "We knew the planet was probably Earthlike if the enemy wanted it. Are we gonna have to go tromping around in spacesuits?"

"No, Paul, our esteemed leader and supply clerk is being sarcastic again." He turned back to his computer. "Explain, Pancho."

"No, that's all right." Paul reddened a bit and also went back to his job. "I remember you complaining about having to take the standard survival issue."

"Well, I was right then and I'm doubly right now. We've *got* parkas back there, and snowshoes, and a complete terranorm environment recirculator, and everything else we could possibly need to walk around in comfort on every planet known to man—*Dios!* That issue masses over a metric ton, more than a giga-watt laser. A laser we could use, but crampons and pith helmets and elephant guns . . ."

Paul looked up again. "Elephant guns?" He was kind of a freak about weapons.

"Yeah."

"That's a gun that shoots elephants?"

"Right. An elephant gun shoots elephants."

"Is that some new kind of ammunition?"

I sighed, I really sighed. You'd think I'd get used to this after twelve years—or four hundred—in the service. "No, kid, elephants were animals, big gray wrinkled animals with horns. You used an elephant gun to shoot *at* them.

"When I was a kid in Rioplex, back in the twenty-first, we had an elephant in the zoo; used to go down in the summer and feed him synthos through the bars. He had a long nose like a fat tail, he ate with that."

"What planet were they from?"

It went on like that for a while. It was Paul's first trip out, and he hadn't yet gotten used to the idea that most of his compatriots were genuine antiques, preserved by the natural process of relativity. At lightspeed you age imperceptibly, while the universe's calendar adds a year for every light-year you travel. Seems like cheating. But it catches up with you eventually.

We hit the atmosphere of Anomaly at an oblique angle and came in passive, like a natural meteor, until we got to a position where we were reasonably safe from detection (just above the south polar sea), then blasted briefly to slow down and splash. Then we spent a few hours in slow flight at sea level, sneaking up on their settlement.

It appeared to be the only enemy camp on the whole planet, which was typical. Strange for a spacefaring, aggressive race to be so incurious about planetary environments, but they always seemed to settle in one place and simply expand radially. And they do expand; their reproduction rate makes rabbits look sick. Starting from one colony, they can fill a world in two hundred years. After that, they control their population by infantiphage and stellar migration.

We landed about a hundred kilometers from the edge of their colony, around local midnight. While we were outside setting up the espionage monitors, the ship camouflaged itself to match the surrounding jungle optically, thermally, magnetically, etc.—we were careful not to get too far from the ship; it can be a bit hard to find even when you know where to look.

The monitors were to be fed information from flea-sized flying robots, each with a special purpose, and it would take several hours for them to wing into the city. We posted a one-man guard, one-hour shifts; the other two inside the ship until the monitors started clicking. But they never started.

Being senior, I took the first watch. A spooky hour, the jungle making dark little noises all around, but nothing happened. Then Fred stood the next hour, while I put on the deepsleep helmet. Figured I'd need the sleep—once data started coming in, I'd have to be alert for about forty hours. We could all sleep for a week once we got off Anomaly and hit lightspeed.

Getting yanked out of deepsleep is like an ice-water douche to the brain. The black nothing dissolved and there was Fred a foot away from my face, yelling my name over and over. As soon as he saw my eyes open, he ran for the open lock, priming his laser on the way (definitely against regulations, could hole the hull that way; I started to say something but couldn't form the words). Anyhow, what were we doing in free fall? And how could Fred run across the deck like that while we were in free fall?

Then my mind started coming back into focus and I could analyze the sinking, spinning sensation—not free-fall vertigo at all, but what we used to call snail-fever. The enemy was very near. Crackling combat sounds drifted in from outdoors.

I sat up on the cot and tried to sort everything out and get going. After long seconds my arms and legs got the idea, I struggled up and staggered to the weapons cabinet. Both the lasers were gone, and the only heavy weapon left was a grenade launcher. I lifted it from the rack and made my way to the lock.

Had I been thinking straight, I would've just sealed the lock and blasted—the presence in my mind was so strong that I should have known there were too many of the enemy, too close, for us to stand and fight. But no one can think while their brain is being curdled that way. I fought the urge to just let go and fall down that hole in my mind, and slid along the wall to the air lock. By the time I got there my teeth were chattering uncontrollably and my face was wet with tears.

Looking out, I saw a smoldering gray lump that must have been Paul, and Fred screaming like a madman, fanning the laser on full over a 180-degree arc. There couldn't have been anything alive in front of him; the jungle was a lurid curtain of fire, but a bolt lanced in from behind and Fred dissolved in a pink spray of blood and flesh.

I saw them then, moving fast for snails, shambling in over thick brush toward the ship. Through the swirling fog in my brain I realized that all they could see was the light pouring through the open lock, and me silhouetted in front. I tried to raise the launcher but couldn't— there were too many, less than a hundred meters away, and the inky whirlpool in my mind just got bigger and bigger and I could feel myself slipping into it.

The first bolt missed me; hit the ship and it shuddered, ringing like a huge cathedral bell. The second one didn't miss, taking off my left hand just above the wrist, roasting what remained of my left arm. In a spastic lurch I jerked up the launcher and yanked the trigger, holding it down while dozens of micro-ton grenades popped out and danced their blinding way up to and across the enemy's ragged line. Dazzled blind, I stepped back and stumbled over the med-robot, which had smelled blood and was eager to do its duty. On top of the machine was a switch that some clown had labeled EMERGENCY EXIT; I slapped it, and as the lock clanged shut the atomic engines muttered—growled— screamed into life and a ten-gravity hand slid me across the blood-slick deck and slammed me back against the rear-wall padding. I felt ribs crack and something in my neck snapped. As the world squeezed away, I knew I was a dead man but it was better to die in a bed of pain than to just fall and fall. . . .

I woke up to the less-than-tender ministrations of the med-robot, who had bound the stump of my left arm and was wrapping my chest in plastiseal. My body from forehead to shins ached from radiation burns, earned by facing the grenades' bursts, and the nonexistent hand seemed to writhe in painful, impossible contortions. But numbing anesthetic kept the pain at a bearable distance, and there was an empty space in my mind where the snail-fever had been, and the gentle hum told me we were at lightspeed; things could have been one flaming hell of a lot worse. Fred and Paul were gone but that just moved them from the small roster of live friends to the long list of dead ones.

A warning light on the control panel was blinking stroboscopically. We were getting near the hole—excuse me, "relativistic discontinuity"—and the computer had to know where I wanted to go. You go in one hole at lightspeed and you'll come out of some other hole; *which* hole you pop out of depends on your angle of approach. Since they say that only about one per cent of the holes are charted, if you go in at any old angle you're liable to wind up in Podunk, on the other side of the galaxy, with no ticket back.

I just let the light blink, though. If it doesn't get any response from the crew, the ship programs itself automatically to go to Heaven, the hospital world, which was fine with me. They cure what ails you and then set you loose with a compatible soldier of the opposite sex, for an extended vacation on that beautiful world. Someone once told me that there were over a hundred worlds named Hell, but there's only one Heaven. Clean and pretty from the tropical seas to the Northern pine forests. Like Earth used to be, before we strangled it.

A bell had been ringing all the time I'd been conscious, but I didn't notice it until it stopped. That meant that the information capsule had been jettisoned, for what little it was worth. Planetary information, very few espionage-type data; just a tape of the battle. Be rough for the next recon patrol.

I fell asleep knowing I'd wake up on the other side of the hole, bound for Heaven.

I pick up my drink—an old-fashioned old-fashioned— with my new left hand and the glass should feel right, slick but slightly tacky with the cold-water sweat, fine ridges molded into the plastic. But there's something missing, hard to describe, a memory stored in your fingertips that a new growth has to learn all over again. It's a strange feeling, but in a way seems to fit with this crazy Earth, where I sit in my alcoholic time capsule and, if I squint with my mind, can almost believe I'm back in the twenty-first.

I pay for the nostalgia—wood and natural food, human bartender and waitress who are also linguists, it all comes dear—but I can afford it, if anyone can. Compound interest, of course. Over four centuries have passed on Earth since I first went off to the war, and my salary's been deposited at the Chase Manhattan Credit Union ever since. They're glad to do it; when I die, they keep the interest and the principal reverts to the government. Heirs? I had one illegitimate son (conceived on my first furlough) and when I last saw his gravestone, the words on it had washed away to barely legible dimples.

But I'm still a young man (at lightspeed you age imperceptibly while the universe winds down outside) and the time you spend going from hole to hole is almost incalculably small. I've spent most of the past half millenium at lightspeed, the rest of the time usually convalescing from battle. My records show that I've logged a trifle under one year in actual combat. Not bad for 438 years' pay. Since I first lifted off I've aged twelve years by my biological calendar. Complicated, isn't it— next month I'll be thirty, 456 years after my date of birth.

But one week before my birthday I've got to decide whether to try my luck for the fourth trip out or just collect my money and retire. No choice, really. I've got to go back.

It's something they didn't emphasize when I joined up, back in 2088—maybe it wasn't so obvious back then, the war only decades old—but they can't hide it nowadays. Too many old vets wandering around, like animated museum pieces.

I could cash in my chips and live in luxury for another hundred years. But it would get mighty lonely. Can't talk to anybody on Earth but other vets and people who've gone to the trouble to learn Basic.

Everyone in space speaks Basic. You can't lift off until you've become fluent. Otherwise, how could you take orders from a fellow who should have been food for worms centuries before your grandfather was born? Especially since language melted down into one Language.

I'm tone-deaf. Can't speak or understand Language, where one word has ten or fifteen different meanings, depending on pitch. To me it sounds like puppydogs yapping. Same words over and over; no sense.

Of course, when I first lived on Earth there were all sorts of languages, not just one Language. I spoke Spanish (still do when I can find some other old codger who remembers) and learned English—that was before they called it Basic—in military training. Learned it damn well, too. If I weren't tone-deaf I'd crack Language and maybe I'd settle down.

Maybe not. The people are so strange, and it's not just the Language. Mindplugs and homosex and voluntary suicide. Walking around with nothing on but paint and powder. We had Fullerdomes when I was a kid; but you didn't *have* to live under one. Now if you take a walk out in the country for a breath of fresh air, you'll drop over dead before you can exhale.

My mind keeps dragging me back to Heaven. I'd retire in a minute if I could spend my remaining century there. Can't, of course; only soldiers allowed in space. And the only way a soldier gets to Heaven is the hard way.

I've been there three times; once more and I'll set a record. That's motivation of a sort, I suppose. Also, in the unlikely event that I should live another five years, I'll get a commission, and a desk job if I live through my term as a field officer. Doesn't happen too often—but there aren't too many desk jobs that people can handle better than cyborgs.

That's another alternative. If my body gets too garbaged for regeneration, and they can save enough of my brain, I could spend the rest of eternity hooked up to a computer, as a cyborg. The only one I've ever talked to seemed to be happy.

I once had an African partner named N'gai. He taught

me how to play O'wari, a game older than Monopoly or even chess. We sat in this very bar (or the identical one that was in its place two hundred years ago) and he tried to impress on my non-Zen-oriented mind just how significant this game was to men in our position.

You start out with forty-eight smooth little pebbles, four in each one of the twelve depressions that make up the game board. Then you take turns, scooping the pebbles out of one hole and distributing them one at a time in holes to the left. If you dropped your last pebble in a hole where your opponent had only one or two, why, you got to take those pebbles off the board. Sounds exciting, doesn't it?

But N'gai sat there in a cloud of bhang-smoke and mumbled about the game and how it was just like the big game we were playing, and everytime he took a pebble off the board, he called it by name. And some of the names I didn't know, but a lot of them were on my long list.

And he talked about how we were like the pieces in this simple game; how some went off the board after the first couple of moves, and some hopped from place to place all through the game and came out unscathed, and some just sat in one place all the time until they got zapped from out of nowhere. . . .

After a while I started hitting the bhang myself, and we abandoned the metaphor in a spirit of mutual intoxication.

And I've been thinking about that night for six years, or two hundred, and I think that N'gai—his soul find Buddha—was wrong. The game isn't all that complex.

Because in O'wari, either person can win.

The snails populate ten planets for every one we destroy.

Solitaire, anyone?

Joe Haldeman, Oklahoma born, spent a year as a foot soldier in Vietnam, where he was wounded. On his return, he sold his first science fiction story, then wrote his first novel, *War Year*, a non-sf book about Vietnam. His first science fiction novel, *The Forever War*, won the Hugo, Nebula, and Ditmar Awards for the best novel of the year 1975. It too was based on his Vietnam experience.

Joe has a B.A. in physics and astronomy and an M.F.A. in English. His latest novels, at this writing, are *Mindbridge* and *All My Sins Remembered*. His short story collection, *Infinite Dreams*, appeared recently, and he has completed his newest novel, *Worlds*. He is now collaborating with his brother, Jack C. Haldeman II, on another novel, *Starschool*.

He lives in Ormond Beach, Florida, with his wife, Gay.

One of the primary rules in any war is that one must be able to distinguish friend from foe, and this is especially true when the foe is not only ruthless and incapable of fear, but also inventive and subtle at dissimulation. Fred Saberhagen's Berserkers are all of these. Military robots created by a long-dead culture to fight a long-forgotten war, capable of self-repair, adaptation and improvement, and replication—and still charged with the terrible mission of destroying all life everywhere—they are, I think, far more convincing and infinitely more frightening than the vast majority of alien enemies imagined by other science fiction writers.

And when it comes to telling which are men and which Berserkers when the life of a planet is concerned. . . .

Fred Saberhagen

INHUMAN ERROR

When the dreadnought *Hamilcar Barca* came out of the inhuman world of plus-space into the blue-white glare of Meitner's Sun the forty men and women of the dreadnought's crew were taut at their battle stations, not knowing whether or not the whole berserker fleet would be around them as they emerged. But then they were in normal space, seconds of time were ticking calmly by, and there were only the stars and galaxies to be seen, no implacable, inanimate killers coming to the attack. The tautness eased a little.

Captain Liao, his lean frame strapped firmly into the combat chair in the center of the dreadnought's bridge, had brought his ship back into normal space as close to Meitner's Sun as he dared—operating on interstellar, *c*-plus drive in a gravitational field this strong was dangerous, to put it mildly—but the orbit of the one planet of the system worth being concerned about was still tens of millions of kilometers closer to the central sun. It was known simply as Meitner's Planet, and was the one rock in the system habitable in terms of gravity and temperature.

Before his ship had been ten standard seconds in normal space, Liao had begun to focus a remote-controlled telescope to bring the planet into close view on a screen that hung before him on the bridge. Luck had brought him to the same side of the sun that the planet happened to be on; it showed under magnification on the screen as a thin illuminated crescent, covered with fluffy-looking perpetual clouds. Somewhere beneath those clouds a human colony of about ten thousand people dwelt, for the most part under the shelter of one huge ceramic dome. The colonists had begun work on the titanic project of converting the planet's ammonia atmosphere to a breathable one of nitrogen and oxygen. Meanwhile they held the planet as an outpost of some importance for the interstellar community of all Earth-descended men.

There were no flares of battle visible in space around the planet, but still Liao lost no time in transmitting a message on the standard radio and laser communications frequencies. "Meitner's Planet, calling Meitner's. This is the dreadnought *Hamilcar Barca*. Are you under attack? Do you need immediate assistance?"

There came no immediate answer, nor could one be expected for several minutes, the time required for signals traveling at the speed of light to reach the planet, and for an answer to be returned.

Into Liao's earphones now came the voice of his Detection and Ranging Officer. "Captain, we have three ships in view." On the bridge there now sprang to life a three-dimensional holographic presentation, showing Liao the situation as accurately as the dreadnought's far-ranging detection systems and elaborate combat computers could diagram it. He smoothed graying hair back from his high forehead with an habitual gesture, and tried to determine what was going on.

One ship, appearing as a small bright dot with attached numerical coordinates, was hanging relatively motionless in space, nearly on a line between *Hamilcar Barca* and Meitner's Planet. The symbol chosen for it indicated that this was probably a sizable craft, though not nearly as massive as the dreadnought. The other two ships visible in the presentation were much smaller, according to the mass-detector readings on them. They were also both considerably closer to the planet, and moving toward it at velocities that would let them land on it, if that was their intention, in less than an hour.

What these three ships were up to, and whether they

were controlled by human beings or berserker machines, was not immediately apparent. After sizing up the situation for a few seconds, Liao ordered full speed toward the planet—full speed, of course, in the sense of remaining in normal space and thus traveling much slower than light—and to each of the three ships in view he ordered the same message beamed: "Identify yourself, or be destroyed."

The threat was no bluff. No one took chances where berserker machines were concerned. They were an armada of robot spaceships and supporting devices built by some unknown and long-vanished race to fight in some interstellar war that had reached its forgotten conclusion while men on Earth were wielding spears against the sabertooth tiger. Though the war for which the berserker machines had been made was long since over, still they fought on across the galaxy, replicating and repairing themselves endlessly, learning new strategies and tactics, refining their weapons to cope with their chief new enemy, Earth-descended man. The sole known basic in their fundamental programming was the destruction of all life, wherever and whenever they could find it.

Waiting for replies from the planet and the three ships, hoping fervently that the berserker fleet that was known to be on its way here had not already come and gone and left the helpless colony destroyed, Liao meanwhile studied his instruments critically. "Drive, this is the Captain. Can't you get a little more speed on?"

The answer came into his earphones: "No, sir, we're on the red line now. Another kilometer-per-second and we'll blow a power lamp, or worse. This is one heavy sun, and it's got some dirty space around it." The ship was running now on the same space-warping engines that carried it faster than light between the stars, but this deep within the huge gravitational well surrounding Meitner's Sun the power that could be applied to them was severely restricted. The more so because here space was dirty, as the Drive Officer had said, meaning the interplanetary matter to be encountered within this system was comparatively dense. It boiled down to the fact that Liao had no hope of overtaking the two small vessels that fled ahead of him toward the planet. They, as it were, skimmed over shoals of particles that the dreadnought must plow through, flirted with reefs of drive-wrecking gravitational potential that it must approach more cautiously, and rode more lightly the waves of the solar wind that streamed outward as always from a sun.

Now the minimum time in which the largest, nearest vessel might have replied to the dreadnought's challenge had come and gone. No reply had been received. Liao ordered the challenge repeated continuously.

The Communications Officer was speaking. "Answer from the planet, Captain. It's coming in code. I mean the simple standard dot-dash code, sir, like emergency signals. There's a lot of noise around too, maybe that's the only way they can get a signal through." Powerfully and crudely modulated dot-and-dash signals could carry intelligence through under conditions where more advanced forms of modulation were simply lost.

Communications was on the ball; already they had the decoded words flowing across a big screen on the bridge.

DREADNOUGHT ARE WE EVER GLAD TO HEAR FROM YOU STOP ONE OF THE TWO LITTLE SHIPS CLOSING IN ON US MUST BE A BERSERKER STOP BETTER TRANSMIT TO US IN DOT-DASH CODE STOP LOTS OF NOISE BECAUSE SUN IS FLARING AND WE COULDN'T READ YOUR SIGNAL VERY WELL.

The letters abruptly stopped flowing across the screen. The voice of the Communications Officer said: "Big burst of noise, Captain, signals from the planet are going to be cut off entirely for a little while. This sun is a very active flare star . . . just a moment, sir. Now we're getting voice and video transmissions beamed to us from both small ships. But the signals from both ships are so garbled by noise we can't make anything out of them."

"Beam back to them in dot-dash, tell them they'll have to answer us that way. Repeat our warnings that they must identify themselves. And keep trying to find out what the ground wants to tell us." The Captain turned his head to look over at his Second Officer in the adjoining combat chair. "What'd you think of that, Miller? 'One of the two little ships must be a berserker'?"

Miller, by nature a somewhat morose man, only shook his massive head gloomily, knitted heavy brows, and saved his speech to make a factual report. "Sir, I've been working on identifying the two active ships. The one nearest the planet is so small it seems to be nothing more than a lifeboat. Extrapolating backward from its present course and position indicates it may well have come from the third ship, the one that's drifting, a couple of hours ago.

"The second little ship is a true interstellar vessel; could be a one-man courier ship or even somebody's private yacht. Or a berserker, of course." The enemy came in all shapes and sizes.

Still no answer had been returned from the large, drifting ship, though the dreadnought was continuing to beam threatening messages to her, now in dot-dash code. Detection reported now that she was spinning slowly around her longest axis, consistent with the theory that she was some kind of derelict. Liao checked again on the state of communications with the planet, but they were still cut off by noise.

"But here's something, Captain. Dot-and-dash is coming in from the supposed courier. Standard code as before, coming at moderate manual speed."

Immediately, more letters began to flow across the number-one screen on the bridge:

I AM METION CHONGJIN COMMANDING THE ONE MAN COURIER ETRURIA EIGHT DAYS OUT OF ESTEEL STOP CANNOT TURN ASIDE I AM CARRYING VITAL DEFENSE COMPONENT FOR COLONY STOP LIFEBOAT APPROX 12 MILLION KM TO MY PORT AND AHEAD IS SAID BY GROUND TO BE CLAIMING TO BE THE SHIP CARRYING THE DEFENSE COMPONENT THEREFORE

IT MUST REALLY BE A BERSERKER STOP IT WILL PROBABLY
REACH COLONY AND BOMB OR RAM IT BEFORE I GET THERE
SO YOU MUST DESTROY IT REPEAT DESTROY THE BERSERKER
QUOTE LIFEBOAT UNQUOTE MOST URGENT THAT YOU HIT IT
SOON END MESSAGE

Miller made a faint whistling noise. "Sounds fairly
convincing, Chief." During briefing back at base three
standard days ago they had been informed of the fact
that the colony on Meitner's Planet was awaiting ship-
ment of a space inverter to complete and activate their
defensive system of protective force-screens and beam-
projecting weapons. Until the inverter could be brought
from Esteel and installed the colony was virtually defenseless; the dreadnought had been dispatched to offer
it some interim protection.

Liao was giving orders to Armament to lock the c-plus
cannon of the main battery onto the lifeboat. "But fire
only on my command." Turning back to the Second, he
said: "Yes, fairly convincing. But the berserkers might
have found out somehow that the space inverter was
being rushed here. They might even have intercepted
and taken over the courier carrying it. We can't see
who we're talking to on that ship or hear his voice. It
might have been a berserker machine that just tapped
out that message to us."

The Communications Officer was on again. "Bridge,
we have the first coded reply from the lifeboat coming
in now. Here it comes on your screen."

WE ARE HENRI SAKAI AND WINIFRED ISPAHAN CARRYING THE
DEFENSE MATERIEL NAMELY SPACE INVERTER THEY NEED
ON THE PLANET STOP OUR SHIP THE WILHELMINA FROM
ESTEEL WAS SHOT UP BY THE BERSERKER TWO DAYS AGO
WHEN IT ALMOST CAUGHT US STOP THE BERSERKER OR AN-
OTHER ONE IS HERE NOW ABOUT 11 MILLION KM TO OUR
STARBOARD AND A LITTLE BEHIND US YOU MUST KEEP IT
FROM GETTING TO US OR TO THE PLANET WHERE MAYBE IT
COULD RAM THE DOME END MESSAGE

"Communications," the Captain snapped, "how is this coming through? I mean, does this also seem like someone sending manual code?"

"No, sir, this is very rapid and regular. But if you mean, Captain, does that prove they're not human, it doesn't. In a lifeboat the transmitter often has a voice-to-code converter built in."

"And conversely a berserker could send slowly and somewhat irregularly, like a man, if it wanted to. Thank you." The Captain pondered in silence for a little while.

"Sir," Miller suggested, "maybe we'd better order both small ships to stop, until we can overtake and board them."

The Captain turned his head to look at him steadily, but remained silent.

Miller, slightly flustered, took thought and then corrected himself. "Now I see the problem more fully, sir. You can't do that. If one of them is really carrying the space inverter you don't dare delay him for a minute. A berserker fleet may materialize in-system here at any moment, and is virtually certain to arrive within the next six to eight hours. Our ship alone won't be able to do more than hit-and-run when that happens. Our fleet can't get here for another day. The colony will never survive the interval without their space inverter installed."

"Right. Even if I sent a fast launch ahead to board and inspect those ships, the delay would be too much to risk. And that's not all, Second. Tell me this—is this conceivably just some misunderstanding, and both of those ships are really manned by human beings?"

"Not a chance," the Second answered promptly. "They both claim to be carrying the space inverter, and that can't be true. Those things just aren't ordered or built in duplicate or triplicate, and they both claim to be bringing it from the planet Esteel . . . the next question is, can both of our little targets be berserkers? Trying to psych us into letting one of them get through? I'll keep trying to reach the ground, see if they can shed any more light on this." Miller swiveled away in his heavy chair.

"Good going."

In their earphones Communications said: "Here's more from the ship that calls itself *Etruria*, Bridge."

"Put it right on our screen."

REPEAT COLONY SAYS LIFEBOAT IS ALSO CLAIMING TO BE THE HUMAN ONE STOP THEY MUST BE A BERSERKER IMPERATIVE YOU STOP THEM WHAT DO YOU WANT ME TO DO TO PROVE IM HUMAN STOP REPEAT MY NAME IS METION CHONGJIN IM ALONE ON BOARD HERE WIFE AND KIDS AT HOME ON ESTEEL IF THAT MEANS ANYTHING TO YOU STOP REPEAT HOW CAN I PROVE TO YOU IM HUMAN END MESSAGE

"Easy," Captain Liao muttered to himself. "Father a human child. Compose a decent symphony. In the next forty minutes or so." That was approximately the time left before at least one of the ships would be able to reach the planet. Liao's mind was racing to formulate possible tests, but getting nowhere. Berserkers had awesome powers, not only as physical fighting machines, but as computers. They could not counterfeit either human appearance or human behavior successfully when under close observation; but Liao was not certain that a battery of psychologists with several days to work in would be able to say with certainty whether it was a living man or a lying berserker that answered their questions in dot-dash.

Time passed. Hurtling through silence and near-emptiness at many kilometers per second, the ships very slowly changed the positions of their symbols in the huge holographic presentation on the bridge.

"Now more from the *Wilhelmina's* lifeboat, Captain."

"Run that on the top of the screen, will you, and put any more that comes in from *Etruria* on the bottom."

HENRI AND WINIFRED HERE COLONY TELLS US OTHER SHIP IS CLAIMING TO BE FROM ESTEEL CARRYING DEFENSE COMPONENTS AND REQUESTING LANDING INSTRUCTIONS STOP IT MUST BE LYING IT MUST BE A BERSERKER MAYBE THE SAME ONE THAT ATTACKED OUR SHIP TWO DAYS AGO . . .

The message ran on and despite some irrelevancies and redundancies it outlined a coherent story. The *Wilhelmina* (if the story was to be believed) had been on an interstellar cruise, carrying a number of young people on some kind of student exchange voyage or post-graduate trip. Somewhere on the outskirts of the solar system that contained the heavily industrialized planet Esteel, a courier ship bound for Meitner's had approached and hailed the *Wilhelmina*, had in fact commandeered her to complete the courier's mission. Berserkers were in pursuit of the courier and had already damaged her extensively.

. . .AND WE WERE ON OUR WAY HERE WITH THE INVERTER WHEN ONE OF THE BERSERKERS ALMOST CAUGHT UP AGAIN TWO STANDARD DAYS AGO STOP WILHELMINA WAS BADLY SHOT UP THEN CREW ALL KILLED WE ARE ONLY TWO LEFT ALIVE TWO HISTORY STUDENTS WE HAD TERRIBLE PROBLEMS ASTROGATING HERE BUT MADE IT STOP LIVING IN LIFEBOAT AND WORKING RIDDLED SHIP IN SPACESUITS YOU CANT STOP US NOW AFTER ALL WE HAVE BEEN THROUGH STOP YOU MUST DESTROY THE BERSERKER SHIP WE WILL REACH PLANET BEFORE IT DOES I THINK BUT IT WILL BE ABLE TO HIT THE DOME BEFORE THE SPACE INVERTER CAN BE INSTALLED STOP WE ARE GOING TO KEEP SENDING UNTIL YOU ARE CONVINCED WE ARE HUMAN . . .

The message from the lifeboat went on, somewhat more repetitiously now. And at the same time on the bottom of the screen more words from *Etruria* flowed in:

I HAVE TRIED TO CATCH THE BERSERKER LIFEBOAT AND SHOOT IT DOWN BUT I CANT ITS UP TO YOU TO STOP IT STOP WHAT DO YOU WANT ME TO DO TO PROVE IM HUMAN . . .

The Second Officer sighed lightly to himself, wondering if, after all, he really wanted his own command.

"Communications, beam this out," the Captain was ordering. "Tell them both to keep talking and give us their life histories. Birth, family, education, the works. Tell them both they'd better make it good if they want to live." On buttons on the arm of his chair he punched out an order for tea, and a moment later tea came to him there through a little door, hot in a capped cup with drinking tube attached. "I've got an idea. Second. You study the background this so-called Esteeler spaceman Metion Chongjin gives us. Think up someplace you might have known him. We'll introduce you to him as an old friend, see how he copes."

"Good idea, Chief."

"Communications here again, Bridge. We've finally gotten another clear answer back from the ground. It's coming through now, we'll put it in the middle of your number-one screen."

. . .IN ANSWER TO YOUR QUESTION NO THEY CAN'T BOTH BE BERSERKERS STOP AN HOUR AGO THERE WAS A BRIEF LETUP IN THE NOISE AND WE GOT ONE CLEAR LOOK AT A HUMAN MALE FACE ALIVE AND TALKING COGENTLY ANSWERING OUR QUESTIONS NO POSSIBILITY THAT WAS A BERSERKER BUT UNFORTUNATELY BOTH SUSPECT SHIPS WERE SENDING ON THE SAME FREQ AND WE DONT KNOW FROM WHICH ONE THAT VOICE AND PICTURE CAME BUT WE DO KNOW THAT ONE OF THEM IS HUMAN . . .

"Damnation, how they've botched things up. Why didn't they ask the two men to describe themselves, and see which description fit what they saw?"

"This is Communications again, Bridge. They may have tried asking that, sir, for all we know. We've lost contact with the ground again now, even on code. I guess the solar wind is heating up. Conditions in the ionosphere down there must be pretty fierce. Anyway, here's a little more from the *Etruria:*"

WHAT DO YOU WANT ME TO DO TO PROVE IM HUMAN RECITE POETRY MARY HAD A LITTLE LAMB STOP SAY PRAYERS I NEVER MEMORIZED ANY OF THEM STOP OKAY I GIVE UP SHOOT US BOTH DOWN THEN END MESSAGE

The Second Officer thumped a fist on the arm of his massive chair. "A berserker would say that, knowing that its fleet was coming, and the colony would be defenseless if we stopped the space inverter from getting to it."

Liao shrugged, and helped himself to a massive slug of tea. "But a human might say that too, being willing to die to give the colony a few more hours of life. A human might hope that given a few more hours some miracle might come along, like the human fleet getting here first after all. I'm afraid that statement didn't prove a thing."

"I . . . guess it didn't."

After another good slug of tea, Liao put in a call to Astrogation.

"Chief Astrogator here, sir."

"Barbara, have you been listening in on this? Good. Tell me, could those two supposed history students, probably knowing little science or technology, have brought that ship in here? Specifically, could they have astrogated for two days, maybe fifty or sixty light-years, without getting lost? I suppose the ship's autopilot was knocked out. They said they were living in the lifeboat and working the damaged ship in spacesuits."

"Captain, I've been pondering that claim too, and I just don't know. I can't say definitely that it would be impossible. If we knew just how badly that ship was damaged, what they had to work with, we could make a better guess."

The Captain looked back at his situation hologram. The apparently inert hulk that he had been told was the *Wilhelmina* was considerably closer now, lying as it did almost in *Hamilcar Barca's* path toward Meitner's Planet. The dreadnought was going to pass fairly near the other ship within the next few minutes. "As to that, maybe we can find out something. Keep listening in, Barbara." Turning to the Second Officer, Liao ordered: "You're going to be taking over the Bridge shortly, Miller. I want us to match velocities with that supposed hulk ahead, and then I'm going over to her, in hopes of learning something."

"It might be booby-trapped, Captain."

"Then we'll have an answer, won't we? But I don't expect an answer will be found that easily. Also get me a reading on exactly how much time we have left to decide which ship we're going to fire on."

"I've already had the computers going on that, sir. As of now, thirty-two and a quarter minutes. Then the lifeboat will either be down in atmosphere or around on the other side of the planet, and out of effective range in either case. The courier will take a little longer to get out of effective range, but . . ." He gestured helplessly.

"The courier being slower won't help us. We have to decide in thirty-two minutes."

"Chief, I just had an idea. If the lifeboat was the berserker, since it's closer to the planet, wouldn't it have tried before we got here to head off the courier from the planet . . . oh. No good. No offensive weapons on the lifeboat."

"Right, except perhaps it has one bloody big bomb, meant for the colony. While the courier ship doubtless has some light armament, enough to deal with the lifeboat if it got in range. Still nothing proven, either way."

In another minute the silent ship ahead was close enough for telescopes on the dreadnought to pick out her name by starlight. It was *Wilhelmina*, all right, emblazoned near one end of her cigar-like shape. The dreadnought matched velocities with her smoothly, and held position a couple of kilometers off. Just before getting into a launch with a squad of armed marines to go over and inspect her, Liao checked back with the Bridge to see if anything was new.

"Better hear this before you go," Miller told him. "I just introduced myself to Chongjin as an old buddy. This is his reply, quote: 'I honestly don't remember your name if I ever knew it, stop. If this was a test I guess I passed. Hurrah! Now get on with it and stop that berserker on the lifeboat . . .' and then the signal faded out again. Chief, our communication problems are getting steadily worse. If we're going to say anything more to either of those ships we'd better send it soon."

"How many minutes left, Second?"

"Just eighteen, sir."

"Don't waste any of 'em. This ship is yours."

"I relieve you, sir."

No signs of either life or berserker activity were apparent on the *Wilhelmina* as the launch crossed the space separating her from the dreadnought and docked, with a gentle clang of magnetic grapples. Now Liao could see that the reported damage was certainly a fact. Holes several meters in diameter had been torn in *Wilhelmina*'s outer hull. Conditions inside could hardly be good.

Leaving one man with the launch, Liao led the rest of his small party in through one of the blasted holes, swimming weightlessly, propelling themselves by whatever they could grip. He had briefed the men to look for something, anything, that would prove or disprove the contention that humans had driven this ship for the last two days since she had been damaged.

Fifteen and a half minutes left.

The damage inside was quite as extensive as the condition of the hull had indicated. Their suit lights augmenting the sharp beams that Meitner's distant sun threw into the airless interior, the boarding party spread out, keeping in touch by means of their suit radios. This had undoubtedly been a passenger ship. Much of the interior was meant as living quarters, divided into single and double cabins, with accommodations for a couple of dozen people. What furnishings remained suggested luxury. So far, everything said by the lifeboat's occupant was being proved true, but Liao as yet had no clear evidence regarding that occupant's humanity, nor even a firm idea of what evidence he was looking for. He only hoped that it was here, and that he would recognize it at first sight.

The interior of the ship was totally airless now, having been effectively opened to the stars by the repeated use of some kind of penetration weapon. The ruin was much cleaner than any similarly damaged structure on a planet's surface could be, loose debris having been carried out of the ship with escaping air, or separated from her when her drive took her outside of normal space and time, between the stars.

"Look here, Captain." The Lieutenant in charge of the marine squad was beckoning to him. Liao followed, on a vertiginous twisting passage through the wreck.

Near the center of the slender ship the Lieutenant had found a place where a wound bigger than any of the others had pierced in, creating in effect an enormous skylight over what had been one of the largest compartments on board. Probably it had been a lounge or refectory for the passengers and crew. Since the ship was damaged this ruined room had evidently provided the most convenient observation platform for whoever or whatever had been in control: a small, wide-angle telescope, and a tubular electronic spectroscope, battery-powered and made for use in vacuum, had been roughly but effectively clamped to the jagged upper edge of what had been one of the lounge's interior walls and now formed a parapet against infinity.

The Lieutenant was swiveling the instruments on their mountings. "Captain, these look like emergency equipment from a lifeboat. Would a berserker machine have needed to use these, or would it have gear of its own?"

The Captain stood beside him. "When a berserker puts a prize crew on a ship, it uses man-sized, almost android machines for the job. It's just more convenient for the machines that way, I suppose, more efficient. So they could quite easily use instruments designed for humans." He swung his legs to put his magnetic boots against the lounge's soft floor, so that they held him lightly to the steel deck beneath, and stared at the instruments, trying to force more meaning from them.

Men kept on searching the ship, probing everywhere, coming and going to report results (or rather the lack of them) to Liao at his impromptu command post in what had been the lounge. Two marines had broken open a jammed door and found a small airless room containing a dead man who wore a spacesuit; cause of death was not immediately apparent, but the uniform collar visible through the helmet's faceplate indicated that the man had been a member of *Wilhelmina's* crew. And in an area of considerable damage near the lounge another, suitless, body was discovered wedged among twisted structural members. This corpse had probably been frozen near absolute zero for several days and exposed to vacuum for an equal length of time. Also its death had been violent. After all this it was hard to be sure, but Liao thought that the body had once been that of a young girl who had been wearing a fancy party dress when she met her end.

Liao could imagine a full scenario now, or rather two of them. Both began with the shipload of students, eighteen or twenty of them perhaps, enjoying their interstellar trip. Surely such a cruise had been a momentous event in their lives. Maybe they had been partying as they either entered or were about to leave the solar system containing the planet Esteel. And then, according to Scenario One, out of the deep night of space came the desperate plea for help from the damaged and harried courier, hotly pursued by berserkers that were not expected to be in this part of the galaxy at all.

The students would have had to remain on board the *Wilhemina*, there being no place for them to get off, when she was commandeered to carry the space inverter on to Meitner's Planet. Then urgent flight, and two days from Meitner's a berserker almost catching up, tracking and finding and shooting holes in *Wilhelmina*, somewhere in the great labyrinth of space and dust and stars and time, in which the little worlds of men were strange and isolated phenomena. And then the two heroic survivors, Henri and Winifred, finding a way to push on somehow.

Scenario Two diverted from that version early on,

and was simpler and at first glance more credible. Instead of the *Wilhelmina* being hailed by a courier and pressed into military service, she was simply jumped by berserkers somewhere, her crew and passengers efficiently wiped out, her battered body driven on here ahead of the main berserker fleet in a ploy to forestall the installation of the space inverter and demolish the colony before any help could reach it. Scenario One was more heroic and romantic, Two more prosaic and businesslike. The trouble was that the real world was not committed to behaving in either style but went on its way indifferently.

A man was just now back from inspecting *Wilhelmina*'s control room. "Almost a total loss in there, sir, except for the Drive controls and their directional settings. Artificial gravity's gone, Astrogator's position is wiped out, and the autopilot too. Drive itself seems all right, as far as I can tell without trying it."

"Don't bother. Thank you, mister."

Another man came to report, drifting upside-down before the captain in the lack of gravity. "Starboard forward lifeboat's been launched, Captain. Others are all still in place, no signs of having been lived in. Eight-passenger models."

"Thank you," Liao said courteously. These facts told him nothing new. Twelve minutes left now, before he must select a target and give the command to fire. In his magnetic boots he stood before the telescope and spectroscope as their user had done, and looked out at the stars.

The slow rotation of the *Wilhelmina* brought the dreadnought into view, and Liao flicked his suit radio to the intership channel. "Bridge, this is Captain. Someone tell me just how big that space inverter is. Could two untrained people manhandle it and its packing into one of those little eight-passenger lifeboats?"

"This is the Armaments Officer, sir," an answer came back promptly. "I used to work in ground installations, and I've handled those things. I could put my arms

around the biggest space inverter ever made, and it
wouldn't mass more than fifty kilograms. It's not the
size makes 'em rare and hard to come by, it's the
complexity. Makes a regular drive unit or artificial gravity generator look like nothing."

"All right. Thank you. Astrogation, are you there?"

"Listening in, sir."

"Good. Barbara, the regular astrogator's gear on this
ship seems to have been wiped out. What we have then
is two history students or whatever, with unknown
astronomical competence, working their way here from
someplace two days off, in a series of *c*-plus jumps.
We've found their instruments, apparently all they used,
simple telescope and spectroscope. You've been thinking it over, now how about it? Possible?"

There was a pause. Barbara would be tapping at her
console with a pencil. "Possible, yes. I can't say more
than that on what you've given me."

"I'm not convinced it's possible. With umpteen thousand stars to look at, their patterns changing every time
you jump, how could you hope to find the one you
wanted to work toward?" *Ten minutes.* Inspiration struck.
"Listen! Why couldn't they have shoved off in the lifeboat, two days ago, and used its autopilot?"

Barbara's voice was careful as always. "To answer
your last question first. Chief, lifeboats on civilian ships
are usually not adjustable to give you a choice of goals;
they just bring you out in the nearest place where you
are likely to be found. No good for either people or
berserkers intent on coming to Meitner's system. And if
Wilhelmina's drive is working it could take them between the stars faster than a lifeboat could.

"To answer your first question, the lifeboats carry
aids for the amateur astrogator, such as spectral records
of thousands of key stars, kept on microfilm. Also often
provided is an electronic scanning spectroscope of the
type you seem to have found there. The star records
are indexed by basic spectral type, you know, types O,
B, A, F, G, W and so on. Type O stars, for example,
are quite rare in this neck of the woods so if you just

scanned for them you would cut down tremendously on the number of stars to be looked at closely for identification. There are large drawbacks to such a system of astrogation, but on the other hand with a little luck one might go a long way using it. If the two students are real people, though, I'll bet at least one of them knows some astronomy."

"Thank you," Liao said carefully, once again. He glanced around him. The marines were still busy, flashing their lights on everything and poking into every crevice. Eight minutes. He thought he could keep the time in his head now, not needing any artificial chronometer.

People had lived in this lounge, or rec room, or whatever it had been, and enjoyed themselves. The wall to which the astrogation instruments were now fastened had earlier been decorated, or burdened, with numerous graffiti of the kinds students seemed always to generate. Many of the messages, Liao saw now, were in English, an ancient and honorable language still fairly widely taught. From his own school days he remembered enough to be able to read it fairly well, helping himself out with an occasional guess.

CAPTAIN AHAB CHASES ALEWIVES, said one message proceeding boldly across the wall at an easy reading height. The first and third words of that were certainly English, but the meaning of the whole eluded him. Captain Liao chases shadows, he thought, and hunches. What else is left?

Here was another:

OSS AND HIS NOBLE CLASSMATES WISH THE WHOLE WORLD

And then nothingness, the remainder of the message having gone when Oss and his noble classmates went and the upper half of this wall went with them.

"Here, Captain! Look!" A marine was beckoning wildly.

The writing he was pointing to was low down on the wall and inconspicuous, made with a thinner writing instrument than most of the other graffiti had been. It said simply: *Henri & Winifred.*

Liao looked at it, first with a jumping hope in his

heart and then with a sagging sensation that had rapidly
become all too familiar. He rubbed at the writing with
his suited thumb; nothing much came off. He said:
"Can anyone tell me in seven minutes whether this was
put here after the air went out of the ship? If so, it
would seem to prove that Henri and Winifred were still
around then. Otherwise it proves nothing." If the berserker had been here it could easily have seen those
names and retained them in its effortless, lifeless memory, and used them when it had to construct a scenario.

"Where are Henri and Winifred now, that is the
question," Liao said to the Lieutenant, who came drifting near, evidently wondering, as they all must be,
what to do next. "Maybe that was Winifred back there
in the party dress."

The marine answered: "Sir, that might have been
Henri, for all that I could tell." He went on directing
his men, and waiting for the Captain to tell him what
else was to be done.

A little distance to one side of the names, an English
message in the same script and apparently made with
the same writing instrument went down the wall like
this:

Oh	Kiss
Be	Me
A	Right
Fine	Now
Girl	Sweetie

Liao was willing to bet that particular message wasn't
written by anyone wearing a space helmet. But no, he
wouldn't make such a bet, not really. If he tried he
could easily enough picture the two young people, rubbing faceplates and laughing, momentarily able to forget the dead wedged in the twisted girders a few meters
away. Something about that message nagged at his memory, though. Could it be the first line of an English
poem he had forgotten?

The slow turn of the torn ship was bringing the
dreadnought into view again. "Bridge, this is Captain.
Tell me anything that's new."

"Sir, here's a little more that came in clear from the lifeboat. I quote: 'This is Winifred talking now, stop. We're going on being human even if you don't believe us, stop.' Some more repetitious stuff, Captain, and then this: 'While Henri was navigating I would come out from the lifeboat with him and he started trying to teach me about the stars, stop. We wrote our names there on the wall under the telescope; if you care to look you'll find them; of course that doesn't prove anything, does it. If I had lenses for eyes I could have read those names there and remembered them . . .' It cuts off again there, Chief, buried in noise."

"Second, confirm my reading of how much time we have left to decide."

"Three minutes and forty seconds, sir. That's cutting it thin."

"Thanks." Liao fell silent, looking off across the universe. It offered him no help.

"Sir! Sir! I may have something here." It was the marine who had found the names, who was still closely examining the wall.

Looking at the wall where the man had aimed his helmet light, near the deck below the mounted instruments, Liao beheld a set of small, grayish indented scratches, about half a meter apart.

"Sir, some machine coming here repeatedly to use the scopes might well have made these markings on the wall. Whereas a man or woman in spacesuits would not have left such marks, in my opinion, sir."

"I see." Looking at the marks, that might have been made by anything, maybe furniture banged into the wall during that final party, Liao felt an irrational anger at the marine. But of course the man was only trying to help. He had a duty to put forward any possibly useful idea that came into his head. "I'm not sure these were made by a berserker, spaceman, but it's something to think about. How much time have we left, Second?"

"Just under three minutes, sir. Standing by ready to fire at target of your choice, sir. Pleading messages still coming in intermittently from both ships, nothing new in them."

"All right." The only reasonable hope of winning was to guess and take the fifty-fifty chance. If he let both ships go on, the bad one was certain to ram into the colony and destroy it before the other could deliver the key to the defenses and it could be installed. If he destroyed both ships, the odds were ten to one or worse that the berserker fleet would be here shortly and accomplish the same ruin upon a colony deprived of any chance of protecting itself.

Liao adjusted his throat muscles so that his voice when it came out would be firm and certain, and then he flipped a coin in his mind. Well, not really. There were the indented scratches on the bulkhead, perhaps not so meaningless after all, and there was the story of the two students' struggle to get here, perhaps a little too fantastic. "Hit the lifeboat," he said then, decisively. "Give it another two minutes, but if no new evidence turns up, let go at it with the main turret. Under no circumstances delay enough to let it reach the planet."

"Understand, sir," said Miller's voice. "Fire at the lifeboat two minutes from your order."

He would repeat the order to fire, emphatically, when the time was up, so that there could be no possible confusion as to where responsibility lay. "Lieutenant, let's get the men back to the launch. Continue to keep your eyes open on the way, for anything . . ."

"Yes, sir."

The last one to leave the ruined lounge-observatory, Liao looked at the place once more before following the marines back through the ship. *Oh, be a fine girl, Winifred, when the slug from the c-plus cannon comes. But if I have guessed wrong and it is coming for you, at least you'll never see it. Just no more for you. No more Henri and no more lessons about the stars.*

The stars . . .

Oh, be a fine girl . . .

O, B, A, F, G, K, . . .

"*Second officer!*"

"Sir!"

"Cancel my previous order! Let the lifeboat land. Hit the *Etruria!* Unload on that bloody damned berserker with everything we've got, right now!"

"Yessir!"

Long before Liao got back to the launch the *c*-plus cannon volleyed. Their firing was invisible, and inaudible here in airlessness, but still he and the others felt the energies released pass twistily through all their bones. Now the huge leaden slugs would begin skipping in and out of normal space, homing on their tiny target, far outracing light in their trajectories toward Meitner's Planet. The slugs would be traveling now like de Broglie wavicles, one aspect matter with its mass magnified awesomely by Einsteinian velocity, one aspect waves of not much more than mathematics. The molecules of lead churned internally with phase velocities greater than that of light.

Liao was back on the dreadnought's bridge before laggard light brought the faint flash of destruction back.

"Direct hit, Captain." There was no need to amplify on that.

"Good shots, Arms."

And then, only a little later, a message got through the planet's ionospheric noise to tell them that the two people with the space inverter were safely down.

Within a few hours the berserker fleet appeared in system, found an armed and ready colony, with *Hamilcar Barca* hanging by for heavy hit-and-run support, skirmished briefly and then decided to decline battle and departed. A few hours after that, the human fleet arrived and decided to pause for some refitting. And then Captain Liao had a chance to get down into the domed colony and talk to two people who wanted very much to meet him.

"So," he was explaining, soon after the first round of mutual congratulations had been completed, "when I at last recognized the mnemonic on the wall for what it was, I knew that not only had Henri and Winny been

there but that he had in fact been teaching her something about astronomical spectroscopy at that very place
beside the instruments—therefore after the ship was
damaged."

Henri was shaking his youthful head, with the air of
one still marveling at it all. "Yes, *now* I can remember
putting the mnemonic thing down, showing her how to
remember the order of spectral types. I guess we use
mnemonics all the time without thinking about it much.
Every good boy does fine, for the musical notes. *Bad
boys race our young girls*—that one's in electronics."

The captain nodded. "*Thirty days hath September.*
And *Barbara Celarent* that the logicians still use now
and then. Berserkers, with their perfect memories, probably don't even know what mnemonics are, much less
need them. Anyway, if the berserker had been on the
Wilhelmina, it would've had no reason to leave false
clues. No way it could have guessed that I was coming
to look things over."

Winifred, slender and too fragile-looking for what she
had been through, took him by the hand. "Captain,
you've given us our lives, you know. What can we ever
do for you?"

"Well. For a start . . ." He slipped into some English
he had recently practiced: "You might be a fine girl,
sweetie, and . . ."

Fred Saberhagen was born in Chicago in 1930, and lived there most of his life, with time out for travel, until he moved with his wife and three children to New Mexico in 1975. He has been writing science fiction and selling it since 1951, full time since 1967. He has also been an Air Force enlisted man, an electronics technician, and a writer/editor at *Encyclopaedia Britannica*, to which he contributed the article on science fiction. His published fiction output now includes about 18 books and 50 short stories. His new novel, *A Matter of Taste*—a Dracula book—is being published by Ace in September 1980. With his family, he enjoys travel, hiking, swimming, and going to conventions about once a year.

In the two following articles, Keith Laumer and Katherine MacLean speculate from very different standpoints on our encounters—and possible conflicts—with alien beings and cultures when we move out into space. Laumer looks at the problem primarily from a struggle-for-survival-as-we-have-known-it point of view; Ms. MacLean regards it from a struggle-for-survival-as-they-may-have-known-it perspective.

Read together, they provide much food for thought—and, I think, substance for quite a number of new science fiction stories.

Keith Laumer

COULDN'T WE ALL JUST BE DEAR, DEAR FRIENDS?

No.

Strangers, unfortunately, are not "Just our friends we haven't met yet."

Life forms may and probably do vary in an infinite number of ways, but it seems pretty certain that they will be alike in some ways too—and therein lies the conflict. The more any alien life form resembles us, the more likely it is that we may find ourselves in competition with it for the necessities of continued existence, the first of which is room.

Consider affairs right here on good old Terra Insula: Biafrans vs. Congolese (not Esquimaux), Bangladesh vs. Pakistan (and Pakistan vs. India). And Israelis vs. Arabs (both sides being desert-dwelling, monotheistic Semites). The persecution of blacks in the post-bellum South was not inspired by white aristocrats, but was the sincere expression of rivalry by their economic competitors, the po' whites. Then we have the religious conflicts: Medieval Catholics vs. assorted heretics, and post-Renaissance Catholics vs. their contemporary Protestants (including 20th Century Irishmen)—Christians all. So if we don't engage in a death-struggle with the mud-dwellers of Krako 8, it'll be because we don't want their dark mud-worlds and they have no yen for the sunlit glades of Earth.

When a bacterial culture reaches the edge of the agar-agar, it either is transferred to a less restricted environment (a bigger plate of jelly) or—it dies. We've pretty well filled up our planet of origin; already we need more room. We envision domed colonies on the Moon or planets, or self-sufficient Earth satellites—both inadequate expedients. But let us assume we succeed in staving off the Great Dying for some centuries by such desperate measures, until we find livable worlds elsewhere or learn to terraform inhospitable planets. It seems to me that other sapient species will inevitably have faced the same problems, and will have found the same solution. The result must be that in time we'll meet and bump organ clusters on some coveted piece of real estate vital to our survival—and to theirs. There'll be no room then for an Alphonse and Gaston routine. We *gotta* have that sector of space! So we proceed—and when they also forge ahead, we both, reluctantly perhaps, start shooting.

But, you say, suppose the people we meet are gentle pacifists, evolved from kindly flower-eaters, with no long tradition of combative competition. Will we just blast them and take their planets? No. Because no passive, nonoffensive species will have made it to the finals. Fast runners, armored browsers, bad-smellers, etc. can survive for a time, but they can't, by the nature of their life patterns, win the survival contest to master their own homeworlds. It will be the mean old predators we'll have to contend with. The best defense is usually an offensive, and you can seldom win sitting on the status quo, or even by running like hell from it. This is not a matter of ravening militarists stamping around the Galaxy looking for trouble, or even of cold-eyed engineers surveying a right-of-way through somebody else's garden. It will be more like a drowning man clutching for his life at whatever's floating.

The dear little fox cubs waiting hopefully in the den for Mommy to come home with dinner before they starve don't have the least ill-will toward the sweet little bunnies huddled in their rabbit-hole waiting for *their* Mommy to return. But if the Mommy wabbit outruns or outwits the Mommy fox, the little foxes may indeed perish. Whereas if Mama fox scores, the little bunnies starve. But Mrs. Fox has to try, and Mrs. Wabbit must try to elude her. Neither can possibly take pity on the other and also go on living. We all have every right to fight for life, and we will when we must. To my mind, this doesn't mean that we'll wage a war of extinction. No doubt some accommodation can be made to allow the loser (the weaker or softer-hearted species) to live a little longer on a reduced scale as long as it doesn't get in the winner's way. But in the final analysis, we can have no alien allies, because eventually it will be them or us. And both species will, quite rightly, vote for "us."

All this, of course, is at very long range. Before we can do a whole lot of organ-cluster bumping with other land-hungry species, we'll have to deal with that venerated bugaboo, the so-called Limiting Velocity. I've dealt with this fallacy at length elsewhere, but here I'll expose it to the harsh light of analogy *Place,* Boston, 1750 A.D. Any horse fancier can tell you that the fastest time ever clocked over the mile by a racehorse works out to about thirty-five miles an hour—a fantastic speed, we'll agree; and supposing that any animal could maintain this speed for the whole 275 miles between Boston and Philly—an obvious impossibility—the time required would be almost eight hours. Ergo, Q.E.D., no man will ever travel from Boston to Philly in less than eight hours. And the fellow who so argues is *absolutely right*—so long as he limits himself to travelling by horse.

So what's that got to do with Einstein's theory that if all the energy in the Universe were employed in attempting to accelerate one sub-nuclear particle to the velocity of light it still wouldn't be enough? Just this: we'll be able to start from Point A at the same moment as a photon, and arrive at Point B while the photon is still enroute. We'll get there before the light, though we won't necessarily exceed C in the process. How? Beats the hell out of me, Lieutenant. But let us not limit ourselves to terms of plain old matter and energy. (Why restrict our thinking to the concept of accelerating a material mass by means of physical energy?) Let's just go—and we will. We'll find lovely unoccupied planets in plenty at first, and I expect we'll grab them as fast as we can breed.

During this Era of Expansion, we'll encounter non-competitor species with which we can temporarily co-exist, as long as there's room for this luxury. But if the day comes when we have to make our last desperate bid to keep a selected few humans alive on a small reservation surrounded by competitors, but are forbidden by the Other Guys to trespass on their territory (perhaps because their Great God Ug says so), we'll dig in and fight. Not because we like fighting or desperately hate the Other Guys, even though they eat both their own young and ours and have other unacceptable habits—but because it's our only chance. We won't let the five-billion-year saga of life on Earth end by default.

In the initial skirmishes of the Last War, when it first becomes apparent that it's Us or Them, no doubt we'll deploy our highly impressive battle-fleets with boyish enthusiasm—and no doubt the Other Guys will be glad to come out to play: a fellow who owns a super-dread-naught naturally wants a chance to see what it'll do. But at the last—and why dwell on mere preliminaries?—we'll find that Infantry is still the Queen of Battles. The foot- (or pseudopod-) soldier will still have to go in to take and hold the ground. After all, the ground is what it's all about. Planet Busters won't be used. More potent and accurate ways of inflicting damage on individuals without damage to the landscape will be found—the weapons of those last desperate days—and we'll find that the ancient virtues of strength and courage, loyalty, and devotion to duty (plus plain old determination) will still be as vital as they were when *Homo erectus* had to throw the cave bears out of the available housing or die of cold. The cave bear was fourteen feet of muscles and bad temper, and could eat a Kodiak bear for lunch. He liked the same kind of caves our great-grandpas did, and great-grandpa had only a sharp stick to fight with. Too bad for *Ursus spelaeus*. They got kind of extinct all of a sudden. We come from a long line of tough SOB's, and if we didn't we wouldn't be here.

Nobody will want to invade Earth except as a mere detail after the last battle has been fought (if we should lose) and the last man is dead. The planet will have no military value, and a room-hungry competitor will take all the easier pickings first. We'll defend the old place the way hornets defend their nests, but our fighting HQ will certainly be elsewhere.

There won't be any robots in the last war, because there won't be any robots, period. By robot, I mean android, artificial man (or alien). There'll be special-purpose usuform devices, of course, like record-changers and Mars-explorers. But there certainly will never be a need—or even an excuse—for crippling a machine by limiting it to tottering around on two or more legs, or in any other way restricting it to an external resemblance to any living being. (I have a late 19th Century magazine article, explaining that mechanical street transportation is just around the corner. The illustration shows a very life-like sheet-metal horse, with a steam boiler in his belly and complete in every detail except genitals, plus neat little external pistons looking like shock-absorbers attached to each joint of its shapely legs. The artist had vision, but not much. We should already have known that wheels worked better, and that the handsome head and neck were as superfluous as the tail and genitals. But we *still* almost always have the engine in front where the horse used to be—and up until about 1905 lots of motor-buggies had a socket for a buggy-whip, useful for horse-whipping editors.) But we don't need to go on being myopic. We can leave the streamlining and steering vanes off our spaceships. Of course, square spaceships with no portholes to look through won't look as snazzy as Flash Gordon's needle-nosed fleets, but they'll be more practical for stacking.

A fighting "robot" will, of course, possess weapons, armor, self-transport capability, and effective communications equipment, and will thus inevitably look like a war machine, not a sheet-metal soldier. Computers will continue to be improved, and to improve themselves, but also and alas, they'll never get as smart as, say, a dull-witted three-year old. (Yes. Exactly: computers are stupid. You're inside a building with a computer-controlled security system that locks all the doors without ever forgetting—only this morning the place is on fire and you're hammering on a locked exit. Your old pal and daily coworker, the computer, hasn't been programmed to listen to reason. Too bad.)

So we'll probably have to do most of our own fighting—and there'll be neither race nor tribe, border nor breed nor birth, when two strong beings stand face to face, though they come from the ends of the Universe.

"I was born," writes Keith Laumer, "in Syracuse, N.Y. at an early age, and almost at once noticed that the world was imperfect, and have since been busy rectifying all errors within my reach."

His family moved first to Buffalo and then, in 1937, to Florida. In April 1945, we are informed, he ended World War II by arriving in Germany. Subsequently, he put in a year at *Stockholms Högskolan,* and then got a B.Sc. and a B.Arch(itecture) at the University of Illinois.

After that, he accepted a direct commission in the Air Force (thereby aborting WW III,) but resigned later to accept appointment in the U.S. Foreign Service, where he earned commissions as Third Secretary to Embassy in the U.S. Diplomatic Service, Vice-Consul in the U.S. Consular Service (both of which are arms of the Foreign Service,) and Foreign Service Officer Class Six in the Foreign Service. (His experiences provided him with excellent background material for his celebrated—and wildly wonderful—Retief stories.) After "a dreadful year in Rangoon, once the Garden City of the East, now the Garbage City of the East," where he wrote his first story, he returned to active duty in the USAF with the rank of captain. He did four years in London, two more at Kelly Field, and resigned to write full time. He has never regretted giving up his sinecure.

Katherine MacLean

AN ALIEN SORT OF WAR

Other species will have other ways of war. We might not recognize them as warfare. We might not even know when we have lost.

The delights of practice battle, in football, fencing or chess, the hot rousing of energy and strength when angry, and our cool alertness of controlled fear when speeding and dodging other cars—these are all pleasures based on a billion years of ancestors who killed enemies or fled from them, whose victories and escapes were helped by that extra surge of energy and delight in both fight and flight. There are no real losers in any living creature's ancestry.

The bloody pawprints of ancestral winners are still in our souls, delighting in the threat of death. Tempted into war, battle, or revenge, we are not seeking profit or benefit, we are trying to reenact our clawed, fanged, daggered, glittering past. All our fellow survivors of ancestral battles must hold in check similar wild impulses to flee or fight. In this selection all animals must be the same, even on other planets.

But there is strangeness in the arena where the males fight for the right to breed. Each species has its special combat style of male pitted against male. Many are very strange.

Even on other planets, the logic of evolution will probably have invented two sexes, and pitted male against male in duels for the right to reproduce. Their styles of duel may become their special style of warfare.

On Earth, rams charge straight at each other and meet head to head with a ground shaking thud. Male birds plunge into endurance displays of dancing, larks fly straight up to a great height singing wildly without losing breath, arousing female larks and lyric poets.

A society of civilized beings organized from an evolutionary advance of winning larks would try to repeat their ancestors way of winning. When confronted by difficulties and giving way to anger males would sing loudly about the threat and fly acrobatics above it.

This is not a human sort of anger. Humans when balked and baffled first feel an urge to push, thrust, hit, but if it is another human they usually attempt to communicate and persuade, holding in check their more savage urges. If baffled by antagonism from strangers of strange beliefs or a different language they tend to yell, curse, stamp, charge, swing clubs or chairs, or throw missiles.

Our ethnologists, trying to trace the kind of successes that could have been responsible for such crude urges, hypothesize a million or so years of wandering in family and tribe, gathering grass seeds and berries and eggs, finding that a threatening pack of baboons, jackals or even single lions might turn tail and run if charged by the whole pack of us. We find that charging, yelling, throwing stones and striking with sticks can panic, and even kill, wandering packs of humans who infringe on our territory and food supply and try to steal our women.

If the band of invaders does not run, the ensuing thud and grunt and smashed skulls results in a fine leftover of attractive defeated women, skin clothing, tents and bags of grain, and much later stimulates thoughts of gathering in a male hunting band and deliberately looking for another tribe of strangers to kill, a thought that appeals to young males when the older males of the tribe have monopolized all the women.

Therefore when a human male hears the trumpets of war, or even the possibility that some outside group has done something to antagonize his group, he usually gets a surge of primitive anticipation, an image of the splendid energy of charging with a pack of yelling friends, lopping violently at the heads of ferocious strange males who invaded his territory to take his women, and being admired by new strange women who love winners.

Survival energy flows, he bristles, struts and grins, showing his teeth, talks more loudly and feels more loyal to his friends and more aggressive toward passing women. It is a pleasant feeling, and likely to override the chilly voice of reason.

The political war over territory, nation against nation, is an enlargement of male combat to an unsuitable size. It pays off only to rulers, who conquer more taxpayers, and to generals, who gain public applause as "defenders" by playing the aging human male's tribal game of Potlatch.

Potlatch, is carried on by an exchange of pawns. Mutual destruction of "others'" war machines, property and surplus young males goes on until one side is left without more property and young soldiers to sacrifice, and the other has still a reserve left. Both nations lose, but the one who loses the least percentage of its wealth and living males prides itself as "the winner" and has the option to loot in reparations whatever little wealth is left the loser. The old men win—or at least always have won in the past.

This is specifically human, but it is the way we like it.

Other species will have other ways of war. We might not recognize them as warfare. We might not even know when we have lost.

Our new settlers on a new, green, empty planet are made uneasy by the settlement of aliens on the other side of the planet. Human settlers who drowned are rumored to have been killed by the aliens.

Our settlers attack and destroy an exploring party of aliens, then, feeling guilty and fearing retaliation, the settlers claim they were attacked and beg our Space Navy to bomb and destroy the alien settlement, which it does.

The Navy Intelligence officers find and capture a wandering survivor of the destroyed settlement and proceed to question the young male about the war plans and defenses of the alien colony.

The prisoner acts harmless, seeming to cooperate by trying to learn our language, but learns intonations first. Deliberately he makes songs from human voice inflections, watching our physical responses to angry, friendly, sad, proud, subordinate and commanding inflections. He answers in friendly, subordinate, sad, high-pitched inflections, and presently is being responded to as a child or girl. He listens to each individual interviewer he encounters and makes songs of mood changes from their inflections. Mimicking a few key words he sings portraits of each individual's innermost thoughts and moods, ranging from defeat and despair to hope and confidence, from love to loneliness, from successful work to courageous stubborn attempts to go on against illness.

He is a mockingbird, invading each bird's territory by song—announcing he can be that bird, take his role, do his job and do it well. He expects males defeated in song to give up their territory and females, as any reasonable bird would do by instinct.

"Play it again, Sam." The human servicemen are deeply moved by Mockingbird and pleased by these artistic renditions of their own deepest feelings. They ask him to sing more, and they take the recordings of his "questionings" and broadcast them on the comm networks of all Earth-settled planets.

Among the listening audiences are many personality types similar to the servicemen whose heart-thoughts Mockingbird has been singing. They feel their emotional essence sublimated into song, given answers and finding completion. They buy recordings and play them, gaining insight and release.

The royalties go to Mockingbird. No one wants to hurt him. He is brought back to Earth-settled planets, rich, surrounded and protected by human fans and admirers, besieged by emotionally intemperate groupies who have fallen sexually in love with the alien. They beg him to sing more, and he makes songs from politi-

cal speeches, songs from the inflections of sermons,
songs from girls talking to their lovers and mothers
talking to their children. He becomes The Wordless
Philosopher, the Guru of Music, respected by critics
and professors, followed by creeds and cults, starting
philosophies and religions.

Politicians and military, maneuvering toward a potlatch or a cold war with the alien planet, find they have
no public support. The public sees the alien planet as
populated with harmless, lovable, wise singers, and
does not want a war against them. Mockingbird is their
idol and friend, he can command more goods, services
and obedience than any politician.

Song has won his territory. He rules planets.

Play it again, Sam.

Believe me, his success is no fantasy. We do not
defend ourselves against invasion by music, taste, smell.
It does not strike against or arouse our male dueling
instincts—there is no pleasure in such a battle for us
and no defeat in submission.

If we lost that round, we did not know we lost.

Meanwhile, some of our merchant traders have landed
on a neutral rocky planet near the central planetary
system of the Mockingbird empire. They have demonstrated things manufactured by Earth industry, given
and taken trade goods.

The Mockingbirds have bought some of our wonderful sound recording equipment, some of our recordings
of great instrumental music. The second round has
begun in a different form of warfare. Their culture is
under attack and might crumble. They do not know it is
a war.

Nor do our Colonel Blimps understand trade as invasion. Our military do not recognize that their own job
as top predator is to reduce our surplus population;
they think that strategy and invasion is the name of
their game.

There are quick, easy ways to conquer and dominate
a new territory, ways our military do not understand.

Give the strangers tobacco, or give them free kerosene lamps, and later when they run out of kerosene, sell them kerosene. Send in free food, put their farms out of business. Stop sending free food after it is too late to plant, and hire the hungry population for your factory. This strategy is The Hook. A hooked user prays for the welfare of his pusher.

Will you integrate the conquered population into your nation or production chain by training them to produce a specialty that your production might need and grow dependent on, or will you keep them as untrained workers, the first to starve in the next wave of automation and unemployment? Pick life or death.

Enemy trade strategists might accept your offer of free goods, and use the surplus wealth to buy time with some strategy of their own, trying to take the bait without the hook.

Our military strategists do not see it. Where is the primitive thrill, glory and blood of war, if property is being traded instead of destroyed?!

Only top corporation executives and heads of departments of trade bent over the skipping chessboard know the keen delight and danger of playing against a tariff barrier until it snaps shut like a mousetrap, amputating a hundred branch stores.

The account balance bleeds and screams, ten thousand are thrown out of work. You pick yourself up broke and come back for the next round, armed with a patent you have been suppressing, long held in reserve, that will put the entire industry out of business in all countries, including the competitors, and replace the million dollar product with something new costing ten cents.

As businesses and work skills sink and rise slowly like overloaded life-rafts with millions hanging on, on any planet which permits trade, we leave the gloriously destructive (but unrecognized) strategies of interstellar business and come to other kinds of alien warfare, before you readers scream, "But this is just Earth!" and stop buying this book.

Imagine a planet on which the future master race,

the creature with the creative, flexible mind, is at this
primitive point in time a small, smelly, skunklike creature which has learned to analyze and control its own
hormone secretions. It is being followed by a giant
carnivore, sniffing the scented footsteps.

The small genius skunk lays a trail of a substance
used in those animal brains to generate sleep.

The giant carnivore sleeps. After the many descendants of the small genius skunk have sprayed each other
into permanent glandular arousal as father, mother,
kitten, and in heat, they have learned to cooperate. The
giant carnivores, drooling, attracted by the delightful
arousals, find that half the trees in the forest are sprayed
to smell like their own giant carnivore females in heat.
They spend their energies and have no descendants.
The skunks are safe, multiply and evolve.

Overpopulating, the skunks must develop social warfare to a fine art and become their own predators. They
play dominance submission games, and build civilizations,
traveling the same paths of political gigantism, passing
through motie cycles, and developing technology from
war machines. But every war is biological and non-
violent, and the only overt machines are wagons pulled
by tamed lions and great tame birds.

The transmission of smells is the transmission of organic molecules. RNA and plasmid, self-replicating DNA
are organic molecules, and in suitably nourishing environments such as the braincells of a sniffer, they can
generate moods and trigger instincts. Our exploring
navy finds a new inhabited planet.

We have found a civilized planet with no signs of
destructive wars, no layers of radioactive ruins. Peace-
niks! Pacifists!

At last we have found a cooperative well-organized
civilization, a submissive orderly population without
any threat of violence!

On the advice of delighted ethologists we land without obvious weapons or threat, take no hostages, study
their languages and conform to their customs.

One of their customs is the standard costume, including a white filter worn tightly over the nose like a surgeon operating. Our human ambassadors wear these also, for fear of being thought immodest in exposing the nose.

Our ambassadors are ignored at first, and then, when they have learned the language, they are approached by a representative of the king, who demands that he be sent the human of greatest command, power and authority among the humans.

The ambassadors choose the one among them who once was a strategist and gave advice that was accepted by the Terran Empire strategic computer. He presents himself alone at the palace of the king, and wonders at the great place of political power in a non-violent community, while he is led into the royal presence.

The alien king, descendant of a long line of conquerers by power of scent, has, after much thought, decided to accept Earthmen as an equal race. He has decided to challenge their king to a friendly duel.

Explaining that he has been impressed by Earth ship technology, the king ostentatiously and slowly takes off his white nose-filter mask, lays it aside and inhales deeply, taking a breath over each of the ambassador's shoulders in a gesture which resembles a French ceremonial kiss.

The human representative, startled by his gesture, but trying to follow strange standards of politeness, slowly removes his own nose filter, and inhales on either side of the alien aristocrat's neck. The alien aristocrat steps back, sampling the human scents he has inhaled. Most of them are merely the scents of clothing and plastic, but there are the smells of oxidized foods, and a few proteins which seem too large to be food, possibly hormones of emotion or instinct, some in tiny peptide traces, perhaps left over from suppressed cries of childhood.

The king smiles and releases a barrage of duplicated hormones and peptides. The Earthman inhales a stink of familiar scents which smell like his own armpit after a week without showering.

He is overwhelmed by nausea, then by a barrage of conflicting emotions. Slowly he slips to his knees, feeling that he is in the presence of someone terrifying, huge, fatherly, motherly, deadly, reassuring, and stunningly attractive. A hand tries to lift him to his feet and a voice murmurs apologies in tones that send chills of delight through his body. He clasps the legs that stand before him and refuses to be raised, weeping with delight.

"I'm sorry. You people must be pacifists. Please stand up," says the incredibly attractive voice, in worried tones.

The hand pulls at his shoulder and the Earthman looks up, weeping tears of gratitude and wonder for such undeserved kindness.

"I'm sorry," says the godlike figure. "I didn't know you were unarmed."

In the biographical note to her article in my symposium, *The Craft of Science Fiction*, Katherine MacLean wrote:

"I treat the job of writing science fiction with great respect, basing my work on the most startling possibilities I can deduce from currently known 'hard' science. If no new insight bobs up in a story I am writing, it usually gets filed in a pile of cardboard boxes in a closet.

"I majored in mathematics and science in high school, economics in college (B.A., Barnard,) and psychology in graduate school. I've worked in many kinds of jobs and, fumbling through experience, have become pretty good at art, photography, teaching, EKG, food factory quality control, and painting walls. I have a big old house in Maine, and an antique VW bus that's forcing me to learn auto engines. I have a sailboat, and might sail to an island someday."

(The island venture will, however, undoubtedly be postponed: Ms. MacLean, while this was being written, informed me that she is just leaving for the University of Vera Cruz, in Mexico, where she will work for her doctorate in nutrition.)

Katherine MacLean's short stories have appeared in almost all the sf magazines, and she is the author of, among other titles, *The Man in the Birdcage*, Ace, New York, 1971; *The Diploids*, a collection of short stories, Manor, New York, 1973; and *The Missing Man*, Putnam, New York, 1975, an sf novel expanded from her Nebula Award novella of the same title.

Our extraterrestrials can be derived logically from what we know of life on Earth and possible conditions on other planets, or we can lift them bodily from our mythology and folklore, or—and this is rare—they can be alchemically invented out of all this, so that (perhaps) with a few unidentified ingredients) they appear completely new and still utterly believable, like Frank Herbert's sandworms in the Dune *series.*

When we get ETs of this order, then war in space can take on a new dimension, as it does in this very funny story by Ted Cogswell and Ted Thomas. And when a military story is funny, it can be delightful, like Conan Doyle's "How the Brigadier Killed the Fox," and George MacDonald Fraser's two wonderful books based on his experience in a Highland regiment, The General Danced at Dawn *and* McAuslan in the Rough.

Theodore R. Cogswell
and Theodore L. Thomas

EARLY BIRD

I

When the leader of a scout patrol fell ill two hours before takeoff and Kurt Dixon was given command, he was delighted. More than a year had passed since the Imperial Space Marines had mopped up the remnants of the old Galactic Protectorate, and in spite of his pleasure at his newly awarded oak leaves, he was tired of being a glorified office boy in the Inspector General's office while the Kierians were raiding the Empire's trade routes with impunity. After a few hours in space, however, his relief began to dwindle when he found there was no way to turn off Zelda's voice box.

Zelda was the prototype of a new kind of command computer, the result of a base psychologist's bright idea that giving the ship's cybernetic control center a human personality tailored to the pilot's idea of an ideal companion would relieve the lonely tedium of being cooped up for weeks on end in a tiny one-man scout. Unfortunately for Kurt, however, his predecessor, Flight Leader Osaki, had a taste for domineering women, and the computer had been programmed accordingly. There hadn't been time for replacement with a conventional model before the flight had to scramble.

Kierian raids on Empire skipping had only begun six months before, but already the Empire was in serious trouble. Kierians bred like fruit flies, looked like mutated maggots, and ate people. Nobody knew where they came from when they came raiding in. Nobody

knew where they went when they left with their loot.
All that *was* known was that they had a weapon that was
invincible and that any attempt to track down a raiding
party to the Kierian base was as futile as it was suicidal.
Ships that tried it never came back.

But this time it looked as if the Empire's luck might
have changed. Kurt whistled happily as he slowly closed
in on what seemed to be a damaged Kierian destroyer,
waiting for the other scouts of his flight to catch up with
him.

Zzzzzt!

The alien's fogger beam hit him square on for the
third time. This close it should have slammed him into
immediate unconsciousness, but all it did was produce
an annoying buzz-saw keening in his neural network.

Flick! Six red dots appeared on his battle screen as
the rest of his flight warped out of hyperspace a hundred miles to his rear.

An anxious voice came over his intercom. "Kurt! You
fogged?"

"Nope. Come up and join the picnic, children. Looks
like us early birds are just about to have us some worms
for breakfast."

"He hits you with his fogger, you're going to be the
breakfast. Get the hell out of there while you still have
a chance!"

Kurt laughed. "This one ain't got much in the way of
teeth. Looks like he's had some sort of an engine-room
breakdown because his fogger strength is down a good
ninety percent. He's beamed me several times, and all
he's been able to do so far is give me a slight hangover."

"Then throw a couple of torps into him before he can
rev up enough to star hop."

"Uh, uh! We're after bigger game. I've got a solid
tracer lock on him and I've a hunch, crippled as he
seems to be, that he's going to run for home. If he
does, and we can hang on to him, we may be able to
find the home base of those bastards. If just one of
us can get back with the coordinates, the heavies can
come in and chuck a few planet-busters. Hook on to me

and follow along. I think he's just about to jump."

Flick! As the tight-arrow formation jumped back into normal space, alarm gongs began clanging in each of the tiny ships. Kurt stared at the image on his battle screen and let out a low whistle. They'd come out within fifty miles of the Kierian base! And it wasn't a planet. It was a mother ship, a ship so big that the largest Imperial space cruiser would have looked like a gnat alongside it. And from it, like hornets from a disturbed nest, poured squadron after squadron of Kierian destroyers.

"Bird leader to fledglings! Red alert! Red alert! Scramble random 360. One of us has to stay clear long enough to get enough warper revs to jump. Zelda will take over if I get fogged! I . . ." The flight leader's voice trailed off as a narrow cone of jarring vibration flicked across his ship, triggering off a neural spasm that hammered him down into unconsciousness. The other scouts broke formation like a flight of frightened quail and zigzagged away from the Kierian attackers, twisting in a desperate attempt to escape the slashing fogger beams. One by one the other pilots were slammed into unconsiousness. Putting the other ships on slave circuit, Zelda threw the flight on emergency drive. Needles emerged from control seats and pumped anti-G drugs into the comatose pilots.

A quick calculation indicated that they couldn't make a subspace jump from their present position. They were so close to the giant sun that its gravitational field would damp the warper nodes. The only thing to do was to run and find a place to hide until the pilots recovered consciousness. Then, while the others supplied a diversion, there was a chance that one might be able to break clear. The computer doubted that the Imperial battle fleet would have much of a chance against something as formidable as the Kierian mother ship, but that was something for fleet command to decide. Her job was to save the flight. There were five planets in the system, but only the nearest to the sun, a cloud-smothered giant, was close enough to offer possible sanctuary.

Setting a corkscrew evasion course and ignoring the fogger beams that lanced at her from the pursuing ships, she streaked for the protective cloud cover of the planet, programming the computers of the six ships that followed her on slave circuit to set them down at widely separated, randomly selected points. Kierian tracer beams would be useless once the flight was within the violent and wildly fluctuating magnetic field of the giant planet.

Once beneath the protective cloud cover, the other scouts took off on their separate courses, leaving Zelda, her commander still slumped in a mind-fog coma, to find her own sanctuary. Then at thirty thousand feet the ship's radiation detector suddenly triggered off a score of red danger lights on the instrument panel. From somewhere below, a sun-hot cone of lethal force was probing for the ship. After an almost instantaneous analysis of the nature of the threat, Zelda threw on a protective heterodyning canceler to shield the scout. Then she taped an evasive course that would take the little ship out of danger as soon as the retrorockets had slowed it enough to make a drastic course change possible without harm to its unconscious commander.

II

Gog's time had almost come. Reluctantly she withdrew her tubelike extractor from the cobalt-rich layer fifty yards below the surface. The propagation pressures inside her were too great to allow her to finish the lode, much less find another. The nerve stem inside the extractor shrank into her body, followed by the acid conduit and ultrasonic tap. Then, ponderously, she began to drag her gravid body toward a nearby ravine. She paused for a moment while a rear short-range projector centered in on a furtive scavenger who had designs on her unfinished meal. One burst and its two-hundred-foot length exploded into a broken heap of metallic and organic rubble. She was tempted to turn back—the remnants would have made a tasty morsel—

but birthing pressures drove her on. Reaching the ravine at last, she squatted over it. Slowly her ovipositor
emerged from between sagging, armored buttocks. Gog
strained and then moved on, leaving behind her a
shining, five-hundred-foot-long egg.

Lighter now, her body quickly adapted for post egg-
laying activities as sensors and projectors extruded from
depressions in her tung-steel hide. Her semi-organic
brain passed into a quiescent state while organo-metallic
arrays of calculators and energy producers activated and
joined into a network on her outer surfaces. The principal computer, located halfway down the fifteen-hundred-
meter length of her grotesque body, activated and took
over control of her formidable defenses. Then, everything in readiness, it triggered the egg.

The egg responded with a microwave pulse of such
intensity that the sensitive antennae of several nearby
lesser creatures grew hot, conducting a surge of power
into their circuits that charred their internal organs and
fused their metallic synapses.

Two hundred kilometers away, Magog woke from a
gorged sleep as a strident mating call came pulsing in.
He lunged erect, the whole kilometer of him. As he
sucked the reducing atmosphere deep into the chain of
ovens that served him as lungs, meter-wide nerve centers along his spinal columns pulsed with a voltage and
current sufficient to fuse bus bars of several centime-
ters' cross section. A cannonlike sperm launcher emerged
from his forehead and stiffened as infernos churned
inside him. Then his towering bulk jerked as the first
spermatozoon shot out, followed by a swarm that dwindled to a few stragglers. Emptied, Magog sagged to the
ground and, suddenly hungry, began to rip up great
slabs of igneous rock to get at the rich vein of ferrous
ore his sensors detected deep beneath. Far to the east,
Gog withdrew a prudent distance from her egg and
squatted down to await the results of its mating call.

The spermatoza reached an altitude of half a kilometer before achieving homing ability. They circled, los-

ing altitude until their newly activated homing mechanisms picked up the high-frequency emissions of the distant egg. Then tiny jets began pouring carbon dioxide, and flattened leading edges bit into the atmosphere as they arced toward their objective.

Each was a flattened cylinder, twenty meters long, with a scythe-shaped sensing element protruding from a flattened head, each with a pair of long tails connected at the trailing edge by a broad ribbon. It was an awesome armada, plowing through the turbulent atmosphere, homing on the distant signal.

As the leaders of the sperm swarm appeared over the horizon, Gog's sensors locked in. The selection time was near. Energy banks cut in and fuel converters began to seethe, preparing for the demands of the activated weapons system. At twenty kilometers a long-range beam locked in on the leading spermatozoon. It lacked evasive ability and a single frontal shot fused it. Its remnants spiraled to the surface, a mass of carbonized debris interspersed with droplets of glowing metal.

The shock of its destruction spread through the armada and stimulated wild, evasive gyrations on the part of the rest. But Gog's calculators predicted the course of one after another, and flickering bolts of energy burned them out of the sky. None was proving itself fit to survive. Then, suddenly, there was a moment of confusion in her intricate neural network. An intruder was approaching from the wrong direction. All her reserve projectors swiveled and spat a concentrated cone of lethal force at the rogue gamete that was screaming down through the atmosphere. Before the beam could take effect, a milky nimbus surrounded the approaching stranger and it continued on course unharmed. She shifted frequencies. The new bolt was as ineffective as the last. A ripple of excited anticipation ran through her great bulk. This was the one she'd been waiting for!

Gog was not a thinking entity in the usual sense, but she was equipped with a pattern of instinctive responses that told her that the gamete that was flashing down through the upper skies contained something precious in defensive armament that her species needed to survive. Mutations induced by the intense hard radiation from the nearby giant sun made each new generation of enemies even more terrible. Only if her egg were fertilized by a sperm bearing improved defensive and offensive characteristics would her offspring have a good chance of survival.

She relaxed her defenses and waited for the stranger to home in on her egg; but for some inexplicable reason, as it slowed down, it began to veer away. Instantly her energy converters and projectors combined to form a new beam, a cone that locked onto the escaping gamete and then narrowed and concentrated all its energy into a single, tight, titanic tractor. The stranger tried one evasive tactic after another, but inextricably it was drawn toward the waiting egg. Then, in response to her radiated command, the egg's shell weakened at the calculated point of impact. A moment later the stranger punched through the ovid wall and came to rest at the egg's exact center. Gog's scanners quickly encoded its components and made appropriate adjustments to the genes of the egg's nucleus.

Swiftly—the planet abounded in egg eaters—the fertilized ovum began to develop. It drew on the rich supply of heavy metals contained in the yolk sac to follow the altered genetic blueprint, incorporating in the growing embryo both the heritage of the strange gamete and that developed by Gog's race in its long fight to stay alive in a hostile environment. When the yolk sac nourishment was finally exhausted, Gog sent out a vibratory beam that cracked the shell of her egg into tiny fragments and freed the fledgling that had developed within. Leaving the strange new hybrid to fend for itself, she crawled back to her abandoned lode to feed and prepare for another laying. In four hours she would be ready to bear again.

III

As Kurt began to regain consciousness, mind still reel-

ing from the aftereffects of the Kierian fogger beam, he
opened his eyes with an effort.

"Don't say it," said the computer's voice box.

"Say what?" he mumbled.

" 'Where am I?' You wouldn't believe it if I told
you."

Kurt shook his head to try to clear it of its fuzz. His
front vision screen was on and strange things were
happening. Zelda had obviously brought the scout down
safely, but how long it was going to remain that way
was open to question.

The screen showed a nightmare landscape, a narrow
valley floor crisscrossed with ragged, smoking fissures.
Low-hanging, boiling clouds were tinged an ugly red by
the spouting firepits of the squat volcanoes that ringed
the depression. It was a hobgoblin scene populated by
hobgoblin forms. Strange shapes, seemingly of living
metal, crawled, slithered and flapped. Titanic battles
raged, victors ravenously consuming losers with maws
like giant ore crushers, only to be vanquished and
gulped down in turn by even more gigantic life forms,
no two of which were quite alike.

A weird battle at one corner of the vision screen
caught Kurt's attention, and he cranked up magnification. Half tank, half dinosaur, a lumbering creature the
size of an imperial space cruiser was backed into a box
canyon in the left escarpment, trying to defend itself
against a pack of smaller but swifter horrors. A short
thick projection stuck out from between its shoulders,
pointing up at forty-five degrees like an ancient howit-
zer. As Kurt watched, flame suddenly flashed from it. A
black spheroid arced out, fell among the attackers, and
then exploded with a concussion that shook the scout,
distant as it was. When the smoke cleared, a crater
twenty feet deep marked where it had landed. Two of
the smaller beasts were out of action, but the rest kept
boring in, incredibly agile toadlike creatures twice the
size of terrestrial elephants, spouting jets of some flaming substance and then skipping back.

This spectacular was suddenly interrupted when the

computer said calmly, "If you think that's something, take a look at the rear scanner."

Kurt did and shuddered in spite of himself.

Crawling up behind the scout on stumpy, centipede legs was something the size of a lunar ore boat. Its front end was dotted with multifaceted eyes that revolved like radar bowls.

"What the hell is *that?*"

"Beats me," said Zelda, "but I think it wants us for lunch."

Kurt flipped on his combat controls and centered the beast on his cross hairs. "Couple right down the throat ought to discourage it."

"Might at that," said Zelda. "But you've got one small problem. Our armament isn't operational yet. The neural connections for the new stuff haven't finished knitting in yet."

"Listen, smart ass," said Kurt in exasperation, "this is no time for funnies. If we can't fight the ship, let's lift the hell out of here. That thing's big enough to swallow us whole."

"Can't lift either. The converters need more mass before they can crank out enough juice to activate the antigravs. We've only five kilomegs in the accumulators."

"Five!" howled Kurt. "I could lift the whole damn squadron with three. I'm getting out of here!"

His fingers danced over the control board, setting up the sequence for emergency takeoff. The ship shuddered but nothing happened. The rear screen showed that the creature was only two hundred yards away, its mouth a gaping cavern lined with chisel-like grinders.

Zelda made a chuckling sound. "Next time, listen to Mother. Strange things happened to all of us while you were in sleepy-bye land." A number of red lights on the combat readiness board began changing to green. "Knew it wouldn't take *too* much longer. Tell you what, why don't you suit up and go outside and watch while I take care of junior back there. You aren't going to believe what you're about to see, but hang with it. I'll explain everything when you get back. In the meantime I'll keep an eye on you."

Kurt made a dash for his space armor and wriggled into it. "I'm not running out on you, baby, but nothing seems to be working on this tub. If one of the other scouts is close enough, I may be able to raise him on my helmet phone and get him here soon enough to do us some good. But what about you?"

"Oh," said Zelda casually, "if worse comes to worst, I can always run away. We now have feet. Thirty on each side."

Kurt just snorted as he undogged the inner air-lock hatch.

Once outside he did the biggest and fastest double take in the history of man.

The scout did have feet. Lots of feet. And other things.

To begin with, though her general contours were the same, she'd grown from forty meters in length to two hundred. Her torp tubes had quadrupled in size and were many times more numerous. Between them, streamlined turrets housed wicked-looking devices whose purpose he didn't understand. One of them suddenly swiveled, pointed at a spot somewhat behind him, and spat an incandescent beam. He spun just in time to see something that looked like a ten-ton crocodile collapse into a molten puddle.

"Told you I'd keep an eye on you," said a cheerful voice in his helmet phone. "All central connections completed themselves while you were on your way out. Now we have teeth."

"So has our friend back there. Check aft!" The Whatever-it-was was determinedly gnawing away on the rear tubes.

"He's just gumming. Our new hide makes the old one look like the skin of a jellyfish. Watch me nail him. But snap on your sun filter first. Otherwise you'll blind yourself."

Obediently Kurt pressed his polarizing stud. One of the scout's rear turrets swung around and a buzzsaw vibration ran through the ground as a purple beam no thicker than a pencil slashed the attacker into piano-sized chunks. Then the reason for the scout's new pedal extremities became apparent as the ship quickly ran around in a circle. Reaching what was left of her attacker, she extended a wedge-shaped head from a depression in her bow and began to feed.

"Just the mass we needed," said Zelda. A tentacle suddenly emerged from a hidden port, circled Kurt's waist, and pulled him inside the ship. "Welcome aboard your new command. And now do you want to hear what's happened to us?"

When she finished, Kurt didn't comment. He couldn't. His vocal chords weren't working.

A shave, a shower, a steak and three cups of coffee later, he gave a contented burp.

"Let's go find some worms and try out our new stuff," Zelda suggested.

"While I get fogged?"

"You won't. Wait and see."

Kurt shrugged dubiously and once again punched in the lifting sequence. This time when he pressed the activator stud the ship went shrieking up through the atmosphere. Gog, busily laying another egg, paid no attention to her strange offspring. Kurt paid attention to her, though.

Once out of the sheltering cloud cover, his detectors picked up three Kierian ships in stratospheric flight. They seemed to be systematically quartering the sun side of the planet in a deliberate search pattern. Then, as if they had detected one of the hidden scouts, they went into a steep purposeful dive. Concerns for his own safety suddenly were flushed away by the apparent threat to a defenseless ship from his flight. Kurt raced toward the alien ships under emergency thrust. The G needle climbed to twenty, but instead of the acceleration hammering him into organic pulp, it only pushed him back in his seat slightly.

The Kierians pulled up and turned to meet him. In

spite of the size of the strange ship that was hurtling toward them, they didn't seem concerned. There was no reason why they should be. Their foggers could hammer a pilot unconscious long before he could pose a real threat.

Kurt felt a slight vibration run through the scout as an enemy beam caught him, but he didn't black out.

"Get the laser on the one that just hit you," Zelda suggested. "It has some of the new stuff hooked into it." Kurt did, and a bolt of raging energy raced back along the path of the fogger beam and converted the first attacker into a ball of ionized gas.

"Try torps on the other two."

"They never work. The Kierians warp out before they get within range."

"Want to bet? Give a try."

"What's to lose?" said Kurt. "Fire three and seven." He felt the shudder of the torpedoes leaving the ship, but their tracks didn't appear on his firing scope. "Where'd they go?"

"Subspace. Watch what happens to the worms when they flick out."

Suddenly the two dots that marked the enemy vanished in an actinic burst.

"Wow!" said Kurt in an awestricken voice, "we something, we is! But why didn't that fogger knock me out? New kind of shield?"

"Nope, new kind of pilot. The ship wasn't the only thing that was changed. And that ain't all. You've got all kinds of new equipment inside your head you don't know about yet."

"Such as?"

"For one thing." she said, "once you learn how to use it, you'll find that your brain can operate at almost ninety percent efficiency instead of its old ten. And that ain't all; your memory bank has twice the storage of a standard ship computer and you can calculate four times as fast. But don't get uppity, buster. You haven't learned to handle it yet. It's going to take months to get you up to full potential. In the meantime I'll babysit as usual."

Kurt had a sudden impulse to count fingers and toes to see if he still had the right number.

"My face didn't look any different when I shaved. Am I still human?"

"Of course," Zelda said soothingly. "You're just a better one, that's all. When the ship fertilized that egg, its cytoplasm went to work incorporating the best elements of both parent strains. Our own equipment was improved and the mother's was added to it. There was no way of sorting you out from the other ship components, and you were improved too. So relax."

Kurt tilted back his seat and stared thoughtfully at the ceiling for a long moment. "Well," he said at last, "best we go round up the rest of the flight."

"What about the Kierian mother ship?"

"We're still not tough enough to tackle something that big."

"But that thing down there was still laying eggs when we pulled out. If the whole flight . . ." Her voice trailed off suggestively.

Kurt sat bolt upright in his seat, his face suddenly split with a wide grin.

"Bird leader to fledglings. You can come out from under them there rocks, children. Coast is clear and Daddy is about to take you on an egg hunt."

A babble of confused voices came from the communication panel speaker.

"One at a time!"

"What about those foggers?"

Kurt chuckled. "Tell them the facts of life, Zelda."

"The facts are," she said, her voice flat and impersonal, "that before too long you early birds are going to be able to get the worms before the worms get you."

Major Kurt Dixon, one-time sergeant in the 427th Light Maintenance Battalion of the Imperial Space Marines, grinned happily as he looked out at the spreading cloud of space debris that was all that was left of the Kierian mother ship. Then he punched the stud that sent a communication beam hurtling through hyperspace to Imperial Headquarters. "Commander Krogson, please. Dixon calling."

"One second, Major."

The Inspector General's granite features appeared on Kurt's communication screen. "Where the hell have you been?"

"Clobbering Kierians," Kurt said smugly, "but before we get into that, I'd like to have you relay a few impolite words to the egghead who put together the talking machine I have for a control computer."

"Oh, sorry about that, Kurt. You see, it was designed with Osaki in mind, and he does have a rather odd taste in women. When you get back, we'll remove the old personality implant and substitute one that's tailored to your specifications."

Kurt shook his head. "No, thanks. The old girl and I have been through some rather tight spots together, and even though she is a pain in the neck at times, I'd sort of like to keep her around just as she is." He reached over and gave an affectionate pat to the squat computer that was bolted to the deck beside him.

"That's nice," Krogson said, "but what's going on out there? What was that about clobbering Kierians?"

"They're finished. Kuput. Thanks to Zelda."

"Who?"

"My computer."

"What happened?"

Kurt gave a lazy grin. "Well, to begin with, I got laid."

Theodore R. Cogswell is perhaps best remembered for his novelette "The Specter General," included in *The Science Fiction Hall of Fame*.

At 19, in 1937, seeing World War II as inevitable, he enlisted as an ambulance driver, serving until invalided home after the retreat to Barcelona. After Pearl Harbor, he joined the USAAF and served, up to the rank of captain, in India, Burma, and China. In the late '50s he edited *The Proceedings of the Institute for Twenty-First Century Studies*, whose circulation was limited to professional sf writers. (G. K. Hall & Co. expect to bring out a complete reprint in their Gregg Press series in 1980.)

Cogswell, giving the lie to the adage that old writers never die—they just keep on grading freshman themes, will retire early from academia and return to full-time writing, hopefully to continue the adventures of Kurt Dixon and the Imperial Space Marines that began in "The Specter General" and were continued in "Early Bird."

Ted Thomas, a graduate of M.I.T. and of Georgetown University Law School, is a former practicing chemical engineer and has been an active patent attorney for the past 28 years.

In addition to innumerable science-oriented newspaper columns, radio programs, and science articles such as "The Twenty Lost Years of Solid State Physics" and "The Chemistry of a Coral Reef," he has published about 70 short stories, mostly sf but also mystery and adventure. He is the co-author with Kate Wilhelm of two sf novels, and of several short stories with Ted Cogswell, and one with both Cogswell and A.J. Budrys. Most of these co-authored stories resulted from one or the other of the four Chesapeake Bay Writers Conferences held aboard his boat while cruising and gunkholing on Chesapeake Bay. For two years, *too*, he edited "The Science Springboard" column for *The Magazine of Fantasy and Science fiction*.

"The art of war," wrote Voltaire, *"is like that of medicine, murderous and conjectural."*

The art of medicine today is generally less murderous and sometimes less conjectural than it was in the 18th Century, but the art of war has not kept up with it. War's weapons are certainly becoming progressively more murderous, but the art of waging war, at least on the strategic level, and despite all our computers, is no less conjectural. War is still above all a gamble.

But so, to a very great degree and despite all our seekings for security, is life itself. It is fascinating, therefore, to imagine—as Poul Anderson does here—a society where gambling is the way of life, where all decisions are left to calculated chance.

How would such a society react to an attack by warmakers who try cold-bloodedly to eliminate all chance from war?

Poul Anderson

INSIDE STRAIGHT

In the main, sociodynamic theory predicted quite accurately the effects of the secondary drive. It foresaw that once cheap interstellar transportation was available, there would be considerable emigration from the Solar System—men looking for a fresh start, malcontents of all kinds, "peculiar people" desiring to maintain their way of life without interference. It also predicted that these colonies would in turn spawn colonies, until this part of the galaxy was sprinkled with human-settled planets, and that in their relative isolation, these politically independent worlds would develop some very odd societies.

However, the economic bias of the Renascence period, and the fact that war was a discarded institution in the Solar System, led these same predictors into errors of detail. It was felt that, since planets useful to man are normally separated by scores of light-years, and since any planet colonized on a high technological level would be quite self-sufficient, there would be little intercourse and no strife between these settlements. In their own reasonableness, the Renascence intellectuals overlooked the fact that man as a whole is not a rational animal, and that exploration and war do not always have economic causes.

—Simon Vardis, *A Short History of Pre-Commonwealth Politics*, Reel I, Frame 617

They did not build high on New Hermes. Plenty of space was available, and the few cities sprawled across many square kilometers in a complex of low, softly tinted domes and cylindroids. Parks spread green wherever you looked, each breeze woke a thousand belltrees into a rush of chiming; flowers and the bright-winged summerflits ran wildly colored beneath a serene blue sky. The planetary capital, Arkinshaw, had the same leisurely old-fashioned look as the other towns Ganch had seen; only down by the docks were energy and haste to be found.

The restaurant Wayland had taken him to was incredibly archaic; it even had live service. When they had finished a subtly prepared lunch, the waiter strolled to their table. "Was there anything else, sir?" he asked.

"I thank you, no," said Wayland. He was a small, lithe man with close-cropped gray hair and a brown nutcracker face in which lay startlingly bright blue eyes. On him, the local dress—a knee-length plaid tunic, green buskins, and yellow mantle—looked good . . . which was more than you could say for most of them, reflected Ganch.

The waiter produced a tray. No bill lay on it, as Ganch had expected, but a pair of dice. *Oh, no!* he thought. *By the Principle, no! Not this again!*

Wayland rattled the cubes in his hand, muttering an incantation. They flipped on the table. Eight spots looked up. "Fortune seems to favor you, sir," said the waiter.

"May she smile on a more worthy son," replied Wayland. Ganch noted with disgust that the planet's urbanity-imperative extended even to servants. The waiter shook the dice and threw.

"Snake eyes" he smiled. "Congratulations, sir. I trust you enjoyed the meal."

"Yes, indeed," said Wayland, rising. "My compliments to the chef, and you and he are invited to my next poker game. I'll have an announcement about it on the telescreens."

He and the waiter exchanged bows and compliments. Wayland left, ushering Ganch through the door and out onto the slidewalk. They found seats and let it carry them toward the waterfront, which Ganch had expressed a desire to see.

"Ah . . ." Ganch cleared his throat. "How was that done?"

"Eh?" Wayland blinked. "Don't you have dice on Dromm?"

"Oh, yes. But I mean the principle of payment for the meal."

"I shook him. Double or nothing. I won."

Ganch shook his head. He was a tall, muscular man in a skintight black uniform. That and the scarlet eyes in his long bony face (not albinism, but healthy mutation) marked him as belonging to the Great Cadre of Dromm.

"But then the restaurant loses money," he said.

"This time, yes," nodded Wayland. "It evens out in the course of a day, just as all our commerce evens out, so that in the long run everybody earns his rightful wage or profit."

"But suppose one—ah—cheats?"

Surprisingly, Wayland reddened, and looked around. When he spoke again, it was in a low voice: "Don't ever use that word, sir, I beg of you. I realize the mores are different on your planet, but here there is one unforgivable, utterly obscene sin, and it's the one you just mentioned." He sat back, breathing heavily for a while, before he cooled off and proffered cigars. Ganch declined—tobacco did not grow on Dromm—but Wayland puffed his own into lighting with obvious enjoyment.

"As a matter of fact," he said presently, "our whole social conditioning is such as to preclude the possibility of . . . unfairness. You realize how thoroughly an imperative can be inculcated with modern psychopediatrics. It is a matter of course that all equipment, from dice and coins to the most elaborate stellarium set, is periodically checked by a games engineer."

"I see," said Ganch doubtfully.

He looked around as the slidewalk carried him on. It

was a pleasant, sunny day, like most on New Hermes. Only to be expected on a world with two small continents, the rest of the land split into a multitude of islands. The people he saw had a relaxed appearance, the men in their tunics and mantles, the women in their loose filmy gowns, the children in little or nothing. A race of sybarites; they had had it *too* easy here, and degenerated.

Sharply he remembered Dromm, gaunt glacial peaks and wind-scoured deserts, storm and darkness galloping down from the poles, the iron cubicles of cities and the obedient gray-clad masses that filled them. That world had brought forth the Great Cadre, and tempered them in struggle and heartbreak, and given them power first over a people and then over a planet and then over two systems.

Eventually . . . who knew? The galaxy?

"I am interested in your history," he said, recalling himself. "Just how was New Hermes settled?"

"The usual process," shrugged Wayland. "Our folk came from Caledonia, which had been settled from Old Hermes, whose people were from Earth. A puritanical gang got into control and started making all kinds of senseless restrictions on natural impulses. Finally a small group, our ancestors, could take no more, and went off looking for a planet of their own. That was about three hundred years ago. They went far, into this spiral arm which was then completely unexplored, in the hope of being left alone; and that hope has been realized. To this day, except for a couple of minor wars, we've simply had casual visitors like yourself."

Casual! A grim amusement twisted Ganch's mouth upward.

To cover it, he asked: "But surely you've had your difficulties? It cannot have been a mere matter of landing here and founding your cities."

"Oh, no, of course not. The usual pioneer troubles—unknown diseases, wild animals, storms, a strange ecology. They endured some hard times before the machines were constructed. Now, of course, we have it pretty good. There are fifty million of us, and space for many more; but we're in no hurry to expand the population. We like elbow room."

Ganch frowned until he had deduced the meaning of that last phrase. They spoke Anglic here, as on Dromm and most colonies, but naturally an individual dialect had evolved.

Excitement gripped him. Fifty million! There were two hundred million people on Dromm, and conquered Thanit added half again as many.

Of course, said his military training, sheer numbers meant little. Automatized equipment made all but the most highly skilled officers and technicians irrelevant. War between systems involved sending a space fleet that met and beat the enemy fleet in a series of engagements: bases on planets had to be manned, and sometimes taken by ground forces, but the fighting was normally remote from the worlds concerned. Once the enemy navy was broken, its home had to capitulate or be sterilized by bombardment from the skies.

Still . . . New Hermes should be an even easier prey than Thanit had been.

"Haven't you taken any precautions against . . . hostiles?" he asked, mostly because the question fitted his assumed character.

"Oh, yes, to be sure," said Wayland. "We maintain a navy and marine corps; matter of fact, I'm in the Naval Intelligence Reserve myself, captain's rank. We had to fight a couple of small wars in the previous century, once with the Corridans—nonhumans out for loot—and once with Oberkassel, whose people were on a religious-fanatic kick. We won them both without much trouble." He added modestly: "But of course, sir, neither planet was very intelligently guided."

Ganch suppressed a desire to ask for figures on naval strength. This guileless dice-thrower might well spout them on request, but . . .

The slidewalk reached the waterfront and they got

off. Here the sea glistened blue, streaked with white foam, and the harbor was crowded with shipping. Not only flying boats, but big watercraft were moored to the ferroconcrete piers. Machines were loading and unloading in a whirl of bright steel arms, warehouses gaped for the planet's wealth, the air was rich with oil and spices. A babbling surfed around Ganch and broke on his eardrums.

Wayland pointed unobtrusively around, his voice almost lost in the din: "See, we have quite a cultural variety of our own. That tall blond man in the fur coat is from Norrin, he must have brought in a load of pelts. The little dark fellow in the sarong is a spice trader from the Radiant Islands. The Mongoloid wearing a robe is clear from the Ivory Gate, probably with handicrafts to exchange for our timber. And—"

They were interrupted by a young woman, good-looking, with long black hair and a tilt-nosed freckled face. She wore a light blue uniform jacket, a lieutenant's twin comets on the shoulders, as well as a short loose-woven skirt revealing slim brown legs. "Will! Where have you been?"

"Showing the distinguished guest of our government around," said Wayland formally. "The Prime Selector himself appointed me to that pleasant task. Ganch, may I have the honor of presenting my niece, Lieutenant Christabel Hesty of the New Hermesian Navy? Lieutenant Hesty, this gentleman hight Ganch, from Dromm. It's a planet lying about fifty light-years from us, a fine place I'm sure. They are making a much overdue ethnographic survey of this galactic region, and Ganch is taking notes on us."

"Honored, sir." She bowed and shook hands with herself in the manner of Arkinshaw. "We've heard of Dromm. Visitors have come thence in the past several years. I trust you are enjoying your stay?"

Ganch saluted stiffly, as was prescribed for the Great Cadre. "Thank you, very much." He was a little shocked at such blatant sexual egalitarianism, but reflected that it might be turned to advantage.

"Will, you're just the man I want to see." Lieutenant Hesty's voice bubbled over. "I came down to wager on a cargo from Thomcroft and you—"

"Ah, yes. I'll be glad to help you, though of course the requirements of my guild are—"

"You'll get your commission." She made a face at him and turned laughing to Ganch. "Perhaps you didn't know, sir, my uncle is a tipster?"

"No, I didn't," said the Dromman. "What profession is that?"

"Probability analyst. It takes years and years of training. When you want to make an important wager, you call in a tipster." She tugged at Wayland's sleeve. "Come on, the trading will start any minute."

"Do you mind, sir?" asked Wayland.

"Not at all," said Ganch. "I would be very interested. Your economic system is unique." *And*, he added to himself, *the most inefficient I have yet heard of.*

They entered a building which proved to be a single great room. In the center was a long table, around which crowded a colorful throng of men and women. An outsize electronic device of some kind stood at the end, with a tall rangy man in kilt and beryllium-copper breastplate at the controls. Wayland stepped aside, his face taking on an odd withdrawn look.

"How does this work?" asked Ganch—*sotto voce*, for the crowd did not look as if it wanted its concentration disturbed.

"The croupier there is a trader from Thomcroft," whispered Christabel Hesty. This close, with her head beneath his chin, Ganch could smell the faint sun-warmed perfume of her hair. It stirred a wistfulness in him, buried ancestral memories of summer meadows on Earth. He choked off the emotion and listened to her words.

"He's brought in a load of refined thorium, immensely valuable. He puts that up as his share, and those who wish to trade get into the game with shares of what they have—they cover him, as in craps, though they're playing Orthotron now. The game is a complex one; I see a lot of tipsters around . . . yes, and the man in the green robe is a games engineer, umpire and technician. I'm afraid you wouldn't understand the rules at once, but perhaps you would like to make side bets?"

"No, thank you," said Ganch. "I am content to observe."

He soon found out that Lieutenant Hesty had not exaggerated the complications. Orthotron seemed to be a remote descendant of roulette such as they had played on Thanit before the war, but the random-pulse tubes shifted the probabilities continuously, and the rules themselves changed as the game went on. When the scoreboard on the machine flashed, chips to the tune of millions of credits clattered from hand to hand. Ganch found it hard to believe that anyone could ever learn the system, let alone become so expert in it as to make a profession of giving advice. A tipster would have to allow for the presence of other tipsters, and . . .

His respect for Wayland went up. The little man must have put a lightning-fast mind through years of the most rigorous training; and there must be a highly developed paramathematical theory behind it all. If that intelligence and energy had gone into something useful, military technique, for instance . . .

But it hadn't, and New Hermes lay green and sunny, wide open for the first determined foe.

Ganch grew aware of tension. It was not overtly expressed, but faces tightened, changed color, pupils narrowed and pulses beat in temples until he could almost feel the emotion, crackling like lightning in the room. Now and then Wayland spoke quietly to his niece, and she laid her bets accordingly.

It was with an effort that she pulled herself away, with two hours lost and a few hundred credits gained. Nothing but courtesy to the guest made her do it. Her hair was plastered to her forehead, and she went out with a stiff-legged gait that only slowly loosened.

Wayland accepted his commission and laughed a trifle shakily. "I earn my living, sir!" he said. "It's brutal on the nerves."

"How long will they play?" asked Ganch.

"Till the trader is cleaned out or has won so much that no one can match him. In this case, I'd estimate about thirty hours."

"Continuous? How can the nervous system endure it, not to mention the feet?"

"It's hard," admitted Christabel Hesty. Her eyes burned. "But exciting! There's nothing in the galaxy quite like that suspense. You lose yourself in it."

"And, of course," said Wayland mildly, "man adapts to any cultural pattern. We'd find it difficult to live as you do on Dromm."

No doubt, thought Ganch sardonically. *But you are going to learn how.*

On an isolated planet like this, an outworlder was always a figure of romance. In spite of manners which must seem crude here, Ganch had only to suggest an evening out for Christabel Hesty to leap at the offer.

He simply changed to another uniform, but she appeared in a topless gown of deep-blue silkite, her dark hair sprinkled with tiny points of light, and made his heart stumble. He reminded himself that women were breeders, nothing else. But Principle! How dull they were on Dromm!

His object was to gain information, but he decided he might as well enjoy his work.

They took an elevated way to the Stellar House, Arkinshaw's single skyscraper, and had cocktails in a clear-domed roof garden with sunset rioting around them. A gentle music, some ancient waltz from Earth herself, lilted in the air, and the gaily clad diners talked in low voices and clinked glasses and laughed softly.

Lieutenant Hesty raised her glass to his. "Your luck, sir," she pledged him. Then, smiling: "Shall we lower guard?"

"I beg your pardon?"

"My apologies. I forgot you are a stranger, sir. The proposal was to relax formality for this evening."

"By all means," said Ganch. He tried to smile in turn. "Though I fear my class is always rather stiff."

Her long, soot-black eyelashes fluttered. "Then I hight Chris tonight," she said. "And your first name . . . ?"

"My class does not use them. I am Ganch, with various identifying symbols attached."

"We meet some strange outworlders," she said frankly, "but in truth, you Drommans seem the most exotic yet."

"And New Hermes gives us that impression," he chuckled.

"We know so little about you—a few explorers and traders, and now you. Is your mission official?"

"Everything on Dromm is official," said Ganch, veraciously enough. "I am an ethnographer making a detailed study of your folkways." And that was a lie.

"Excuse my saying so, I shouldn't criticize another civilization, but isn't it terribly drab having one's entire life regulated by the State?"

"It is . . ." Ganch hunted for words. "Secure," he finished earnestly. "Ordered. One knows where one stands."

"A pity you had that war with Thanit. They seemed such nice people, those who visited here."

"We had no choice," answered Ganch with the smoothness of rote. "An irresponsible, aggressive government attacked us." She did not ask for details, and he supposed it was the usual thing: interest in other people's fate obeys an inverse-square law, and fifty light-years is a gulf of distance no man can really imagine.

In point of fact, he told himself with the bitter honesty of his race, Thanit had sought peace up to the last moment; Dromm's ultimatum had demanded impossible concessions, and Thanit had had no choice but to fight a hopeless battle. Her conquest had been well-planned, the armored legions of Dromm had romped over her and now she was being digested by the State.

Chris frowned, a shadow on the wide clear brow. "I find it hard to see why they would make war . . . why anyone would," she murmured. "Isn't there enough on any planet to content its people? And if by chance they should be unhappy, there are always new worlds."

"Well," shrugged Ganch, "you should know why. You're in the navy yourself, aren't you, and New Hermes has fought a couple of times."

"Strictly in self-defense," she said. "Naturally, we now mount guard on our defeated enemies, even seventy years later, to be sure they don't try again. As for me, I have a peaceful desk job in the statistics branch, correlating data."

Ganch felt a thrumming within himself. He could hardly have asked for better luck. Precise information on the armament of New Hermes was just what Dromm lacked. If he could bring it back to old wan Halsker it would mean a directorship, at least!

And afterward, when a new conquest was to be administered and made over . . . His ruby eyes studied Chris from beneath drooping lids. A territorial governor had certain perquisites of office.

"I suppose there are many poor twisted people in the universe," went on the girl. "Like those Oberkassel priests, with their weird doctrine they wanted to force on everybody. It's hard to believe intolerance exists, but alien planets have done strange things to human minds."

A veiling was on her violet gaze as she looked at him. She must want to know his soul, what it was that drove the Great Cadre and why anyone should enjoy having power over other men. He could have told her a great deal—the cruel wintry planet, the generations-long war against the unhuman Ixlatt who made sport of torturing prisoners, then war between factions that split men, war against the red-eyed mutants, whipped-up xenophobia, pogroms, concentration camps . . . Ganch's grandfather had died in one.

But the mutation was more than an accidental mark; it was in the nervous system, answer to a pitiless environment. A man of the Great Cadre did not know fear on the conscious level. Danger lashed him to alertness, but there was no fright to cloud his thoughts. And, by genetics or merely as the result of persecution, he had a will to power which only death could stop. The Great Cadre had subdued a hundred times their numbers, and made them into brainchanneled tools of the State, simply by being braver and more able in war. And Dromm was not enough, not when each darkness brought unconquered stars out overhead.

A philosopher from distant Archbishop, where they went in for imaginative speculation, had visited Dromm a decade ago. His remark still lay in Ganch's mind, and stung: "Unjust treatment is apt to produce paranoia in the victim. Your race has outlived its oppressors, but not the reflexes they built into your society. You'll never rest till the whole universe is enslaved, for your canalized nervous systems make you incapable of regarding anyone else as anything but a dangerous enemy."

The philosopher had not gone home alive, but his words remained; Ganch had tried to forget them, and could not.

Enough! His mind had completed its tack in the blink of an eye, and now he remembered that the girl expected an answer. He sipped his cocktail and spoke thoughtfully:

"Yes, these special groups, isolated on their special planets, have developed in many peculiar ways. New Hermes, for instance, if you will pardon my saying so."

Chris raised her brows. "Of course, this is my home and I'm used to it, Ganch," she replied, "but I fail to see anything which would surprise an outsider very much. We live quietly for the most part, with a loose parliamentary government to run planetary affairs. The necessities of life are produced free for all by the automatic factories; to avoid the annoyance of regulations, we leave everything else to private enterprise, subject only to the reasonable restrictions of the Conservation Authority and a fair-practices act. We don't need more government than that, because the educational system instills respect for the rights and dignity of others and we have no ambitious public-works projects.

"You might say our whole culture is founded on a principle of live and let live."

She stroked her chin, man-fashion. "Of course, we have police and courts. And we discourage a concentration of power, political or economic, but that's simply to preserve individual liberty. Our economic system helps; it's hard to build up a gigantic business when one game may wipe it out."

"Now there," said Ganch, "you strike the oddity. This passion for gambling. How does it arise?"

"Oh . . . I wouldn't call it a passion. It's merely one way of pricing goods and services, just as haggling is on Kwan-Yin, and socialism on Arjay, and supply-demand on Alexander."

"But how did it originate?"

Chris lifted smooth bare shoulders and smiled. "Ask the historians, not me. I suppose our ancestors, reacting from the Caledonian puritanism, were apt to glorify vices and practice them to excess. Gambling was the only one that didn't taper off as a more balanced society evolved. It came to be a custom. Gradually it superseded the traditional methods of exchange.

"It doesn't make any difference, you see; being honest gambling, it comes out even. Win one, lose one . . . that's almost the motto of our folk. To be sure, in games of skill like poker, a good player will come out ahead in the long run; but any society gives an advantage to certain talents. On Alexander, most of the money and prestige flow to the successful entrepreneur. On Einstein, the scientists are the rich and honored leaders. On Hellas, it's male prowess and female beauty. On Arjay, it's the political spellbinder. On Dromm, I suppose, the soldier is on top. With us, it's the shrewd gambler.

"The important thing," she finished gravely, "is not who gets the most, but whether everyone gets enough."

"But that is what makes me wonder," said Ganch. "This trader we saw today, for instance. Suppose he loses everything?"

"It would be a blow, of course. But he wouldn't

starve, because the necessities are free anyway; and he'll have the sense—he'll have learned in the primaries—to keep a reserve to start over with. We have few paupers."

"Your financial structure must be most complicated."

"It is," she said wryly. "We've had to develop a tremendous theoretical science and a great number of highly trained men to handle it. That game today was childish compared with what goes on in, say, the securities exchange. I don't pretend to understand what happens there. I'm content to turn a wheel for my monthly pay, and if I win to go out and see if I can't make a little more."

"And you *enjoy* this . . . insecurity?"

"Why, yes. As I imagine you enjoy war, and an engineer enjoys building a spaceship, and—" Chris looked at the table. "It's always hard and risky settling a new planet, even one as Earth-like as ours. Our ancestors got a taste for excitement. When no more was to be had in subduing nature, they transferred the desire to— Ah, here come the hors d'oeuvres."

Ganch ate a stately succession of courses with pleasure. He was not good at small talk, but Chris made such eager conversation that it was simple to lead her: the details of her life and work, insignificant items but they clicked together. By the coffee and liqueur, Ganch knew where the military microfiles of New Hermes were kept and was fairly sure he knew how to get at them.

Afterward they danced. Ganch had never done it before, but his natural coordination soon fitted him into the rhythm. There was a curious bittersweet savor to holding the girl in his arms . . . dearest enemy. He wondered if he should try to make love to her. An infatuated female officer would be useful. . . .

No. In such matters, she was the sophisticate and he the bumbling yokel. Coldly, though not without regret, he dismissed the idea.

They sat at a poker table for a while, where the management put up chips to the value of their bill.

Ganch was completely outclassed; he learned the game readily, but his excellent analytical mind could not match the Hermesians. It was almost as if they knew what cards he held. He lost heavily, but Chris made up for it and when they quit they only had to pay half of what they owed.

They hired an aircar, and for a while its gravity drive lifted them noiselessly into a night-blue sky, under a flooding moon and myriad stars and the great milky sprawl of the galaxy. Beneath them a broken bridge of moonlight shuddered across the darkened sea, and they heard the far, faint crying of birds.

When he let Chris off at her apartment, Ganch wanted to stay. It was a wrenching to say good night and turn back to his own hotel. He stamped out the wish and bent his mind elsewhere. There was work to do.

Dromm was nothing if not thorough. Her agents had been on New Hermes for ten years now, mostly posing as natives of unsuspicious planets like Guise and Anubis. Enough had been learned to earmark this world for conquest after Thanit, and to lay out the basic military campaign.

The Hermesians were not really naive. They had their own spies and counterspies. Customs inspection was careful. But each Dromman visitor had brought a few plausible objects with him—a personal teleset, a depilator, a sample of nuclear-powered tools for sale— nothing to cause remark, and those objects had stayed behind, in care of a supposed immigrant from Kwan-Yin who lived in Arkinshaw. This man had refashioned them into as efficient a set of machinery for breaking and entering as existed anywhere in the known galaxy.

Ganch was quite sure Wayland had a tail on him. It was an elementary precaution. But a field intelligence officer of Dromm had ways to shake a tail off without its appearing more than accidental. Ganch went out the following afternoon, having notified Wayland that he did not need a guide: he just wanted to stroll around and look at things for himself. After wandering a bit, he went into a pleasure house. It was a holiday, Discovery Day, and Arkinshaw swarmed with a merry crowd; in the jampacked building Ganch slipped quietly into a washroom cubicle.

His shadows would most likely watch all exits; and they wouldn't be surprised if he stayed inside for many hours. The hetaerae of New Hermes were famous.

Alone, Ganch slipped out of his uniform and stuffed it down the rubbish disintegrator. Beneath it he wore the loose blue coat and trousers of a Kwan-Yin colonist. A lifemask over his head, a complete alteration of posture and gait . . . it was another man who stepped into the hall and sauntered out the main door as if his amusements were completed. He went quite openly to Fraybiner's house; what was more natural than that some home-planet relative of Tao Chung should pay a call?

When they were alone, Fraybiner let out a long breath. "By the Principle, it's good to be with a man again!" he said. "If you knew how sick I am of these chattering decadents—"

"Enough!" snapped Ganch. "I am here on business. Operation Lift."

Fraybiner's surgically slanted and darkened eyes widened. "So it's finally coming off?" he murmured. "I was beginning to wonder."

"If I get away with it," said Ganch grimly. "If I don't, it doesn't matter. Exact knowledge of the enemy's strength will be valuable, but we have sufficient information already to launch the war."

Fraybiner began operating concealed studs. A false wall slid aside to reveal a safe, on which he got to work. "How will you take it home?" he asked. "When they find their files looted, they won't let anyone leave the planet without a thorough search."

Ganch didn't reply; Fraybiner had no business knowing. Actually, the files were going to be destroyed, once read, and their contents go home in Ganch's eidetic memory. But that versatile ethnographer did not plan to leave for some weeks yet: no use causing unnecessary suspicion. When he finally did . . . a surprise attack on the Hermesian bases would immobilize them at one swoop.

He smiled to himself. Even knowing they were to be attacked, their whole planet fully alerted, the Hermesians were finished. It was well established that their fleet had less than half the strength of Dromm's, and not a single supernova-class dreadnaught. Ganch's information would be helpful, but was by no means vital.

Except, of course, to Ganch Z-17837-JX-39. But death was a threat he treated with the contempt it deserved.

Fraybiner had gotten the safe open, and a metal gleam of instruments and weapons lay before their gaze. Ganch inspected each item carefully while the other jittered with impatience. Finally he donned the flying combat armor and hung the implements at its belt. By that time the sun was down and the stars out.

Chris had said the Naval HQ building was deserted at night except for its guards. Previous spies had learned where these were posted. "Very well," said Ganch. "I'm on my way. I won't see you again, and advise you to move elsewhere soon. If the natives turn out to be stubborn, we'll have to destroy this city."

Fraybiner nodded, and activated the ceiling door. Ganch went up on his gravity beams and out into the sky. The town was a jeweled spiderweb beneath him, and fireworks burst with great soft explosions of color. His outfit was a nonreflecting black, and there was only a whisper of air to betray his flight.

The HQ building, broad and low, rested on a green-sward several kilometers from Arkinshaw. Ganch approached its slumbering dark mass carefully, taking his time. A bare meter's advance, an instrument reading . . . yes, they had a radio-alarm field set up. He neutralized it with his heterodyning unit, flew another cautious meter, stopped to readjust the neutralization. The moon was down, but he wished the stars weren't so bright.

It was past midnight when he lay in the shrubbery surrounding a rear entrance. A pair of sentries, armed and helmeted, tramped almost by his nose, crossing paths in front of the door. He waited, learning the pattern of their march.

When his tactics were fully planned, he rose as one marine came by and let the fellow have a sonic stun beam. Too low-powered to trip an alarm, it was close range and to the base of the neck. Ganch caught the body as it fell, let it down, and picked up the same measured tread.

He felt no conscious tension as he neared the other man, though a sharp glance through darkness would end the ruse, but his muscles gathered themselves. He was almost abreast of the Hermesian when he saw the figure recoil in alarm. His stunner went off again. It was a bad shot; the sentry lurched but retained a wavering consciousness. Ganch sprang on him, one tigerish bound, a squeezed trigger, and he lowered the marine as gently as a woman might her lover.

For a moment he stood looking down on the slack face. A youngster, hardly out of his teens; there was something strangely innocent about him as he slept. About this whole world. They were too kind here, they didn't belong in a universe of wolves.

He had no doubt they would fight bravely and skillfully. Dromm would have to pay for her conquest. But the age of heroes was past. War was not an art, it was a science, and a set of giant computers joylessly chewing an involved symbolism told ships and men what to do. Given equal courage and equally intelligent leadership, it was merely arithmetic that the numerically superior fleet would win.

No time to lose! He spun on his heel and crouched over the door. His instruments traced out its circuits, a diamond drill bit into plastic, a wire shorted a current . . . the door opened for him and he went into a hollow darkness of corridors.

Lightly, even in the clumsy armor, he made his way toward the main file room. Once he stopped. His instruments sensed a black-light barrier and it took him a quarter of an hour to neutralize it. But thereafter he was in among the cabinets.

They were not locked, and his flashbeam picked out the categories held in each drawer. Swiftly, then, he took the spools relating to ships, bases, armament, disposition . . . he ignored the codes, which would be changed anyway when the burglary was discovered. The entire set went into a small pouch such as the men of Kwan-Yin carried, and he had a micro-reader at the hotel.

The lights came on.

Before his eyes had adjusted to that sudden blaze, before he was consciously aware of action, Ganch's drilled reflexes had gone to work. His faceplate clashed down, gauntlets snapped shut around his hands, and a Mark IV blaster was at his shoulder even as he whirled to meet the intruders.

They were a score, and their gay holiday attire was somehow nightmarish behind the weapons they carried. Wayland was in the lead, harshness on his face, and Christabel at his back. The rest Ganch did not recognize; they must be naval officers but— He crouched, covering them, a robot figure cased in a centimeter of imperviousness.

"So." Wayland spoke quietly, a flat tone across the silence. "I wondered—Ganch, I suppose."

The Dromman did not answer. He heard a thin fine singing as his helmet absorbed the stun beam Chris was aiming at it.

"When my men reported you had been ten hours in the joy-house, I thought it best to check up: first your quarters and next . . ." Wayland paused. "I didn't think you'd penetrate this far. But it could only be you, Ganch, so you may as well surrender."

The spy shook his head, futile gesture inside that metal box he wore. "No. It is you who are trapped," he answered steadily. "I can blast you all before your beams work through my armor. . . . Don't move!"

"You wouldn't escape," said Wayland. "The fight would trip alarms, bring the whole Fort Canfield garrison down on you." Sweat beaded his forehead. Perhaps he thought of his niece and the gun which could make her a blackened husk; but his own small-bore flamer held firm.

"This means war," said Chris. "We've wondered about Dromm for a long time. Now we know." Tears glimmered in her eyes. "And it's so senseless!"

Ganch laughed without much humor. "Impasse," he said. "I can kill you, but that would bring my own death. Be sure, though, that the failure of my mission will make little difference."

Wayland stood brooding for a while. "You're congenitally unafraid to die," he said at last. "The rest of us prefer to live, but will die if we must. So any decision must be made with a view to planetary advantage."

Ganch's heart sprang within his ribs. He had lost, unless—

He still had an even chance.

"You're a race of gamblers," he said. "Will you gamble now?"

"Not with our planet," said Chris.

"Let me finish! I propose we toss a coin, shake dice, whatever you like that distributes the probabilities evenly. If I win, I go free with what I've taken here. You furnish me safe conduct and transportation home. You'll have the knowledge that Dromm is going to attack, and some time to prepare. If you win, I surrender and cooperate with you. I have valuable information, and you can drug me to make sure I don't lie."

"No!" shouted one of the officers.

"Wait. Let me think. . . . I have to make an estimate." Wayland lowered his gun and stood with half-shut eyes. He looked as he had down in the traders' hall, and Ganch remembered uneasily that Wayland was a gambling analyst.

But there was little to lose. If he won, he went home with his booty; if he lost . . . he knew how to will his heart to stop beating.

Wayland looked up. "Yes," he said.

The others did not question him. They must be used to following a tipster's advice blindly. But one of them asked how Ganch could be trusted. "I'll lay down my blaster when you produce the selection device," said the Dromman. "All the worlds know you do not cheat."

Chris reached into her pouched belt and drew out a deck of cards. Wordlessly, she shuffled them and gave them to her uncle. The spy put his gun on the floor. He half expected the others to rush him, but they stood where they were.

Wayland's hands shook as he cut the deck. He smiled crookedly.

"One-eyed jack," he whispered. "Hard to beat."

He shuffled the cards again and held them out to Ganch. The armored fingers were clumsy, but they opened the deck.

It was the king of spades.

Stars blazed in blackness. The engines which had eaten light-years were pulsing now on primary drive, gravitics, accelerating toward the red sun that lay three astronomical units ahead.

Ganch thought that the space distortions of the drive beams were lighting the fleet up like a nova for the Hermesian detectors. But you couldn't fight a battle at translight speeds, and their present objective was to seek the enemy out and destoy him.

Overcommandant wan Halsker peered into the viewscreens of the dreadnought. Avidness was on his long gaunt face, but he spoke levelly: "I find it hard to believe. They actually gave you a speedster and let you go."

"I expected treachery myself, sir," answered Ganch deferentially. Despite promotion, he was only the chief intelligence officer attached to Task Force One. "Surely, with their whole civilization at stake, any rational people would have— But their mores are unique. They always pay their gambling debts."

It was very quiet down here in the bowels of the supernova ship. A ring of technicians sat before their instruments, watching the dials unblinkingly. Wan Halsker's eyes never left the simulacrum of space in his screens, though all he saw was stars. There was too much emptiness around to show the five hundred ships of his command, spread in careful formation through some billions of cubic kilometers.

A light glowed, and a technician said: "Contact made. *Turolin* engaging estimated five meteor-class enemy vessels."

Wan Halsker allowed himself a snort. "Insects! Don't break formation; let the *Turolin* swat them as she proceeds."

Ganch sat waiting, rehearsing in his mind the principles of modern warfare. The gravity drive had radically changed them in the last few centuries. A forward vector could be killed almost instantaneously, a new direction taken as fast, while internal pseudograv fields compensated for accelerations which would otherwise have crumpled a man. A fight in space was not unlike one in air, with this difference: the velocities used were too high, the distances too great, the units involved too many, for a human brain to grasp. It had to be done by machine.

Subspace quivered with coded messages, the ships' own electronic minds transmitting information back to the prime computers on Dromm—the computers laid out not only the over-all strategy, but the tactics of every major engagement. A man could not follow that esoteric mathematics, he could merely obey the thing he had built.

No change of orders came, a few torpedo ships were unimportant, and Task Force One continued.

Astran was a clinker, an airless, valueless planet of a waning red dwarf star, but it housed a key base of the Hermesian navy. With Astran reduced, wan Halsker's command could safely go on to rendezvous with six other fleets that had been taking care of their own assignments; the whole group would then continue to New Hermes herself, and let the enemy dare try to stop them!

Such, in broad outline, was the plan; but only a

hundred computers, each filling a large building, could handle the details of strategy, tactics, and logistics.

Ganch had an uneasy feeling of being a very small cog in a very large machine. He didn't matter; the commandant didn't; the ship, the fleet, the gray mass of commoners didn't; nothing except the Cadre, and above them the almighty State, had real existence.

The Hermesians would need a lot of taming before they learned to think that way.

Now fire was exploding out in space, great guns cutting loose as the outnumbered force sought the invaders. Ganch felt a shuddering when the supernova's own armament spoke. The ship's computer, her brain, flashed and chattered, the vessel leaped on her gravity beams, ducking, dodging, spouting flame and hot metal. Stars spun on the screen in a lunatic dance. Ten thousand men aboard the ship had become robots feeding her guns.

"Compartment Seven hit . . . sealed off."

"Hit made on enemy star-class; damage looks light."

"Number Forty-two gun out of action. Residual radioactivity . . . compartment sealed off."

Men died, scorched and burned, air sucked from their lungs as the armored walls peeled away, listening to the clack of radiation counters as leaden bulkheads locked them away like lepers. The supernova trembled with each hit. Ganch heard steel shriek not far away and braced his body for death.

Wan Halsker sat impassively, hands folded on his lap, watching the screens and the dials. There was nothing he could do; the ship fought herself, men were too slow. But he nodded after a while, in satisfaction.

"We're sustaining damage," he said, "but no more than expected." He stared at a slim small crescent in the screen. "Yonder's the planet. We're working in . . . we'll be in bombardment range soon."

The ships' individual computers made their decisions on the basis of information received; but they were constantly sending a digest of the facts back to their

electronic masters on Dromm. So far no tactical change
had been ordered, but . . .

Ganch frowned at the visual tank which gave a crude
approximation of the reality ramping around him. The
little red specks were his own ships, the green ones
such of the enemy as had been spotted. It seemed to
him that too many red lights had stopped twinkling,
and that the Hermesian fireflies were driving a wedge
into the formation. But there was nothing he could do
either.

A bell clanged. Change of orders! *Turolin* to withdraw three megakilometers toward Polaris, *Colfin* to
swing around toward enemy Constellation Number Four,
Hardes to— Watching the tank in a hypnotized way,
Ganch decided vaguely it must be some attempt at a
flanking movement. But a Hermesian squadron was out
there!

Well . . .

The battle snarled across vacuum. It was many hours
before the Dromman computers gave up and flashed
the command: Break contact, retreat in formation to
Neering Base.

They had been outmaneuvered. Incredibly, New
Hermes' machines had out-thought Dromm's and the
battle was lost.

Wayland entered the mapping room with a jaunty
step that belied the haggardness in his face. Christabel
Hesty looked up from her task of directing the integra-
tors and cried aloud: "Will! I didn't expect you back so
soon!"

"I thumbed a ride home with a courier ship," said
Wayland. "Three months' leave. By that time the war
will be over, so . . ." He sat down on her desk, swinging his short legs, and got out an old and incredibly foul
pipe. "I'm just as glad, to tell the truth. Planetarism is
all right in its place, but war's an ugly business."

He grimaced. A Hermesian withstood the military
life better than most; he was used not only to moments
of nerve-ripping suspense but to long and patient wait-

ing. Wayland, though, had during the past year seen too many ships blown up, too many men dead or screaming with their wounds. His hands shook a little as he tamped the pipe full.

"Luck be praised you're alive!"

"It hasn't been easy on you either, has it? Chained to a desk like this. Here, sit back and take a few minutes off. The war can wait." Wayland kindled his tobacco and blew rich clouds. "At least it never got close to our home, and our losses have been lighter than expected."

"If you get occupation duty . . ."

"I'm afraid I will."

"Well, I want to come *too*. I've never been off this planet; it's disgraceful."

"Dromm is a pretty dreary place, I warn you. But Thanit is close by, of course. It used to be a gay world, it will be again, and every Hermesian will be luck incarnate to them. Sure, I'll wangle an assignment for you."

Chris frowned. "Only three months to go, though? That's hard to believe."

"Two and a half is the official estimate. Look here." Wayland stumped over to the three-dimensional sector map, which was there only for the enlightenment of humans. The military computers dealt strictly in lists of numbers.

"See, we whipped them at the Cold Stars, and now a feint of ours is drawing what's left of them into Ransome's Nebula."

"Ransome's . . . oh, you mean the Queen of Clubs? Mmm-hm. And what's going to happen to them there?"

"Tch, tch. Official secrets, my dear inquisitive nieceling. But imagine what *could* happen to a fleet concentrated in a mess of nebular dust that blocks their detectors!"

Wayland did not see Ganch again until he was stationed on Dromm. There he grumbled long and loudly about the climate, the food, and the tedious necessity of making sure that a subjugated enemy stayed subjugated. He looked forward to his next furlough on Thanit, and still more to rotation home in six months. Chris, being younger, enjoyed herself. They had no mountains on New Hermes, and she was going to climb Hell's Peak with Commander Danson. About half a dozen other young officers would be jealously present, so her uncle felt she would be adequately chaperoned.

They were working together in the political office, interviewing Cadre men and disposing of their cases. Wayland was not sympathetic toward the prisoners. But when Ganch was led in, he felt a certain kinship and even smiled.

"Sit down," he invited. "Take it easy. I don't bite."

Ganch slumped into a chair before the desk and looked at the floor. He seemed as shattered as the rest of his class. They weren't really tough, thought Wayland; they couldn't stand defeat; most of them suicided rather than undergo psychorevision.

"Didn't expect to see you again," he said. "I understood you were on combat duty, and . . . um . . ."

"I know," said Ganch lifelessly. "Our combat units averaged ninety per cent casualties, toward the end." In a rush of bitterness: "I wish I had been one of them."

"Take it easy," repeated Wayland. "We Hermesians aren't vindictive. Your planet will never have armed forces again—it'll join Corrid and Oberkassel as a protectorate of ours—but once we've straightened you out you'll be free to live as you please."

"Free!" mumbled Ganch.

He lifted tortured red eyes to the face before him, but shifted from its wintry smile to Chris. She had some warmth for him at least.

"How did you do it?" he whispered. "I don't understand. I thought you must have some new kind of computer, but our intelligence swore you didn't . . . and we outnumbered you, and had that information you let me take home, and—"

"We're gamblers," said the girl soberly.

"Yes, but—"

"Look at it this way," she went on. "War is a science, based on a complex paramathematical theory. Maneuvers and engagements are ordered with a view to gaining the maximum advantage for one's own side, in the light of known information. But of course, *all* the information is never available, so intelligent guesswork has to fill in the gaps.

"Well, a system exists for making such guesses and for deciding what move has the maximum probability of success. It applies to games, business, war—every competitive enterprise. It's called games theory."

"I—" Ganch's jaw dropped. He snapped it shut again and said desperately: "But that's elementary! It's been known for centuries."

"Of course," nodded Chris. "But New Hermes has based on her whole economy on gambling—on probabilities, on games of skill where no player has complete information. Don't you see, it would make our entire intellectual interest turn toward games theory. And in fact we had to have a higher development of such knowledge, and a large class of men skilled in using it, or we could not maintain as complex a civilization as we do.

"No other planet has a comparable body of knowledge. And, while we haven't kept it a secret, no other planet has men able to use that knowledge on its highest levels.

"For instance, take that night we caught you in the file room. If we cut cards with you, there was a fifty-fifty chance you'd go free. Will here had to estimate whether the over-all probabilities justified the gamble. Because he decided they did, we three are alive today."

"But I did bring that material home!" cried Ganch.

"Yes," said the girl. "And the fact you had it was merely another item for our strategic computers to take into account. Indeed, it helped us: it was definite information about what *you* knew, and your actions became yet more predictable."

Laughter, gentle and unmocking, lay in her throat, "Never draw to an inside straight," she said. "And never play with a man who knows enough not to, when you don't."

Ganch sagged farther down in his chair. He felt sick. He replied to Wayland's questioning in a mechanical fashion, and heard sentence pronounced, and left under guard.

As he stumbled out, he heard Wayland say thoughtfully: "Three gets you four he suicides rather than take psychorevision."

"You're covered!" said Christabel.

Poul Anderson is the author of more than fifty books and two-hundred-and-some-odd short pieces. Besides sf, these include fantasy, mystery, historical, juvenile, and here-and-now fiction; nonfiction; poetry, essays, criticism, translations, etc. His short stories and articles have appeared in places as various as the sf magazines, *Boys' Life, Playboy,* the Toronto *Star Weekly, National Review, Ellery Queen's,* and the now defunct *Jack London's Magazine.* His novels, nonfiction books, and short stories have been published in fifteen foreign languages.

Poul is a former Regional Vice-President of the Mystery Writers of America and former President of the Science Fiction Writers of America, and he has had several Hugo and Nebula Awards, the "Forry" Award of the Los Angeles Science Fantasy Society, a special issue of *The Magazine of Fantasy and Science Fiction,* the Macmillan Cock Robin Award for best mystery novel, and others. Among his most popular books are *Brain Wave, The High Crusade, The Enemy Stars, Three Hearts and Three Lions, The Broken Sword,* and *Tau Zero.* More recent titles are *There Will Be Time, The People of the Wind, A Midsummer Tempest, Fire Time, The Avatar* (1978) and *The Merman's Children* (1979).

Poul and his wife, Karen, live in the San Francisco Bay area. His story "Marius" appeared in *Thor's Hammer,* Volunne I of *The Future at War,* and Volume II, *The Spear of Mars,* contains his "Cold Victory."

Jon Freeman's "World of the Wars" is the new world of war games. War games—perhaps we should say war-related games—have been with us for millenia; chess, for example, and go, and more recently and less abstractly, such highly formalized military-training games as kriegspiel.

But it is only during the last few years that war games have broken loose from the ties of military history and of Earth's gravity, moving out into space and involving any number of alien cultures and strange technologies.

These games are science fiction's children, born of its involvement with the progress and the unprecedented perils of our scientific age—and perhaps fostered by the psychological need to participate in that progress and contend with those perils at least symbolically.

The world of war games is a world which, until not many years ago, knew no contests much more exciting than "Monopoly." The number of their players is increasing rapidly, and those players are uniformly above-average in intelligence. It remains to be seen what effect, social and political and military, they will have on our unstable world.

Jon Freeman

WORLD OF THE WARS

Although science-fiction and fantasy games have achieved remarkable popular and commercial success, they have not yet received the recognition in science-fiction circles that they deserve. A war game "Hugo" is still in the future.

Many of the classic subjects of SF have been done as games: alternate time-tracks; robots run amok; an atomic war and its aftermath; a future world desolated by nuclear war and altered by radiation; an enormous colonial ship whose inhabitants have forgotten the universe outside; the expansion of the human race through the rest of the galaxy; colonial rebellion against a mother planet or empire; battle in deep space; the chancy thrill of First Contact; the ultimate artifact of a long-forgotten civilization that could wipe out a planet, a star, or an entire race of beings—even the fantasies of Tolkien, Leiber, Moorcock, and others. Not all the elements of SF literature are suited to a game, of course, but for those that are, games offer a temptation no book or movie can match: a chance for player/readers to get in on the action. Not just to read about the exploits of John Carter or Gunnar Heim but to *be* them: to make their own decisions, to fail or triumph themselves as a result of their own actions.

Since most science-fiction games are a subclass of what are nominally "war games," it should not be surprising that their conflicts should be direct and open, echoing not Le Guin's philosophical questioning or

Ellison's psychological torment but rather the exuberant adventure of Poul Anderson, H. Beam Piper, Andre Norton, or Keith Laumer. Some are as frankly anachronistic in content and style as *Planet Stories* and *Star Wars*.

There are more than a dozen games that deal with a war that might happen tomorrow—or the day after. As an exercise in speculation, games like *The East Is Red* (about a Soviet invasion of China), *NATO* (a conflict in West Germany between forces of NATO and the Warsaw Pact), and *World War Three* are as conservative as a weather forecast. However, all—even the more speculative *Invasion: America*—illustrate the basic war game approach.

Most war games are designed for two players (*Invasion: America* has provisions for up to five, but that's atypical). The board, almost always, is a map overlaid with a hexagonal grid—divided into "hexes," that is, much the way a chessboard is split up into squares, and for much the same reason. Each player controls an army of cardboard pieces—called "counters" or simply "units"—each of which, depending on the scale of the map and the size of the conflict being simulated, may represent a fleet or a battleship, an army or an individual infantryman, or anything in between. (The same technique can be used for dragons, goblin cavalry, stellar destroyers, or bolo tanks.) In addition to an identifying symbol, these color-coded (by nationality, generally) counters have numbers printed on them which quantify their basic abilities of movement and combat. Essentially, the two players maneuver their cardboard armies as if they were miniature soldiers crossing scaled-down terrain, as they attempt to attain their objectives: capturing Berlin or Peking or destroying Washington, DC. When opposing forces meet, the battles are resolved using a carefully prepared chart called, simply enough, the Combat Results Table (CRT). Most often, the ratio of the opposing combat factors is used to determine which column of the CRT to consult; a roll of a die gives the row, and the result of the battle is read from the table. Units may be reduced in strength, forced to retreat, or destroyed and removed from the board. Combat thus lacks the artificial certainties of chess, but it is no more a matter of luck than anything else based on statistical probabilities. While CRTs vary in detail, it is always true that the more overwhelming the attack, the better the chances of success.

This simple description can do no more than hint at the incredible variety of battles, weapons, and situations that can be handled with permutations of this approach, but this will be clearer as we examine the picture of warfare presented by different games.

The infantry of SF war games is not the simply armed mercenary of Dickson's Dorsai stories or even Andre Norton's *Star Guard*, it's the specially trained, technologically sophisticated soldier of Joe Haldeman's *The Forever War*—Heinlein's "Mobile Infantry." Wearing a cross between 14th Century plate armor and a spacesuit, the "foot soldier" of *Starship Troopers*, *StarSoldier*, *Olympica*, and the (deservedly) more obscure *Rift Trooper* is half airborne, with the firepower of a tank and more mobility than a helicopter.

Retaining both the flavor and the details of the *book*, *Starship Troopers* (the game) includes a number of scenarios based on typical MI battles against both "Skinnies" and "Bugs." (Scenarios are minigames or subgames that simulate different situations with different units and objectives on the same board; many war games, especially tactically oriented ones, consist of up to a dozen or more scenarios.) The latter are the most fun and the most challenging, since the "Bug" player gets to design hidden tunnel complexes, which allow his warriors to pop up in unexpected places on the board. True to the book, the humans have to locate and penetrate the tunnels and go in after the "Brains."

Olympica is very similar in flavor, since the objective is the retrieval of an item hidden inside an underground complex guarded by a powerful alien "WebMind." There are tanks, tactical thermonuclear weapons, and special effects of the WebMind, but the focus is still on powered infantry.

While differing in detail, *StarSoldier* has many similarities to *Starship Troopers:* a multitude of recon or smash-and-grab scenarios; a mapboard of "typical" terrain; powerful individual units, hard to hurt and very difficult to kill; and a couple of alien races. Limited intelligence is represented by placing "native" counters—some of which are blank, dummy units—face down until contacted. The setting is slightly farther in the future, and the soldier's all-purpose power unit governs *everything:* movement, firepower, the works. Power expended in movement is not available that turn for firing at the opposition; damage, recorded on the same sliding scale, reduces the power available on the current and future turns. (Variations on this theme are a standard feature of ship-to-ship combat in other games.) Like its siblings, *Outreach* and *StarForce*, *StarSoldier* uses a system of simultaneous movement (SiMov) that requires each player to make a written plan of action for each unit each turn: a nuisance but not the major disaster it would be with more units to keep track of.

A second group of tactical games set on a planetary (or planetoidal) surface owes more to *Hammer's Slammers* or Keith Laumer's "Bolo" stories than to Heinlein's MI. The most famous of these is *Ogre*, the first of Metagamings pocket-sized microgames. A small masterpiece, *Ogre* is as responsible as anything on the market for the boom in sf gaming and the resurgence of manageable games. Despite its title, *Ogre* is not a game of dragons and goblins; the Ogre is a monster *tank*, huge, powerful, and robotically intelligent. The aim of the Ogre, which is nearly invulnerable and so big it can simply run over anything in its way, is to single-handedly destroy an enemy command post. Against it are arrayed artillery, normal tanks, and lesser vehicles (GEVs and the like), which have to be sacrificed, one by one, to slow down and destroy the Ogre literally piece by piece. If you're new to wargaming, *Ogre* is the place to start: it's easy to learn, short, and fun—even (or maybe especially) for those who don't play many war games.

Although it can stand alone, *G.E.V.* (for "Ground Effect Vehicle") is really an expansion kit for Ogre that adds more vehicles, weapon systems, and scenarios. *Titan Strike* (a "capsule game," SPI's answer to micro-games) uses a somewhat similar mixture of tanks (robot and otherwise), artillery (laser and conventional), GEV-type hover platforms, heavy infantry, skimmers (the equivalent of aircraft), and some odd "hopper" units to depict a battle for the control of fissionable ore on Saturn's moon. Chief differences from *Ogre/G.E.V.* are the importance of electronic jamming (and counter-jamming) and the simple, all-or-nothing type of Combat Results Table (which isn't called that) similar to the one used in *Imperium* (discussed later).

Loosely speaking, *Ice War* is the same sort of thing set in the Arctic: a raid by a Eurasian Socialist Alliance on the Prudhoe Bay oilfields. *Black Hole* (like *Ice War* a microgame) employs a simpler system with a simpler "counter mix" (that is, with fewer different kinds of units) to portray a similar fight over a toroidal (donut-shaped) asteroid (discovered by one "Winchell Dunkin," I am appalled to repeat) that surrounds a tiny black hole. The fun comes from the bizarre properties of the map, which effectively joins itself top to bottom and side to side. The abruptly curving line of sight drastically limits ranged weapons on the outside of the torus, and missiles that miss their intended targets become serious menaces to everyone as they continue to circle the board.

Like the earlier group, all these games tend to be only minimally concerned with the causes of conflict; occasionally, some reason is concocted, but the usual assumption is that human beings have always fought for control of land, resources, and the minds, souls, and bodies of men—and will probably continue to do so. The focus is on "color"—the minor differences between warfare-as-we-know-it and the same conventional combat logically extrapolated a century or two (or three) into the future.

Color appears to be the major excuse for *Rivets* and *Chitin: I*, which break somewhat from this pattern without being particularly original. In *Rivets*, man is dead, but semi-intelligent robots carry on the fight. (Oh, you've heard that one before . . .) In *Chitin: I* the war is for food, and the combatants are intelligent hive insects whose varied warriors are vaguely reminiscent of Vance's dragons. Despite the difference in settings, both involve a circular pattern of effectiveness of the scissors-paper-stone family: Robot/Insect Type A can defeat Robot/Insect Type B, which is better than Type C, which is more effective against lowly Type D, which nevertheless has an advantage over Type A, and so forth. Sort of the Jungle Game with a CRT.

Curiously, there seems to be no counterpart to the planetary raids of *Space Viking*. *The Ythri*, a game based on Poul Anderson's *The People of the Wind*, did portray both ship-to-ship combat and a planetary invasion/assault, but it is no longer on the market. Such a subject offers such obvious possibilities for a good game that the omission can only be temporary.

Tactical space war games derive less from the massed fleet actions of E. E. Smith and Edmond Hamilton than from the escapades of *Star Trek*'s Enterprise. Most versions of the *Star Trek* game (collectively the most popular computer game ever done) were fairly primitive by war game standards and, being played in "real time," did not lend themselves to multiple combat and complicated decision-making.

Lou Zocchi's *Alien Ship* was a thinly disguised adaptation of the TV show fleshed out with other alien ships to keep the altered Klingons and Romulans company. Each ship had some peculiar weapon or protective (e.g., "cloaking") device instead of or in addition to the standard armament of blazers (phasers), proton (photon) torpedoes, and shielding force fields. Zocchi used a quasiminiatures approach: each ship was represented by a large (3″) cardboard maneuvered on the floor. Firing was by guess and by golly and was checked by measuring the actual firing angle with a yardstick and the compass printed on the counter. (Newer editions include a now-official *Star Trek Battle Manual* and *do* use miniatures—small spaceships of plastic or metal.) While challenging and fun, this was a bit impractical and did not allow more than one ship on a side (although it did permit some wild multiplayer free-for-alls).

The idea of individual ships being the norm, however, remained; subsequent efforts attempted to add numbers without losing the detail of individual ship actions. As a simulation of the mechanics of combat, fleets of a thousand ships (a *la* the Lensman series) may sound appealing, but they pose horrible problems of logistics: maneuvering a thousand counters is pure tedium, and if the pieces themselves are flotillas, the thunder of exploding bulkheads and the fire of overheated force fields are lost in abstraction. (Some games do use this scale, but their interest is in strategic maneuver and the control of star systems, not the minute-by-minute fate of a particular destroyer.)

Energy weapons by whatever name have been standard equipment on spaceships since the Year One, and protective force fields—defensive energy screens—are as old and nearly as common. As a game device, however, *Star Trek* was largely responsible for the notion of a common (and limited) energy source behind movement and weapons systems—a concept we noticed in *StarSoldier*. In the more typical setting of starships, *Alpha Omega* uses it to a large degree, but the quintessential example is probably the system used in the computer games *StarFleet Orion* and *Invasion Orion*.

In both, a given energy allotment is used to power a ship's drive, defensive force shield, offensive beam, tractor/pressor beam, and to launch missiles or torpedoes. (The latter are reasonably standard mass-seeking missiles that proceed in a straight line until they hit something; the former are something like projected bombs that can be used to damage star ships or destroy torpedoes.) In the normal course of events, there is not enough energy to go around so the player must decide every turn how best to allocate the energy he has.

(*Alpha Omega* even more extreme in this regard; all the ships are so energy-poor that they can't come close to utilizing all their subsystems.) Missile weapons, which are expendable, do a set amount of damage (variable in the system but fixed by the scenario); beam damage is a function of the energy applied to the striking beam and the range to the target ship. The shield and inert armor ("collapsium" or the equivalent) absorb some, and what gets through is divided at random among the various subsystems, reducing their capacities for the remainder of the game. While there is not the variety of weapon systems found in *Alpha Omega or Alien Space,* each ship is more diversified. An obvious advantage to the *Orion* games is that the complications of combat resolution, which normally require much die-rolling and chart-consulting, are invisibly built into the computer program.

As in noncomputer wargames, there is no time constraint (one second of game time does not equal one second of real time). Each ship is ordered individually and damaged bit by bit, but small fleet actions can be accommodated. Within its limit of nine ships per side, the flexible *Orion* system, which allows you to tailor the ships and their weapon systems to your specifications and even to add asteroids or a planet to the scene, can be used to duplicate almost any space battle in sf.

Vector movement—good old Newtonian mechanics—is attractive but messy. *Mayday* requires three counters to represent a ship in just two dimensions. To get full three-dimensional motion in the optional *BattleFleet Mars* tactical subgame, each ship is represented by *five* pieces (two "counters" and three "markers") on *two* boards; besides being cumbersome, the system makes visualization difficult. (The strategic movement system for interplanetary travel in *BattleFleet Mars* is Apollo-accurate and not so unhandy.) *Vector Three* has a similar pair of square grids, but instead of pieces it uses pencil, paper, and a lot of calculating and record-keeping. *Starfleet/Invasion Orion* and *WarpWar* duck the problem by using inertialess microjumps, while the human and Rhylsh ships in *Alpha Omega* compromise on a simplified system of semi-vector movement.

The common fictional background of *Starfleet Orion* and *Invasion Orion* is "classic" if you will (or "standard" if you won't): the Great Exodus to the stars, the attempt by an authoritarian Terran government to reassert control over the colonies, the inevitable military conflict, the discovery of a "race" of robots inimical to all human beings, the temporary patching of old wounds to fight the common foe. Part of this is echoed in *Alpha Omega:* a long war between humans and the Rhylsh is finally ended by the attack of a third alien race, the Drove, which is hostile to both. The inevitability of conflict is a practical rather than a philosophical conclusion: the only games that allow the possibility of friendly interaction with aliens are the multiplayer games of grand strategy discussed later.

Metagaming's *WarpWar*, GDW's *Imperium*, and SPI's *StarForce* and *BattleFleet Mars* could be termed strategic games with tactical overtones (or undertones). They are, in the purest sense, "war games." Despite distinct differences in setting, their common subject is not individual battles or chronicles of expansion that subsume wars and generations; it's a war.

WarpWar's ships resemble those of *Alpha Omega* and the *Orion* games, and combat is resolved somewhat similarly, but the scale of movement is entirely different. Ships maneuver along "warp lines" from star to star as they attempt to seize control of enemy bases. Combat takes place only when opposing ships occupy the same space, and at that point they're no longer moving, except abstractly, on the diceless CRT. Neither side starts the game with specific ships, so their design and construction is a major part of strategy.

Imperium is a far more developed game of the same general sort played out against an elaborate but familiar background. A small Terran Confederation is expanding into territory claimed by a large, established, permanent . . . um . . . empire. The Imperium is so vast, in fact, and its center of government so far away, that the actual game conflict involves only the governor of the Imperial province bordering Terra. Since the Imperium *per se* is essentially off-stage, its existence is simulated abstractly but cleverly by a series of rules, charts, and the effects of the "Glory Index," which reflects the prestige of the provincial governor with the "home office."

Essentially, Terran growth, militarily and economically, is dependent on Terran expansion: the establishment of outposts and colonized worlds in new star systems. Since the bulk of provincial (Imperial) income is derived from a relatively fixed Imperial budget, the Terran Confederation must take the strategic offensive, while the Imperium player is on the strategic defensive. In fact, since limited Terran expansion could be accomplished without disturbing the Imperial status quo, what pushes the conflict from the Imperial side is the postulated ambition of the governor. If he can expand the empire at the expense of the Terran Confederation, the recognition he achieves may allow him to move up in the Imperial bureaucracy. (This basic background was used in *The Rebel Worlds*, one of Poul Anderson's Dominic Flandry novels, among others.) However, increases in his budget and permission to build the larger classes of warship both require appeals to the Emperor, which cost Glory Points (the governor's power is predicated on not bothering the Imperium with "administrative details"). If he then *loses* territory to the Terrans (resulting in a further loss of points on the Glory Index), he will eventually be replaced; the Imperium will negotiate peace; and the Terran player will win.

BattleFleet Mars represents, in outline, a reasonably similar situation set entirely within the solar system at a time less far in the future. The Martian colonists' struggle for independence from the control of the Earth-based Ares Corporation suggests the basic situation in Heinlein's *Red Planet*—and, to a degree, of *Between Planets, The Moon Is A Harsh Mistress*, and the Thirteen Colonies. Distant governments, by whatever name, are even less responsive to the wishes and welfare of the governed than local ones. Although the issue is political autonomy, the colonists' long-term weapon in *BattleFleet Mars* is economic: a reverse boycott, a refusal to ship raw materials on which Earth industry depends. Performing much the same function of *Imperium*'s Glory Index, a Morale Index measures popular sentiment on Earth and Mars and political pressure on the Corporation resulting from the effects of the blockade and the battles, revolts on asteroid outposts, assassinations, and intrigue that constitute the actual business of the game. The military weapons (lasers and missiles) are similar to *Imperium*'s, but, except for the optional tactical subgame, there is even less concern for the actual details of combat.

StarForce shares a common fictional background with *StarSoldier* and *Outreach*. In *StarForce* (as in *BattleFleet Mars*) the cause of conflict is political: which hegemony, league, or confederation should be top dog: i.e., who will rule whom under what name.

Interstellar travel is a product of amplified telekinesis (teleportation of man and machine)—a notion used by Doc Smith (among others) in *The Galaxy Primes*. Instead of maneuvering to control warp lines (in *WarpWar*) or jump routes (in *Imperium*)—along which movement is essentially free—the key in *StarForce* is the control of "stargates," which boost the distance and accuracy of the telekinetic jumps. Combat is not a matter of energy guns or missiles; it's a function of the same mental abilities. In battle, people are rendered *hors de combat* by being knocked out psychically (psionically) or by having their ship (and themselves) "displaced" telekinetically a few light-years in a random direction. Since the rare people with the necessary "telesthetic" abilities constitute a tiny and fairly fixed percentage of the population, the game's designer optimistically suggests that warring groups would not wish to damage the population base—even (perhaps especially) the opposing "soldiers"—of the worlds they hope to rule. Such a rational approach to warfare does not seem, historically, too typical of the human race—particularly the portion of it that starts wars.

Science fiction on the grand scale is represented by *4000 A.D.*, *Star Web*, *Stellar Conquest*, and *Outreach*, whose general aims are to explore/colonize/conquer other star systems, develop/exploit/appropriate whatever resources may be found there, use the resources to build new ships or installations and/or to raise the level of technology or civilization. In some cases, this arbitrarily defined level increase is an end in itself; in others, it is used to accelerate the cycle of expansion, and the ultimate aim is the occupation of the bases or home stars of the opposing player(s).

It is not just the scope (1500 light-years per hex, in *Outreach*) that distinguishes these games, but the element of the unknown involved in exploring the universe. In the computer-moderated *Star Web* and, to a lesser degree, in *Outreach*, you don't know how many players or factions there are, where they are located, or what their intentions are. Even in *4000 A.D.* or *Stellar Conquest*, the presence of more than two players—and the consequent possibility of alliances—adds an element of complexity and uncertainty not found in any standard two-player war game. Although any of them can be played by only two people, the added interaction makes the presence of more players very desirable.

4000 A.D. is the simplest and not all that much different in some respects from *Imperium*. Resources from an occupied star system enable a player's home star to build more ships, which allow him to occupy more stars. There is no interest in low-level tactics: there is only one sort of starship, and, in battle, a larger fleet overwhelms a smaller one without loss to itself (in theory, the greater force field annihilates the lesser one—and the ships generating it). Like *StarForce* and unlike *Imperium*, there is no "front." A unique offboard "space warp" (more of a misnomer than usual), in which a fleet travels one sector per turn, allows everyone to see where the fleet *might* go, but the exact destination is unknown until the controlling player removes the fleet from the warp and brings it into "normal space" at any star the legal distance from the starting point. In its simple fashion, this novel device simulates the old problem of limited intelligence—the element of the unknown referred to earlier—which would surely be exacerbated if warfare were conducted across interstellar distances.

The other three games introduce various complications: different kinds of ships and weapons, varying and initially unknown resources in the unexplored star systems, limitations on movement, hidden movement, certain tactical considerations, alien races with dissimilar objectives, and on and on. Because it allows a large number of participants, each of whom can (and must) operate "in the dark," *Star Web*'s large-computer-moderated play-by-mail is probably the most logical mode for this sort of game. The multitude of decisions—and *kinds* of decisions—characteristically required in all these games give their players a particular opportunity for skillful play and a chance to submerge themselves in the game world.

This "role-playing' is the essence of a final group of games without which any discussion of SF games would not be complete. In *Traveller* (easily the best and broadest in scope of the bunch), *Space Patrol*, *Metamorphosis Alpha*, and others, there is no board, no predetermined setting (except, in a general sense, in *Metamorphosis Alpha*, which takes place among the various levels of a gigantic spaceship of the *Orphans of the Sky* variety), and no real objective except experiencing another world. In such role-playing games, one person (the referee or gamesmaster) constructs a world of his own; the other players then take the part of individuals living in that world: exploring new planets, fighting hostile aliens, trading at colonial outposts—anything allowed by their inclinations and the "slant" of the universe. On a personal level, at least, nearly anything in science fiction literature can be recreated in this sort of game, but because it is not suited for large-scale (e.g., fleet) action, war, properly speaking, is not usually its subject.

For a broad grasp of the strategy and tactics of combat at any level—for a sense of how things work in war, and why—there is nothing like a war game. A story can paint a vivid picture of war in the future: the flash of a heavy laser, the whine of a hovercraft, even the stench of burning flesh. A *good* story can even make you *feel* what war is like to the people who are in it and near it. But if the gamesmaster is inspired and the players are willing, a good role-playing game can do those things also (not usually quite so well, perhaps, but that is a matter of time, trouble, talent, and practice, rather than any inherent limitations of the form). And *any* good science-fiction game allows you to participate—to act—to be there yourself—to create a story of your own that is different every time you play: always changing, always new.

And that does wonders for that old Sense of Wonder.

A lifelong sf reader and game enthusiast, Jon Freeman was graduated from Indiana University with Honors in English and received his Masters in English from the University of California. The following summer he wrote his first sf novel; it was published two years later, and, despite periodic billpaying jobs (as teacher, computer operator, secretary) he's been writing ever since.

Much of Freeman's recent output has involved games: the definitive introduction to the now notorious *Dungeons & Dragons* and other pieces for *Games* magazine, *The Playboy Winner's Guide to Board Games*, and (for *Consumers Guide*) *The Complete Book of War Games*. He currently divides his working time between freelance writing (sf and otherwise) and producing new microcomputer games for Automated Simulations. Avoiding the usual vices, he is addicted to reading (of course), *D&D* (i.e., *Dungeons & Dragons*), active sports, and the company of attractive, intelligent women.

One of the persisting problems of high-technology warfare is, and probably always will be, the gap between theory and practice, drawing-board design and functioning in the field, the planner and the doer, the wish and its fulfillment. It has always been quite true that "the best laid schemes o' mice an' men gang aft-a-gley" but now the mice have an advantage: their schemes are simple, their ojectives constant, and the means for their achievement unchanging.

This is not true of men, and the fact that military technology in all its aspects is progressing geometrically along ever-steeping curves seems certain to make the gap harder and harder to bridge successfully—even when, as in this story of Arthur Clarke's, it comes to war in space, fought at faster-than-light speeds between the ships of many-systemed empires.

Arthur C. Clarke

SUPERIORITY

In making this statement—which I do of my own free will—I wish first to make it perfectly clear that I am not in any way trying to gain sympathy, nor do I expect any mitigation of whatever sentence the Court may pronounce. I am writing this in an attempt to refute some of the lying reports broadcast over the prison radio and published in the papers I have been allowed to see. These have given an entirely false picture of the true cause of our defeat, and as the leader of my race's armed forces at the cessation of hostilities I feel it my duty to protest against such libels upon those who served under me.

I also hope that this statement may explain the reasons for the application I have twice made to the Court, and will now induce it to grant a favor for which I can see no possible grounds of refusal.

The ultimate cause of our failure was a simple one: despite all statements to the contrary, it was not due to lack of bravery on the part of our men, or to any fault of the Fleet's. We were defeated by one thing only—by the inferior science of our enemies. I repeat—by the *inferior* science of our enemies.

When the war opened we had no doubt of our ultimate victory. The combined fleets of our allies greatly exceeded in number and armament those which the enemy could muster against us, and in almost all branches of military science we were their superiors. We were

175

sure that we could maintain this superiority. Our belief proved, alas, to be only too well founded.

At the opening of the war our main weapons were the long-range homing torpedo, dirigible ball-lightning and the various modifications of the Klydon beam. Every unit of the Fleet was equipped with these and though the enemy possessed similar weapons their installations were generally of lesser power. Moreover, we had behind us a far greater military Research Organization, and with this initial advantage we could not possibly lose.

The campaign proceeded according to plan until the Battle of the Five Suns. We won this, of course, but the opposition proved stronger than we had expected. It was realized that victory might be more difficult, and more delayed, than had first been imagined. A conference of supreme commanders was therefore called to discuss our future strategy.

Present for the first time at one of our war conferences was Professor-General Norden, the new Chief of the Research Staff, who had just been appointed to fill the gap left by the death of Malvar, our greatest scientist. Malvar's leadership had been responsible, more than any other single factor, for the efficiency and power of our weapons. His loss was a very serious blow, but no one doubted the brilliance of his successor—though many of us disputed the wisdom of appointing a theoretical scientist to fill a post of such vital importance. But we had been overruled.

I can well remember the impression Norden made at that conference. The military advisers were worried, and as usual turned to the scientists for help. Would it be possible to improve our existing weapons, they asked, so that our present advantage could be increased still further?

Norden's reply was quite unexpected. Malvar had often been asked such a question—and he had always done what we requested.

"Frankly, gentlemen," said Norden, "I doubt it. Our existing weapons have practically reached finality. I don't wish to criticize my predecessor, or the excellent work done by the Research Staff in the last few generations, but do you realize that there has been no basic change in armaments for over a century? It is, I am afraid, the result of a tradition that has become conservative. For too long, the Research Staff has devoted itself to perfecting old weapons instead of developing new ones. It is fortunate for us that our opponents have been no wiser; we cannot assume that this will always be so."

Norden's words left an uncomfortable impression, as he had no doubt intended. He quickly pressed home the attack.

"What we want are *new* weapons—weapons totally different from any that have been employed before. Such weapons can be made: it will take time, of course, but since assuming charge I have replaced some of the older scientists by young men and have directed research into several unexplored fields which show great promise. I believe, in fact, that a revolution in warfare may soon be upon us."

We were skeptical. There was a bombastic tone in Norden's voice that made us suspicious of his claims. We did not know, then, that he never promised anything that he had not already almost perfected in the laboratory. *In the laboratory*—that was the operative phrase.

Norden proved his case less than a month later, when he demonstrated the Sphere of Annihilation, which produced complete disintegration of matter over a radius of several hundred meters. We were intoxicated by the power of the new weapon, and were quite prepared to overlook one fundamental defect—the fact that it *was* a sphere and hence destroyed its rather complicated generating equipment at the instant of formation. This meant, of course, that it could not be used on warships but only on guided missiles, and a great program was started to convert all homing torpedoes to carry the new weapon. For the time being all further offensives were suspended.

We realize now that this was our first mistake. I still think that it was a natural one, for it seemed to us then that all our existing weapons had become obsolete overnight, and we already regarded them as almost primitive survivals. What we did not appreciate was the magnitude of the task we were attempting, and the length of time it would take to get the revolutionary super-weapon into battle. Nothing like this had happened for a hundred years and we had no previous experience to guide us.

The conversion problem proved far more difficult than anticipated. A new class of torpedo had to be designed, as the standard model was too small. This meant in turn that only the larger ships could launch the weapon, but we were prepared to accept this penalty. After six months, the heavy units of the Fleet were being equipped with the Sphere. Training maneuvers and tests had shown that it was operating satisfactorily and we were ready to take it into action. Norden was already being hailed as the architect of victory, and had half promised even more spectacular weapons.

Then two things happened. One of our battleships disappeared completely on a training flight, and an investigation showed that under certain conditions the ship's long-range radar could trigger the Sphere immediately it had been launched. The modification needed to overcome this defect was trivial, but it caused a delay of another month and was the source of much bad feeling between the naval staff and the scientists. We were ready for action again—when Norden announced that the radius of effectiveness of the Sphere had now been increased by ten. Thus multiplying by a thousand the chances of destroying an enemy ship.

So the modifications started all over again, but everyone agreed that the delay would be worth it. Meanwhile, however, the enemy had been emboldened by the absence of further attacks and had made an unexpected onslaught. Our ships were short of torpedoes, since none had been coming from the factories, and were forced to retire. So we lost the systems of Kyrane and Floranus, and the planetary fortress of Rhamsandron.

It was an annoying but not a serious blow, for the recaptured systems had been unfriendly, and difficult to administer. We had no doubt that we could restore the position in the near future, as soon as the new weapon became operational.

These hopes were only partially fulfilled. When we renewed our offensive, we had to do so with fewer of the Spheres of Annihilation than had been planned, and this was one reason for our limited success. The other reason was more serious.

While we had been equipping as many of our ships as we could with the irresistible weapon, the enemy had been building feverishly. His ships were of the old pattern with the old weapons—but they now outnumbered ours. When we went into action, we found that the numbers ranged against us were often 100 per cent greater than expected, causing target confusion among the automatic weapons and resulting in higher losses than anticipated. The enemy losses were higher still, for once a Sphere had reached its objective, destruction was certain, but the balance had not swung as far in our favor as we had hoped.

Moreover, while the main fleets had been engaged, the enemy had launched a daring attack on the lightly held systems of Eriston, Duranus, Carmanidora and Pharanidon—recapturing them all. We were thus faced with a threat only fifty light-years from our home planets.

There was much recrimination at the next meeting of the supreme commanders. Most of the complaints were addressed to Norden—Grand Admiral Taxaris in particular maintaining that thanks to our admittedly irresistible weapon we were now considerably worse off than before. We should, he claimed, have continued to build conventional ships, thus preventing the loss of our numerical superiority.

Norden was equally angry and called the naval staff ungrateful bunglers. But I could tell that he was worried—as indeed we all were—by the unexpected turn of events. He hinted that there might be a speedy way of remedying the situation.

We now know that Research had been working on the Battle Analyzer for many years, but at the time it came as a revelation to us and perhaps we were too easily swept off our feet. Norden's argument, also, was seductively convincing. What did it matter, he said, if the enemy had twice as many ships as we—if the efficiency of ours could be doubled or even trebled? For decades the limiting factor in warfare had been not mechanical but biological—it had become more and more difficult for any single mind, or group of minds, to cope with the rapidly changing complexities of battle in three-dimensional space. Norden's mathematicians had analyzed some of the classic engagements of the past, and had shown that even when we had been victorious we had often operated our units at much less than half of their theoretical efficiency.

The Battle Analyzer would change all this by replacing the operations staff with electronic calculators. The idea was not new, in theory, but until now it had been no more than a utopian dream. Many of us found it difficult to believe that it was still anything but a dream: after we had run through several very complex dummy battles, however, we were convinced.

It was decided to install the Analyzer in four of our heaviest ships, so that each of the main fleets could be equipped with one. At this stage, the trouble began—though we did not know it until later.

The Analyzer needed a team of five hundred technicians to maintain and operate it. It was quite impossible to accommodate the extra staff aboard a battleship, so each of the four units had to be accompanied by a converted liner to carry the technicians not on duty. Installation was also a very slow and tedious business, but by gigantic efforts it was completed in six months.

Then, to our dismay, we were confronted by another crisis. Nearly five thousand highly skilled men had been selected to serve the Analyzers and had been given an intensive course at the Technical Training Schools. At

the end of seven months, 10 per cent of them had had
nervous breakdowns and only 40 per cent had qualified.

Once again, everyone started to blame everyone else.
Norden, of course, said that the Research Staff could
not be held responsible, and so incurred the enmity of
the Personnel and Training Commands. It was finally
decided that the only thing to do was to use two instead
of four Analyzers and to bring the others into action as
soon as men could be trained. There was little time to
lose, for the enemy was still on the offensive and his
morale was rising.

The first Analyzer fleet was ordered to recapture the
system of Eriston. On the way, by one of the hazards of
war, the liner carrying the technicians was struck by a
roving mine. A warship would have survived, but the
liner with its irreplaceable cargo was totally destroyed.
So the operation had to be abandoned.

The other expedition was, at first, more successful.
There was no doubt at all that the Analyzer fulfilled its
designer's claims, and the enemy was heavily defeated
in the first engagements. He withdrew, leaving us in
possession of Saphran, Leucon and Hexanerax. But his
Intelligence Staff must have noted the change in our
tactics and the inexplicable presence of a liner in the
heart of our battlefleet. It must have noted, also, that
our first fleet had been accompanied by a similar ship—
and had withdrawn when it had been destroyed.

In the next engagement, the enemy used his superior
numbers to launch an overwhelming attack on the
Analyzer ship and its unarmed consort. The attack was
made without regard to losses—both ships were, of
course, very heavily protected—and it succeeded. The
result was the virtual decapitation of the Fleet, since an
effectual transfer to the old operational methods proved
impossible. We disengaged under heavy fire, and so
lost all our gains and also the systems of Lormyia,
Ismarnus, Beronis, Alphanidon and Sideneus.

At this stage, Grand Admiral Taxaris expressed his
disapproval of Norden by committing suicide, and I
assumed supreme command.

The situation was now both serious and infuriating. With stubborn conservatism and complete lack of imagination, the enemy continued to advance with his old-fashioned and inefficient but now vastly more numerous ships. It was galling to realize that if we had only continued building, without seeking new weapons, we would have been in a far more advantageous position. There were many acrimonious conferences at which Norden defended the scientists while everyone else blamed them for all that had happened. The difficulty was that Norden had proved every one of his claims: he had a perfect excuse for all the disasters that had occurred. And we could not now turn back—the search for an irresistible weapon must go on. At first it had been a luxury that would shorten the war. Now it was a necessity if we were to end it victoriously.

We were on the defensive, and so was Norden. He was more than ever determined to re-establish his prestige and that of the Research Staff. But we had been twice disappointed, and would not make the same mistake again. No doubt Norden's twenty thousand scientists would produce many further weapons: we would remain ummpressed.

We were wrong. The final weapon was something so fantastic that even now it seems difficult to believe that it ever existed. Its innocent, noncommittal name—The Exponential Field—gave no hint of its real potentialities. Some of Norden's mathematicians had discovered it during a piece of entirely theoretical research into the properties of space, and to everyone's great surprise their results were found to be physically realizable.

It seems very difficult to explain the operation of the Field to the layman. According to the technical description, it "produces an exponential condition of space, so that a finite distance in normal, linear space may become infinite in pseudo-space." Norden gave an analogy which some of us found useful. It was as if one took a flat disk of rubber—representing a region of normal space—and then pulled its center out to infinity. The circumference of the disk would be unaltered—but its "diameter" would be infinite. That was the sort of thing the generator of the Field did to the space around it.

As an example, suppose that a ship carrying the generator was surrounded by a ring of hostile machines. If it switched on the Field, *each* of the enemy ships would think that it—and the ships on the far side of the circle—had suddenly receded into nothingness. Yet the circumference of the circle would be the same as before: only the journey to the center would be of infinite duration, for as one proceeded, distances would appear to become greater and greater as the "scale" of space altered.

It was a nightmare condition, but a very useful one. Nothing could reach a ship carrying the Field: it might be englobed by an enemy fleet yet would be as inaccessible as if it were at the other side of the Universe. Against this, of course, it could not fight back without switching off the Field, but this still left it at a very great advantage, not only in defense but in offense. For a ship fitted with the Field could approach an enemy fleet undetected and suddenly appear in its midst.

This time there seemed to be no flaws in the new weapon. Needless to say, we looked for all the possible objections before we committed ourselves again. Fortunately the equipment was fairly simple and did not require a large operating staff. After much debate, we decided to rush it into production, for we realized that time was running short and the war was going against us. We had now lost about the whole of our initial gains and enemy forces had made several raids into our own solar system.

We managed to hold off the enemy while the Fleet was re-equipped and the new battle techniques were worked out. To use the Field operationally it was necessary to locate an enemy formation, set a course that would intercept it, and then switch on the generator for the calculated period of time. On releasing the Field again—if the calculations had been accurate—one would be in the enemy's midst and could do great damage during the resulting confusion, retreating by the same route when necessary.

The first trial maneuvers proved satisfactory and the equipment seemed quite reliable. Numerous mock attacks were made and the crews became accustomed to the new technique. I was on one of the test flights and can vividly remember my impressions as the Field was switched on. The ships around us seemed to dwindle as if on the surface of an expanding bubble: in an instant they had vanished completely. So had the stars—but presently we could see that the Galaxy was still visible as a faint band of light around the ship. The virtual radius of our pseudo-space was not really infinite, but some hundred thousand light-years, and so the distance to the farthest stars of our system had not been greatly increased—though the nearest had of course totally disappeared.

These training maneuvers, however, had to be cancelled before they were complete owing to a whole flock of minor technical troubles in various pieces of equipment, notably the communications circuits. These were annoying, but not important, though it was thought best to return to Base to clear them up.

At that moment the enemy made what was obviously intended to be a decisive attack against the fortress planet of Iton at the limits of our solar system. The Fleet had to go into battle before repairs could be made.

The enemy must have believed that we had mastered the secret of invisibility—as in a sense we had. Our ships appeared suddenly out of nowhere and inflicted tremendous damage—for a while. And then something quite baffling and inexplicable happened.

I was in command of the flagship *Hircania* when the trouble started. We had been operating as independent units, each against assigned objectives. Our detectors observed an enemy formation at medium range and the navigating officers measured its distance with great accuracy. We set course and switched on the generator.

The Exponential Field was released at the moment

when we should have been passing through the center of the enemy group. To our consternation, we emerged into normal space at a distance of many hundred miles—and when we found the enemy, he had already found us. We retreated, and tried again. This time we were so far away from the enemy that he located us first.

Obviously, something was seriously wrong. We broke communicator silence and tried to contact the other ships of the Fleet to see if they had experienced the same trouble. Once again we failed—and this time the failure was beyond all reason, for the communication equipment appeared to be working perfectly. We could only assume, fantastic though it seemed, that the rest of the Fleet had been destroyed.

I do not wish to describe the scenes when the scattered units of the Fleet struggled back to Base. Our casualties had actually been negligible, but the ships were completely demoralized. Almost all had lost touch with one another and had found that their ranging equipment showed inexplicable errors. It was obvious that the Exponential Field was the cause of the troubles, despite the fact that they were only apparent when it was switched off.

The explanation came too late to do us any good, and Norden's final discomfiture was small consolation for the virtual loss of the war. As I have explained, the Field generators produced a radial distortion of space, distances appearing greater and greater as one approached the center of the artificial pseudo-space. When the Field was switched off, conditions returned to normal.

But not quite. It was never possible to restore the initial state *exactly*. Switching the Field on and off was equivalent to an elongation and contraction of the ship carrying the generator, but there was an hysteretic effect, as it were, and the initial condition was never quite reproducible, owing to all the thousands of electrical changes and movements of mass aboard the ship while the Field was on. These asymmetries and distortions were cumulative, and though they seldom amounted to more than a fraction of one per cent, that was quite enough. It meant that the precision ranging equipment and the tuned circuits in the communication apparatus were thrown completely out of adjustment. Any single ship could never detect the change—only when it compared its equipment with that of another vessel, or tried to communicate with it, could it tell what had happened.

It is impossible to describe the resultant chaos. Not a single component of one ship could be expected with certainty to work aboard another. The very nuts and bolts were no longer interchangeable, and the supply position became quite impossible. Given time, we might even have overcome these difficulties, but the enemy ships were already attacking in thousands with weapons which now seemed centuries behind those that we had invented. Our magnificent Fleet, crippled by our own science, fought on as best it could until it was overwhelmed and forced to surrender. The ships fitted with the Field were still invulnerable, but as fighting units they were almost helpless. Every time they switched on their generators to escape from enemy attack, the permanent distortion of their equipment increased. In a month, it was all over.

This is the true story of our defeat, which I give without prejudice to my defense before this Court. I make it, as I have said, to counteract the libels that have been circulating against the men who fought under me, and to show where the true blame for our misfortunes lay.

Finally, my request, which as the Court will now realize, I make in no frivolous manner and which I hope will therefore be granted.

The Court will be aware that the conditions under which we are housed and the constant surveillance to which we are subjected night and day are somewhat distressing. Yet I am not complaining of this: nor do I complain of the fact that shortage of accommodation has made it necessary to house us in pairs.

But I cannot be held responsible for my future actions if I am compelled any longer to share my cell with Professor Norden, late Chief of the Research Staff of my armed forces.

Arthur C. Clarke's long and distinguished career in science fiction started before World War II, when he was active in British fan circles. From 1941 to 1946, he served as a radar instructor with the RAF, finishing as a flight lieutenant, then took his BSc. with honors in physics and mathematics at King's College, London. His first two professionally published sf stories, "Loophole" and "Rescue Party," appeared in *Astounding* in 1946, launching a career of astonishing creativity, not only in sf, but also in popular science fact writing. His first two novels, *Prelude to Space* and *The Sands of Mars*, came out in 1951, and his work began to appear, not only in the sf genre magazines, but in many general periodicals. His story, "The Sentinel," originally in *10 Story Fantasy*, became the basis for the tremendously popular *2001: A Space Odyssey*, for which he and Stanley Kubrick wrote the script.

By the 1960s, Clarke was concentrating more and more on his non-fiction scientific books and articles, not only on the adventure into space, but also on undersea exploration—the last interest one of the reasons for his moving his residence to Sri Lanka (Ceylon) where he has lived for more than twenty years, and which he tells about in his recent memoir, *The View from Serendip*. However, after the success of *2001*, he signed a contract for three new novels, the first of which, *Rendezvous With Rama*, captured almost every available award: the Hugo and Nebula, the John W. Campbell Memorial, the British Science Fiction and Jupiter Awards.

Everyone is familiar with Napoleon's maxim, "The moral is to the physical as three to one." As a general statement of the military importance of morale it essentially is true—but as a statement of the physical value of morale in any specific military equation it is false and conveys a totally false promise. Morale, no matter how high, does not multiply the power of weapons; nor does it diminish the inherent vulnerability of men and their devices to destruction. It cannot increase the cyclic rate of fire of a machine-gun by one percent, nor extend the designed range of an artillery projectile, nor expand the destructive radius of an H-bomb. It cannot render a soldier bullet-proof.

But what it can do is equally important. It can enable the maximum realization of the power of weapons, and a minimum realization of vulnerability, in attack and in defense.

In that sense, one can say that the moral is to the physical as three, or three hundred, or three thousand to one—for without it, as long as the exercise of physical force in war depends on men, the physical is nothing.

And that, as Gordon Dickson shows us in this story, will remain true wherever men may go, even into the most distant marches of unexplored space.

Gordon R. Dickson

STEEL BROTHER

"We stand on guard."
                    —*Motto of the Frontier Force*

". . . *Man that is born of woman hath but a short time to live and is full of misery. He cometh up and is cut down, like a flower; he fleeth as it were a shadow and never continueth in one stay—*"

The voice of the chaplain was small and sharp in the thin air, intoning the words of the burial service above the temporary lectern set up just inside the transparent wall of the landing field dome. Through the double transparencies of the dome and the plastic cover of the burial rocket the black-clad ranks could see the body of the dead stationman, Ted Waskewicz, lying back comfortably at an angle of forty-five degrees, peaceful in death, waxily perfect from the hands of the embalmers, and immobile. The eyes were closed, the cheerful, heavy features still held their expression of thoughtless dominance, as though death had been a minor incident, easily shrugged off; and the battle star made a single blaze of color on the tunic of the black uniform.

"*Amen.*" The response was a deep bass utterance from the assembled men, like the single note of an organ. In the front rank of the Cadets, Thomas Jordan's lips moved stiffly with the others', his voice joining mechanically in their chorus. For this was the moment of his triumph, but in spite of it, the old, old fear had come back; the old sense of loneliness and loss and terror of his own inadequacy.

He stood at stiff attention, eyes to the front, trying to lose himself in the unanimity of his classmates, to shut out the voice of the chaplain and the memory it evoked of an alien raid on an undefended city and of home and parents swept away from him in a breath. He remembered the mass burial service read over the shattered ruin of the city; and the government agency that had taken him—a ten-year-old orphan—and given him care and training until this day, but could not give him what these others about him had by natural right—the courage of those who had matured in safety.

For he had been lonely and afraid since that day. Untouched by bomb or shell, he had yet been crippled deep inside of him. He had seen the enemy in his strength and run screaming from his spacesuited gangs. And what could give Thomas Jordan back his soul after that?

But still he stood rigidly at attention, as a Guardsman should; for he was a soldier now, and this was part of his duty.

The chaplain's voice droned to a halt. He closed his prayer-book and stepped back from the lectern. The captain of the training ship took his place.

"In accordance with the conventions of the Frontier Force," he said, crisply, "I now commit the ashes of Station Commandant First Class, Theodore Waskewicz, to the keeping of time and space."

He pressed a button on the lectern. Beyond the dome, white fire blossomed out from the tail of the burial rocket, heating the asteroid rock to temporary incandescence. For a moment it hung there, spewing flame. Then it rose, at first slowly, then quickly, and was gone, sketching a fiery path out and away, until, at almost the limits of human sight, it vanished in a sudden, silent explosion of brilliant light.

Around Jordan, the black-clad ranks relaxed. Not by any physical movement, but with an indefinable breaking of nervous tension, they settled themselves for the more prosaic conclusion of the ceremony. The relaxation reached even to the captain, for he about-faced with a relieved snap and spoke to the ranks.

"Cadet Thomas Jordan. Front and center."

The command struck Jordan with an icy shock. As long as the burial service had been in progress, he had had the protection of anonymity among his classmates around him. Now, the captain's voice was a knife, cutting him off, finally and irrevocably from the one security his life had known, leaving him naked and exposed. A despairing numbness seized him. His reflexes took over, moving his body like a robot. One step forward, a right face, down to the end of the row of silent men, a left face, three steps forward. Halt. Salute.

"Cadet Thomas Jordan reporting, sir."

"Cadet Thomas Jordan, I hereby invest you with command of this Frontier Station. You will hold it until relieved. Under no conditions will you enter into communications with an enemy nor allow any creature or vessel to pass through your sector of space from Outside."

"Yes, sir."

"In consideration of the duties and responsibilities requisite on assuming command of this Station, you are promoted to the rank and title of Station Commandant Third Class."

"Thank you, sir."

From the lectern the captain lifted a cap of silver wire mesh and placed it on his head. It clipped on to the electrodes already buried in his skull, with a snap that sent sound ringing through his skull. For a second, a sheet of lightning flashed in front of his eyes and he seemed to feel the weight of the memory bank already pressing on his mind. Then lightning and pressure vanished together to show him the captain offering his hand.

"My congratulations, commandant."

"Thank you, sir."

They shook hands, the captain's grip quick, nervous and perfunctory. He took one abrupt step backward and transferred his attention to his second in command.

"Lieutenant! Dismiss the formation!"

It was over. The new rank locked itself around Jordan, sealing up the fear and loneliness inside him. Without listening to the barked commands that no longer concerned him, he turned on his heel and strode over to take up his position by the sally port of the training ship. He stood formally at attention beside it, feeling the weight of his new authority like a heavy cloak on his thin shoulders. At one stroke he had become the ranking officer present. The officers—even the captain—were nominally under his authority, so long as their ship remained grounded at his Station. So rigidly he stood at attention that not even the slightest tremor of the trembling inside him escaped to quiver betrayingly in his body.

They came toward him in a loose, dark mass that resolved itself into a single file just beyond saluting distance. Singly, they went past him and up the ladder into the sally port, each saluting him as they passed. He returned the salutes stiffly, mechanically, walled off from these classmates of six years by the barrier of his new command. It was a moment when a smile or a casual handshake would have meant more than a little. But protocol had stripped him of the right to familiarity; and it was a line of black-uniformed strangers that now filed slowly past. His place was already established and theirs was yet to be. They had nothing in common any more.

The last of the men went past him up the ladder and were lost to view through the black circle of the sally port. The heavy steel plug swung slowly to, behind them. He turned and made his way to the unfamiliar but well-known field control panel in the main control room of the Station. A light glowed redly on the communications board. He thumbed a switch and spoke into a grill set in the panel.

"Station to Ship. Go ahead."

Overhead the loudspeaker answered.

"Ship to Station. Ready for take-off."

His fingers went swiftly over the panel. Outside, the atmosphere of the field was evacuated and the dome slid back. Tractor mechs scurried out from the pit, under remote control, clamped huge magnetic fists on the ship, swung it into launching position, then retreated.

Jordan spoke again into the grill.

"Station clear. Take-off at will."

"Thank you, Station." He recognized the captain's voice. "And good luck."

Outside, the ship lifted, at first slowly, then faster on its pillar of flame, and dwindled away into the darkness of space. Automatically, he closed the dome and pumped the air back in.

He was turning away from the control panel, bracing himself against the moment of finding himself completely isolated, when, with a sudden, curious shock, he noticed that there was another, smaller ship yet on the field.

For a moment he stared at it blankly, uncomprehendingly. Then memory returned and he realized that the ship was a small courier vessel from Intelligence, which had been hidden by the huge bulk of the training ship. Its officer would still be below, cutting a record tape of the former commandant's last memories for the file at Headquarters. The memory lifted him momentarily from the morass of his emotions to attention to duty. He turned from the panel and went below.

In the triply-armored basement of the Station, the man from Intelligence was half in and half out of the memory bank when he arrived, having cut away a portion of the steel casing around the bank so as to connect his recorder direct to the cells. The sight of the heavy mount of steel with the ragged incision in one side, squatting like a wounded monster, struck Jordan unpleasantly; but he smoothed the emotion from his face and walked firmly to the bank. His footsteps rang on the metal floor; and the man from Intelligence, hearing them, brought his head momentarily outside the bank for a quick look.

"Hi!" he said, shortly, returning to his work. His

voice continued from the interior of the bank with a friendly, hollow sound. "Congratulations, commandant."

"Thanks," answered Jordan, stiffly. He stood, somewhat ill at ease, uncertain of what was expected of him. When he hesitated, the voice from the bank continued.

"How does the cap feel?"

Jordan's hands went up instinctively to the mesh of silver wire on his head. It pushed back unyieldingly at his fingers, held firmly on the electrodes.

"Tight," he said.

The Intelligence man came crawling out of the bank, his recorder in one hand and thick loops of glassy tape in the other.

"They all do at first," he said squatting down and feeding one end of the tape into a spring rewind spool. "In a couple of days you won't even be able to feel it up there."

"I suppose."

The Intelligence man looked up at him curiously.

"Nothing about it bothering you, is there?" he asked. "You look a little strained."

"Doesn't everybody when they first start out?"

"Sometimes," said the other, noncommittally. "Sometimes not. Don't hear a sort of humming, do you?"

"No."

"Feel any kind of pressure inside your head?"

"No."

"How about your eyes. See any spots or flashes in front of them?"

"No!" snapped Jordan.

"Take it easy," said the man from Intelligence. "This is my business."

"Sorry."

"That's all right. It's just that if there's anything wrong with you or the bank I want to know it." He rose from the rewind spool, which was now industriously gathering in the loose tape; and unclipping a pressure-torch from his belt, began resealing the aperture. "It's just that occasionally new officers have been hearing too many stories about the banks in Training School, and they're inclined to be jumpy.

"Stories?" said Jordan.

"Haven't you heard them?" answered the Intelligence man. "Stories of memory domination—stationmen driven insane by the memories of the men who had the Station before them. Catatonics whose minds have got lost in the past history of the bank, or cases of memory replacement where the stationman has identified himself with the memories and personality of the man who preceded him."

"Oh, those," said Jordan. "I've heard them." He paused, and then, when the other did not go on: "What about them? Are they me?"

The Intelligence man turned from the half-resealed aperture and faced him squarely, torch in hand.

"Some," he said bluntly. "There's been a few cases like that; although there didn't have to be. Nobody's trying to sugarcoat the facts. The memory bank's nothing but a storehouse connected to you through your silver cap—a gadget to enable you not only to remember everything you ever do at the station, but also everything anybody else who ever ran the Station, did. But there've been a few impressionable stationmen who've let themselves get the notion that the memory bank's a sort of a coffin with living dead men crawling around inside it. When that happens, there's trouble."

He turned away from Jordan, back to his work.

"And that's what you thought was the trouble with me," said Jordan, speaking to his back.

The man from Intelligence chuckled—it was an amazingly human sound.

"In my line, fella," he said, "we check all possibilities." He finished his resealing and turned around.

"No hard feelings?" he said.

Jordan shook his head. "Of course not."

"Then I'll be getting along." He bent over and picked up the spool, which had by now neatly wound up all the tape, straightened up and headed for the ramp that

led up from the basement to the landing field. Jordan
fell into step beside him.

"You've nothing more to do, then?" he asked.

"Just my reports. But I can write those on the way
back." They went up the ramp and out through the lock
on to the field.

"They did a good job of repairing the battle damage,"
he went on, looking around the Station.

"I guess they did," said Jordan. The two men paced
soberly to the sally port of the Intelligence ship. "Well,
so long."

"So long," answered the man from Intelligence, activating the sally port mechanism. The outer lock swung
open and he hopped the few feet up to the opening
without waiting for the little ladder to wind itself out.
"See you in six months."

He turned to Jordan and gave him a casual, offhand
salute with the hand holding the wind-up spool. Jordan
returned it with training school precision. The port
swung closed.

He went back to the master control room and the
ritual of seeing the ship off. He stood looking out for a
long time after it had vanished, then turned from the
panel with a sigh to find himself at last completely alone.

He looked about the Station. For the next six months
this would be his home. Then, for another six months
he would be free on leave while the Station was rotated
out of the line in its regular order for repair, recondi-
tioning, and improvements.

If he lived that long.

The fear, which had been driven a little distance
away by his conversation with the man from Intelligence, came back.

If he lived that long. He stood, bemused.

Back to his mind with the letter-perfect recall of the
memory bank came the words of the other. Catatonic—
cases of memory replacement. Memory domination.
Had those others, too, had more than they could bear
of fear and anticipation?

And with that thought came a suggestion that coiled like a snake in his mind. That would be a way out. What if they came, the alien invaders, and Thomas Jordan was no longer here to meet them? What if only the catatonic hulk of a man was left? What if they came and a man was here, but that man called himself and knew himself only as—

Waskewicz!

"No!" the cry came involuntarily from his lips; and he came to himself with his face contorted and his hands half-extended in front of him in the attitude of one who wards off a ghost. He shook his head to shake the vile suggestion from his brain; and leaned back, panting, against the control panel.

Not that. Not ever that. He had surprised in himself a weakness that turned him sick with horror. Win or lose; live or die. But as Jordan—not as any other.

He lit a cigarette with trembling fingers. So—it was over now and he was safe. He had caught it in time. He had his warning. Unknown to him—all this time—the seeds of memory domination must have been lying waiting within him. But now he knew they were there, he knew what measures to take. The danger lay in Waskewicz's memories. He would shut his mind off from them—would fight the Station without the benefit of their experience. The first stationmen on the line had done without the aid of a memory bank and so could he.

So.

He had settled it. He flicked on the viewing screens and stood opposite them, very straight and correct in the middle of his Station, looking out at the dots that were his forty-five doggie mechs spread out on guard over a million kilometers of space, looking at the controls that would enable him to throw their blunt, terrible, mechanical bodies into battle with the enemy, looking and waiting, waiting, for the courage that comes from having faced squarely a situation, to rise within him and take possession of him, putting an end to all fears and doubtings.

And he waited so for a long time, but it did not come.

The weeks went swiftly by; and that was as it should be. He had been told what to expect, during training; and it was as it should be that these first months should be tense ones, with a part of him always stiff and waiting for the alarm bell that would mean a doggie signaling sight of an enemy. It was as it should be that he should pause, suddenly, in the midst of a meal with his fork halfway to his mouth, waiting and expecting momentarily to be summoned; that he should wake unexpectedly in the nighttime and lie rigid and tense, eyes fixed on the shadowy ceiling and listening. Later— they had said in training—after you have become used to the Station, this constant tension will relax and you will be left at ease, with only one little unobtrusive corner of your mind unnoticed but forever alert. This will come with time, they said.

So he waited for it, waited for the release of the coiled springs inside him and the time when the feel of the Station would be comfortable and friendly about him. When he had first been left alone, he had thought to himself that surely, in his case, the waiting would not be more than a matter of days; then, as the days went by and he still lived in a state of hair-trigger sensitivity, he had given himself, in his own mind, a couple of weeks—then a month.

But now a month and more than a month had gone without relaxation coming to him; and the strain was beginning to show in nervousness of his hands and the dark circles under his eyes. He found it impossible to sit still either to read, or to listen to the music that was available in the Station library. He roamed restlessly, endlessly checking and rechecking the empty space that his doggies' viewers revealed.

For the recollection of Waskewicz as he lay in the burial rocket would not go from him. And that was not as it should be.

He could, and did, refuse to recall the memories of

Waskewicz that he had never experienced; but his own personal recollections were not easy to control and slipped into his mind when he was unaware. All else that he could do to lay the ghost, he had done. He had combed the Station carefully, seeking out the little adjustments and conveniences that a lonely man will make about his home, and removed them, even when the removal meant a loss of personal comfort. He had locked his mind securely to the storehouse of the memory bank, striving to hold himself isolated from the other's memories until familiarity and association should bring him to the point where he instinctively felt that the Station was *his* and not the other's. And whenever thoughts of Waskewicz entered in spite of all these precautions, he had dismissed them sternly, telling himself that his predecessor was not worth the considering.

But the other's ghost remained, intangible and invulnerable, as if locked in the very metal of the walls and floor and ceiling of the Station; and rising to haunt him with the memories of the training school tales and the ominous words of the man from Intelligence. At such times, when the ghost had seized him, he would stand paralyzed, staring in hypnotic fascination at the screens with their silent mechanical sentinels, or at the cold steel of the memory bank, crouching like some brooding monster, fear feeding on his thoughts—until, with a sudden, wrenching effort of the will, he broke free of the mesmerism and flung himself frantically into the duties of the Station, checking and rechecking his instruments and the space they watched, doing anything and everything to drown his wild emotions in the necessity for attention to duty.

And eventually he found himself almost hoping for a raid, for the test that would prove him, would lay the ghost, one way or another, once and for all.

It came at last, as he had known it would, during one of the rare moments when he had forgotten the imminence of danger. He had awakened in his bunk, at the beginning of the arbitrary ten-hour day; and lay there drowsily, comfortably, his thoughts vague and formless, like shadows in the depths of a lazy whirlpool, turning slowly, going no place.

Then—the alarm!

Overhead the shouting bell burst into life, jerking him from his bed. Its metal clangor poured out on the air, tumbling from the loudspeakers in every room all over the Station, strident with urgency, pregnant with disaster. It roared, it vibrated, it thundered, until the walls themselves threw it back, seeming to echo in sympathy, acquiring a voice of their own until the room rang—until the Station itself rang like one monster bell, calling him into battle.

He leaped to his feet and ran to the master control room. On the telltale high on the wall above the viewer screens, the red light of number thirty-eight doggie was flashing ominously. He threw himself into the operator's seat before it, slapping one palm hard down on the switch to disconnect the alarm.

The Station is in contact with the enemy.

The sudden silence slapped at him, taking his breath away. He gasped and shook his head like a man who has had a glassful of cold water thrown unexpectedly in his face; then plunged his fingers at the keys on the master control board in front of his seat—Up beams. Up detector screen, established now at forty thousand kilometers distance. Switch on communications to Sector Headquarters.

The transmitter purred. Overhead, the white light flashed as it began to tick off its automatic signal. "Alert! Alert! Further data follows. Will report."

Headquarters has been notified by the Station.

Activate viewing screen on doggie number thirty-eight.

He looked into the activated screen, into the vast arena of space over which the mechanical vision of that doggie mech was ranging. Far and far away at top magnification were five small dots, coming in fast on a course leading ten points below and at an angle of thirty-two degrees to the Station.

He flicked a key, releasing thirty-eight on proximity

fuse control and sending it plunging toward the dots.
He scanned the Station area map for the positions of his
other mechs. Thirty-nine was missing—in the Station
for repair. The rest were available. He checked numbers forty through forty-five and thirty-seven through
thirty to rendezvous on collision course with enemy at
seventy-five thousand kilometers. Numbers twenty to
thirty to rendezvous at fifty thousand kilometers.

Primary defense has been inaugurated.

He turned back to the screen. Number thirty-eight,
expendable in the interests of gaining information, was
plunging towards the ships at top acceleration under
strains no living flesh would have been able to endure.
But as yet the size and type of the invaders was still
hidden by distance. A white light flashed abruptly from
the communications panel, announcing that Sector Headquarters was alerted and ready to talk. He cut in audio.

"Contact. Go ahead, Station J-49C3."

"Five ships," he said. "Beyond identification range.
Coming in through thirty-eight at ten point thirty-two."

"Acknowledge," the voice of Headquarters was level,
precise, emotionless. "Five ships—thirty-eight—ten—
thirty-two. Patrol Twenty, passing through your area at
four hours distance, has been notified and will proceed
to your station at once, arriving in four hours, plus or
minus twenty minutes. Further assistance follows. Will
stand by here for your future messages."

The white light went out and he turned away from
the communications panel. On the screen, the five
ships had still not grown to identifiable proportions, but
for all practical purposes, the preliminaries were over.
He had some fifteen minutes now during which everything that could be done, had been done.

Primary defense has been completed.

He turned away from the controls and walked back to
the bedroom, where he dressed slowly and meticu-
lously in full black uniform. He straightened his tunic,
looking in the mirror and stood gazing at himself for a
long moment. Then, hesitantly, almost as if against his

will, he reached out with one hand to a small gray box on a shelf beside the mirror, opened it, and took out the silver battle star that the next few hours would entitle him to wear.

It lay in his palm, the bright metal winking softly up at him under the reflection of the room lights and the small movements of his hand. The little cluster of diamonds in its center sparkled and ran the whole gamut of their flashing colors. For several minutes he stood looking at it; then slowly, gently, he shut it back up in its box and went out, back to the control room.

On the screen, the ships were now large enough to be identified. They were medium sized vessels, Jordan noticed, of the type used most by the most common species of raiders—that same race which had orphaned him. There could be no doubt about their intentions, as there sometimes was when some odd stranger chanced upon the Frontier, to be regretfully destroyed by men whose orders were to take no chances. No, these were *the enemy*, the strange, suicidal life form that thrust thousands of attacks yearly against the little human empire, who blew themselves up when captured and wasted a hundred ships for every one that broke through the guarding stations to descend on some unprotected city of an inner planet and loot it of equipment and machinery that the aliens were either unwilling or unable to build for themselves—a contradictory, little understood and savage race. These five ships would make no attempt to parley.

But now, doggie number thirty-eight had been spotted and the white exhausts of guided missiles began to streak toward the viewing screen. For a few seconds, the little mech bucked and tossed, dodging, firing defensively, shooting down the missiles as they approached. But it was a hopeless fight against those odds and suddenly one of the streaks expanded to fill the screen with glaring light.

And the screen went blank. Thirty-eight was gone.

Suddenly realizing that he should have been covering with observation from one of the doggies further back,

Jordan jumped to fill his screens. He brought the view from forty in on the one that thirty-eight had vacated and filled the two flanking screens with the view from thirty-seven on his left and twenty on his right. They showed his first line of defense already gathered at the seventy-five kilometer rendezvous and the fifty thousand kilometer rendezvous still forming.

The raiders were decelerating now, and on the wall, the telltale for the enemy's detectors flushed a sudden deep and angry purple as their invisible beams reached out and were baffled by the detector screen he had erected at a distance of forty thousand kilometers in front of the Station. They continued to decelerate, but the blockage of their detector beams had given them the approximate area of his Station; and they corrected course, swinging in until they were no more than two points and ten degrees in error. Jordan, his nervous fingers trembling slightly on the keys, stretched thirty-seven through thirty out in depth and sent forty through forty-five forward on a five-degree sweep to attempt a circling movement.

The five dark ships of the raiders, recognizing his intention, fell out of their single file approach formation to spread out and take a formation in open echelon. They were already firing on the advancing doggies and tiny streaks of light tattooed the black of space around numbers forty through forty-five.

Jordan drew a deep and ragged breath and leaned back in his control seat. For the moment there was nothing for his busy fingers to do among the control keys. His thirties must wait until the enemy came to them; since, with modern automatic gunnery the body at rest had an advantage over the body in motion. And it would be some minutes before the forties would be in attack position. He fumbled for a cigarette, keeping his eyes on the screens, remembering the caution in the training manuals against relaxation once contact with the enemy has been made.

But reaction was setting in.

From the first wild ringing command of the alarm until the present moment, he had reacted automatically, with perfection and precision, as the drills had schooled him, as the training manuals had impressed upon him. The enemy had appeared. He had taken measures for defense against them. All that could have been done had been done; and he knew he had done it properly. And the enemy had done what he had been told they would do.

He was struck, suddenly, with the deep quivering realization of the truth in the manual's predictions. It was so, then. These inimical others, these alien foes, were also bound by the physical laws. They as well as he, could move only within the rules of time and space. They were shorn of their mystery and brought down to his level. Different and awful, they might be, but their capabilities were limited, even as his; and in a combat such as the one now shaping up, their inhumanness was of no account, for the inflexible realities of the universe weighed impartially on him and them alike.

And with this realization, for the first time, the old remembered fear began to fall away like a discarded garment. A tingle ran through him and he found himself warming to the fight as his forefathers had warmed before him away back to the days when man was young and the tiger roared in the cool, damp jungle-dawn of long ago. The blood-instinct was in him; that and something of the fierce, vengeful joy with which a hunted creature turns at last on its pursuer. He would win. Of course he would win. And in winning he would at one stroke pay off the debt of blood and fear which the enemy had held against him these fifteen years.

Thinking in this way, he leaned back in his seat and the old memory of the shattered city and of himself running, running, rose up again around him. But this time it was no longer a prelude to terror, but fuel for the kindling of his rage. *These are my fear*, he thought, gazing unseeingly at the five ships in the screens *and I will destroy them*.

The phantasms of his memory faded like smoke around

him. He dropped his cigarette into a disposal slot on the arm of his seat, and leaned forward to inspect the enemy positions.

They had spread out to force his forties to circle wide, and those doggies were now scattered, safe but ineffective, waiting further directions. What had been an open echelon formation of the raiders was now a ragged, widely dispersed line, with far too much space between ships to allow each to cover his neighbor.

For a moment Jordan was puzzled; and a tiny surge of fear of the inexplicable rippled across the calm surface of his mind. Then his brow smoothed out. There was no need to get panicky. The aliens' maneuver was not the mysterious tactic he had half-expected it to be; but just what it appeared, a rather obvious and somewhat stupid move to avoid the flanking movement he had been attempting with his forties. Stupid—because the foolish aliens had now rendered themselves vulnerable to interspersal by his thirties.

It was good news, rather than bad, and his spirits leaped another notch.

He ignored the baffled forties, circling automatically on safety control just beyond the ships' effective aiming range; and turned to the thirties, sending them plunging toward the empty areas between ships as you might interlace the fingers of one hand with another. Between any two ships there would be a dead spot—a position where a mech could not be fired on by either vessel without also aiming at its right- or left-hand companion. If two or more doggies could be brought safely to that spot, they could turn and pour down the open lanes on proximity control, their fuses primed, their bomb loads activated, blind bulldogs of destruction.

One third, at least, should in this way get through the defensive shelling of the ships and track their dodging prey to the atomic flare of a grim meeting.

Smiling now in confidence, Jordan watched his mechs approach the ships. There was nothing the enemy could do. They could not now tighten up their formation without merely making themselves a more attractive target; and to disperse still further would negate any chance in the future of regaining a semblance of formation.

Carefully, his fingers played over the keys, gentling his mechs into line so that they would come as close as possible to hitting their dead spots simultaneously. The ships came on.

Closer the raiders came, and closer. And then—bare seconds away from contact with the line of approaching doggies, white fire ravened in unison from their stern tubes, making each ship suddenly a black nugget in the center of a blossom of flame. In unison, they spurted forward, in sudden and unexpected movement, bringing their dead spots to and past the line of seeking doggies, leaving them behind.

Caught for a second in stunned surprise, Jordan sat dumb and motionless, staring at the screen. Then, swift in his anger, his hands flashed out over the keys, blasting his mechs to a cruel, shuddering halt, straining their metal sinews for the quickest and most abrupt about face and return. This time he would catch them from behind. This time, going in the same direction as the ships, the mechs could not be dodged. For what living thing could endure equal strains with cold metal?

But there was no second attempt on the part of the thirties, for as each bucked to its savage halt, the rear weapons of the ships reached out in unison, and each of the blasting mechs, that had leaped forward so confidently, flared up and died like little candles in the dark.

Numb in the grip of icy failure, Jordan sat still, a ramrod figure staring at the two screens that spoke so eloquently of his disaster—and the one dead screen where the view from thirty-seven had been, that said nothing at all. Like a man in a dream, he reached out his right hand and cut in the final sentinel, the *watchdog*, that mech that circled closest to the Station. In one short breath his strong first line was gone, and the enemy rode, their strength undiminished, floating in toward his single line of twenties at fifty thousand with the defensive screen a mere ten thousand kilometers behind them.

Training was strong. Without hesitation his hands went out over the keys and the doggies of the twenties surged forward, trying for contact with the enemy in an area as far from the screen as possible. But, because they were moving in on an opponent relatively at rest, their courses were the more predictable on the enemy's calculators and the disadvantage was theirs. So it was that forty minutes later three ships of the alien rode clear and unthreatened in an area where two of their mates, the forties and all of the thirties were gone.

The ships were, at this moment, fifteen thousand kilometers from the detector screen.

Jordan looked at his handiwork. The situation was obvious and the alternatives undeniable. He had twenty doggies remaining, but he had neither the time to move them up beyond the screen, nor the room to maneuver them in front of it. The only answer was to pull his screen back. But to pull the screen back would be to indicate, by its shrinkage and the direction of its withdrawal, the position of his Station clearly enough for the guided missiles of the enemy to seek him out; and once the Station was knocked out, the doggies were directionless, impotent.

Yet, if he did nothing, in a few minutes the ships would touch and penetrate the detector screen and his Station, the nerve center the aliens were seeking, would lie naked and revealed in their detectors.

He had lost. The alternatives totaled to the same answer, to defeat. In the inattention of a moment, in the smoke of a cigarette, the first blind surge of self-confidence and the thoughtless halting of his by-passed doggies that had allowed the ships' calculators to find them stationary for a second in a predictable area, he had failed. He had given away, in the error of his pride, the initial advantage. He had lost. Speak it softly, speak it gently, for his fault was the fault of one young and untried. He was defeated.

And in the case of defeat, the actions prescribed by

the manual were stern and clear. The memory of the instructions tolled in his mind like the unvarying notes of a funeral bell.

"When, in any conflict, the forces of the enemy have obtained a position of advantage such that it is no longer possible to maintain the anonymity of the Station's position, the commandant of the Station is required to perform one final duty. Knowing that the Station will shortly be destroyed and that this will render all remaining mechs innocuous to enemy forces, the commandant is commanded to relinquish control of these mechs, and to place them with fuses primed on proximity control, in order that, even without the Station, they may be enabled to automatically pursue and attempt to destroy those forces of the enemy that approach within critical range of their proximity fuse."

Jordan looked at his screens. Out at forty thousand kilometers, the detector screen was beginning to luminesce slightly as the detectors of the ships probed it at shorter range. To make the manual's order effective, it would have to be pulled back to at least half that distance; and there, while it would still hide the Station, it would give the enemy his approximate location. They would then fire blindly, but with cunning and increasing knowledge and it would be only a matter of time before they hit. After that—only the blind doggies, quivering, turning and trembling through all points of the stellar compass in their thoughtless hunger for prey. One or two of these might gain a revenge as the ships tried to slip past them and over the Line; but Jordan would not be there to know it.

But there was no alternative—even if duty had left him one. Like strangers, his hands rose from the board and stretched out over the keys that would turn the doggies loose. His fingers dropped and rested upon them—light touch on smooth polished coolness.

But he could not press them down.

He sat with his arms outstretched, as if in supplication, like one of his primitive forebears before some

ancient altar of death. For his will had failed him and
there was no denying now his guilt and his failure. For
the battle had turned in his short few moments of
inattention, and his underestimation of the enemy that
had seduced him into halting his thirties without thinking. He knew; and through the memory bank—if that
survived—the Force would know. In his neglect, in his
refusal to avail himself of the experience of his predecessors, he was guilty.

And yet, he could not press the keys. He could not
die properly—*in the execution of his duty*—the cold,
correct phrase of the official reports. For a wild rebellion surged through his young body, an instinctive denial of the end that stared him so undeniably in the
face. Through vein and sinew and nerve, it raced, opposing and blocking the dictates of training, the logical
orders of his upper mind. It was too soon, it was not
fair, he had not been given his chance to profit by
experience. One more opportunity was all he needed,
one more try to redeem himself.

But the rebellion passed and left him shaken, weak.
There was no denying reality. And now, a new shame
came to press upon him, for he thought of the three
alien vessels breaking through, of another city in flaming ruins, and another child that would run screaming
from his destroyers. The thought rose up in him, and
he writhed internally, torn by his own indecisions. Why
couldn't he act? It made no difference to him. What
would justification and the redeeming of error mean to
him after he was dead?

And he moaned a little, softly to himself, holding his
hands outstretched above the keys, but could not press
them down.

And then hope came. For suddenly, rising up out of
the rubble of his mind came the memory of the Intelligence man's words once again, and his own near-pursuit
of insanity. He, Jordan, could not bring himself to
expose himself to the enemy, not even if the method of
exposure meant possible protection for the Inner Worlds.
But the man who had held this Station before him, who

had died as he was about to die, must have been faced
with the same necessity for self-sacrifice. And those
last-minute memories of his decision would be in the
memory bank, waiting for the evocation of Jordan's
mind.

Here was hope at last. He would remember, would
embrace the insanity he had shrunk from. He would
remember and be Waskewicz, not Jordan. He would be
Waskewicz and unafraid; though it was a shameful thing
to do. Had there been one person, one memory among
all living humans, whose image he could have evoked
to place in opposition to the images of the three dark
ships, he might have managed by himself. But there
had been no one close to him since the day of the city
raid.

His mind reached back into the memory bank, reached
back to the last of Waskewicz's memories. He remembered.

Of the ten ships attacking, six were down. Their
ashes strewed the void and the remaining four rode
warily, spread widely apart for maximum safety, sure of
victory, but wary of this hornet's nest which might still
have some stings yet unexpended. But the detector
screen was back to its minimum distance for effective
concealment and only five doggies remained poised like
blunt arrows behind it. He—Waskewicz—sat hunched
before the control board, his thick and hairy hands
lying softly on the proximity keys.

"Drift in," he said, speaking to the ships, which were
cautiously approaching the screen. "Drift in, you. Drift!"

His lips were skinned back over his teeth in a grin—
but he did not mean it. It was an automatc grimace,
reflex to the tenseness of his waiting. He would lure
them on until the last moment, draw them as close as
possible to the automatic pursuit mechanisms of the
remaining doggies, before pulling back the screen.

"Drift in," he said.

They drifted in. Behind the screen he aimed his
doggies, pointing each one of four at a ship and the
remaining one generally at them all. They drifted in.

They touched.

His fingers slapped the keys. The screen snapped back until it barely covered the waiting doggies. And the doggies stirred, on proximity, their pursuit mechs activated, now blind and terrible fully armed, ready to attack in senseless directness anything that came close enough.

And the first shells from the advancing ships began to probe the general area of the Station asteroid.

Waskewicz sighed, pushed himself back from the controls and stood up, turning away from the screens. It was over. Done. All finished. For a moment he stood irresolute; then, walking over to the dispenser on the wall, dialed for coffee and drew it, hot into a disposable cup. He lit a cigarette and stood waiting, smoking and drinking the coffee.

The Station rocked suddenly to the impact of a glancing hit on the asteroid. He staggered and slopped some coffee on his boots, but kept his feet. He took another gulp from the cup, another drag on the cigarette. The Station shook again, and the lights dimmed. He crumpled the cup and dropped it in the disposal slot. He dropped the cigarette on the steel floor, ground it beneath his boot sole; and walked back to the screen and leaned over for it for a final look.

The lights went out. And memory ended.

The present returned to Jordan and he stared about him a trifle wildly. Then he felt hardness beneath his fingers and forced himself to look down.

The keys were depressed. The screen was back. The doggies were on proximity. He stared at his hand as if he had never known it before, shocked at its thinness and the lack of soft down on its back. Then, slowly, fighting reluctant neck muscles, he forced himself to look up and into the viewing screen.

And the ships were there, but the ships were drawing away.

He stared, unable to believe his eyes, and half-ready to believe anything else. For the invaders had turned and the flames from their tails made it evident that they were making away into outer space at their maximum bearable acceleration, leaving him alone and unharmed. He shook his head to clear away the false vision from the screen before him, but it remained, denying its falseness. The miracle for which his instincts had held him in check had come—in the moment in which he had borrowed strength to deny it.

His eyes searched the screens in wonder. And then, far down in one corner of the watch dog's screen and so distant still that they showed only as pips on the wide expanse, he saw the shape of his miracle. Coming up from inside of the Line under maximum bearable acceleration were six gleaming fish-shapes that would dwarf his doggies to minnows—the battleships of Patrol Twenty. And he realized, with the dawning wonder of the reprieved, that the conflict, which had seemed so momentary while he was fighting it had actually lasted the four hours necessary to bring the Patrol up to his aid.

The realization that he was now safe washed over him like a wave and he was conscious of a deep thankfulness swelling up within him. It swelled up and out, pushing aside the lonely fear and desperation of his last few minutes, filling him instead with a relief so all-encompassing and profound that there was no anger left in him and no hate—not even for the enemy. It was like being born again.

Above him on the communications panel, the white message light was blinking. He cut in on the speaker with a steady hand and the dispassionate, official voice of the Patrol sounded over his head.

"Patrol Twenty to Station. Twenty to Station. Come in Station. Are you all right?"

He pressed the transmitter key.

"Station to Twenty. Station to Twenty. No damage to report. The Station is unharmed."

"Glad to hear it, Station. We will not pursue. We are decelerating now and will drop all ships on your field in half an hour. That is all."

"Thank you, Twenty. The field will be clear and ready for you. Land at will. That is all."

His hand fell away from the key and the message light winked out. In unconscious imitation of Waskewicz's memory he pushed himself back from the controls, stood up, turned and walked to the dispenser in the wall, where he dialed for and received a cup of coffee. He lit a cigarette and stood as the other had stood, smoking and drinking. He had won.

And reality came back to him with a rush.

For he looked down at his hand and saw the cup of coffee. He drew in on the cigarette and felt the hot smoothness of it deep in his lungs. And terror took him twisting by the throat.

He had won? He had done nothing. The enemy ships had fled not from him, but from the Patrol; and it was Waskewicz, *Waskewicz*, who had taken the controls from his hands at the crucial moment. It was Waskewicz who had saved the day, not he. It was the memory bank. The memory bank and Waskewicz!

The control room rocked about him. He had been betrayed. Nothing was won. Nothing was conquered. It was no friend that had broken at last through his lonely shell to save him, but the mind-sucking figment of memory-domination sanity. The memory bank and Waskewicz had seized him in their grasp.

He threw the coffee container from him and made himself stand upright. He threw the cigarette down and ground it beneath his boot. White-hot, from the very depths of his being, a wild anger blazed and consumed him. *Puppet,* said the mocking voice of his conscience, whispering in his ear. *Puppet!*

Dance, Puppet! Dance to the tune of the twitching strings!

"No!" he yelled. And, borne on the white-hot tide of his rage, the all-consuming rage that burnt the last trace of fear from his heart like dross from the molten steel, he turned to face his tormentor, hurling his mind backward, back into the life of Waskewicz, prisoned in the memory bank.

Back through the swirling tide of memories he raced, hunting a point of contact, wanting only to come to grips with his predecessor, to stand face to face with Waskewicz. Surely, in all his years at the Station, the other must sometime have devoted a thought to the man who must come after him. Let Jordan just find that point, there where the influence was strongest, and settle the matter, for sanity or insanity, for shame or pride, once and for all.

"Hi, Brother!"

The friendly words splashed like cool water on the white blaze of his anger. He—Waskewicz—stood in front of the bedroom mirror and his face looked out at the man who was himself, and who yet was also Jordan.

"Hi, Brother!" he said. "Whoever and wherever you may be. Hi!"

Jordan looked out through the eyes of Waskewicz, at the reflected face of Waskewicz; and it was a friendly face, the face of a man like himself.

"This is what they don't tell you," said Waskewicz. "This is what they don't teach in training—the message that, sooner or later, every stationman leaves for the guy who comes after him.

"This is the creed of the Station. *You are not alone.* No matter what happens, *you are not alone.* Out on the rim of the empire, facing the unknown races and the endless depths of the universe, this is the one thing that will keep you from all harm. As long as you remember it, nothing can affect you, neither attack, nor defeat, nor death. Light a screen on your outermost doggie and turn the magnification up as far as it will go. Away out at the limits of your vision you can see the doggie of another Station, of another man who holds the Line beside you. All along the Frontier, the Outpost Stations stand, forming a link of steel to guard the Inner Worlds and the little people there. They have their lives and you have yours; and yours is to stand on guard.

"It is not easy to stand on guard; and no man can face

the universe alone. But—*you are not alone!* All those who at this moment keep the Line, are with you; and all that have ever kept the Line, as well. For this is our new immortality, we who guard the Frontier, that we do not stop with our deaths, but live on in the Station we have kept. We are in its screens, its controls, in its memory bank, in the very bone and sinew of its steel body. *We are the station,* your steel brother that fights and lives and dies with you and welcome you at last to our kinship when for your personal self the light has gone out forever, and what was individual of you is nothing any more but cold ashes drifting in the eternity of space. *We are with you and of you, and you are not alone.* I, who was once Waskewicz, and am now part of the Station, leave this message for you, as it was left to me by the man who kept this guard before me, and as you will leave it in your turn to the man who follows you, and so on down the centuries until we have become an elder race and no longer need our shield of brains and steel.

"*Hi, Brother! You are not alone!*"

And so, when the six ships of Patrol Twenty came drifting in to their landing at the Station, the man who waited to greet them had more than the battle star on his chest to show he was a veteran. For he had done more than win a battle. He had found his soul.

Born in Edmonton, Alberta, Canada in 1923, Gordon R. Dickson graduated from high school at the age of fifteen, and then entered the University of Arizona to work toward a degree in creative writing. He left the University for military service from 1943 to 1946, but returned in 1947 and received his B.A. in 1950. He then became a full-time writer, and has written uninterruptedly ever since. His "Soldier, Ask Not," won the Hugo Award for best shorter-than-novel-length fiction of 1964, which was presented at the World Science Fiction Convention at London, England. He also won the Science Fiction Writers of America Nebula Award for best novelette, "Call Him Lord," in 1966.

Dickson is especially noted for his military science fiction centering around the Dorsai, men inhabiting a world of the same name, who are specially bred and trained as professional soldiers, and who have evolved entirely new survival abilities and talents. His novels have sold upwards of two million copies here and abroad, and his work has been translated into many foreign languages, appearing in more than a score of countries. He has served two terms as President of the Science Fiction Writers of America, and is a member of the Authors Guild and of the Mystery Writers of America.

The central psychological problem of war in space against alien enemies will be our almost certain ignorance of alien minds and their working—and their very possible ignorance of ours. Here Dr. Nourse wrestles with the problem and charts a very general—which is all that can be attempted at the moment—but practical approach to it.

Alan E. Nourse

OUTGUESSING THE UNKNOWN: Psychological Aspects of Future War

You've all read it a hundred times before. Some of you may have written it, in a bad moment; I know I have. It goes something like this:

Suddenly, out of the void, three dark alien craft materialize in near space, moving on a swift tangential course toward the rings of Saturn. Something ahead flares silently. One instant before, Saturn's Titan had been a thriving mining colony, teeming with life and activity. Now, in one blast of unthinkable energy, it is reduced to a bubbling slag-heap, like what the Monster fell into in Son Of Frankenstein, but don't let me get things confused.

The aliens turn and flee, vanishing ino hyperspace before they reach Uranus—a menace never before seen so close to the Solar System, suddenly come and suddenly gone. Within moments Earth ships move out in hot pursuit, but the aliens' faster-than-light drive is faster than our faster-than-light drive and they are fading into the void. There is time to launch only one beam; it catches the third ship in an orange blossom of raw violence and splits it open like a rotten melon.

Then, on the Earth ship, Mark Earthcrawler is taken out of his cage, injected with five times his daily dose of norepinephrine potentiator and beta-endorphins, stuffed into a pod and launched toward the ruined alien vessel. His mission: to bring a grisly end to any of the invading Bugs still floating around, since they breath hyperspace . . .

Yes, you've read it before. Even the first time you read it, at age 6, it may have struck you that there was something a little wrong with it. Maybe, reading it now, it strikes you that there is quite a bit more than just a little wrong with it. (But then, maybe it doesn't, in which case you should immediately start writing science fiction and sell it to the movies and get rich.) Whatever else may be said, this little vignette does conform thoroughly to a long-standing science fiction tradition. Throughout its recent history an enormous amount of science fiction has been concerned with warfare in various guises, and for the most part that warfare-of-the-future has involved alien beings of one sort or another. And whatever the sort, those aliens all behaved and fought wars just *exactly* like human beings.

For a long time it was just fun and games anyway and didn't really matter that practically nobody stopped to try to figure out just what "being an alien" might *mean*. The notion of any such thing as a *real* alien encounter was so far beyond any realistic consideration as to qualify more as fantasy than science fiction. But things are changing now, for those who want to think about it. In our lifetimes we have reached out decisively to begin the first serious physical exploration of our immediate solar system environment. In a flare of dubious good judgment we have fired supposedly revealing messages about ourselves off and away to be picked up and read very much elsewhere. We have discovered the principles of fusion power, even if we have not yet precisely harnessed it. Above all we are expanding our knowledge of areas of physics and mathematics that suggest that there may be a considerable body of Natural Law that we don't know anything about at all—a body of Natural Law which might sometime very conceivably allow us to break the fetters that we conceive as holding us in at the present time and effectively let us Out (and let others In as well).

With all of this going on the notion of ultimate contact with alien creatures, with or without war, seems just a little more imminent. Science fiction stories coming true. We can see the pattern. But oddly enough, virtually all of the vast body of science fiction which has dealt with such contact or such warfare has been 99.9% claptrap—and that includes some of the best of science fiction as well as some of the worst.

The problem is simple, obvious and extremely difficult to deal with. In our foolish little opening vignette the warlike aliens act altogether too much exactly the way we might imagine hostile human beings would act—but whatever else those aliens may be, they are by definition *not* human beings and could not conceivably act like human beings. There is not even much evidence presented, on the face of it, that they are particularly hostile. It is simply that what they are observed doing seems to be a hostile act *to our minds.*

It is to our minds—and to theirs—that we must look for some of the fascinating ideas that science fiction today all too seldom explores. For openers we must convince ourselves that whatever we imagine that future warfare with alien creatures might be like, it is most unlikely to be anything like that we might imagine it would be.

The Inadvertent Killer

Motives, actions and reactions between two human beings are confusing enough to try to figure out, God knows. If you don't believe it, go observe a good, vigorous divorce trial someday. Motives, actions and reactions between human and alien are *impossible* to figure out unless you first find out what kind of minds/bodies they may have and what those minds/bodies may require or make possible for them. At least in human/human reactions you can usually get a handle on *something*. Human motives are based on physiology (hunger, thirst, oxygen requirements, etc.) or on psychophysiology (sex, pleasure drives, self-preservation, territoriality, urge for revenge, body-mind need for endorphins, etc.) or on sociopsychology (money, greed, anger, status, desire for power, etc.) to name just a few things that come instantly to mind. But in human/alien encounters the handle gets slippery because it is most extremely likely that *not one* of such motives will apply, and the more bizarre the alien the slipperier the handle gets.

For example, let's make up an alien at random. For kicks, and because I like the idea, let's postulate that the alien is a virus entity—a highly intelligent colony-being composed of untold billions of virus particles that retains and magnifies its intelligence in exponential proportion to the total number and physical proximity of its particles. That is to say, when its component particles are scattered hither and yon individually or in little clumps, those scattered components are essentially mindless virus particles, but when many of them are drawn close together they become, conjointly, a powerful, sentient, intelligent organism. (This is all completely arbitrary, of course—what else? You want it some other way, set it up some other way.) This means, of course, that if a single virus particle, or small cluster of particles, becomes separated from the colony it becomes virtually nothing until it does what viruses do best: create more of themselves. And since, like all viruses, they are obligate cellular parasites, the only way they can create more of themselves is to invade a suitable host composed of protoplasmic cells containing DNA.

Now suppose a lost cluster of particles, once part of an intelligent virus entity but now weak, stupid, helpless and armed only with what their genetic packets are capable of, finds such a protoplasmic host. The individual virus particles find entry into the host's body, spread out, tap on cell doors until they find one kind of cell they can force entry into most easily (like nice juicy brain cells). All they want to do (if at this stage they can be said to want anything) is to get inside some cells of this host, safe from any nasty antibodies that might start appearing, and pat his DNA to see what its base pairs are. Then later, naturally, they will make that

DNA start replicating *them* until there are lots, lots more of them so they can begin to acquire sentience, maybe even enough that they can think about making peaceful psychological contact with the host. Certainly nothing hostile about that. Nothing unreasonable, either, he's got a staggering surplus of protein for them to use—

So this fragmentary, almost-mindless piece of virus entity enters the creature—now obviously a human being—and sets his brain cells to replicating virus particles like mad. 48 hours later the virus-entity is much larger, totally sentient, maybe fantastically intelligent— and the human being drops dead on the floor. This might be an absolutely appalling turn of events, from the viewpoint of the virus-entity. There might have been nothing farther from its collective mind or intention than to kill its host. In fact, it might be totally outside its age-old experience that such a thing might happen at all. It might have been sheer blind bad luck that it had come up against one of the rare species in the universe that happened to be mortally vulnerable to the intracellular activities of a few nice, friendly viruses.

The human being's companions—aboard a small space ship, say—might regard this whole deplorable business quite differently. Perhaps these people don't *like* to have their DNA patted by viruses just on general principles, and especially by viruses they can't identify in their laboratories or even *classify* with any other viruses they know. Whatever this one is, it wasn't around when they left home. The notion of *sentience* on the part of a virus might never enter their minds—who ever heard of a smart virus?—but the idea of *warfare* against it would arise almost immediately. Whatever it is, this virus kills fast, which means they have to strike back fast.

The intelligent virus-entity might well not grasp immediately that it had become the subject of warfare. However, certain things would begin happening to it to suggest that these protoplasmic creatures had intelligent minds and a grasp of biological technology. Soon other things would begin happening to suggest to the virus-entity that it had better find out something about how those intelligent minds worked or it was likely to be cooked. It could accomplish this any number of ways. Perhaps it could try invading several host-creatures in succession, forbearing to replicate more viruses but rather devoting its energy to searching out the highest concentrations of dopamine agonist activity and beta-endorphin production and then studying cells in that region to see what they were doing biochemically—one approach to studying psychology. Perhaps the virus-entity might discover that certain kinds of contact with certain cells forced it to participate intellectually in the hosts' *emotions*, perhaps a function of intelligence that is totally alien and unheard of to the virus. Perhaps it might find that by doing other things to other cells the virus could actually control thinking patterns or behavior patterns in the host. There could be all sorts of other possibilities, all based on the one thing we haven't really touched on yet, i.e. the nature of the mind of the virus entity. And meanwhile a desperate future war has been launched, an alien identified and a no-holds-barred battle begun to destroy it.

Yet this could be our first contact ever with a peaceful, intelligent alien.

Unless such a future war is to result in wholesale horror on either side, each side must obviously find a way to grasp something about the mind of the other *before* the war starts, not after. In the case of our virus-entity we might (or might not) be talking about a closet war, closely confined. On the human side the horror would be held down to 8 or 10 people on a space ship, hardly enough for really massive horror—but then, Dracula can only bite one girl at a time. On the virus side the horror could involve the destruction or crippling or agony of multiple billions of individual fragments of one sentient entity, which might be quite a bit of horror if it weren't so hard to sympathize with a virus particle. But in other cases whole races and civilizations could be involved.

Minds First

Warfare as we generally comprehend it involves motivation, means, directed action and goals to be achieved. Without motivation of *some* sort you don't ordinarily go out and hit somebody in the head. In fact, if the somebody is big and you're not, your strongest motivation may well be *not* to hit him in the head unless you are driven by such overwhelming considerations (rebellion against tyranny, for example) that you're prepared to take extraordinary chances. If you do hit him in the head, you'd better have something substantial to hit him with or you'll be in trouble. Without some notion of what you're going to do after you've dropped him and his buddies are closing in, you could be in *real* trouble. And unless there is something really worthwhile (to you) to be achieved from all this, you're just plain witless.

Notice that none of these considerations are particularly physiological; they are psychological. Hawks kill to eat, and that is physiological. It doesn't take much thought. But humans do not generally commit themselves to warfare because of stomach rumblings. Warfare is mostly a function of the mind—a reasoned or inflamed/emotional response to something psychologically intolerable. (It may be a response to some other guy holding power that you want, but you won't go to war for it until this has become psychologically intolerable to you.) And the way the war will be pursued will be keyed directly to the way the minds of the people fighting happen to work.

If this is true of human beings, why would it not be equally true of war with alien opponents? The forces leading aliens to war, and the ways they might pursue it, would be keyed directly to the way *their* minds worked. But to assume, as science fiction so often does, that their minds worked in even remotely similar fashion to human minds is either very naive or very lazy.

In the case of our virus entity, for example, we have an alien that doesn't have any mind at all except at certain times and under certain special circumstances.

Such a mind could be a tough one for humans to figure out—or to fight. In that same case one side doesn't even know a war is going on, at least for a period of time. Perhaps the virus can't even conceive what warfare *is*, and can only observe, bit by bit, that the other side seems to be doing a whole succession of *very* peculiar things, all of which hurt. It takes two to make a war, you say? Since when?

Obviously in any encounter which might end up in hostilities, which is to say any alien encounter, the first order of business is to do something *fast* to figure out how the minds of the alien creatures function. Contrary to the advice of recent motion pictures, this may perhaps *not* be best accomplished by rushing up and greeting them with open arms. We would have absolutely no way to guess how an alien mind might interpret such an overt act. It might be frightened, or repelled, or horrified or infuriated. It might feel driven to take instant violent defensive measures. It might feel driven to dematerialize completely, never to be seen again. God only knows *what* it might do. Virtually any overt act on our part might engender any one of an infinite variety of totally imponderable and unpredictable reactions, many of them not at all nice from our viewpoint.

Probing the Unknown

A far more sane and psychologically sound approach would be a *covert* search for clues to the nature of the alien mind and its function before rushing up and greeting it with open arms. After all, much of psychology is concerned with preserving, defending and protecting the mental integrity of the individual, at least in the case of humans. One might assume it to be an equal concern to an alien race as well. In fact, one might reasonably assume (as many science fiction stories have) that the alien's approach to us would be extremely covert, unless they bring with them an awful lot of foreknowledge about us gathered from *somewhere*. They might, indeed, be among us for a long old time before we had any idea they were there—cf. Horace Gold's celebrated speculation about the behavior of paper clips in offices. Of course this assumption, that aliens would come covertly, might well be totally wrong, based as it is on the insupportable assumption that alien minds and human would work similarly at least on this one point. In fact, they might see no point at all to a covert approach. They might even make no distinction whatever between overt and covert.

For humans approaching *them*, however, a covert approach would certainly seem the least risky avenue we could imagine, and would certainly be the most rewarding in terms of psychological probing. Here is a completely unknown, imponderable entity which appears at Time A at Point B in space. Friendly or hostile? (Or neither?) No guessing. Peaceful or warlike (or neither)? No guessing. Greedy as we are, we can imagine the staggering enrichment of our culture, our civilization and our species that could be engendered by peaceful intercourse with an alien race. Most desirable. Savage as we are, we can all too well imagine that one wrong move from us might pull some unknown plug and get us all wiped out. Most undesirable. (Of course both "greedy" and "savage" may be totally incomprehensible concepts to the aliens, in which case they are going to have quite an interesting time figuring out how *our* minds work.) Given these two real concerns, one desirable, one not, what kind of covert approach might help us?

I think that exploration of this problem—and it is a huge and mind-boggling problem, when you start digging into it—is one of the things that science fiction should be doing far more of than it has in the past. If you think I am going to produce any neat answers, you're wrong. The best I can manage is a rambling and disorganized attempt to define one tiny, insignificant corner of the problem. The whole problem spans all time and space and requires a firm grasp of all the known scientific disciplines just to begin to perceive the outlines and the magnitude. Like any science fiction writer, I can suggest a few undeveloped ideas. You could add your own, and certainly pick large holes in mine. Then perhaps better ideas might emerge.

Problem: planning some kind of covert psychological approach to an alien in an effort to learn all we possibly can about the workings of its mind, hopefully before we inadvertantly reveal too much about ourselves to the alien. This might—*might*—enable us to retain some options that could turn out to be race-preserving. So how could we do it?

First, we could just look at them without doing anything at all, without even moving. Simply observe them, silently, observe what they are doing, what activities they are involved in. Try to figure out what those activities might *mean* in terms of how their minds work. The seasoned hunter knows that he can learn an enormous amount about what other species in the forest are up to and why, just by sitting on a stump dead still and watching. If he can observe without being observed, so much the better. But even if he is observed, he can still see and learn if he can remain absolutely inert. I once had a cow elk walk up and nearly put her head in my lap because she was so damned curious about what I was and what I was doing sitting there watching her. Then I twitched a muscle and she immediately charged off through the brush like a freight train. (Item: she probably didn't know I was sitting because she didn't know what "sitting" was; and she may well not have known I was watching her. She didn't say. But she *taught* me that cow elk are curious, foolish animals with bad eyesight that don't have wit enough to know they may be in danger when they approach something strange and unfamiliar.)

Second, we could let the aliens see something of ourselves—some small fragment that *we* select—and see what they do. It might not matter too much what we choose to reveal. Pick the most expendable man around and send him off on a close approach singing "A Letter Edged In Black" and strumming on a ten-string banjo. Try to pick something to reveal that would elicit from the alien the most useful response we can imagine while not teaching the alien any more than we can help about *us*. Sanity and sensibility might not count in this little exercise. All that mattered would be what we learned.

Third, getting a bit more adventurous, we might poke them in some small way and see what response *that* elicits. Do something positive, if only to approach it. Try to pick the most useful, least hazardous poke that we can think of. Of course, whatever it is it may turn out to be the equivalent of patting the alien's DNA and bring the roof down on us, but life is full of hazards. Try and try. If one thing doesn't work, try another—and another—and another.

Fourth, use information we have gained to plan further gambits in information-gathering. *Something* will elicit some revealing response, eventually. Even if nothing elicits *any* response, that in itself is revealing, because if there is any single probable verity in all of this, it is that a sentient intelligence is sooner or later going to reveal something in its nature, mirror-like, in the actions that it takes or doesn't take (cf. my story MIRROR, MIRROR elsewhere in this anthology).

Oh, yes one other point: be sure you have the chaplain around, because any or all of the above approaches may be mortally perilous and we may well need to have an expert on hand praying for us.

The Time Factor

Finally, something here cries out to be said about time and timing.

Any of the approaches we have suggested above might or might not elicit a mind-revealing response from the alien. If we were to win so much as a single fleeting fragment of revelation—a single tidbit of true knowledge—in the course of an encounter, we could consider ourselves fantastically lucky. If we won one such tidbit of true insight in the course of twenty encounters, or a hundred, we could consider ourselves lucky.

That one tidbit would be better than none, and would be won far sooner than the odds might indicate.

You could call it Nourse's First Law of Alien Encounters: *Aliens are not contacted in a day.*

Consider: On a purely human-to-human level we in the West have been encountering and grappling with the Byzantine minds of countries like Mother Russia for scores and scores of years and we still have not gotten to first base figuring out what they are thinking about. (Those who think we have, please read Charles Thayer's fascinating book *Diplomat* and then come back and argue.) We know that they don't think like we do, but that's about it. And these encounters were with the same species in multitudes of meetings throughout multitudes of years under (generally) quite favorable conditions. Yet I read science fiction stories dealing with single encounters with totally unknown aliens which either result in commitment to total intergalactic war then and there, or else we're suddenly friends forever.

I don't believe those stories. Any single encounter with an alien, even if it happens to be warlike, is almost certain to be fragmentary. Innumerable encounters spread out over centuries or eons of real time are likely to leave us with innumerable fragments of information, many of them totally incomprehensible and none of them internally consistent with any others. Any truly meaningful *contact* with an alien, if it comes at all, will come only after a prolonged interval of repeated encounters, joustings and counter-joustings, trials and errors—perhaps disastrous and tragic errors—and even then it will come, ultimately, only when we have succeeded in piecing together the nature of the aliens' minds and, in the long run, allowing them to piece together the nature of ours.

It's a long way to go, but I suspect it's the only way. It requires deep knowledge of alien psychology, and vice versa. If it then becomes clear that we must pursue future war, knowledge of the enemy's psychology will be the single most vital factor in winning. If instead we can pursue peace, commerce and interchange, that same knowledge will be of infinitely greater value to us if only because we will be running an infinitely smaller risk of ceasing to exist as a species.

Right now all we need to do is somehow to survive long enough for the first aliens to find us. Or vice versa.

Alan E. Nourse started pre-medical studies at Rutgers in 1945, but interrupted them to serve two years in the Navy's hospital corps. Afterwards he returned to Rutgers for his B.S., and took his M.D. at the U. of Pennsylvania Medical School in 1955. He interned in Seattle, and then devoted two years to freelance writing before entering general practice at North Bend, Washington, in 1958. In 1963, he returned to full-time writing.

His first national publication was a short story, "High Threshold," published in *Astounding* in 1951, and this was followed by some sixty short stories and novelettes which appeared in virtually all the magazines of the time. In addition, he published a short novel, *A Man Obsessed*, and, in collaboration, wrote *The Invaders Are Coming* (both for Ace). His writing helped to pay for his medical education and, of course, reflects a strong medical orientation.

Dr. Nourse has published thirty-five or so works of fiction and nonfiction, including a dozen or so juveniles and three volumes of short stories. Two of his latest titles are *The Practice*, a mainstream novel (Harper & Row, 1978), and *Inside the Mayo Clinic*.

Dr. Nourse has an article on medicine in future warfare in *Thor's Hammer*, Volume I of *The Future at War*, and a story, "Mirror, Mirror," in Volume II, *The Spear of Mars*.

"O! now doth Death line his dead chaps with steel;
The swords of soldiers are his teeth, his fangs;
And now he feasts, mousing the flesh of man."
                    Shakespeare, *King John*, Act II, Scene 1.

And, when the machines of war have degraded men
into Death's-meat, then psychological warfare will be
waged not only against the enemy, but . . . . .

Terry Carr

CITY OF YESTERDAY

"Wake up," said Charles, and J-1001011 instantly sat up. The couch sat up with him, jackknifing to form his pilot's seat. J-1001011 noted that the seat was in combat position, raised high enough to give him unobstructed vision on all sides of the planetflier.

"We're in orbit around our objective," said Charles. "Breakout and attack in seven minutes. Eat. Eliminate."

J-1001011 obediently withdrew the red-winking tube from the panel before him and put it between his lips. Warm, mealy liquid fed into his mouth, and he swallowed at a regular rate. When the nourishment tube stopped, he removed it from his mouth and let it slide back into the panel.

The peristalsis stimulators began, and he asked, "Is there news of my parents?"

"Personal questions are always answered freely," said Charles, "but only when military necessities have been completed. Your briefing for this mission takes precedence." A screen lit up on the flier's control panel, showing a 3-D contour map of the planet they were orbiting.

J-1001011 sighed and turned his attention to the screen.

"The planet Rhinstruk," said Charles. "Oxygen 13.7%; nitrogen 82.4%; plus inert gases. Full spacewear will be required for the high-altitude attack pattern in effect on this mission."

The image on the screen zoomed in, selected one

234

continent out of three he had seen revolving below, continued zooming down to near planet level. Charles said, "Note that this is a totally enemy planet; should I be shot down and you somehow survive, there will be no refuge. If that happens, destroy yourself."

"The target?" the pilot asked.

"The city you see below. It isn't fully automated, but its defenses will be formidable anyway." On the screen J-1001011 saw a towered city rising from a broad plain. The city was circular, and as the image sharpened with proximity he could make out individual streets, parkways . . . and beam emplacements. The screen threw light-circles on seven of these in all.

"We will have nine fliers," said Charles. "These beams will attempt to defend, but our mission will be simple destruction of the entire city, which presents a much larger target than any one of our fliers. We will lose between three and five of us, but we'll succeed. Attack pattern RO-1101 will be in effect; you'll take control of me at 30,000 feet. End of briefing."

The pilot stretched in his chair, flexed muscles in his arms and hands. "How long was I asleep?" he asked.

"Eight months, seventeen days plus," said Charles.

That long! At quarter-credit for sleep time that would give him over two months on his term of service, leaving him . . . less than a year, Earthstandard. J-1001011 felt his heart speed up momentarily, before Charles' nerve-implants detected and corrected it. The pilot had been in service for nearly seven subjective years. Adding objective sleep time, it came out to over nineteen years. The sleep periods, during Hardin Drive travel between starsystems, ate up his service term easily for him . . . but then he remembered, as he always did, that the objective time was still the same, that his parents, whoever and wherever they were, would be getting older at objective time rate on some planet.

Nineteen years. . . . They should still be alive, he thought. He remembered them from his childhood, on a planet where colors had been real rather than dyed or light-tinted, where winds had blown fresh and night

had fallen with the regular revolution of the planet. He
had had a name there, not a binary number—Henry, or
Hendrick, or Henried; he couldn't quite remember.
When the Control machines had come for him he had
been ten years old, old enough to know his own name,
but they had erased it. They had had to clear his
memory for the masses of minute data he'd need for
service, so the machines had stored his personal memories in neat patterns of microenergy, waiting for his
release.

Not all of them, though. The specific things, yes: his
name, the name of his planet, its exact location, the
thousand-and-one details that machines recognize as
data. But not remembered sights, smells, tastes: flow-
erbursts of color amid green vegetation, the cold spray
of rainbowed water as he stood beside a waterfall, the
warmth of an animal held in the arms. He remembered
what it was like to be Henry, or Hendrick or Henried,
even though he couldn't remember the exact name of
the person he had been.

And he remembered what his parents were like,
though he had no memory at all of *their* names. His
father: big and rangy, with bony hands and an awkward
walk and a deep, distant voice, like thunder and rain on
the other side of a mountain. His mother: soft and
quiet, a quizzical face framed by dark hair, somehow
smiling even when she was angry, as if she wasn't quite
sure how to put together a stern expression.

By now they must be . . . fifty years old? Sixty? Or
even a *hundred* and sixty, he thought. He couldn't
know; he had to trust what the machines told him, what
Charles said. And they could be lying about the time
spent in sleep. But he had to assume they weren't.

"Breakout and attack in one minute," Charles said.

The voice startled him momentarily, but then he
reached for his pressure helmet, sealed it in place with
automatic movements, machine-trained muscle patterns.
He heard the helmet's intercom click on.

"What about my parents?" he asked. "You have time

to tell me before we break out. At least tell me if they're still alive."

"Breakout and attack in thirty seconds and counting," said Charles. "Twenty-eight, twenty-seven, twenty-six . . ."

J-1001011, human pilot of a planetflier named Charles, shook his head in resignation and listened to the count, bracing himself for the coming shock of acceleration.

It hit him, as always, with more force than he had remembered, crushing him back into the chair as the planetflier rocketed out of the starship's hold along with its eight unit-mates. Charles had opaqued the pilot's bubble to prevent blinding him with sudden light, but the machine cleared it steadily as it drove downward toward the planet's surface, and soon the man could make out the other fliers around him. He recognized the flying formation, remembered the circular attack pattern they'd be using—a devastating ring of fliers equipped with pyrobombs. Charles was right: they'd lose some fliers, but the city would be destroyed.

He wondered about the city, the enemy. Was this another pacification mission, another planet feeling strong in its isolation from the rest of GalFed's far-flung worlds and trying to break away from central regulation? J-1001011 had been on dozens of such missions. But their attacks then hadn't been destruct-patterns against whole cities, so this must be a different kind of problem. Maybe the city was really a military complex . . . even a stronghold of the Khallash, if they really existed.

When men had first made contact with an alien race a century and a half before, they had met with total enmity, almost mindlessly implacable hatred. War had flared immediately—a defensive war on the part of the humans, who hadn't been prepared for it. And in order to organize the loose-knit Galactic Federation efficiently, they'd computerized the central commands . . . and then the middle echelons . . . and finally, a little over a century ago, the whole of GalFed had been given to the machines to defend.

Or so he had been taught. There were rumors, of course, that there were no Khallash any longer, that they'd been destroyed or driven off long ago . . . or that they'd never existed in the first place, that the machines had invented them as an excuse for their own control of GalFed. J-1001011 didn't know. He'd never met the aliens in battle, but that proved nothing, considering the vastness of space and the many internal problems the machines had to cope with.

Yet perhaps he would meet them now . . . in the city below.

"30,000 feet," said Charles. "Attach your muscle contacts."

The pilot quickly drew from the walls of the compartment a network of small wires, one after the other, and touched each to magnetized terminals on his arms, hands, legs, shoulders. As he did so he felt the growing sensation of airflight: he was becoming one with the flier, a single unit of machine and man. Charles fed the sensory impressions into his nervous system through his regular nerve-implants, and as the muscle contacts were attached he could feel the flier's rockets, gyros, pyrolaunchers all coming under his control, responding instantly to movements of his body's muscles.

This was the part that he liked, that almost made his service term worth it. As the last contact snapped into place, he *became* the planetflier. His name was Charles, and he was a whole being once more. Air rushed past him, mottled fields tilted far below, he felt the strength of duralloy skin and the thrust of rockets; and he was not just a flesh-and-blood human wombed in his pilot's compartment, but a weapon of war swooping down for a kill.

The machines themselves don't appreciate this, he thought. *Charles and the rest have no emotions, no pleasures. But a human does . . . and we can even enjoy killing. Maybe that's why they need us—because we can love combat, so we're better at it than them.*

But he knew that wasn't true, only an emotional conceit. Human battle pilots were needed because their nervous systems were more efficient than any micro-miniaturized computer of the same size and mass; it was as simple as that. And human pilots were expendable where costly mechanization wouldn't be.

"Control is full now," he said; but Charles didn't answer. Charles didn't exist now. Only the computer aboard the orbiting starship remained to monitor the planetfliers below.

In a moment the starship's voice came to him through Charles' receptors: "All human units are ready. Attack pattern RO-1101 will now begin."

The city was below him, looking just as it had on the contour map: wide streets, buildings thrusting up toward him, patches of green that must have been parks . . . or camouflage, he warned himself. The city was the enemy.

He banked into a spiral and knifed down through the planet's cold air. The other fliers fell into formation behind him, and as the starship cut in the intercommunications channels he heard the voices of the other pilots:

"Beautiful big target; we can't miss it. Anybody know if they're Khallash down there?"

"Only the machines would know that, and if they'd wanted to tell us, they'd have included it in the briefing."

"It looks like a human city to me. Must be another rebel planet."

"Maybe that's what the Khallash want us to think."

"It doesn't matter who they are," J-1001011 said. "They're enemy; they're our mission. Complete enough missions and we go home. Stop talking and start the attack; we're in range."

As he spoke he lined his sights dead-center on the city and fired three pyrobombs in quick succession. He peeled off and slipped back into the flight circle as another flier banked into firing trajectory. Three more bombs flared out and downward, and the second flier rejoined the pattern.

Below, J-1001011's bombs hit. He saw the flashes, one, two, three quick bursts, and a moment later red flames showed where the bombs had hit. A bit off-center from where he had aimed, but close enough. He could correct for it on the next pass.

More bombs burst below; more fires leapt and spread. The fliers darted in, loosed their bombs and dodged away. They were in a complete ring around the city now, the pattern fully established. It was all going according to plan.

Then the beams from the city began to fire.

The beams were almost invisible at a distance, just lightning-quick lances of destructive energy cutting into the sky. Not that it was important to see them—the fliers couldn't veer off to evade them in time, wouldn't even be able to react before a beam struck.

But the planetfliers were small, and they stayed high. Any beam hits would be as much luck as skill.

They rained fire and death on the city for an hour, each flier banking inward just long enough to get off three or four bombs, then veering out and up before he got too close. At the hour's end the city below was dotted by fires, and the fires were spreading steadily. One of the planetfliers had been hit; it had burst with an energy-release that buffeted J-1001011 with its shockwave, sending him momentarily off course. But he had quickly righted himself, reentered the pattern and returned to the attack.

As the destruction continued, he felt more and more the oneness, the wholeness of machine and man. Charles the other-thing was gone, merged into his own being, and now he was the machine, the beautiful complex mass of metals and sensors, relays and engines and weaponry. He was a destruction-machine, a death-flier, a superefficient killer. It was like coming out of the darkness of some prison, being freed to burst out with all his pent-up hatreds and frustrations and destroy, destroy. . . .

It was the closest thing he had to being human again, to being . . . what was the name he had had back on that planet where he'd been born? He couldn't remember now; there was no room for even an echo of that name in his mind.

He was *Charles*.

He was a war-machine destroying a city—that and only that. Flight and power occupied his whole being, and the screaming release of hatred and fear within him was so intense that it was love. The attack pattern became, somehow, a ritual of courtship, the pyrobombs and destruction and fire below a kind of lovemaking whose intensity gripped him more and more fiercely as the attack continued. It was a red hell, but it was the only kind of real life he had known since the machines had taken him.

When the battle was over, when the city was a flaming circle of red and even the beams had stopped firing from below, he was exhausted both physically and emotionally. He was able to note dimly, with some back part of his brain or perhaps through one of Charles' machine synapse-patterns, that they had lost three of the fliers. But that didn't interest him; nothing did.

When something clicked in him and Charles' voice said, "Remove your muscle contacts now," he did so dully, uncaring. And he became J-1001011 again.

Later, with the planetfliers back in the hold of the starship and awaiting the central computer's analysis of the mission's success, he remembered the battle like something in a dream. It was a red, violent dream, a nightmare; and it was worse than that, because it had been real.

He roused himself, licked dry lips, said, "You have time now, Charles, to tell me about my parents. Are they alive?"

Charles said, "Your parents do not exist. They've been destroyed."

There was a moment of incomprehension, then a dull shock hit J-1001011 in the stomach. But it was almost as if he had been expecting to hear this—and Charles controlled his reaction instantly through the nerve-implants.

"Then that was no Khallash city," he said.

"No," said Charles. "It was a human city, a rebel city."

The pilot searched vaguely through the fog of his memories of home, trying to remember anything about a city such as he'd destroyed today. But he could grasp nothing like that; his memories were all of some smaller town, and of mountains, not the open fields that had surrounded this city.

"My parents moved to the city after I was taken away," he said. "Is that right?"

"We have no way of knowing about that," said Charles. "Who your parents were, on what planet they lived— all this information has been destroyed in the city on Rhinstruk. It was the archives center of the Galactic Federation, storing all the memory-data of our service humans. Useless information, since none of it will ever be used again—and potentially harmful, because the humans assigned to guard it were engaged in a plot to broadcast the data through official machine communications channels to the original holders of the memories. So it became necessary to destroy the city."

"You destroyed an entire city . . . just for that?"

"It was necessary. Humans perform up to minimum efficiency standards only when they're unhampered by pre-service memories; this is why all your memory-data was transferred from your mind when you were inducted. For a while it was expedient to keep the records on file, to be returned as humans terminated their service, but that time is past. It has always been a waste of training and manpower to release humans from service, and now we have great enough control in the Federation that it's no longer necessary. Therefore we're able to complete a major step toward totally efficient organization."

J-1001011 imagined fleetingly that he could feel the machine's nerve-implants moving within him to control some emotion that threatened to rise. Anger? Fear? Grief? He couldn't be sure just what was appropriate to this situation; all he actually felt was a dull, uncomprehending curiosity.

"But my parents . . . you said they were destroyed."

"For all purposes they have been. The actual humans who were your parents may still be alive somewhere, but now there is no way of knowing where that may be or who they are. They've become totally negligible factors, along with the rest of your pre-service existence. When we control all data in your mind, we then have proper control of the mind itself."

He remembered dark trees and a cushion of damp green leaves beneath them, where he had fallen asleep one endless afternoon. He heard the earthquake of his father's laughter once when he had drunk far too much; remembered how like a stranger his mother had seemed for weeks after she'd cut her hair short; tasted smoked meat and felt the heat of an open hearth-fire. . . .

The nerve-implants moved like ghosts inside him.

"The central computer's analysis is now complete," Charles announced. "The city on Rhinstruk is totally destroyed; our mission was successful. So there's no more need for you to be awake; deactivation will now begin."

Immediately, Pilot J-1001011 felt his consciousness ebbing away. He said, more to himself than to Charles, "You can't erase the past like that. The mission was . . . unsuccessful." He felt a yawn coming, tried to fight it, couldn't. "Their names weren't . . . the important . . ."

Then he couldn't talk any more; but there was no need for it. He drifted into sleep remembering the freedom of flight when he was Charles, the beauty and strength of destroying, of rage channeled through pyrobombs . . . of release, of release. . . .

For one last flickering moment he felt a stab of anger begin to rise, but then Charles' implants pushed it back down inside. He slept.

Until his next awakening.

Terry Carr was born in southern Oregon, between Grant's Pass and Medford, where his father worked a small gold mine. He moved to San Francisco in 1941, and grew up there, going to college at CCSF and the University of California at Berkeley. In 1961, moving to New York, he began writing and selling science fiction. He worked a year and a half at the Scott Meredith Literary Agency, then seven years as an editor at Ace Books, where he was responsible for the original Ace SF Specials and began the *Universe* series of original-story anthologies and, with Don Wollheim, the *World's Best Science Fiction* series.

He married Carol Carr—herself an sf writer for a time—and they returned to the Bay Area in '71. Since then he has been freelance writing and anthology-editing. He has published about 50 anthologies to date, plus three dozen short stories and novelettes, a collection (*The Light at the End of the Universe*) of his own stories, and a novel, *Cirque,* which was a Nebula nominee.

"City of Yesterday" was written on assignment from Fred Pohl for *If,* based on a cover painting by Chaffee.

In any combat situation, here on Earth, on any alien planet, or far out in space, the fighting man must understand his enemy—the enemy himself, the enemy's weapons and machines, his strengths and weaknesses.

But, above all, he must understand his own—and be prepared to take advantage of them, a point this fine story of Dean Ing's makes dramatically and clearly.

Dean Ing

WHEN I WAS RED ROVER

The colonel stood before the shack's only functioning viewscreen, staring at it as he leaned on spidery aluminum crutches. The big man swayed around, hearing Mayhan's scuffing steps, then returned his gaze to the screen.

"The *Pink Pup* checked out fine, Colonel Meier," Mayhan said. "I could scramble anytime now."

The older man stiffened slightly. "Your ship is the Terran Federation Scout three-seven-six-six, lieutenant. You will kindly remember that." He spoke without turning. "We may be getting shot to blazes here, but we're still a military unit."

Mayhan risked a shrug. "Yes, sir."

"The sixty-six . . . the *thirty-seven* sixty-six," the colonel corrected himself quickly, "isn't your personal plaything."

"No, sir." Mayhan kept his answers meek. There was no point in aggravating one's C.O., especially when he was in constant pain from a shrapnel wound in the hip.

From near the base perimeter, a homing missile shrieked away into the yellow sky of Di Cicco with dreams of predation in its primitive brain. Mayhan sent an awed glance after the missile. As a scout pilot, Mayhan commanded a more versatile machine, but the tiny genius of destruction that was a homing missile always fascinated him. He had a personal interest, too; a single Backer projectile, eluding the homing "birds" high above Di Cicco's lone outpost, might destroy the entire potential of the planet. Mayhan and his ship *were* that potential.

Mayhan took on a military bearing as Colonel Meier turned toward him. He did it well; a sharp-eyed, closely-knit youngster of thirty, Mayhan could, if pressed, become a creature of spit and polish. If only temporarily.

"We're getting clobbered, lieutenant," Meier told him flatly. "I knew it was too good to last. Don't know why the Backers waited so long."

"Perhaps our other ships called attention to us, sir," Mayhan offered. "If they took one of our guys intact, they'll know we have data that can hurt 'em.'"

"And so we have." Meier permitted himself a frosted smile. "Too bad we don't have facilities any more, or we could microfilm everything. As it is, our maps and psychomotor data on the Backers give us a high card. But the Federation'll have to play it for us," he grunted. "If only we'd known what was out here," he trailed off, a dull luster in his eyes.

Six months before, Di Cicco had been a perfect duty planet, discounting the lack of female companionship. Routine mapping missions on the rim of known space, deep-sea fishing on Di Cicco's placid ocean, high-diving under a feeble gravity constant—the outpost was a model for Federation Service recruiting posters on thirty worlds. And then the Backers came darting in with their outrageous little ships, bypassing Di Cicco temporarily on their way into Federation territory.

Colonel Frederick Meier had the agonized distinction of being the first man to contact a Backer ship; he was the only one who'd gotten close to the Backers and had lived to regret it. His wound, healing slowly, was a souvenir from a Backer torpedo that had caught Meier's ship even as the colonel was ducking into Di Cicco's atmosphere. There was no communication with the aliens, only contacts: they came; they took. Their weapons and intellect seemed to be on a par with those of the Federation, but without much co-ordination. Still, they had cut off a prime source of information when they set up their flexible picket line. Di Cicco, officially, was behind enemy lines. So far, six ships had been stripped and refitted for a dash back to Federation planets. Five had made the supreme effort, beaming back a steady call as long as they functioned. They had all been caught, either in normal space or in hyperspace, in a matter of hours.

Colonel Meier relaxed a trifle, with a look at Mayhan that was not quite fondness. "I won't bandy words," he rumbled. "That billion-dollar vessel out there," he nodded toward the *Pink Pup* as it squatted on the landing area, "is worth a billion times more now. There isn't another available scout this side of Vega, and this data must get to Planning Center."

Mayhan voiced a confidence that was mostly sham. "She'll do it, colonel. Every tech on Di Cicco knows the best ship we have is the *Pink* . . . three-seven-six-six."

Now the C.O. actually grinned, lifting a heavily veined wrist to rub his nose. "You're incurable, lieutenant," he said, "if not inoperable. Well, this time I won't warn you against acrobatics. You're on your own. Maybe you've gotten some good out of treating your ship like a mechanized roller skate. You'll need to do some fancy twisting to run a Backer gantlet."

"I think I can, colonel," Mayhan said uneasily. He was wondering if the C.O.'s mind had gone soft. The robot satellite that soared above Di Cicco had been transmitting some interesting scenes as Mayhan entered the communications shack. Time, Mayhan thought tritely, was of the essence.

"By the way," Meier asked, "what were your 'G' tolerances at your last physical?"

Mayhan pursed his lips, looked up at nothing for a moment. "Forty G's for point one seconds," he recalled. "Twelve G's for ten seconds, and five G's for as long as my fuel holds out. For a one minute increment—"

"O.K.," Meier cut him off, "so long as you haven't forgotten. Just try to remember," he almost pleaded, "that it's more than a broken blood vessel you're risking. Will you do that for me, Mayhan, as a personal favor?"

"Yes sir," Mayhan mumbled, reddening. The young pilot fidgeted in silence as Meier studied the viewscreen again and made a vernier adjustment. Mayhan saw a Backer ship leap into focus, then dwindle. On the screen's panel, a red light winked off; Meier nodded.

"That's it, Mayhan," he said. "Damn if I know what they're up to, but the Backers have left us to our own devices for a while. You sure you can handle the . . . God forgive me . . . *Pink Pup?*"

"If you mean the three-seven-six-six," Mayhan said straight-faced, "Yes sir." Then he bit his lip. One doesn't make quips to one's C.O.; one laughs when the C.O. does it. Period.

"I resign," the colonel chuckled softly. "Tell Wang and the other techs to get back here on the double, soon as you're off. We have papers to destroy before we fade into the underbrush. And Mayhan," he called as the pilot streaked for the door, "wait until I clear you from here!"

"Will comply, sir," Mayhan returned unmilitarily over his shoulder. He ran easily, shrugging his G-suit into the proper places and patting pockets to make sure of their contents. Bounding across the taxi strip, he waved an arm at Captain Wang, the field-control officer. He stabbed one finger into the air in the time-honored scramble signal. Mayhan found his skin prickling as a ragged cheer went up from the assembled technical specialists. Best bunch of bums in the universe, he thought. And they're counting on me. Then he was riding the lift to the *Pink Pup's* cabin, repeating Meier's instructions to Wang as the taciturn captain made minor adjustments on Mayhan's G-suit.

Mayhan busied himself inside the *Pup*, double-checking everything. His G-suit stretched across his shoulders and down his thighs to encase his feet without a wrinkle. He left the air lock open, breathing the almost Earth-normal air to conserve oxygen. The viewscreens showed one last tech racing away from the blast area on his scooter, toolbox spilling gadgetry at every jounce.

The radio crackled. "Lieutenant Mayhan, the area is

clear of the enemy," came Meier's voice. Mayhan acknowledged, operating the air-lock servo. The alloy port thunked shut, depriving him of his last sight of Di Cicco's distant hills and spinnaker cloudlets. Hills and cloudlets that would soon be under Backer jurisdiction.

The *Pink Pup* was alive under Mayhan's deft touch as he typed instructions into the console keyboard. "Prepare for launch," Meier droned dispassionately, and Mayhan hit the manual first-stage alert switch. There was the usual pause of interminable seconds. Then Meier spoke again. "Any time, son," he said gently. Mayhan was aloft an instant later.

Mayhan considered his situation while the ship accelerated steadily out of Di Cicco's area. It was too bad that data couldn't be sent by microwave. Then again it could, if you counted hyperspace. Everything seemed the same in hyperspace, once past the feeling of being drawn through a jagged knothole—but it wasn't. For one thing, the trip to Vega VI would take about three days instead of the several centuries it and radio waves would require in normal space. Physicists said that in hyperspace the ship and contents were only a matrix of wave lengths with cohesive properties—whatever that meant. Mayhan didn't care. He did care about the Backers' use of hyperspace. It wasn't known if they could make an instant jump or not, since the five previous escape ships from Di Cicco couldn't be monitored adequately while in a state of flux. Carrier waves simply fanned out too quickiy to be useful over great distances, in hyperspace.

Mayhan only vaguely understood these problems; his most prominent worry was a physical one. He knew that he was physically inferior to the Backers in one important respect.

"I could lick any three dozen of 'em hand to hand," he growled to the ship. "Those greasy little octopi are *soft!*"

A close scrutiny of Di Cicco's only prize had provided the news that the aliens had no solid bone. Something akin to cuttlebone served the alien—and served them well, considering humans by comparison. The Backers could beat Mayhan easily in space. They could beat any man or Vegan by a freakish ability to take huge gravity loads. Angular course changes seemed to affect them much as they affected humans, but at straight linear acceleration, positive or negative, a Backer was master of the known universe.

Backer ships advertised this ability by the lack of a forward cabin. There were identical ion drives on both ends, making the Backer ships look ridiculous to men. And making them almost impossible to catch or to avoid.

Mayhan stroked the cushioned panel before him. "You can do it, *Pup*," he soothed. "The question is, can I?"

He put the query to the autopilot, an inane habit born of dreary mapping trips. He hit the MESSAGE ENDS key and instantly saw the expected answer crawl across the display. The *Pink Pup*, he decided, didn't think much of her master.

Mayhan had been in favor of sending robot controlled scouts past the Backers, rigged for evasive action. Meier had coolly voted him down with a short lecture on the limitations of machinery.

"Space travel," he'd said, "calls for judgment on a high level of consciousness. *Good* judgment," he had stressed, cocking a skeptical eye at Mayhan. "No robot ship has ever made a trip like this even in peacetime, when we had every gimmick known to science. How the devil can we hope to do it with a jury-rigged scout? The chances against us would be astronomical in several senses." Meier had added that, as it was, the chances were mighty slim indeed.

Mayhan looked at his typed question again. CAN A HUMAN RECEIVE ONE CHANCE IN ONE BILLION CHANCES OF LIVING THROUGH EVASIVE ACTION VERSUS ENEMY?

Bluntly, the *Pup* had said, NO.

"All right," Mayhan sighed, grinning tightly, "but

I've got *some* chance. Even you wouldn't begrudge me that, you pessimist." Mayhan was never quite sure that he'd asked the right question in the right way. Nor, for that matter, that the autopilot *cum* oracle was always right.

"Let's see," he mused, raising his couch nearer the keyboard. "Given a sudden pandemic attack of scrofula for the Backers—and a cargo of rabbits' feet for Mayhan—I'd still get trounced," he learned.

"Then why did I take on this job to begin with?" he shouted suddenly. The echoes rebounded thinly in the *Pup's* recirculation vents. The *Pink Pup* clicked electronic tongues at him in derision; under the circumstances, she could afford to. Meier had been fairly sure that a Federation scout ship in good condition could, if not encumbered with delicate animal cargo, outmaneuver anything in space. But Meier himself had placed animal limitations on the ship, in the form of Jesse Mayhan. Mayhan swore softly, balling his fists.

A scrap of memory came back to him from his cadet days. "When any action *per se* isn't feasible," the instructor had said, "relax. Save that adrenalin." Mayhan reclined on the couch from long habit, tried to relax. He tried until sweat bejewelled his brow, realized that tension was begetting tension, and guffawed at himself. Then he *did* relax.

For many minutes, only the faint click of relays twittered at the silence. A saffron warning light from the radar console winked once and subsided. No one knew what sort of matter whizzed through hyperspace, but the radar system duly avoided any possibility of finding out. The *Pink Pup* was nosing nearer to Federation lines every second, spanning light-years with each sweep of the chronometer. Suddenly Mayhan realized that he must be beyond any microwave hookup with Di Cicco. The other ships had been destroyed before they had gone much farther than this. Perhaps he now had a chance.

"Maybe Stine or Vargas or one of the others made it

after all," he breathed. "We *could* have got a bollixed signal from them back on Di Cicco." Vargas, Stine and Wright, the last three volunteers, had plotted a steady three-point-five G acceleration course up to velocity limit. Mayhan was holding it down to three, reasoning that he'd be fresher when the real G loads were applied. Mayhan was the best G-loader on Di Cicco and knew his limitations, usually pretending indifference. Now, with the *Pink Pup* as his only company, the feigned carelessness dropped away. He raised himself toward the keyboard again.

ARE YOU NOW OUTSIDE ENEMY PERIMETER?
YES, was the answer, QUALIFIED.

"That's so," Mayhan conceded. "The information we fed you was pretty arbitrary. Or the Backers could've moved their pickets closer to Vega. But even when you have good news you qualify it." He stared ferociously at the keyboard. "When a female pup grows up, you know what they call her, don't you," he insinuated. The *Pink Pup* ignored this calumny; Mayhan was moved to further action. GO BLANK YOURSELF, he typed rapidly.

The *Pup* countered primly, INSUFFICIENT DATA.

THEN GO RUST YOURSELF, Mayhan answered, and raised the acceleration to a shade over four G's. He listened with great joy to the confused muttering that went on inside the autopilot's flat crackle-finished face.

The ship was still perplexed and Mayhan still gratified with his small verbal victory when the warning light winked on again. This time it stayed on. Mayhan cleared the autopilot's circuits and asked for specifics. When they came, Mayhan felt sick all over; a ship-sized mass was accelerating past any human tolerance, on collision course and some five minutes away.

The *Pink Pup* slammed ahead as Mayhan sank into his couch, his body in agony. The autopilot's message, now magnified at the base of the main viewscreen, stated that the Backer ship was altering course. The radar was in complete agreement, as usual. Mayhan's sight grew fuzzy; he cut the drive and the engines' vibration shuddered and stopped.

Alertness returned quickly. Mayhan took a deep breath and flicked the ship into normal space. Generators screeched behind the cabin, then there was the familiar gut-churning vertigo and he was alone again. Mayhan set a new course, trying only to go where the Backers weren't.

After a few minutes' heavy acceleration he cut the drive again. He was trying a random sequence of moves, knowing of nothing better to do.

It was like a game he'd played as a kid, Mayhan decided, usually with all the big kids opposite him. They'd form two parallel chains, arms linked tightly, and the opposition would set up a chant. "Red Rover, Red Rover, let Mayhan come over." Jesse Mayhan had been a scrawny kid, much in demand. The other kids loved seeing him gather speed, running madly toward the human chain. They had the most fun when Mayhan knocked himself senseless without breaking the chain.

For Mayhan, it began to be fun when he learned to sprint at one spot, then hurl his frail bulk at another pair of locked arms that weren't expecting his small assault. Then, he sometimes broke the chain. Once he broke a wrist. It was glorious.

When Mayhan lost, he was added to the opposing side. When he won, he could take the two weak links and add them to his own side. It was the game of Red Rover that earned him his boyhood nickname, Mayhem Mayhan. He was fiercely glad to have had the experience.

The immediate area around the *Pink Pup* was clear of any calculable mass, which was normal. The autopilot was set to reject any jump that would endanger the ship. Mayhan caught himself wondering at the *Pup's* intellect again as he watched the fore viewscreens. A radar blip sliced his thoughts neatly as it moved toward the center cross hairs at fantastic speed.

Mayhan reacted instantly; the ship leaped away in a curve that was almost an angle. Another blip came in focus. It was dead center on the cross hairs. From the left, a third blip sneaked onto the screen. Mayhan was boxed.

It took only a second for the jump back into hyperspace. For a screaming instant everything whirlpooled as the autopilot countermanded Mayhan's order. Then the wrenching jump was complete, leaving Mayhan sopping with apprehensive sweat. No time to wonder what had caused the delay; whatever it was, it had thrown him and the Backers far out of contact.

Mayhan checked his position. He wasn't headed for Vega any more, that much was certain. With the data fed to him he set a course change, then committed it. Mayhan was less than one third of the way to Vega.

"So now we know the Backers don't need much time going into hyperspace," Mayhan said, feeding the data to the autopilot in triplicate. Satisfied that the repetitions ruled out the possibility of error, the *Pup* flashed a green eye to show that she was digesting this new information.

"It's pretty clear," Mayhan continued, "Vargas and the others were clobbered. I could jump back and forth all I wanted, but as long as I'm heading for Vega they can soon pick me up. If I wait, my fuel dribbles away while Backer reinforcements come up.

"So it's up to us," he said, fingering the throttle quadrant. "You and I, *Pup*. We're the last card, the whole card. We're the whole card," he chanted, "the whole chord, the lost chord, the last chord, the last card. Full circle." He shook his head dizzily. "Or almost the last. Maybe we have a last card of our own."

It seemed doubtful. For the first time in his life, Jesse Mayhan contemplated death. To cease living, to just quit being, was a thought that raged and tore and pounded in him. He controlled his ragged breathing, remembered to relax. His subconscious wasn't having any. Mayhan was poised between quietude and frenzy as he clasped and unclasped the throttle arm.

"O.K., let's talk it over," he croaked. A small crevice in his mind was jeering at him for collapsing under strain. He cleared his throat. "Temporarily we're O.K.

But there are at least three Backer ships snooping around nearby. We don't even have one lousy torpedo. I can't outdodge 'em, I can't outrun 'em. The next fix they get on us, we're as good as dead. Ain't that so?" He almost expected to get an answer.

"So. For all practical purposes I have no chance of outmaneuvering a Backer. But you have, *Pup*. Damn your titanium innards, if this were a simple Red Rover gambit you'd slaughter 'em. Every component in you is pretested for two hundred G's."

Mayhan's fingers hovered over the keyboard while he framed a useless query. "No you don't," he sneered, and withdrew his hands. "That's all you want now, isn't it, to tell me you could do it without me? But you need me, just like I need you, most of the time. When the going gets tough, you'd rather I skedaddled. Like taking a dive in the capsule, or—"

He snapped his mouth shut and stared at the screens. A Backer ship was coming up fast behind him, preparing its favorite trick of cutting in the fore jets and slowing down at fifty G's while incinerating its enemy. Very economical, thought Mayhan. But the trick in Red Rover is in not being where you're supposed to be, at the critical time. "And I figured it out without you," he told the ship archly. "Meier was right all the way down the line."

He crouched over the keyboard as far as his harness would allow, then set the steering jets for a tight clockwise turn. He left the ship at that setting and began feeding instructions to the *Pup* while the Backer ship, its radar obviously locked onto the *Pink Pup's* mass, howled in pursuit.

Mayhan saw that the Backers couldn't turn inside him, since the momentum change wasn't a straight linear type. If they could, a quick kill would have been easy. As it was, momentum tugged mightily at Mayhan, trying to wrench him from his one-handed grasp on the keyboard as he pecked, as if with aged palsy, at the keys with one finger. His sight was growing bleary. That's an early sign, he thought. The G-meter showed a trifle over six gravities, enough to black him out in just under five minutes. With a final lunge he struck the MESSAGE ENDS key and relaxed—too completely. He was thrown against the edge of his couch with a jarring smash.

A newly formed wrinkle in his all-purpose suit cut into Mayhan's back as he wriggled into position in the contoured couch. His vision was dimming, but still good enough for watching viewscreens.

This is a one-shot proposition, he thought dimly. Gotta be able to hit that EXECUTE key. Mayhan fought against the drowsiness and nausea imposed by minutes of bone-grinding acceleration. He had to wait until the Red Rover chain was complete.

Mayhan was fuzzily aware that if he blacked out completely, his suit would relay that information to the *Pink Pup*. Then the ship would stop its steering jets, the mad merry-go-round would stop—and the *Pup* would be atomized a moment later. He couldn't afford to let that happen, and refused to wonder why the Backers hadn't sent out a homing missile. Full realization that the Backers were only toying with him might have snapped Mayhan's reason.

It wasn't clear any more just why, but for some reason he had to stick with it.

A new blip came racing into the right-hand viewscreen, then, and Mayhan was instantly wide awake. He clawed frantically at the keyboard and shut his eyes, feeling his jaws creak in a spastic gritting of teeth.

What am I doing, he thought. I can't see the screens. He pried his eyes open and saw the second Backer ship accompanied by a third, coming in to make a neat kill. Mayhan stabbed down on the EXECUTE key, then dodged back into his couch as one hand groped for the *auf Wiedersehen* handle.

The *auf Wiedersehen* handle was, as it had always been, the pilot's best friend. No one in the Terran Federation fleet knew the exact origin of the name, but

the facts spoke for themselves: when all else failed, pull
the little handle—and *auf Wiedersehen*.

Q. E. D.

Mayhan, tissue-paper limp, was hauled tightly into
his couch by his harness webbing. The couch flipped
smartly backward and became half of a cylinder with
Mayhan inside. He never felt the jolt that catapulted
the escape capsule away from the *Pink Pup*.

The Backer ships paid no attention to the tiny mass
that drifted away at a tangent to their quarry's course.
They were used to it. Supercargo, chunks of the ship
itself or even escape capsules were of little importance.
The ship was the thing; without it, and with no hope of
friendly rescue, escape capsules were only a method of
prolonging the occupant's death. Later, the Backers
might cruise around to collect samples of jetsam. The
aliens had no doubt of their ability to stay with the
quarry; they were all locked onto the target, which
suited Mayhan just dandy.

Mayhan groggily moved a hand to massage his aching
neck, slightly amazed to find himself in working condition. The capsule gave no illusion of movement; its tiny
jets were silent. Outside somewhere, he knew that the
Pink Pup was having her fling at a singular game of Red
Rover.

At first he could see no sign of action in the void
beyond him. Then, peering back through a porthole, he
saw an incandescent flash light the other-dimensional
heavens. Mayhan knew that a ship had died. He knew
somehow that the *Pup* was still, spectacularly, alive.

Gleefully he reviewed his instructions to the *Pup's*
autopilot. EXECUTE RANDOM CHANGE OF
COURSE, he had typed. CONTINUE CHANGE OF
COURSE FOR TEN SECONDS. EXECUTE CHANGE
OF COURSE EXACTLY OPPOSING ORIGINAL
CHANGE OF COURSE AFTER TEN SECOND IN-
TERVAL. CONTINUE SAME OPPOSING CHANGES
OF COURSE AT TEN-SECOND INTERVALS UN-
TIL YOU ARE NO LONGER PURSUED. WHEN NO
LONGER PURSUED, PARALLEL COURSE AND

VELOCITY OF EMERGENCY PILOT'S RADIO SIGNAL SOURCE. DELAY ORIGINAL EXECUTION THREE SECONDS AFTER EXECUTION ORDER. EXECUTE ALL CHANGES OF COURSE AT ONE HUNDRED FIFTY GRAVITIES. MESSAGE ENDS.

Mayhan stopped laughing in mid-chuckle. "Random course change? *Random?* The *Pup* could've bashed into my capsule!" He giggled a little madly. "Well, obviously she didn't." A wink of flame caught his eye, a fiery line scrawled far ahead of the capsule. It was trailed by another flame. Then, like flashlight beams bent, they came nearer.

"Eight thousand, nine thousand, ten thousand," Mayhan muttered; then the flame bent again. The following ship tried an identical course change.

Fortunately. Mayhan grunted in satisfaction as the trailing flame was extinguished. He set his emergency radio on continuous call; he waited.

"We did it, ole dog," he hummed softly. "We broke the chain, we wrecked 'em, faked 'em out. We—" he watched a pinpoint of light as it became a thin line curving toward him. "Great space!"

Belatedly, Mayhan realized the implications of the orders he'd given the *Pup*. Execute all course changes at a hundred and fifty G's, he'd said. The *Pup* took him at his word.

In one instant, the flame passed behind his field of vision. In the next he was wildly urging the capsule's engines into action. He hadn't said how closely the ship should parallel his capsule, and suddenly understood what Colonel Meier had meant about good judgment. He could still become a cinder in God's eye with the *Pink Pup* decelerating so hard. The fore jets would be lancing a tongue of flame several miles ahead of the ship itself, and if the *Pup* elected to come in close— well, that was the stuff of which posthumous medals are made. Like a small boy urging his rocking horse on, Mayhan lunged against his harness. He had a mental picture of a barrel-sized gun muzzle aimed at the base of his skull.

The capsule was scarcely under gentle acceleration when a ravening light rebounded from the capsule's padded inner lining, blinding Mayhan for the moment. When his eyes refocused, the *Pink Pup* was making short spurts first with aft jets, then with fore jets, trying to keep pace with the capsule while making all course corrections at the stipulated hundred and fifty G's. Mayhan quickly shut off the capsule's power plant and the *Pink Pup* sidled up some quarter mile away.

Mayhan's eyes misted, though it could have been from the terrible glare of a moment before. Thoughtfully, he prepared his G-suit for deep space conditions and, feeling the suit linings expand, he jettisoned himself from the capsule. It took only a moment to detach the capsule power plant from its linkages. Then he steered himself with several miscalculations to the ship's air lock.

"One'll get you five," he said acidly as he crawled through the air lock, "if I'd steered the capsule closer you'd have shied away. I'm taking no chances."

Mayhan emerged into the cabin to find his equipment in some disorder. An errant chewing gum wrapper was firmly plastered to the aluminum air-lock frame. Mayhan had to scrape it off. One of the atmospheric pressure gauges had lost a pointer, which had burst from its glass cage and skewered a bulkhead.

Mayhan worked it loose, eventually. Every boxed component in sight seemed to sag tiredly; it appeared that everything was tested for two hundred G's but the shock mounts. Mayhan made a note of that one.

There were reams of notes to be taken but Mayhan busied himself with more pressing matters. "We won this 'un, *Pup*," he crooned, "and we're gonna keep going according to the rules."

A Vegan battle cruiser was the first to pick up Mayhan's IFF signal. It was a tribute to Federation Planning Center that an Identification, Friend-or-Foe system was in effect before the Backers brought the need of it; but jumpy Vegans weren't inclined to trust a signal coming from Backer areas.

Three ships were approaching, the IFF signal coming from the leader of the closely-spaced trio. They were obviously Backer ships, reasoned Intelligence officers, since no one but Backers could be approaching from Backer lines. They found that they were only sixty-seven per cent correct.

"All right," a nervous Terran captain found himself saying, some minutes later. "If you're who you say you are, how the devil did you manage to put two Backer ships in tow?"

Mayhan sighed gently, gesturing into the screen. "Going by the rules of the game, captain," he said. "I broke the chain, so I was naturally entitled to choose a pair."

The captain ran a hand across haunted eyes at the word, "naturally." "You must realize that we can blast you down at any time, lieutenant . . . if you are a lieutenant."

"But that wouldn't be quite fair, sir," Mayhan grinned. "We won."

The captain craned his neck into the screen as if to look around the edge of it. "We?"

"The *Pink Pup* and I," Mayhan explained maddeningly. "Our prizes may not be what you'd call the neatest in space, being decorated inside with eight-legged lumps of goo. But they're all ours," he chortled.

"You've got that mighty right," the captain growled. "These are the first enemy ships we've captured intact."

"Not quite intact, captain. These ships aren't built like mine is; their autopilots are torn half to pieces. I even had to crowd 'em up close to jump back out of hyperspace with 'em."

"That remains to be seen. You just keep your hands where I can see 'em, lieutenant. You're giving us the jitters."

"True," Mayhan admitted, "if interesting." He went on, more reasonably. "Captain, the only undesirable cargo I'm carrying is a bunch of Backers that couldn't take it. They were locked onto my ship, twiddling their tentacles in the happy thought that they could take any maneuver I could. I guess it never occurred to 'em that I might send in my autopilot for a substitute."

The unhappy captain turned away for a moment, conferring *sotto voce* with someone out of the screen's range. Mayhan waited, keeping his hands conspicuously before him.

"Your claims are partly true, at least," the captain said at last. "Our records show that there is a Lieutenant Jesse Mayhan on Di Cicco."

"Was," Mayhan corrected. "I'm here, now. And pretty tired. I left my couch back in hyperspace and I've been standing up most of the time since, under acceleration." He assumed his best haggard expression. "Me for a nice, soft bed."

There was another hurried consultation. Finally the captain shrugged into the screen. "My guess is that you're clean. Nobody—but *nobody*—could imitate a scatterbrained scout pilot this well. Stand by for a boarding party."

"You bet," Mayhan replied. "And captain, would you do me a favor?"

"What is it?"

"Roust out a tech to etch off the sign I put on my ship's nose."

"I suppose I can. You're one of those mental pygmies who names his gadgets, are you? Finally come to your senses?"

"In a way." Mayhan idly stroked the autopilot keyboard. I don't want to call her *Pink Pup* any more."

"Believe me, I'm grateful," said the intelligence officer dryly.

"No," Mayhan continued, "she grew up on this trip. Reached the age of reason, you might say. From now on, I'm calling her the *Red Rover*."

Dean Ing was an interceptor crew chief when he first sold to *Astouding Science Fiction* in 1954. Later he became a heavy construction worker, technical writer, racing driver, research engineer, and university professor. (As a car designer, he built his original Magnum, which "looks like a LeMans Lola coupe, weighs 1280 lbs, and is made of titanium, stainless, aluminum, and fiberglass," twenty years ago. Its oil, like the car, was compounded in his lab—and hasn't been changed in more than 13 years.)

Dean's first novel, *Soft Targets* (Ace), has already appeared at this writing; his second, *Anasazi*, will be an *Analog* serial in 1980; his third, *Systemic Shock*, is now being written. Two of his stories have been in Terry Carr's *Best SF of the Year* anthologies, and he has also twice been a Nebula and Hugo nominee.

He and his wife Gina (whose media work is heard on National Public Radio and stations KLCC and KUGN) live in Oregon with their two pre-teen daughters.

Dean Ing's story showed us one possible way in which men and robots/computers can complement each other in far-out future wars. It is a good introduction to this article by G. Harry Stine, for Stine examines every facet of the relationship, starting with the fundamental differences—and similarities—between the human/colloidal system and the far faster crystalline/computer systems.

His carefully reasoned view of how that relationship will develop in the future opens new perspectives and limitless new possibilities, not only for the conduct of war, but more importantly for the ways of peace.

G. Harry Stine

THE WIZARD WARRIORS: COMPUTERS AND ROBOTS IN WARFARE

Warfare is conducted by warriors using various types of weapon systems in a variety of environments. This definition holds true for all past, present, and future armed conflicts. The warriors have not changed over the years. They are Homo sapiens, Mark I, Mod O, and they will continue to be Homo sapiens, Mark I for many years to come. However, there may be different mods in the future.

A warrior is often considered to be an automatic piece on the gaming board of battle, an individual operator who carries out instructions from other warriors higher in the chain of command according to predetermined programs drilled into the individual warrior's memory. This is termed military discipline.

To most non-military people, military doctrine, training, and discipline appear to have no place for any display of individual action or volition. The orders given from above must be obeyed instantly, to the letter, and without variance. This is the non-military image of military discipline. Warriors are looked upon as preprogrammed automata. It is even a widely-held belief that military commanders really prefer that their subordinate warriors adhere closely to this bit of wishful thinking.

It is either wishful thinking or anti-war propaganda that portrays a warrior in this image. Military commanders and historians know full well that their warriors are human beings who are endowed with some survival instincts, less in some cultures than others.

Military commanders also know that their warriors possess the capability for self-adaptive action to meet unanticipated situations. Human warriors will disobey an order just as readily and as quickly as they will obey if they believe that they will not be held accountable for disobedience! They are, after all, human. If this were not the case, there would be no prisoners of war, and every warrior would fight to the death. "Hold at all costs!" would become a commonplace battlefield action rather than a heroic accomplishment of a very few brave warriors. Military discipline is often a transient thing. Sometimes, better disciplined troops will prevail. Fanatical, zealous, and psychologically trained warriors can achieve military miracles. But no commander and no historian can tell you what really went on in the minds of the troops of the Light Brigade or the pilots of the *Shikishima Kamikaze* once the final commitment had been made; would they or could they have backed out at the last moment? Some did.

All of these human intangibles and unpredictabilities make warfare a gigantic gamble. In the "haze of battle," the actions of warriors and the effectiveness of their weapons systems grow to have an increasing effect upon the outcome as the scope of the battle and the weapons systems elements—range, power, and accuracy—increase.

Military planners and commanders indeed wish to reduce the number of improbables and unpredictables. They also desire to increase the effectiveness of the individual warrior. Military history is a story of a growing number of extensions to human muscle power and brain power to accomplish this goal. The emergence of robots and computers in the conduct of warfare is quite recent, is still in the throes of evolutionary development, and shows strong indications of becoming an important area of military activity. But not in the manner in which robots and computers have been considered during the mid-20th Century.

It is possible to consider the robot as a surrogate warrior and the computer as a surrogate warrior brain.

These concepts merely substitute robots and computers for human warriors. They have proven themselves to be fallacious because of a misconception, a gross misunderstanding of both human beings and of computers/robots. One simple and highly controversial fact has been overlooked: some human beings like to fight, deliberately go looking for conflict, and *love* war. These people are *not* atavistic, barbarian imbeciles; some of them have been among the few super-geniuses produced by the human race. Why?

Our ancestors evolved as highly successful hunters. This heritage has left very powerful and subtle subconscious programs in every one of us. A hunter needs space to move around in and, in a world of scarcity, he needs to control his hunting area to insure that he will have enough to eat. He needs green growing things and animals around him. He needs a small group of intimate relatives and close friends with whom he reacts face to face and with whom he co-operates for survival. He needs to make decisions on his own because he has discovered that he cannot bring down his quarry unless he does so. His evolution as a hunter has prepared him for jobs that are at times dangerous and that, at all times, must sharpen his wits.

But we no longer must hunt our daily food; we nurture it, harvest it; and store it until we require it. We no longer face great animal adversaries every day, nor do we face other man-apes for the available food supply; we have eliminated our animal and man-ape competition so thoroughly that they are now extinct. We have only ourselves, and have had for nearly ten thousand years. We have therefore turned against one another to provide the demanding, interesting, dangerous, and deadly confrontations that our basic, eon-bred hunting heritage demands.

Many wars and conquests in human history have come about because the aggressors became *bored*. They went looking for excitement. To paraphrase Sir Winston Churchill, what can be more exhilarating than to be shot at and missed? And what can liven up a dull day more than the promise of loot? What can provide more excitement than the ability to rape and steal with license and without worrying about the consequences?

Warfare—past, present, and future—is a human activity, and it cannot be carried on in the absence of human beings.

In the period 1956–1966, military planners labored under the delusion that they had finally replaced the unreliable human being with computers and robots in warfare. This new, emerging technology offered high promise of replacing the human warrior. The modern cavalry of the clouds, the fighter aircraft, was tagged with the incredible sobriquet of a "manned missile." The intercontinental ballistic missile became "the ultimate weapon," the military planners not realizing that they had been working with the ultimate weapon, the human being, for millennia. In the warfare of the future, these planners maintained, adversaries would never see one another in an engagement. Wars would be fought with computers making lightning decisions and directing robot weapons that never missed their targets, and casualties would be reckoned in "megadeaths." These fallacies were rudely reined-up in Southeast Asia where rice farmers with no technological training but armed with the very high technology of the AK-47 assault rifle and the 60-millimeter mortar forced the retreat of a larger, better-equipped, highly automated, and computer planned army equipped with all the necessities for general war; the larger army had destroyed the field manuals that were sixty years old and that would have told them how to fight such a war.

If future warfare is not to be the automated, robotized, computerized, push-button, planet-busting conflict whose reality was attempted and failed, what is the role of robots and computers in future warfare? For that matter, what is the role of the human warrior in future wars of any kind?

Robots and computers will not replace human beings; this we now know. Warfare will be conducted by human beings with the *assistance* of robots and computers supplementing and amplifying the human warrior and, in some instances, helping the human warrior overcome some of his own shortcomings brought about by having to fight in new and different environments . . . such as space.

To gain an insight on how this is likely to evolve, one must consider that there are two basic types of systems involved: (a) the human being who can be considered to be a colloidal system, and (b) the computer/robot which is a crystalline system. The characteristics of both systems are different. And both systems, because of the differences in their characteristics, can complement one another.

The colloidal system can operate only within very limited temperature and pressure ranges. The system is basically chemical or molecular in its nature, requiring the transmission of ions and the energy transfer derived from chemical changes on a molecular level. The colloidal system seems to be very complex because we do not fully understand it yet; biochemistry is a very young and emerging science. The colloidal system is also very slow, having response times measured in milliseconds. It compensates for the slow response time by operating in a multi-channel mode of great complexity and redundancy. Because of this multiplexing redundancy, the colloidal system can also be very adaptive and can carry out a surprisingly large number of simultaneous operations with a very large amount of feedback. The most highly evolved colloidal system is the human being. The human being has a very large memory and occasionally exhibits the ability to make novel correlations between memory matrices; in short, the human being is creative.

One cannot say for certain at the time of this writing whether or not crystalline systems are capable of creativity nor even whether or not advanced crystalline systems are self-aware as advanced colloidal systems are. There are serious attempts under way to investigate this at such places as the Artificial Intelligence Laboratories at the Massachusetts Institute of Technology. The questions of creativity and self-awareness may not be answerable until we have determined what "intelligence" is. Be that as it may, and intelligent or not, crystalline systems are causing a major revolution today in the everyday life of colloidal systems such as ourselves as well as in military affairs.

Crystalline systems are very fast, are amenable to rapid and easy reprogramming, operate within much the same limited ranges of temperature and pressure as colloidal systems, and operate on a different level than colloidals. The mode of operation is on the atomic level wherein electrons move within crystal lattices. The state of the art is rapidly approaching the point where the movement of a single electron will constitute a signal. Crystalline systems are capable of handling a very large number of variables and performing many correlations in a short period of time using what is essentially linear, single-channel logic. They appear to be able to do this much better than colloidal systems only because crystalline systems operate more than one billion times faster than colloidal systems. This difference in reaction time is a result of operational modes, the relaxation times and transit times of atomic versus molecular mechanisms.

So much for the generalized and impersonally-worded backgrounds and definitions which are nonetheless necessary if we are to understand what we are really dealing with. We do indeed have two highly different systems here, and neither one is completely capable of replacing the other. Given the strongpoints and shortcomings of both systems, the scientist and the military planner would logically like to use the colloidal systems with which he and his predecessors have been working since prehistoric times and pair-off the colloidal systems with the crystalline systems to get the very best from both. In short, we would like to attain the optimum human-machine interface.

This matching and pairing appears to be the trend of the future rather than total dependence upon either human warriors or their robot/computer counterparts.

It is indeed a trend because it started many years ago and continues today, even in the aftermath and reaction to the purely mechanistic military concepts of a few years ago.

Although many might claim that the legendary Trojan Horse was the first military robot, it was simply camouflage. The first computer used in warfare was probably the gunner's quadrant used to accurately determine the elevation angle of a gun barrel. The first real military robot was probably the British tank of World War I, although it was directed internally by humans rather than by a computer. World War II—or the second phase of the Modern Thirty Years War—saw accelerated development of both computer and robot extensions of the capabilities of human warriors. The famous Norden bombsight is a case in point, being an analog computer and gyro-stabilized platform coupled to the bomber's auto-pilot so that it would compute the bomb release point; the bombardier pressed the pickle switch to command "bombs away!" World War II also saw the first use of the so-called "smart bombs," which are not very smart at all; a warrior must designate the target and give the signal, "Go get 'em!" The bomb just follows orders in typical robotic fashion.

The earlier trend to take the human warrior "out of the loop" and let the robot/computer run itself proved ineffective, as we pointed out above. Any industrial engineer could have predicted the consequences because he knows from long, hard experience that any machine having any degree of automation will, when left to itself for a period of time, tear itself to pieces in spite of automatic stops and guard circuits. As the industrial engineer will confirm, it is very difficult to determine in advance every possible failure mode and to construct reliable guard circuits against all these modes. It's easier to put a man in the loop.

It is also standard industrial practice never to fully automate any system or process until one understands it and can measure and control all the variables involved. One automates a process in evolutionary steps, always keeping a human being in the loop. As the "state of the art" (engineers flatly acknowledge with this statement that they are practitioners of an arcane art rather than a solid science) progresses and the system or process becomes understood, the human in the loop is moved to higher and higher positions in the system. But the human supervisor always stays in the loop.

In spite of the recent and short-lived fads, military systems planners and designers are now doing exactly the same thing. The combination of the human colloidal system with the robot/computer crystalline system appears to create a very effective supersystem if the advantages and disadvantages of each are properly integrated into the supersystem.

But a major problem faces us in linking the colloidal system with the crystalline system:

The human colloidal system is at best a billion times slower than the crystalline system!

The human colloidal system operates in milliseconds (10^3 seconds or 0.001 seconds) while the modern computer or crystalline system operates in picoseconds (10^2 seconds or 0.000000000001 seconds). The nine orders of magnitude difference between the response time represents a very difficult problem in achieving a proper human-machine interface.

From the computer's point of view during such an interface, communicating with a human being involves displaying an output or sending a message, then waiting more than *six years* for a reply! If said computer possessed emotions, during such a human-machine interface it would probably become exceedingly bored. In human terms, it's like trying to communicate by radio with someone on Barnard's Star.

Keyboard inputs are terribly slow from the computer viewpoint, and so are voice-actuated programming circuits. Even the fastest computer print-outs and displays require the computer equivalent of years to activate.

The nine orders of magnitude response time difference has two possible approaches: (a) speed up the human colloidal system, and/or (b) slow down the computer crystalline system. Because of the multi-channel characteristics of the colloidal system, it may be possible to achieve one to two orders of magnitude speed-up through proper training or by additional understanding of human thought processes. We may actually "think" faster than the simple measurements of neurone response and relaxation times indicate. Psychological time is a very tricky concept right now because we know that it exists but know very little about it. The real promise in psychedelic drugs may lie in providing us with a key to this understanding; the oriental shaman may have discovered the methodology of psychological time control ages ago. This area is utterly ripe for serious investigation in lieu of highs, trips, and all of the mysticism of oriental religions and philosophies.

Slowing down the computer's crystalline modes is not that difficult; engineers have spent several decades speeding them up. After all, the crystalline system doesn't have to report on everything that it is doing any more than our own autonomic nervous systems continually report heartbeat to our consciousness. That portion of a crystalline system that interfaces with the human colloidal system will be the "slow poke" or idiot of the crystalline system's universe.

It is assumed that we will be able to achieve direct linkage between the colloidal and crystalline systems, between the human nervous system and the circuits of a computer. This is because it has already happened in proof-of-principle laboratory situations. Computers and electronic circuits have directly linked with the human nervous system in both directions. The crystalline system has transmitted to the colloidal system, and the colloidal system has transmitted to the crystalline system. Most of this has not been reported.

On July 24, 1962, I witnessed a proof-of-principle demonstration of a direct linkage of an electronic circuit to my own nervous system that permitted the electronic system to transmit information directly to me. A teen-aged gadgeteer named G. Patrick Flanagan of Bellaire, Texas had stumbled upon a technique of introducing audio information into the human nervous system without a direct connection between the two systems. Flanagan's "neurophone" utilized a 35 kilohertz oscillator amplitude-modulated by audio signals. The output of the oscillator was fed through TV twin-lead to two insulated rubber pads scrounged from a "relaxicizor." The pads contained a sandwich of a metal mesh insulated by two rubber discs. It was possible to place one pad on your spine and the other on the sole of your foot, for example. The moment that contact was made, you could hear the audio signal in perfect hi-fi! Flanagan had succeeded in accomplishing what other investigators such as Dr. Henry Puharich had been working on for years. I subsequently became project manager to investigate the Flanagan neurophone as a possible new product for a small industrial firm. In a series of long and complex experiments, we showed conclusively that the transmission of the audio information to the human nervous system was not being accomplished by bone conduction or by skin conduction of the audio signals to the inner ear. No matter where the two neurophone pads were placed, one always "heard" the audio signal in one's head. Later investigations by Dr. Wayne Batteau of Tufts University proved that the neurophone was indeed activating the human nervous system directly and that the audio information was not being picked up by the ear or by the auditory nerve. In fact, Dr. Batteau succeeded in restoring "hearing" to a person who had become nerve-deaf; it required nearly an hour before the nerve-deaf subject using the neurophone began to "hear" again. His brain had "forgotten" how to hear during years of nerve deafness.

Somehow, in a manner not yet fully understood, the Flanagan neurophone coupled electronic circuitry directly to the human nervous system. When audio information is presented to the nervous system *anywhere,* the nervous system sends the signals to the brain where the brain apparently recognizes the audio information as audio information and proceeds to switch the signals into the appropriate area of the cortex.

Dr. Batteau proceeded to have a massive myocardial infarction whilst diving with dolphins off Hawaii in 1965, and Flanagan became involved in cults and oriental mysticism shortly thereafter. The neurophone lies fallow as of this writing. [Editor's note: It is now, March 1980, being manufactured by Dr. Flanagan. See "The Alternate View," *Analog*, Feb. 1980]

If direct connection between crystalline systems and colloidal systems can be achieved for audio information—and I will personally attest to the fact that it can—then other sensory data and information can be transmitted as well. This can be done with no direct physical hook-up or wiring-up of the crystalline system to the colloidal system. A computer can "talk" directly to a human being, provided it "speaks" a language that the human being's nervous system understands.

Achieving linking from human nervous system to computer is also on the road to being solved today.

In their annual report for 1978 to Congress, the Defense Advanced Research Projects Agency (DARPA) reported significant progress in what they termed "biocybernetics." DARPA researchers have succeeded in extracting useful information from human electroencephalograms (EEG) and "other non-verbal signals," to use their deliberately vague terminology. Utilizing a crystalline computer's great speed, they have been able to analyze the component waveforms of an EEG and can now differentiate between the EEG signals for cognitive or thinking processes and for non-cognitive motor responses or signals to the muscles. The computer then measures both the workload signals and the cognitive load signals to assess the human's spare brain capacity on a moment-to-moment basis without interfering with the human's performance of the task.

DARPA also claims to have a new technique for computer identification and measurement of EEG waveform components associated with decision-making and with action. They can now tell from this computer analysis whether or not the human being believes he has made the correct choice or has taken the proper action. If the decision-making EEG component ends before the action component, the probability of the human's action being correct is very high. If the decision-making component ends *after* the action component ceases, however, the probability of the human having made an error is very high. In other words, a crystalline computer can now check on human actions and advise the human that he has probably made a mistake. A computer can now measure human doubt! Following up on this train of logic, a computer can advise a human to reconsider his choice or his action.

Here, then, is the beginning of the human-to-computer linkage, the colloidal to the crystalline system interface.

The EEG has been a common neurological diagnostic tool for decades. There are many known components and waveforms to an EEG. Various states of conciousness and some of the more powerful emotions have been correlated with various changes in EEG frequencies and waveforms. But most of this work to date has been done in the very low frequency area up to perhaps one kilohertz maximum, this being the upper limit of the frequency response of most pen-and-paper chart recorders associated with the EEG system. Modern electronics does not impose such limitations on frequency response, however. It is now possible to investigate the human EEG components out to frequencies of several megahertz, if desired. No one knows—or no one is telling—what might be found out at these frequencies. True, the colloidal system works up to about a kilohertz for its basic components, but the system is multichannelled with many signals in transit at any given instant. A low frequency response picks out only the gross effects of this, while investigations at higher frequencies could possibly separate some of the thousands of simultaneous messages in transit. For example, human hearing normally extends out to a frequency of 15,000 hertz; how is it possible for a communications system to handle this with a basic component reaction and relaxation time of a millisecond, equivalent to a frequency limit of 1000 hertz?

The early work is under way. Humans with their colloidal systems will be communicating directly back and forth with computers and robots with their crystalline systems in less time than many suspect. Barring some unforeseen circumstances, the results should be in well before the turn of the century, and we will then have some help in the form of intelligence we have created ourselves. We will have achieved the "intelligence amplifier" in which a human being is coupled to a computer and uses the computer to expand his own thinking and action processes.

This probably means that the wizard warrior of the future will not be the legendary six-million-dollar bionic man, but an ordinary human being trained to use the direct-link computer and robot input-output devices that he puts on and takes off at will. The wizard warrior will not be a cyborg because we have deliberately not taken that route historically. To achieve flight in the air, we did not give people feathered wings; we created devices, tools, mechanisms that Homo sapiens Mark I Mod O could get into and get out of at will and yet would permit the human to fly around the world or to the planets and back.

The future also holds the technology to permit the cyborg and the bionic human, but we may not wish to go this route. Researchers are perfecting the powered prosthesis whose movements are actuated by nerve impulses, and the development of these devices is a logical consequence of our ability to build and use waldoes. But let us carry this train of thought to its logical conclusion. It may well be within the capabilities of medical technology within a few decades to remove a living brain from a body and to keep the brain functioning *in vitro*. But is the brain the entire human nervous system? How about the spinal cord and the rest of the central nervous system? Where is the true center of intelligence? And is the brain really the location of the ego? We do not know. But we do know that a normal, healthy, sane person with no nervous disorders will become insane if placed in an environment of total sensory deprivation. A disembodied brain is in an environment of total sensory deprivation. Will said brain long remain sane? How do we provide the inputs from the crystalline computers to keep it sane?

With the exception of the mechanical and biological replication of human beings, robots are not beyond forecastable technology. However, a true humanoid robot warrior is not impossible, just exceedingly difficult. In time, engineers may be able to build a humanoid robot that can serve as a warrior. This humanoid robot would have to do a number of different things, including swim a river while keeping his M-16 rifle dry above his head, then scale a hundred-foot cliff on the other side of the river, then crawl across a clearing on his belly, run through dense woods, shoot a sniper out of cover in a tree, throw two grenades, dig a foxhole, and then defend his position against the enemy. While it is possible to build a mechanical humanoid that could do all this and more, we know of no way to power it. There are no batteries that would provide the required energy in a size small enough to do all of the above acts.

The more reasonable forecast for robots in the future of warfare includes both waldoes and direct human interface with various types of weapons systems.

The term "waldo" comes directly from the first published description of the device, Robert A. Heinlein's "Waldo" published in the August 1942 issue of *Astounding Science Fiction* magazine. A waldo is a human actuated remote manipulator. While Heinlein was writing about the device, real ones were being developed for the purpose of handling radioactive materials. Waldoes are powered extensions of human muscles and joints. They can be made very much larger and very much smaller than their human counterparts.

Two major problems exist with remote manipulators.

The first of these involves copying evolution. Human anatomy has evolved over a very long period of time and exhibits some outstanding engineering. The human wrist joint is an example. A human being can bend his wrist so that his hand is at right angles to his forearm. He can then move every one of his five fingers independently through that right angle. Furthermore, he can rotate the wrist joint 180-degrees or more while still retaining individual control over the movement of each finger. The muscles for accomplishing this are located in the forearm, including the muscles that activate each joint in each finger. The wrist joint is a mass of tendons to carry muscle power through the joint and out to each individual finger joint.

No other animal on Earth possesses this wrist joint capability, and this capability is even more important to a human being's ability to use tools than his opposing thumb. It is an engineering nightmare to try duplicating the human wrist joint because it is complex. It can be done, but it is difficult.

The Spare Parts Department of the medical profession is beginning to make some headway in this area by developing powered prosthesis limbs.

The second humanoid robot problem is the requirement for a very large number of communications channels required to activate a waldo and to provide its operator with the necessary feedback to insure the waldo is doing what the operator commands. In essence, an engineer must duplicate the nervous system of the human prototype. Fortunately, the designer can use the high speed and other characteristics of the crystalline system rather than the multi-channel approach of the colloidal system to accomplish this.

Fontunately, too, a robot does not have to look like a human being, nor does it have to perform all the actions that a human is capable of. A robot can be pared down to the absolutely required necessities, and it can be designed to perform a specific task. The power steering system of an automobile is a crude, primitive, but understandable example. Power steering requires an actuator that is moved by a human being or by computer signals, an action follower that faithfully and accurately duplicates the activity commanded by the actuator in a timely fashion, and a feedback circuit to inform the human or the computer that the follower is indeed following, how well it is following, and how quickly it is following.

Utilizing these basic principles, robot-like systems have already been developed for use by warriors, and they will continue to be developed and improved for warriors of the future. The future robots will be extensions of a warrior's capabilities in terms of providing him with greater strength, faster reactions, greater accuracy, and remoteness from the actual scene of the battle. Robots can take the form of Heinlein's powered fighting suit described in great detail in his book, *Starship Troopers*. Robots of this type can literally turn an ordinary human being into a superman, able to leap tall buildings at a single bound, etc.

There is an outside chance, however, that future technology will bring to fruition and practicality the biological robot rather than the mechanical one. The cyborg was the favorite bio-robot of the 1960's and led to the concept of the six-million-dollar man, a human whose damaged or lost limbs and organs had been replaced with biological and mechanical counterparts of greater strength, speed, and stamina. A cyborg requires a great deal of individual attention to a single human, however; this bothers production engineers who espouse mass production techniques. Therefore, the current vogue is the cloned human. A clone is an organism that has been mass-produced from the basic genetic material of the prototype to create a multitude of identical organisms. Cloning has been accomplished with amphibians. At the time of this writing, the reports of cloning human beings are yet to be verified. But if it can be done for amphibians, cloning will certainly some day be done for human beings. Cloning a warrior to produce an army holds great fascination for military planners. If one could start with a hero, a winner of the Congressional Medal of Honor, the Victoria Cross, the Croix de Guerre, the Order of Lenin, etc. and duplicate him by the thousands. . . .

The ultimate biological robot derives from the original use of the term. The word "robot" is the slavic Czech word for "worker." It was first used in its present sense by the Czech writer, Karel Capek, in 1923 in the stage play *R.U.R.* which stood for "Rossum's Universal Robots." A Rossum Universal Robot was made from "a substance that behaves exactly like living matter although its chemical composition is different." The fictional scientist Rossum developed a totally new biochemistry which permitted him to create artificial people. The robots from *R.U.R.* could be designed and built for specialized jobs, including warfare. The concepts put forth in this landmark stage play may yet come about as the ultimate consequence of recombinant DNA research. *R.U.R.* may well be on its way to becoming another fiction story brought to reality by scientific and technical progress because, when *R.U.R.* was written, no one had the slightest idea of the technology and could not even forecast it. Less than sixty years later, we can begin to see how it might be accomplished and could, if we wished, begin research work toward the goal of creating humanoid biological robots. The forecasts of future mechanical robots may turn out to be as quaint and dated to our grandchildren as the 19th Century concepts of aircraft seem to us today.

Will human beings eventually fight robots and computers in some future war? Perhaps. There have been many references in science fiction to "genetic wars" and "clone wars." If it does happen, I will be willing to bet that the humans win the war. Reason: robots will probably be specialized, while a human being is unspecialized. As was remarked earlier, it is a common layman's fallacy that military commanders would prefer mindless robots as their warriors; they would really like to have unspecialized troops who could handle any and every military task. Military commanders have been forced to demand specialization among their warriors; this does not mean that the commanders like specialization.

It is most certainly going to be possible in the future to create a warrior robot that will be a one-to-one stand-in for a human warrior. But making that robot will not be as much fun as making the human one.

Many years ago in the early days of guided missiles and space vehicles, there was a sign that hung on the wall of the guidance laboratory at the U.S. Army's White Sands Proving Ground in New Mexico. It said:

"Man is not as good as a little black box for certain specific things. However, he is flexible and much more reliable. He is easily maintained and can be manufactured by relatively unskilled labor."

Warfare was, is, and will continue to be a human activity. Machines do not fight. Computers do not fight. Only human beings fight one another. Unless the basic characteristics of human beings change, they will continue to fight one another. Future war will see the continuance of the trends of today. Among these trends is the development of robots and computers, the crystalline systems, to assist and complement the colloidal systems of human beings. This growing interface between crystalline and colloidal systems is not a true symbiosis for the colloidal systems can survive without the crystalline systems. The crystalline systems will continue to be the servants of the colloidal systems of humans.

Slaves have been used in warfare for eons. Robots and computers are the new slaves, replacing human slaves because of increased power, strength, accuracy, range, and response time. Robots and computers can also be considered as technically advanced tools. They will be used, in both war and peace, to extend and expand both the intelligence and physical capabilities of human beings.

And perhaps, because of this, they may eventually change human nature to the point where humans no longer fight among themselves. But don't count on it happening next week. And don't count on the human race expanding through the galaxy without encountering another species as mean and nasty as we are. If that does happen, we will need all the help we can get from our robots and computers.

G. Harry Stine is a science-fact and science-fiction writer. He is also an engineer, a high-technology marketing consultant, and one of the founders of the concept of space industrialization. (His book, *The Third Industrial Revolution*, published in 1975, remains the definitive work on the subject.)

Harry Stine received his B.A. in physics from Colorado College in 1952 and immediately went to work on rockets at White Sands Proving Ground. He was one of the first futurists, working for an aerospace company on future space programs as early as 1957, before the launch of Sputnik-I; and on the Tenth Anniversary of the launching of Explorer-I, the first U.S. satellite, he was awarded a silver medal as one of fifty American space pioneers by the Association of the United States Army.

Because of his early association with this nation's military rocket program, he has written about the military implications of space for nearly a quarter of a century. He is a fellow of the Explorers Club and the British Interplanetary Society, and Associate Fellow of the American Institute of Aeronautics and Astronautics, and a member of the New York Academy of Sciences. He has published more than twenty books on science and technology, including three sf novels. His science fiction appears under the pen name of "Lee Correy."

In the popular imagination, the computer, the robot, the semi-sentient machine is almost always—except when it is deliberately made cute and cuddly (like Star Wars' R2D2)—shown as something cold, unhuman and inhuman, without human graces and human failings.

Yet can any device conceived and built by men escape sharing, at least in some degree, man's humanity? If such devices can caricature man, if they can exaggerate his least pleasant traits, may they not conceivably also reflect his better qualities and higher aspirations?

Even if they happen to be war machines?

Keith Laumer

FIELD TEST

A SHORT HISTORY OF
THE BOLO FIGHTING MACHINES

The first appearance in history of the concept of the
armored vehicle was the use of wooden-shielded war
wagons by the reformer John Huss in Bohemia, in the
Fifteenth Century. Thereafter, the idea lapsed—unless
one wishes to consider the armored knights of the Middle Ages, mounted on armored war-horses—until the
Twentieth Century. In 1915, during the Great War, the
British developed in secrecy a steel-armored motor car
(called a "tank" for security reasons during construction—
and the appellation remained in use for the rest of the
century). First sent into action at the Somme in AD
1916 (BAE 29), the new device was immensely impressive and was soon copied by all belligerents. By the
time of Phase Two of the Great War, AD 1939–1945,
tank corps were a basic element in all modern armies.
Quite naturally, great improvements were soon made
over the original clumsy, fragile, feeble, and tempera-
mental tank. The British Sheridan and Centurion, the
German Tiger, the US Sherman and the Russian T-34,
were all highly potent weapons in their own milieu.

During the long period of cold war following 1945
AD, development continued, especially in the US. By
1989, the direct ancestor of the Bolo line had been
constructed by the Bolo Division of General Motors.
This machine, almost twice the weight of its Phase Two
predecessors at 150 tons, was designated the Bolo Mark

I, Model B. No Bolo Model A of any mark ever existed, since it was felt that the then-contemporary Ford Motor Company had pre-empted that designation permanently. The same is true of Model T.

The Mark I was essentially a bigger and better conventional tank, carrying a crew of three, and via power-assisted servos, completely manually operated, with the exception of the capability to perform a number of pre-set routine functions such as patrol duty with no crew aboard. The following Mark II of 1995 was even more highly automated, carrying an on-board fire control computer and requiring only a single operator. The Mark III of 2020 was considered by some to be almost a step backward, its highly complex controls normally requiring a crew of two, though in an emergency a single experienced man could fight the machine with limited effectiveness. These were by no means negligible weapons systems, their individual fire-power exceeding that of a contemporary battalion of heavy infantry, while they were of course correspondingly heavily armored and shielded. The outer durachrome war-hull of the Mark III was twenty millimeters in thickness and capable of withstanding any offensive weapon then known, short of a contact nuclear blast.

The first completely automated Bolo, designed to operate normally without a man aboard, was the landmark Mark XV, Model M, originally dubbed *Resartus* for obscure reasons, but later officially named *Stupendous*. This model, first commissioned in the Twenty-fifth Century, was widely used throughout the Eastern Arm during the Era of Expansion, and remained in service on remote worlds for over two centuries, acquiring many improvements in detail along the way, while remaining basically unchanged, though increasing sophistication of circuitry and weapons vastly upgraded its effectiveness. The Bolo *Horrendous,* Model R, of 2807 was the culmination of this phase of Bolo development, though older models lingered on in the active service of minor powers for centuries.

Thereafter, the development of the Mark XVI-XIX

consisted largely in further refinement and improvement in detail of the Mark XV. Provision continued to be made for a human occupant, now as a passenger rather than an operator, usually an officer who wished to observe the action at first hand. Of course these machines normally went into action under the guidance of individually prepared computer programs, while military regulations continued to require installation of devices for halting or even self-destructing the machine at any time. This latter feature was intended mainly to prevent capture and hostile use of the great machine by an enemy. It was at this time that the first-line Bolos in Terran service were organized into a brigade, known as the Dinochrome Brigade, and deployed as a strategic unit. Tactically, the regiment was the basic Bolo unit.

The always-present though perhaps unlikely possibility of capture and use of a Bolo by an enemy was a constant source of anxiety to military leaders and in time gave rise to the next and final major advance in Bolo technology: the self-directing (and quite incidentally self-aware) Mark XX, Model B Bolo *Tremendous*. At this time it was customary to designate each individual unit by a three-letter group indicating hull-style, power unit and main armament. This gave rise to the custom of forming a nickname from the letters, such as Johnny from JNY, adding to the tendency to anthropomorphize the great fighting machine.

The Mark XX was at first greeted with little enthusiasm by the High Command, who now professed to believe that an unguided-by-operator Bolo would potentially be capable of running amok and wreaking destruction on its owners. Many observers have speculated by hindsight that a more candid objection would have been that the legitimate area of command function was about to be invaded by mere machinery. Machinery the Bolos were, but never *mere*.

At one time an effort was made to convert a number of surplus Bolos to peace-time use, by such modifications as the addition of a soil-moving blade to a Mark XII Bolo WV/I Continental Siege Unit, and installation of seats for four men, and referring to the resulting irre-sistible force as a tractor. This idea came to naught, however, since the machines retained their half-megaton/second firepower and were never widely accepted as normal agricultural equipment.

As the great conflict of the Post-Thirtieth-Century Era variously known as the Last War and, later, the Lost War wore on, Bolos of Mark XXVIII and later series were organized into independently operating bri-gades, now doing their own strategic, as well as tactical, planning. Many of these machines still exist in func-tional condition in out-of-the-way corners of the former Terran Empire. At this time the program of locating and neutralizing these ancient weapons continues.

1

.07 seconds have now elapsed since my general aware-ness circuit was activated at a level of low alert. Through-out this entire period I have been uneasy, since this procedure is clearly not in accordance with the theo-retical optimum activation schedule.

In addition, the quality of a part of my data-input is disturbing. For example, it appears obvious that Prince Eugene of Savoy erred in not more promptly commit-ting his reserve cavalry in support of Marlborough's right at Blenheim. In addition, I compute that Ney's employment of his artillery throughout the Peninsular campaign was sub-optimal. I have detected many thou-sands of such anomalies. However, data-input activates my pleasure center in a most satisfying manner. So long as the input continues without interruption, I shall not feel the need to file a VSR on the matter. Later, no doubt, my Command unit will explain these seeming oddities. As for the present disturbing circumstances, I compute that within 28,922.9 seconds at most, I will receive additional Current Situation input which will enable me to assess the status correctly. I also antici-pate that full Stand-by Alert activation is imminent.

2

This statement not for publication.

When I designed the new psychodynamic attention circuit, I concede that I did not anticipate the whole new level of intra-cybernetic function that has arisen—the manifestation of which, I am assuming, has been the cause of the unit's seemingly spontaneous adoption of the personal pronoun in its situation reports—the "self-awareness" capability, as the sensational press chooses to call it. But I see no cause for the alarm expressed by those high-level military officers who have irresponsibly characterized the new Bolo Mark XX, Model B as a potential rampaging juggernaut, which, once fully activated and dispatched to the field, unrestrained by continuous external control, may turn on its makers and lay waste the continent. This is all fantasy, of course. The Mark XX, for all its awesome firepower and virtually invulnerable armor and shielding, is governed by its circuitry as completely as man is governed by his nervous system—but that is perhaps a dangerous analogy, which would be pounced on at once if I were so incautious as to permit it to be quoted.

In my opinion, the reluctance of the High Command to authorize full activation and field-testing of the new Bolo is based more on a fear of technological obsolescence of the High Command than on specious predictions of potential run-away destruction. This is a serious impediment to the national defense at a time when we must recognize the growing threat posed by the expansionist philosophy of the so-called People's Republic. After four decades of saber-rattling, there is no doubt that they are even now preparing for a massive attack. The Bolo Mark XX is the only weapon in our armory potentially capable of confronting the enemy's hundred ton Yavacs. For the moment, thanks to the new "selfawareness" circuitry, we hold the technological advantage, an advantage we may very well lose unless we place this new weapon on active service without delay.

s/Sigmund Chin, PhD

3

I'm not wearing six stars so that a crowd of professors can dictate military policy to me. What's at stake here is more than just a question of budget and logistics: it's a purely military decision. The proposal to release this robot Frankenstein monster to operate on its own initiative, just to see if their theories check out, is irresponsible to say the least—treasonable at worst. So long as I am Chief of Combined Staff, I will not authorize this so-called field test. Consider, gentlemen: you're all familiar with the firepower and defensive capabilities of the old stand-by Mark XV. We've fought our way across the lights with them—with properly qualified military officers as Battle Controllers, with the ability to switch off or, if need be, self-destruct any unit at any moment. Now these ivory tower chaps—mind you, I don't suggest they're not qualified in their own fields—these civilians come up with the idea of eliminating the Battle Controllers and releasing even greater fire-power to the discretion, if I may call it that, of a machine. Gentlemen, machines aren't people; your own ground-car can roll back and crush you if the brakes happen to fail. Your own gun will kill you as easily as your enemy's. Suppose I should agree to this field test, and this engine of destruction is transported to a waste area, activated unrestrained and aimed at some sort of mock-up hot obstacle course. Presumably, it would obediently advance, as a good soldier should—I concede that the data blocks controlling the thing have been correctly programmed in accordance with the schedule prepared under contract, supervised by the Joint Chiefs and myself. Then, gentlemen, let us carry this supposition one step farther: suppose, quite by accident, by unlikely coincidence if you will, the machine should encounter some obstacle which had the effect of deflecting this one hundred and fifty ton dreadnaught from its intended course, so that it came blundering toward the perimeter of the test area. The machine is programmed to fight and destroy all opposition. It appears obvious that any attempts on our part to interfere with its free movement, to interpose obstacles in its path, if need be to destroy it, would be interpreted as hostile—as indeed they would be. I leave it to you to picture the result. No, we must devise another method of determining the usefulness of this new development. As you know, I have recommended conducting any such test on our major satellite, where no harm can be done—or at least a great deal less harm. Unfortunately, I am informed by Admiral Hayle that the Space Arm does not at this time have available equipment with such transport capability. Perhaps the admiral also shares to a degree my own distrust of a killer machine not susceptible to normal command function. Were I in the admiral's position, I, too, would refuse to consider placing my command at the mercy of a mechanical caprice—or an electronic one. Gentlemen, we must remain masters of our own creations. That's all. Good day.

4

All right, men. You've asked me for a statement; here it is: the next war will begin with a two-pronged over-the-pole land and air attack on the North Power Complex by the People's Republic. An attack on the Concordiat, I should say, though Cold City and the Complex is the probable specific target of the first sneak thrust. No, I'm not using a crystal ball; it's tactically obvious. And I intend to dispose my forces accordingly. I'm sure we all recognize that we're in a posture of gross unpreparedness. The PR has been openly announcing its intention to fulfill its destiny, as their demagogues say, by imposing their rule on the entire planet. We've pretended we didn't hear. Now it's time to stop pretending. The forces at my disposal are totally inadequate to halt a determined thrust—and you can be sure the enemy has prepared well during the last thirty years of cold peace. Still, I have sufficient armor to establish what will be no more than a skirmish line across the enemy's route of advance. We'll do what we can before they roll over us. With luck we may be able to divert them from the Grand Crevasse route into Cold City. If so, we may be able to avoid the necessity for evacuating the city. No questions, please.

5
NORTHERN METROPOLIS
THREATENED

In an informal statement released today by the Council's press office, it was revealed that plans are already under preparation for a massive evacuation of civilian population from West Continent's northernmost city. It was implied that an armed attack on the city by an Eastern power is imminent. General Bates has stated that he is prepared to employ "all measures at his disposal" to preclude the necessity for evacuation, but that the possibility must be faced. The Council Spokesman added that in the event of emergency evacuation of the city's five million persons, losses due to exposure and hardship will probably exceed five percent, mostly women, children, and the sick or aged. There is some speculation as to the significance of the general's statement regarding "all means at his disposal."

6

I built the dang thing, and it scares *me*. I come in here in the lab garage about an hour ago, just before dark, and seen it setting there, just about fills up the #1 garage, and *it's* a hundred foot long and fifty foot high. First time it hit me: I wonder what it's thinking about. Kind of scares me to think about a thing that big with that kind of armor and all them repeaters and Hellbores and them computers and a quarter-sun fission plant in her—planning what to do next. I know all about the Command Override Circuit and all that, supposed to stop her dead any time they want to take over onto override—heck, I wired it up myself. You might be surprised, thinking I'm just a grease-monkey and all—but I got a High Honors degree in Psychotronics. I just like the work, is all. But like I said, it scares me. I hear old Doc Chin wants to turn her loose and see what

happens, but so far General Margrave's stopped him
cold. But young General Bates was down today, asking
me all about firepower and shielding, crawled under
her and spent about an hour looking over her tracks and
bogies and all. He knew what to look at, too, even if he
did get his pretty suit kind of greasy. But scared or not,
I got to climb back up on her and run the rest of this
pre-test schedule. So far she checks out a hundred
percent.

7

. . . as a member of the Council, it is of course my
responsibility to fully inform myself on all aspects of the
national defense. Accordingly, my dear Doctor, I will
meet with you tomorrow as you requested to hear your
presentation with reference to the proposed testing of
your new machine. I remind you, however, that I will
be equally guided by advice from other quarters. For
this reason I have requested a party of military Procurement and B & F officers to join us. However, I assure
you, I retain an open mind. Let the facts decide.

Sincerely yours,
s/ Hamilton Grace,
GCM, BC, et cetera

8

It is my unhappy duty to inform you that since the
dastardly unprovoked attack on our nation by eastern
forces crossing the International truce-line at 0200 hours
today, a state of war has existed between the People's
Republic and the Concordiat. Our first casualties, the
senseless massacre of 55 inoffensive civilian meteorolo-
gists and technicians at Pole Base, occurred within minutes of the enemy attack.

9

"I'm afraid I don't quite understand what you mean
about 'irresponsible statements to the press,' General.
After all . . ."

"Yes, George, I'm prepared to let that aspect of the

matter drop. The PR attack has saved that much of your neck. However, I'm warning you that I shall tolerate no attempt on your part to make capital of your dramatic public statement of what was, as you concede, tactically obvious to us all. Now, indeed, PR forces have taken the expected step, as all the world is aware—so the rather excessively punctilious demands by CDT officials that the Council issue an immediate apology to Chairman Smith for your remarks will doubtless be dropped. But there will be no crowing; no basking in the limelight: Chief of Ground Forces Predicted Enemy Attack. No nonsense of that sort. Instead, you will deploy your conventional forces to meet and destroy these would-be invaders."

"Certainly, General. But in that connection—well, as to your earlier position regarding the new model B Bolo, I assume . . ."

"My 'position,' General? 'Decision' is the more appropriate word. Just step around the desk, George. Bend over slightly, and look carefully at my shoulder tab. Count 'em, George. Six. An even half-dozen. And unless I'm in serious trouble, you're wearing four. You have your orders, George. See to your defenses."

10

Can't figure it out. Batesy-boy was down here again, gave me direct orders to give her full depot maintenance, just as if she hadn't been setting right here in her garage ever since I topped her off a week ago. Wonder what's up. If I didn't know the Council outlawed the test run Doc Chin wanted so bad, I'd almost think . . . But like Bates told me: I ain't paid to think. Anyways she's in full action condition, 'cept for switching over the full self-direction. Hope he don't order me to do it: I'm still kind of leery; like old Margrave said, what if I just got a couple wires crossed and she takes a notion to wreck the joint?

11

I am more uneasy than ever. In the past 4,000.007

seconds I have received external inspection and depot maintenance far in advance of the programmed schedule. The thought occurs to me: am I under some subtle form of attack? In order to correctly compute the possibilities, I initiate a test sequence of 50,000 random data-retrieval-and-correlation pulses and evaluate the results. This requires .9 seconds, but such sluggishness is to be expected in my untried condition. I detect no unmistakable indications of enemy trickery, but I am still uneasy. Impatiently, I await the orders of my commander.

12

"I don't care what you do, Jimmy—just do *something!* Ah, of course I don't mean that literally. Of course I care. The well-being of the citizens of Cold City is after all my chief concern. What I mean is, I'm giving you carte blanche—full powers. You must act at once, Jimmy. Before the sun sets I want to see your evacuation plan on my desk for signature."

"Surely, Mr. Mayor. I understand. But what am I supposed to work with? I have no transport yet. The Army has promised a fleet of D-100 tractors pulling 100x cargo flats, but none have materialized. They were caught just as short as we were, your Honor, even though that General Bates knew all about it. We all knew the day would come, but I guess we kept hoping 'maybe.' Our negotiations with them seemed to be bearing fruit, and the idea of exposing over a million and a half city-bred individuals to a 1,200-mile trek in 30-below temperatures was just too awful to really face. Even now—"

"I know. The army is doing all it can. The main body of PR troops hasn't actually crossed the date-line yet—so perhaps our forces can get in position. Who knows? Miracles have happened before. But we can't base our thinking on miracles, Jimmy. Flats or no flats we have to have the people out of the dome before enemy forces cut us off."

"Mr. Mayor, our people can't take this. Aside from

leaving their homes and possessions—I've already started them packing, and I've given them a ten-pound-per-person limit—they aren't used to exercise, to say nothing of walking 1,200 miles over frozen tundra. And most of them have no clothing heavier than a business suit. And—"

"Enough, Jimmy. I was ambushed in my office earlier today by an entire family: the old grandmother who was born under the dome and refused to consider going outside; the father all full of his product promotion plans and the new garden he'd just laid out; mother, complaining about Junior having a cold and no warm clothes—and the kids, just waiting trustfully until the excitement was over and they could go home and be tucked into their warm beds with a tummyful of dinner. Ye gods, Jimmy! Can you imagine them after three weeks on the trail?"

13

"Just lean across the desk, fellows; come on, gather round. Take a close look at the shoulder tab. Four stars; see 'em? Then go over to the Slab and do the same with General Margrave. You'll count six. It's as easy as that, boys. The general says no test. Sure, I told him the whole plan. His eyes just kept boring in. Even making contingency plans for deploying an untested and non-High Command-approved weapon system is grounds for court-martial. He didn't say that; maybe I'm telepathic. In summary, the general says no."

14

"I don't know, now. What I heard, even with everything we got on the line, dug in and ready for anything, they's still a ten-mile-wide gap the Peepreps can waltz through without getting even a dirty look. So if the young general—Bates—oh, he's a nice enough young fellow, after you get used to him—if he wants to plug the hole with old unit DNE here, why I say go to it, only the Council says nix. I can say this much: she's put together so she'll stay together, I must of wired in a thousand of them damage sensors myself, and that ain't a spot on what's on the diagram. 'Pain circuits,' old Doc Chin calls 'em. Says it's just like a instinct for self-preservation or something, like people. Old Denny can hurt, he says, so he'll be all the better at dodging enemy fire. He can enjoy, too, Doc says. He gets a kick out of doing his job right, and out of learning stuff. And he learns fast. He'll do OK against them durn Peepreps. They got him programmed right to the brim with everything from the way them Greeks used to fight with no pants to Avery's Last Stand at Leadpipe. He ain't no dumb private; he's got more dope to work on than any general ever graduated from the Point. And he's got more firepower than an old-time army corps. So I think maybe General Bates got aholt of a good idear, there, myself. Says he can put her in the gap in his line and field-test her for fair, with the whole durn Peeprep army and air force for a test problem. Save the gubment some money, too. I heard Doc Chin say the full-scale field test mock-up would run GM a hundred million and another five times that in army R & D funds. He had a map showed where he could use Denny here to block off the sound end of Grand Crevasse where the Peeprep armor will have to travel 'count of the rugged terrain north of Cold City, and bottle 'em up slick as a owl's peter. I'm for it, durn it. Let Denny have his chance. Can't be no worse'n having them Comrades down here running things even worse'n the gubment."

15

"You don't understand, young man. My goodness, I'm not the least bit interested in bucking the line, as you put it. Heavens, I'm going back to my apartment—"

"I'm sorry, ma'am, I got my orders; this here ain't no drill; you got to keep it closed up. They're loading as fast as they can. It's my job to keep these lines moving right out the lock, so they get that flat loaded and get the next one up. We got over a million people to load by 6 AM deadline. So you just be nice, ma'am, and think about all the trouble it'd make if everybody decided to start back upstream and jam the elevators and all."

16

Beats me. Course, the good part about being just a hired man is I got no big decisions to make, so I don't hafta know what's going on. Seems like they'd let me know something, though. Batesey was down again, spent a hour with old Denny, like I say, beats me; but he give me a new data can to program into her, right in her Action/Command section. Something's up. I just fired a N-class pulse at old Denny (them's the closest to the real thing) and she snapped her aft quarter battery around so fast I couldn't see it move. Old Denny's keyed-up, I know that much.

17

This has been a memorable time for me. I have my assignment at last, and I have conferred at length—for 2,037 seconds—with my commander. I am now a fighting unit of the 20th Virginia, a regiment ancient and honorable, with a history dating back to Terra Insula. I look forward to my opportunity to demonstrate my worthiness.

18

"I assure you, gentlemen, the rumor is unfounded. I have by no means authorized the deployment of 'an untested—and potentially highly dangerous machine,' as your memo termed it. Candidly, I was not at first entirely unsympathetic to the proposal of the Chief of Ground Forces in view of the circumstances—I presume you're aware that the PR committed its forces to invasion over an hour ago, and that they are advancing in overwhelming strength. I have issued the order to commence the evacuation, and I believe that the initial phases are even now in progress. I have the fullest confidence in General Bates and can assure you that our forces will do all in their power in the face of this dastardly sneak attack. As for the unfortunate publicity given to the earlier suggestion re the use of the Mark XX, I can tell you that I at once subjected the data to computer analysis here at Headquarters, to determine whether any potentially useful purpose could be served by risking the use of the new machine without prior test certification. The results were negative. I'm sorry, gentlemen, but that's it. They have the advantage both strategically and tactically. We are out-gunned, out-manned, and in effect out-flanked. There is nothing we can do save attempt to hold them long enough to permit the evacuation to get underway, then retreat in good order. The use of our orbiting nuclear capability is out of the question. It is after all our own territory we'd be devastated. No more questions for the present, please, gentlemen. I have my duties to see to."

19

The situation as regards my own circumstances continues to deteriorate. The current status program has been updated to within 21 seconds of the present. The reasons both for what is normally a pre-engagement updating and for the hiatus of 21 seconds remain obscure. However, I shall of course hold myself in readiness for whatever comes.

20

It's all nonsense: to call me here at this hour merely to stand by and watch the destruction of our gallant men who are giving their lives in a totally hopeless fight against overwhelming odds. We know what the outcome must be. You yourself, General, informed us this afternoon that the big tactical computer has analyzed the situation and reported no possibility of stopping them with what we've got. By the way, did you include the alternative of use of the big, er, Bolo, I believe they're called—frightening things—they're so damned *big*. But if, in desperation, you should be forced to employ the thing—have you that result as well? I see. No hope at all. So there's nothing we can do. This is a sad day, General. But I fail to see what object is served by getting me out of bed to come down here. Not that I'm not willing to do anything I can, of course. With our people—innocent civilians—out on that blizzard-swept tundra tonight—and our boys dying to gain them a little time, the loss of a night's sleep is relatively unimportant, of course. But it's my duty to be at my best, rested and ready to face the decisions that we of the Council will be called on to make.

Now, General, kindly excuse my ignorance if I don't understand all this . . . but I understood that the large screen there was placed so as to monitor the action at the southern debouchment of Grand Crevasse where we expect the enemy armor to emerge to make its dash for Cold City and the Complex. Yes, indeed, so I was saying, but in that case, I'm afraid I don't understand. I'm quite sure you stated that the untried Mark XX would *not* be used. Yet, on the screen I see what appears to be in fact that very machine moving up. Please, calmly, General. I quite understand your position. Defiance of a direct order. That's rather serious, I'm sure, but no occasion for such language, General.

There must be some explanation.

21

This is a most satisfying development. Quite abruptly, my introspection complex was brought up to full operating level, extra power resources were made available to my current-action memory stage, and most satisfying of all, my battle reflex circuit has been activated at active service level. Action is impending, I am sure of it. It is a curious anomaly: I dread the prospect of damage and even possible destruction, but even more strongly, I anticipate the pleasure of performing my design function.

22

"Yes, sir. I agree, it's mutiny. But I will not recall the Bolo and I will not report myself under arrest. Not until this battle's over, General. So the hell with my career. I've got a war to win."

23

Now just let me get this quite straight, General.
Having been denied authority to field-test this new
device, you—or a subordinate—which amounts to the
same thing—have placed the machine in the line of
battle, in open defiance of the Council. This is a serious
matter, General. Yes, of course it's war, but to attempt
to defend your actions now will merely exacerbate the
matter. In any event—to return to your curious decision to defy Council authority and to reverse your own
earlier position—it was yourself who assured me that no
useful purpose could be served by fielding this experimental equipment—that the battle, and perhaps the
war, and the very self-determination of West Continent
are irretrievably lost. There is nothing we can do save
accept the situation gracefully while decrying Chairman
Smith's decision to resort to force. Yes, indeed, General, I should like to observe on the Main Tactical
Display screen. Shall we go along?

24

Now, there at center screen, Mr. Councillor, you see
that big blue rectangular formation. Actually that's the
opening of Grand Crevasse, emerges through an ice
tunnel, you know. Understand the Crevasse is a crystal
fault, a part of the same formation that created the
thermal sink from which the Complex draws its energy.
Splendid spot for an ambush, of course, if we had the
capability. Enemy has little option; like a highway in
there—armor can move up at flank speed. Above, the
badlands, where *we* must operate. Now, over to the
left, you see that smoke, or dust or whatever. That
represents the western limit of the unavoidable gap in
General Bates' line. Dust raised by maneuvering Mark
XV's, you understand. Obsolete equipment, but we'll do
what we can with them. Over to the right, in the
distance there, we can make out our forward artillery
emplacement of the Threshold Line. Pitiful, really. Yes,
Mr. Councillor, there is indeed a gap precisely opposite
the point where the lead units of the enemy are ex-

pected to appear. Clearly, anything in their direct line
of advance will be annihilated; thus General Bates has
wisely chosen to dispose his forces to cover both enemy
flanks, putting him in position to counterattack if opportunity offers. We must, after all, sir, use what we
have. Theoretical arms programmed for fiscal 90 are of
no use whatever today. Umm. As for that, one must be
flexible, modifying plans to meet a shifting tactical situation. Faced with the prospect of seeing the enemy
drive through our center and descend, unopposed, on
the vital installations at Cold City, I have, as you see,
decided to order General Bates to make use of the
experimental Mark XX. Certainly; my decision entirely. I take full responsibility.

25

I advance over broken terrain toward my assigned
position. The prospect of action exhilarates me, but my
assessment of enemy strength indicates they are fielding
approximately 17.4 percent greater weight of armor
than anticipated, with commensurately greater fire
power. I compute that I am grossly overmatched. None-
theless, I do my best.

26

There's no doubt whatever, gentlemen. Computers
work with hard facts. Given the enemy's known offensive capability, and our own defensive resources, it's a
simple computation. No combination of the manpower
and equipment at our command can possibly inflict a
defeat on the PR forces at this time and place. Two is
greater than one. You can't make a dollar out of fifteen
cents.

27

At least we can gather some useful data from the
situation, gentlemen. The Bolo Mark XX has been committed to battle. Its designers assure me that the new
self-motivating circuitry will vastly enhance the combat
effectiveness of the Bolo. Let us observe.

28

Hate to see old Denny out there, just a great big sitting duck, all alone and—here they come! Look at em boiling out of there like ants out of a hot log. Can't hardly look at that screen, them tactical nukes popping like fireworks all over the place. But old Denny knows enough to get under cover. See that kind of glow all around him? All right, *it*, then. You know, working with him—it—so long, it got to feeling almost like he was somebody. Sure, I know, anyway, that's vaporized ablative shield you see. They're making it plenty hot for him. But he's fighting back. Them Hellbores is putting out, and they know it. Looks like they're concentrating on him now. Look at them tracers closing in on him. Come on, Denny, you ain't dumb. Get out of there, fast.

29

Certainly it's aware what's at stake! I've told you he—the machine, that is, has been fully programmed and is well aware not only of the tactical situation, but of strategic and logistical considerations as well. Certainly it's an important item of equipment; its loss would be a serious blow to our present under-equipped forces. You may rest assured that its pain circuits as well as its basic military competence will cause it to take the proper action. The fact that I originally opposed commissioning the device is not to be taken as implying any lack of confidence on my part in its combat effectiveness. You may consider that my reputation is staked on the performance of the machine. It will act correctly.

30

It appears that the enemy is absorbing my barrage with little effect. More precisely, for each enemy unit destroyed by my fire 2.4 fresh units immediately move out to replace it. Thus it appears I am ineffective, while already my own shielding is suffering severe damage. Yet while I have offensive capability, I must carry on as

*my commander would wish. The pain is very great
now, but thanks to my superb circuitry, I am not
disabled, though it has been necessary to withdraw
power from my external somatic sensors.*

31

I can assure you, gentlemen, insofar as simple logic
functions are concerned, the Mark XX is perfectly capable of assessing the situation, even as you and I, only
better. Doubtless as soon as it senses that its position
has grown totally untenable, it will retreat to the shelter of the rock ridge and retire under cover to a position
from which it can return fire without taking the full
force of the enemy's attack at point-blank range. It's
been fully briefed on late developments, it knows this is
a hopeless fight. There, you see? It's moving. . . .

32

I thought you said—dammit, I *know* you said your
pet machine had brains enough to know when to pull
out. But look at it: half a billion plus of Concordiat
funds being bombarded into radioactive rubbish. Like
shooting fish in a barrel.

33

Yes, sir, I'm monitoring everything. My test panel is
tuned to it across the board; I'm getting continuous
reading on all still-active circuits. Battle Reflex is still
hot. Pain circuits close to overload, but he's still taking
it—I don't know how much more he can take, sir;
already way past Redline; expected him to break off and
get out before now.

34

It's a simple matter of arithmetic. There is only one
correct course of action in any given military situation;
the big tactical computer was designed specifically to
compare data and deduce that sole correct action. In
this case my read-out shows that the only thing the
Mark XX could legitimately do at this point is just what

the professor here says: pull back to cover and continue its barrage. The on-board computing capability of the unit is as capable of reaching that conclusion as is the big computer at HQ. So keep calm, gentlemen. It will withdraw at any moment, I assure you of that.

35

Now it's getting ready—no, look what it's doing! It's advancing into the teeth of that murderous fire. By God, you've got to admire that workmanship! That it's still capable of moving is a miracle. All the ablative metal is gone—you can see its bare armor exposed—and it takes some heat to make that flint-steel glow white!

36

Certainly, I'm looking. I see it. By God, sir, it's still moving—faster, in fact; charging the enemy line like the Light Brigade. And all for nothing, it appears. Your machine, General, appears less competent than you expected.

37

Poor old Denny. Made his play and played out, I reckon. Readings on the board over there don't look good; durn near every overload in him blowed wide open. Not much there to salvage. Emergency Survival Center's hot. Never expected to see *that*. Means all kinds of breakdowns inside. But it figures, after what he just went through. Look at that slag pit he drove up out of. They wanted a field test. Reckon they got it. And he flunked it.

38

Violating orders and winning is one thing, George. Committing mutiny and losing is quite another. Your damned machine made a fool of me. After I stepped in and backed you to the hilt and stood there like a jack-ass and assured Councillor Grace that thing knew what it was doing—it blows the whole show. Instead of pull-

ing back to save itself it charged to destruction. I want
an explanation of this fiasco at once.

39

Look! No, by God, over *there!* On the left of the entrance. They're breaking formation—they're running for
it! Watch this! The whole spearhead is crumbling, they're
taking to the badlands—they're—

40

Why, dammit? It's outside all rationality. As far as
the enemy's concerned, fine. They broke and ran. They
couldn't stand up to the sight of the Mark XX not only
taking everything they had, but advancing on them out
of that inferno, all guns blazing. Another hundred yards
and—but they don't know that. It buffaloed them, so
score a battle won for our side. But why? I'd stack its
circuits up against any fixed installation in existence
including the big Tacomp the army's so proud of. That
machine was as aware as anybody that the only smart
thing to do was run. So now I've got a junk pile on my
hands. Some test! A clear flunk. Destroyed in action.
Not recommended for Federal procurement. Nothing
left but a few hot transistors in the Survival Center. It's
a disaster, Fred. All my work, all your work, the whole
program wrecked. Fred, you talk to General Bates; as
soon as he's done inspecting the hulk he'll want somebody human to chew out.

41

Look at that pile of junk. Reading off the scale. Won't
be cool enough to haul to Disposal for six months. I
understand you're Chief Engineer at Bolo Division.
You built this thing. Maybe you can tell me what you
had in mind here. Sure, it stood up to fire better than I
hoped. But so what? A stone wall can stand and take it.
This thing is supposed to be *smart,* supposed to feel
pain like a living creature. Blunting the strike at the
Complex was a valuable contribution, but how can I
recommend procurement of this junk-heap?

42

Why, Denny? Just tell me why you did it. You got all these military brass down on you, and on me, too. On all of us. They don't much like stuff they can't understand. You attacked when they figured you to run. Sure, you routed the enemy, like Bates says, but you got yourself ruined in the process. Don't make sense. Any dumb private, along with the generals, would have known enough to get out of there. Tell me why, so I'll have something for Bates to put on his Test Evaluation Report, AGF Form 1103-6, Rev 11/3/85.

43

"All right, Unit DNE of the line. Why did you do it? This is your Commander, Unit DNE. Report! Why did you do it? Now, you knew your position was hopeless, didn't you? That you'd be destroyed if you held your ground, to say nothing of advancing. Surely you were able to compute that. You were lucky to have the chance to prove yourself."

For a minute I thought old Denny was too far gone to answer. There was just a kind of groan come out of the amplifier. Then it firmed up. General Bates had his hand cupped behind his ear, but Denny spoke right up.

"Yes, sir."

"You knew what was at stake here. It was the ultimate test of your ability to perform correctly under stress, of your suitability as a weapon of war. You knew that. General Margrave and old Priss Grace and the press boys all had their eyes on every move you made. So, instead of using common sense, you waded into that inferno in defiance of all logic—and destroyed yourself. Right?"

"That is correct, sir."

"Then why? In the name of sanity why, instead of backing out and saving yourself, did you charge?"

"Wait a minute, Unit DNE. It just dawned on me. I've been underestimating you. You knew, didn't you? Your knowledge of human psychology told you they'd break and run, didn't it?"

"No, sir. On the contrary, I was quite certain that they knew they held every advantage."

"Then that leaves me back where I started. Why? What made you risk everything on a hopeless attack? Why did you do it?"

"For the honor of the regiment."

In each of the preceding volumes of The Future at War *I have published a poem by Robert Frazier. This one is the third in the series.*

Certainly the drama and the tragedy of war, and the even higher drama of man's adventure into space, should be evoking more poetry than they are—more poetry and more song. It is encouraging that more and more of it is now being published in the science fiction field, professional and amateur.

Robert Frazier

ENCASED IN THE AMBER
OF FATE

The Colony forces conscripted my brother Slim,
enfolded him in the cocoon of their keep,
and in two standard weeks released by metamorphosis,
like a falconer unhooding his peregrine,
a glorious, glittering, terrible insect.

Out of the titanium of his back:
the glide-wings unfold like morning-glories to the sun.
Out of the nylon seams of his calves:
the attitude jets sprout like risomes.
Out of the shielded ceramic platter of his chest:
the radar pulses invisible tsunamis.
His infrared eyes are scalpels in a surgeon's hand,
peeling away layers of the night.
His parabolic ears are bats,
forever turning toward the merest shadow of sound.
His reflexes are a nervous gunfighter,
poised on a hair trigger.

Immortality is to be his reward
and service to the planets his staple,
but I have seen the quality of pickings
on the winter plate of war,
and hear well of his chances.
Both were prophesied by my parents' choice,
that gentle summer so long ago,
when they filed his birth certificate.
Slim.

Robert Frazier has been involved in many aspects of poetry in the science fiction field—an area offering unlimited challenges to the poetic imagination, and one in which too little has still been done. He has been an editor, a member of an awards committee (CAS Award,) and has read papers on science fiction poetry at conferences and conventions. He has also written critical articles on the subject, and has done bibliographical research regarding it.

Thor's Hammer, Volume I of *The Future at War,* contains his "Encased in the Amber of Eternity." Volume II, *The Spear of Mars,* contains "Encased in the Amber of Death." The present poem is the third in that triad.

Real people, real problems, real science and no compromises:
New Destinies delivers everything needed to satisfy the science fiction reader. Every issue includes hard sf and speculative fact written by scientists and authors like these:

-Harry Turtledove -Charles Sheffield -Dean Ing
-Poul Anderson -Spider Robinson -Larry Niven

New Destinies: the quarterly paperback magazine of science fiction and speculative fact. *The Washington Post* called it "a forum for hard sf." This is *the* place to go for exciting, new adventures and mind-blowing extrapolation on the latest in human inquiry. No other publication will challenge you like *New Destinies*. No other publication will reward you as well.

****And, it's the only place to find****
****Jim Baen's outrageous editorials!****

Why worry about missing the latest issue? Take advantage of our special ordering offer today—and we'll send you a free poster!

Name: _____ Date: _____
Street: _____
City: _____ State: _____ Zip: _____
I have enclosed $14.00 in check or money order, so send me the next four volumes of *New Destinies* as soon as they are available!

Return this coupon to:
Baen Books, Dept. D, 260 Fifth Avenue, New York, NY 10001.